THE RIVER GIRLS

A Mercy Harbor Thriller: Book One

MELINDA WOODHALL

Cover Designed by Michael Rehder

Melinda Woodhall
Visit my website at www.MelindaWoodhall.com

Printed in the United States of America

First Printing: November 2018
Creative Magnolia

ISBN: 9781731293923

For Linda Jean

Other books by Melinda Woodhall

Girl Eight
Catch the Girl
Girls Who Lie
Her Last Summer
Her Final Fall
Her Winter of Darkness
Her Silent Spring
Her Day to Die

Sign up for the Melinda Woodhall Thrillers Newsletter to receive bonus scenes and insider details at www.melindawoodhall.com/newsletter

CHAPTER ONE

The key slipped into the lock, turning with a soft metallic click that made the man's heart race. He inched the door open and stepped inside, pausing to listen for any sound from within the dark room.

Had the girl heard? Was she awake?

As always, the smell of moldy carpet and stale cigarette smoke greeted him, assailing his senses. His nostrils flared in distaste.

What a dump.

He knew the motel had been selected for that very reason. Families and professionals were less likely to stop at a cheap, run-down motel that still used actual metal keys instead of those little plastic cards. Fewer conveniences and luxuries meant fewer guests who might care enough to ask questions.

After the harsh light of the motel's corridor, the darkness of the room enveloped him. He opened his eyes wide, impatient for them to adjust. Following the glowing numbers on the bedside clock, he moved across the room and leaned over to feel the rough bedspread and lumpy pillows. The bed was empty.

Disappointment surged through him as he threw the scratchy cover to the floor.

You waited too long, an angry voice spoke in his head. It sounded so close, so real, that he spun around and faced the room. Was someone there in the dark? Had someone been waiting for him? He switched on the bedside lamp, knowing even as he did that no one would be there. A pale circle of light lit up the small, empty room. He saw the navy-blue bedspread laying in a heap where he'd thrown it on the stained carpet. A wooden table with two mismatched chairs sat under the window. Thick curtains were tightly drawn, protecting the room from any nosy passersby.

"No, she *was* here," he whispered into the quiet room. "How can she be gone?"

He raised his hand in a clenched fist, tempted to slam the table lamp to the floor when he heard a faint retching coming from the bathroom. He couldn't see light under the door, but she must be in there. He could hear her begin to gag and cough. Relief, mixed with the stirrings of anticipation, made his hands start to tremble.

The poor girl must be coming down hard.

He'd expected her to still be out of it, still be sleeping off the effects of her last hit. He thought she'd be laying down, maybe even unconscious. It would be easier that way. Less risk of something going wrong. Less likely that the girls in the room next door might hear something.

He hadn't counted on her being awake and alert, at least not at the beginning, but it was too late to turn back. His pulse quickened as the bathroom door opened and the girl stepped into the room.

"What the hell...why are *you* here?" Her blood-shot eyes widened at the sight of him. "I'm supposed to have the night off."

She clutched her stomach and shuffled toward the bed. The oversized t-shirt she was wearing had once been white, but it appeared gray in the dim light of the room, and the man could see the front of the shirt had a variety of stains on it, some still wet.

"Look, I'm sick. I need a fix bad." The girl sunk onto the bed and held out her arm.

A pattern of angry red track marks contrasted with the pale skin. He looked into her face and saw a new bruise, a big purple one on her left cheek. Her eyes were puffy and wet.

He took in her bleached blonde hair, the ends dry and tangled, the grown-out roots dark and greasy. Rage started to simmer in his belly as he surveyed her. How could they have done this to her? She'd been so beautiful, so fresh. Sure, she'd had problems, needed help. But what had they done? Instead of helping her, they'd ruined her.

She's a poor substitute for Tiffany, the inner voice taunted, and he flinched, feeling the urge to punch the wall, or maybe break the lamp after all. Taking a deep breath, he stopped himself from giving in to his impulse. It wouldn't do for the girl to think he was violent or unstable. Not if he hoped to save her from this mess.

But the thought of Tiffany lingered. Her image filled his mind, made his blood pump faster through his veins. Tiffany had been his first girl; the perfect girl that had once been his obsession; the girl who still haunted his dreams.

He'd waited three long years to find another girl like Tiffany, and he knew this girl might be the one. He had decided to save her the moment he had seen her two weeks ago. She had been pretty and blonde and new. Not yet tarnished and beaten down like the other girls at the motel. He had seen right away that she was special, and that she'd gotten herself into the kind of trouble that she couldn't begin to understand.

"Come on, hook me up." The girl's voice trembled, not from fear but with need. Her pleading eyes searched his face, perhaps hoping to find some sign of kindness, some hint of compassion for her suffering.

A small, sad smile played around his mouth as he unbuckled his thin leather belt, pulled it free of his belt loops, and slid the end through the buckle to make a noose. The girl's eyes shone with gratitude as she lay back and held up her arm, ready for the tourniquet that meant an injection was coming and relief was on its way.

"Yeah, I'll help you," he whispered as one strong finger reached out and caught a lock of her hair and caressed it.

He moved closer, then recoiled at the stench from her shirt.

That wouldn't do at all.

He grabbed the bottom of the shirt and wrenched it up and over her head in one movement, the shirt sleeves trapping her arms behind her back. She yelled out in surprise, but he slipped the belt around her neck before she could inhale or produce a second sound.

"Shh...quiet. We don't want anyone bothering us, do we?"

Her startled eyes bulged in fear and she produced a coarse gurgling sound.

"From this angle, you really do look like Tiffany," he said, his voice low and thick with excitement. He settled himself over her, his strong leg muscles keeping her body firmly in place.

His hands pulled the belt tighter around her throat. "Only she was prettier...and cleaner."

A long-denied need moved in him and ignited into a clawing hunger as he writhed against her, his body shaking with frustration. Suddenly scared that he would end things too soon, he forced himself to loosen the belt and shift the bulk of his body weight to his knees.

He looked down at her and saw that her eyes were closed, her face red and puffy. But he could hear her wheezing in and out, and feel her chest moving under him. It wasn't over yet.

Her eyes blinked open and he thought he saw a flash of relief. Maybe she knew he was saving her, that her suffering would be over. Or perhaps she was hoping he was just playing some sick game.

But this was no game, and he was no pathetic john out for a cheap thrill. No, he had a mission: he was going to save her from the shame that she'd brought upon herself. He was like the good

Samaritan in his mother's stories, the kind of man she had wanted him to be. He was bringing relief to the suffering.

Keeping his eyes on her face, the man tightened the belt again, watching her gasp for air, feeling her body begin to convulse underneath him.

Almost there, almost time. But not yet.

He loosened the belt again, relieving the pressure.

This time the girl turned her head to the side, no longer hoping, no longer trying to resist. He could see that she was struggling to say something but couldn't get the words out. Reining in his growing need, the man put his ear close to her lips to listen.

"Help...me," she managed to rasp out before a weak cough silenced her attempt to say more.

"Yes, oh yes, I'll help you," the man panted, his voice soft but shaking with emotion.

He tightened the belt using all his strength. Satisfaction coursed through his body, making even the hateful voice inside his head recede underneath the roar of bliss that consumed him. He watched her eyes glaze over, felt her heat and energy fade.

Then, as he collapsed with his full weight on her limp body, the sensations diminished and began to fade away. He raised his head and looked into the girl's dead eyes. Something felt wrong. He felt like he'd been cheated somehow. The experience hadn't been as powerful as he had remembered.

This time the rush hadn't been as good as he'd gotten with Tiffany. Maybe it was because this girl had been sick and stoned, only half-conscious really. She hadn't even known what was going on, couldn't appreciate the fact that he was freeing her, redeeming her.

Tiffany had stayed alert until the end, and then her energy had flooded into him, filled him, stayed with him. With Tiffany, he had been satiated for a long time. But this time his need hadn't been quenched. This time he was left unfulfilled.

Maybe the poor girl wasn't the right one after all.

Too late to think about that now though. He needed to figure out how to get rid of her body before anyone came to the room. The other girls would be back soon. He knew if he was caught, he would likely end up in prison, either on death row or serving a life sentence.

Men like him didn't do well in prison. And the outcome for him would be even worse if the guys in Miami found out. They didn't tolerate anyone stealing from them, whether it be girls, drugs, or whatever else they happened to be dealing.

They were savages, irredeemable degenerates, and they would never understand that he'd been compelled to rescue the girl from the life of depravity they'd intended for her.

His head began to ache as he planned out his next move. He would make it looked like she had fallen into the canal, or maybe jumped, just in case her body was discovered. The other girls would confirm that she'd been sick and depressed. She'd likely been begging to go home. They all wanted to go home at the end.

He looked around the room and saw a pile of clothes in the corner. He picked up a skirt and a tank top and dressed the thin, bruised body. He looked around for shoes but couldn't find any, and he couldn't risk spending any more time looking for them.

If they find her, they'll just think her shoes floated away.

He wrapped the rough blue bedspread around the girl and dragged her toward the door. He parted the curtains and peered out into the corridor. It was empty. The cover of the dark awaited past a few feet of dirty concrete. And past that was a short walk to the water's edge.

The water would cleanse them both, erase all traces of their sins. If luck was with him, the girl would be washed out to the river and into the bay before anyone came looking for her. He assured himself that his mission had been worth the risk; no one could ever hurt the girl again.

CHAPTER TWO

Eden Winthrop looked at the clock and grimaced. She would be home late again. Guilt pierced her as she thought of Hope and Devon eating dinner and preparing for bed without her. Thank goodness she had Sage now to make sure her niece and nephew ate their veggies and washed behind their ears.

After a string of nannies had failed to fit in with their unconventional family, Eden had been relieved to find Sage Parsons, a young woman who possessed a calm, unflappable kindness that seemed to make Hope and Devon feel safe.

And no one needs to feel safe more than those poor kids, Eden thought, the guilt resurfacing on cue. *Which is why I should be home with them instead of here.*

Eden bit her lip and turned back to her computer. How could she go home when there was so much left to do? During the last twelve hours social services had called in five separate requests for emergency placements, and Eden had been determined to help all the women find shelter.

Each woman had escaped an abusive partner. Three of the women had children. One woman had custody of her four grandchildren. They all needed a place to sleep and food to eat, and she had been relieved to find enough rooms available within the foundation's network of safe houses.

An hour earlier she had settled the last woman into the 1408 Shutter Street location and was sitting in the facility's reception office reviewing the current status of rooms and resources on the foundation's computer. She noted that only one room was still unoccupied and available.

What will happen if tomorrow is another busy day?

Her biggest fear was having to turn someone away. Someone who might not have anywhere else to go. Someone like Mercy.

Eden shook her head to clear the unwanted thoughts, determined not to go down that path again. She stared at a spreadsheet of volunteers, wishing she could make the available resources somehow magically match those needed.

Why are the shelters always so full this time of year? she wondered.

It seemed summer was always an especially busy time. Perhaps the blistering Florida heat pushed already hot tempers over the boiling point, or maybe it was the daily thunderstorms that rolled through Willow Bay each afternoon, the torrential rain trapping residents inside their houses. Whatever the cause, the increase in domestic violence was stretching the foundation's resources to their limit.

"Motion detected at door number one," an automated voice announced, just as a wall-mounted security monitor displayed a small, pale face dominated by an alarmingly swollen black eye.

The face was ringed by a halo of messy platinum blonde curls. Duke stirred at Eden's feet, his big, dark eyes blinking as both he and Eden stared at the monitor.

Eden was accustomed to seeing the aftermath of violence on the faces of women seeking shelter at the safe house, but she wasn't used to women showing up unannounced and alone. Standard protocol required staff to call security when any unknown person passed the *No Trespassing* sign on the perimeter gate.

Eden's hand hovered over the telephone then hesitated. There was something familiar about that bruised face, something in the defiant tilt of the swollen chin. Her finger impulsively pushed the intercom button.

"Hello, how can I help you?" Eden said, not taking her eyes off the monitor, watching for the girl's reaction. Had there been a mix-up? Could this be a new resident Eden hadn't met yet?

The girl turned her head toward the sound of Eden's voice and tried to focus on the camera positioned above the door.

"Let me in!" The girl's voice was urgent, but the words came out as little more than a hoarse whisper. She looked over her shoulder as if worried she had been followed, and said, "I got away, but they'll come after me. I need a place to stay. Please..."

Letting the girl inside would break an ironclad rule: never open the safe house door to a stranger. Eden hesitated, her eyes moving from the security monitor to the large, framed portrait on the wall above the desk. A serene young woman with laughing blue eyes and a shy smile looked back. Those same blue eyes had been bruised and swollen shut when her sister's body had been found.

If someone had helped you that day, Mercy, maybe you'd still be here, Eden thought for the millionth time. *If only I'd gotten there in time.*

Her hand moved to the intercom. "Hold on, I'm coming out."

Eden rose from the chair, and Duke stood up and trotted over to the door, ready to accompany her wherever she was going. She smiled at the golden retriever's enthusiasm, but she felt a pang of doubt settle in her stomach as she moved across the room.

"Stay here, Duke," she told the dog before opening the door. She didn't know who the girl was, or if she was a threat. Duke was an emotional support animal, not a guard dog, and she didn't want to put him in danger.

Duke's eyes reproached her. "I'll be back soon," she said, wondering who she was trying to reassure more, herself or Duke.

* * *

"Come on in," Eden said, as the girl scurried past her into the brightly lit foyer. She leaned out and surveyed the dark street, wincing as the hot, humid air encircled her. Security lights shone on the wrought iron fence and firmly closed gate.

The girl must be a good climber, Eden thought, wondering what had made her desperate enough to scale the tall fence.

The street beyond the gate was quiet as usual. A single car drove past, and Eden watched the red tail lights recede into the dark before closing the door.

"Okay, follow me," Eden said over her shoulder as she led the girl down a hall and into the shelter's last empty resident room. Matching homemade quilts covered twin beds, and two straight-backed chairs flanked a small table. A wicker basket on the table had been filled with packets of nuts and an assortment of granola bars. The cozy room was illuminated with soft light from a floor lamp in the corner.

"I'm Eden Winthrop, and..." Eden hesitated. She didn't want to give the girl any information without first finding out who she was and how she'd found the house. Best to keep it simple. "And I work here."

The location of each safe house operated by the Mercy Harbor Foundation was closely guarded. If the address of one of the houses was divulged to the wrong person, all the residents would have to be immediately relocated to a different location.

The house at 1408 Shutter Street was their largest facility, occupying a renovated building that had previously contained twelve private apartments and a leasing office. A security breach and the resulting relocation effort would mean uprooting a dozen women and their children.

"Sit down and catch your breath." Eden motioned to one of the chairs and opened a bottle of water. "Have a drink, and then tell me what's happened to you."

She studied the girl's discolored, swollen eye, then let her gaze drift down to a trail of angry red puncture marks on the girl's pale inner arm. Eden knew those marks were the telltale sign of an intravenous drug user.

Mercy Harbor wasn't a rehab facility, and the staff members weren't equipped to deal with addicts. Eden was beginning to suspect she'd made a mistake letting the girl inside.

How did she find us anyway?

Eden waited for the girl to collect her thoughts and take a few sips from the bottle.

Has she been here before? Is that how I know her?

She could see that the black eye wasn't fresh. Someone had hit the girl a few days ago. The yellowish tinge of her swollen chin also indicated that the injuries were starting to heal.

"My name is Sta...Star," the girl stammered and hugged herself as if scared, or perhaps cold.

No, it's not Star, but that sounds close, Eden thought, keeping her expression neutral and open, trying to remember where she'd seen the girl's face before. She tried to imagine her face as it would look if it were fresh and undamaged.

"Okay, Star, glad to meet you," Eden said, pulling open a drawer and removing a blanket.

The summer night was hot and humid, but constant air conditioning kept the big building cold, and Star looked as if she didn't have an ounce of extra flesh to keep her warm. Her skimpy tank top and tiny shorts didn't offer much in the way of coverage or warmth either. At least the girl was wearing a solid-looking pair of tennis shoes.

Eden wrapped the blanket over Star's shoulders, pulled up a chair, and sat down. "Now, can you tell me what happened?"

"My boyfriend..." Star paused and seemed to reconsider her words. "Well, Hollywood, that's what we call him, he's sort of my boyfriend. At least I thought he was. Anyway, he did this." Star pointed to her eye and then looked down at her lap.

"How old are you?" Eden tried to keep her tone non-judgmental. Star was still a teenager, she couldn't be more than sixteen or seventeen years old, so Eden knew the girl was most likely a runaway, and that she may try to hide her real age.

"You still living at home?"

"Um...I'm eighteen. I've been staying with Hollywood. He set me up in a room with some other girls." Star didn't make eye contact. Her hands fidgeted with the edge of the blanket.

"Does your family know where you've been living?" Eden sensed that Star wanted to say more, but she didn't want to spook her by asking too many questions just yet.

"Nah, I didn't tell my mom where I was going. She's...busy. I wish I had though." Star suddenly looked straight into Eden's eyes.

"I wish I'd never met him. I hate him!" A tear trickled down the girl's cheek, dripping off her bruised chin.

"So, this Hollywood, he's the one that hit you? He's the one you think might try to follow you?" Eden asked, her suspicions growing that Star was the victim of more than just an abusive boyfriend.

"Yeah, he got mad when I wouldn't go with this old man he knows. He wanted me to...to work. But I was sick. The junk he gave me was bad or something and I got sick. He...*oh my god*...I think...I think he may have *killed* Jess."

Star's words hung in the air, stunning Eden into a silent pause. She then leaned over and put her hand on Star's shaking arm.

"Who's Jess? Is she one of the other girls that lives with you? What happened to her?"

Star covered her face with her hands, muffling her hoarse voice. "Jess was my friend. She just wanted to go home. But they wouldn't let her." Star stood up and shrugged off the blanket, her fists clenched at her sides.

"I woke up...and Jess...she was on the bed, and she wasn't moving. I shook her, but she wouldn't wake up." Star was shaking her head from side to side as if refusing to believe her own words.

"Hollywood said she'd had too much smack, that she just needed to sleep it off. He made me leave, and when I came back...she was gone. Most of her stuff was there, but she was just...gone."

"Is that when you ran away?" Eden asked, trying to piece together the timeline.

"No, I waited a few days. I hoped she'd come back," Star said, "but then yesterday Hollywood brought in a new girl and gave her all Jess' clothes, even her shoes. I mean, come on, they were the only shoes she had. Where could she go without shoes?"

Eden made herself take a deep breath before asking, "Did you ask Hollywood where Jess had gone?"

"Yeah, that first night I asked him a bunch of times. He just said that Jess wasn't coming back and that she wouldn't need her stuff anymore. When I begged him to tell me where she'd gone, he gave me this."

Star's hand went to her swollen eye.

Eden had heard enough. She reached for the phone. "I've got to call the police, Star. We've got to report this."

"No, you can't!" Star croaked out, grabbing the phone from Eden's hand and flinging it across the room. The phone hit the wall and slid behind one of the twin beds. "If Hollywood knows I'm here, that I've snitched, he'll tell Sig, and they'll...they'll make *me* disappear, like Jess."

Eden's pulse began to pound, and she backed away, suddenly wishing she had let Duke follow them into the room. Not that he'd be able to protect her, but he could soothe her anxiety, help her stay calm so that she could figure out what to do.

She counted on Duke now, had counted on him ever since Reggie had introduced them in the aftermath of her first acute panic attack.

She'd ended up in the emergency room at Willow Bay General Hospital, consumed by fear and guilt over her sister's death. In the months that followed, the dog's gentle presence had helped her regain control over her emotions, but she knew that Duke wasn't going to be able to solve this dilemma.

Looking at Star's stricken face, Eden decided it was time to summon additional help. It was time to call in a professional.

"It's okay, Star." Eden kept her voice low and calm even as anxiety tightened her chest and constricted her throat. "I just want to help you. And help Jess if possible."

Suddenly falling silent, Star sat down on one of the twin beds and wrapped her frail arms around her body once again, rocking back and forth, before reclining on the bed, then curling into a fetal position. Eden crossed over and looked down at her.

Is she in shock? Eden wondered, knowing all too well how fragile the human psyche could be, especially when faced with the type of trauma and abuse Star had experienced. Star's eyes closed, and her breathing grew quiet.

Eden decided she'd let Star sleep for now. She bent over and untied Star's shoes and put them on the floor beside the bed, before tucking the blanket around the girl's sleeping form.

The poor girl doesn't look much older than Hope, Eden mused, her heart clenching at the thought of her innocent young niece ever being in such a position, ever being so alone and abused.

"Star, I'm going to leave you here to sleep for a little while. I need to go get someone who can help you," Eden said, in what she hoped was a reassuring tone. "You stay here and sleep. I'll be right back."

CHAPTER THREE

Star heard the door close behind the tall blonde woman. What was her name? Did she say it was Eden? Yes, Eden Winthrop. The woman that had been so nice to her and Zane when they'd stayed at this same house with their mother. Had it already been two years since the woman had led them on a tour of the building and assured her mother they'd be safe? Memories stirred. A lot had changed for her since then.

Two years ago she'd been Stacey Moore, and she'd had a mother and a brother with her. Of course, they'd been terrified that Buddy would find them, but at least they'd all been together.

Tonight, she was just Star, and she was all alone. The house still had that same clean smell, the same cool, quiet chill in the air. It had been the first place she'd thought of when she'd left the stifling, stinking motel room and escaped into the moonless night.

Once she'd gotten safely outside, she'd been tempted to scream for help, but her survival instincts had kept her mouth shut, kept her quiet. She had to stay silent if she had any hope of making it past Hollywood and Sig and their creepy friends. She couldn't let them see her, couldn't let them follow her.

She didn't know how they always found her. She'd tried to run before, but each time they managed to find her before she'd made it out of the motel parking lot. This time she'd left only after Hollywood had passed out. This time she'd made it to the highway.

Star had suddenly wanted to go home more than anything, even if her mother had started seeing Buddy again. No matter what had happened in the past, she knew she needed to be with her mother and little brother. Needed to know they were okay.

But she had to be sure she hadn't been seen, wasn't being tracked. She needed a safe place to hide, and she had remembered just where she could find one.

Star knew the location of the safe house was supposed to be some big secret, but she'd seen the street address a few times during the two weeks she'd lived there, and for some reason, she had always remembered it. It hadn't even been hard to find. Not once the man who'd offered her a ride at the gas station had used his satnav. And she had just wanted to stay a day or two, just to make sure she wouldn't bring trouble home with her.

But then she had to go and run her big mouth and tell Eden about Hollywood and Jess. The thought of Jess made Star's eyes water again. Poor sweet Jess had been so sad at the end. The image of her tormented eyes had lingered in Star's mind, had finally given her the strength to try to run again. It was as if Jess had been warning her to leave before it was too late.

But what *had* happened to Jess? Star still wasn't sure. Not a hundred percent certain. She'd thought she could see Jess breathing when she'd left the room. Thought she'd seen her chest moving ever so slightly up and down. She was almost sure of it. But then when she got back, Jess was gone.

Had the smack killed her? Or had Hollywood and his friends taken her somewhere? All Star knew was that Jess only had one pair of shoes. She always hid them under the bed with her stash. Star had seen that both the shoes and the stash had been sitting right where Jess had left them. So, wherever Jess had gone, she likely hadn't been walking on her own.

Star opened her eyes and looked at the door, uncertain what to do. If Eden did call the police, Hollywood would know she'd snitched on them. They'd find her, and they'd kill her. Star sat up and stretched. She was reaching for her shoes when it dawned on her. Suddenly she knew how they would find her.

"How could I be so stupid?" she whispered, knowing without a doubt that she only had a few minutes to get away.

They would be coming for her soon, and she'd better be gone when they showed up. Star stood up and crossed the room. Without making a sound, she opened the door and stepped out into the hall.

CHAPTER FOUR

Eden dialed Reggie's number for the third time, and once again got her voicemail. She listened to the recorded greeting. "You've reached Dr. Regina Horn's voicemail. Feel free to leave your name, number, and reason for calling and Dr. Horn will return your call as soon as possible."

Eden waited for the beep, deciding she'd better leave a message this time. Her mind raced. *Where was Reggie?* Although Eden knew that Reggie wasn't officially on call, the foundation's director was usually quick to answer her phone in case one of the residents needed her.

"Reggie, please call me back. I've got a situation here and I need your help. Please, call my cell as soon as you get this." Eden ended the call and dropped her cell phone onto the desk. Duke sat at her feet looking up expectantly. It was well past time for them to head home and he was probably hungry and in need of a walk. He'd been cramped up all evening.

"Sorry, Duke, I guess I should have left you at home with Hope and Devon," Eden said, scratching behind his ears and looking into his doleful eyes. But she knew that Duke would prefer to be with her, even if that meant dinner had to wait. He'd been with her for the last four years, and they now spent most of their time together. Neither of them liked to be apart for long.

"Let's go to the kitchen and get you some water while we wait for Reggie to call back," Eden said, opening the office door and walking down the hall to the kitchen with Duke fast on her heels.

As she turned on the faucet to fill Duke's bowl, and then waited for him to eagerly lap up the cool water, she wasn't there to hear the automated voice telling the empty office that motion had been detected at door number four. She didn't see the security monitor display the image of Star hurrying down the back lawn toward the dock. She didn't see the girl slip into the shadows beside the Willow River.

By the time Eden and Duke got back to the office, the room was quiet, and the monitor was dark.

Eden sat down in front of the computer, rested her fingers on top of the keyboard, and closed her eyes. She needed to think, but exhaustion seeped in, making her head feel heavy. How long had it been since she'd had a good night's sleep?

She shook herself and reached for her coffee cup. Not a good time to be dozing off. She needed her wits about her if she was going to figure out why Star looked so familiar.

Star must have stayed at the safe house before. How else would she have known where to find it? And the girl's real name must have been saved somewhere in the foundation's database, but how could she find it without going through each record? *I'm sure I've met her; I must have seen her before. Why can't I remember?*

Eden tried to meet all the women that came through the foundation's programs. She wasn't interested in seeing only names and statistics on a report. She needed to know that she was making a difference to real people.

Eden stared over at Mercy's portrait again and read the inscription underneath it: *Whoever saves a single life, saves the world entire.* It was a quote from the Talmud that she'd heard many times before her sister had been killed, but it wasn't until she was standing beside Mercy's coffin, racked with guilt and grief, that she had grasped at the hope of redeeming herself by saving other women.

The idea had grown into the Mercy Harbor Foundation. It was the inspiration that had sustained her in her darkest moments. So long as there was a chance to save other lives, Mercy had not died in vain.

Eden would never know for sure how many lives they'd saved from suffering her sister's fate, but Mercy Harbor had provided shelter to hundreds of at-risk women in the four years it had been operating. She believed the foundation was making a difference, and that Mercy would have approved. But now it was time to save Star. If only Eden could remember her real name.

"Why can't I remember?" Eden muttered, frustrated by a name that seemed just out of reach.

She had always credited her ability to recall and memorize massive amounts of data for getting her through graduate school and helping her build a successful tech start-up. But Mercy's death had left its scars, and her memory, once so good, now seemed damaged, often failing her in moments of stress.

"Star...Star..." Eden murmured the name and tried to picture the girl's face, but the image in her mind was dominated by a cloud of platinum blonde hair and vivid purple bruises. She focused on the girl's light brown eyes and her lightly freckled nose.

Most likely she'd come in with her mother. No matter what Star had said, Eden knew in her gut the girl couldn't be eighteen. That meant she was too young to have been in the safe house on her own, otherwise, child protective services would have been called in, and they would have sent her elsewhere. Children normally only stayed at Mercy Harbor if they were with a custodial parent or guardian.

Eden opened a search window and was entering in criteria when the phone rang. It was Reggie.

"Where's the fire, dear?" Reggie asked, and Eden felt a lessening of tension at just hearing the warm, familiar voice.

"We've had an unexpected visitor tonight here at Shutter Street. A girl knocked on the door about thirty minutes ago. She's still here, and she's in pretty bad shape," Eden said, steeling herself for Reggie's reaction.

"Who is she?" Reggie asked, her voice indignant but still calm. "No one called me about sending over another new resident tonight."

"I'm not sure who she is, but she wasn't sent over by social services." Eden tried not to sound defensive.

"She came on her own and says her name is Star. But I think that's a nickname, or maybe her street name. She has been beaten pretty badly, and she's got tracks on her arms. They look recent."

"And you let this girl in without question?" Reggie was beginning to get the picture, and she wasn't happy. "No vetting? No idea who she is and who could have sent her?"

"I know, Reggie, I feel awful," Eden said. "It's just she needs help, and she looks familiar. She's just a kid..."

"I'll be right there," Reggie said, and the resigned sigh in her voice filled Eden with guilt faster than any reprimand could have. "My wheels are already heading in your direction."

Eden set the phone down and turned to Duke. "Well, boy, looks like I'm the one in the doghouse tonight."

Duke dropped his head on his paws and closed his eyes, and Eden, feeling chastened by both Reggie and Duke, sighed and trained her eyes on the blank security monitor. Just a few more minutes and Reggie would be there to help. She'd know what to do next.

Eden glanced at the clock again; it was half-past ten. The kids would hopefully be in bed by now, but Eden had the feeling it would be a long time before she'd be home to check on them.

CHAPTER FIVE

Reggie Horn smashed her foot down on the brake pedal of her Mini Cooper just as it hurtled up to the gate outside the house on Shutter Street. She tapped in her security code with a long red-lacquered fingernail, and when the gate rolled open, she maneuvered the tiny car into an equally tiny parking space before cutting off the engine.

Take a deep breath and count to ten, Reggie told herself, knowing that Eden was likely already in a heightened state of anxiety and wouldn't respond well to more stress coming from her.

Deliberately stopping herself from blowing into the room like a tiny force of nature as she usually did, she instead stepped into the office with a graceful flourish, her canary-yellow caftan billowing around her short, thin frame. She swung her enormous red leather messenger bag onto the desk and turned to face Eden.

"So, where is she?" Reggie asked, searching the room with a perplexed expression, her eyes big behind red-framed glasses, her ebony skin luminous in the soft glow of the desk lamp.

"She's sleeping in unit 1B. It's been empty since Tilda Collingsworth moved out last week," Eden replied, already moving toward the door. Duke jumped up to follow her.

"Stay here, Duke," Eden said, stepping into the hall without giving Reggie the chance to ask further questions.

Reggie patted the disappointed golden retriever on the head before following Eden out and closing the door behind her. She could see right away that the door to unit 1B was closed, but when Eden tried the knob it was unlocked, and she opened the door and stepped into the room.

Reggie pushed past her to see that both the twin beds were empty. A pair of tennis shoes lay on the floor, laces untied, along with an empty bottle of water.

"There's a light on in the bathroom," Reggie said, motioning for Eden to knock.

"Star? Everything all right?" Eden called, tapping on the door twice. When Star didn't respond, Eden knocked again. "Star? Are you okay?"

"Is she even in there?" Reggie asked. "I don't hear anything."

"Maybe she passed out," Eden said, looking back at Reggie with wide, green eyes.

Reggie could hear the tremor of anxiety in Eden's voice and felt her own heart begin to pump faster in response. She reached over and jiggled the doorknob; it wasn't locked. She pushed open the door and stared into the brightly lit room. No one was standing in front of the small sink or sitting on the toilet. She crossed the floor and drew back the mint green shower curtain. The bathtub was freshly cleaned and completely empty.

"Looks like she did a runner." Reggie's tone was matter-of-fact; she wasn't surprised.

"She was sleeping," Eden said, returning to the main room and looking around, as if she may have missed Star standing in a corner.

Reggie ignored Eden's comment and headed back toward the office. "We can check the security tapes first to see if she left the building. If we don't see anything we'll have to search room to room."

"But I was watching the monitor. There's no way she got past the camera," Eden insisted as she followed Reggie back into the office, but there was a hint of doubt in her voice.

Reggie began clicking away on the mouse next to the display. She opened a folder and clicked on a thumbnail image. A video clip of the back entrance and lawn appeared. In the video the back door was open and a slim girl with messy platinum curls slipped out and closed the door behind her, before darting toward the river. Within seconds she had disappeared into the shadows.

"I presume that was Star?" Reggie asked, looking back at Eden, feeling a rush of sympathy at the crestfallen expression on Eden's face.

"Yes, that was Star," Eden responded, staring back at Reggie. "She just...left. Why'd she leave like that? And why would she go without her shoes?"

Before Reggie could remind her that drug-addicted teenagers didn't always need a reason to disappear, Eden turned and hurried down the hall and through the back door calling Star's name. Reggie scrambled after her, arriving at the back door just in time to see Eden reach the lawn and start to run. Fear surged through Reggie as she saw Eden slip into the pitch-black shadows by the shore.

"Eden, wait!" Reggie yelled, returning to the office to grab a flashlight out of the utility closet, then running down the hall and out the backdoor toward the dock. She cursed herself for wearing her favorite strappy sandals as the kitten-heels sunk into the soft, wet ground near the river.

"Star!" Eden called again, and then as Reggie approached, cried out, "What if she's thrown herself into the river, Reggie? What if she wants to kill herself?"

The image of the untied shoes abandoned by the bed played in Reggie's mind as she aimed the beam of the flashlight toward the dock. Something was different. What was it?

"The boat," Eden said, turning to Reggie. "The little rowboat is gone. She must have taken the boat."

"If she's in the boat, then she should be safe on the water. I'm sure she'll find a place to dock," Reggie said, putting a hand on Eden's shoulder. "Come on, let's go back inside."

"But what if she tips over and drowns? Or what if they catch her...whoever *they* are?" Eden's voice caught in her throat, and her eyes filled with tears.

"I know, honey, I know," Reggie said, guiding Eden back toward the building. "But you did what you could."

"She's so young," Eden moaned, and Reggie cringed inwardly, knowing better than most the type of abuse some people were capable of inflicting on those weaker than themselves. She also knew that many victims of abuse ended up returning to their abuser. She didn't want to worry Eden even more, but a thought nagged in the back of her head.

Was the poor girl running back to the man who had hurt her?

"I know you want to, but you just can't save everyone." Reggie stepped in front of Eden and looked into her friend's haunted eyes, recognizing the guilt and regret that always seemed to hover just under the surface.

"You have to forgive yourself for...well, for not saving Mercy. You have to let it go."

"This isn't about Mercy or about me." Eden stared out into the dark water. "This is about that girl out there, on her own."

Eden began to walk toward the safe house. Her shoulders were slumped, and Reggie thought she looked somehow deflated, her energy seeming to have deserted her.

Reggie turned to look back into the shadows. She strained to hear, hoped to detect the sound of oars breaking the surface of the river, but the night was quiet and only the croaking of frogs and chirping of crickets could be heard in the dark. Star was gone.

CHAPTER SIX

Hollywood sat in the passenger seat of Vinny's old silver sedan and checked his phone again. She was still in there, he was sure of it. They'd driven by just in time to see Star disappear into what looked like some type of big apartment house on Shutter Street.

Someone had been standing in the doorway looking out when they'd gone past, so he'd had to duck down and tell Vinny to keep driving. But when they circled back around, the front door was closed, the gate leading up the front walk was locked, and Star had disappeared into the house.

"She's in there," Hollywood said to Vinny, without taking his eyes off the house. "Just a matter of time until she has to come out."

"At least she didn't run to the cops," Vinny said, drumming his fingers on the steering wheel, looking around at the other houses on the block.

"She ain't going to the cops," Hollywood snorted. "No way."

Hollywood had already decided it was safe to stake out the house, at least for now. The block didn't have street lamps, and most of the houses were dark. No one seemed to be out walking their dog or jogging, and no other cars had driven by. It was a quiet neighborhood. So why had Star run here?

Hollywood didn't know what she was planning, but he needed to find out. If Star did rat them out, the whole operation at the Old

Canal Motel would be in jeopardy, and next week's shipment would have to be called off. Sig wouldn't be happy.

"I'd better call Sig," Hollywood said, looking over at Vinny. His mouth twitched as he said, "Sorry, pal, but I gotta let him know you screwed up and Star got away."

Vinny jerked his head around and stared at Hollywood.

"You're the one that passed out, man. I wasn't even there."

"Exactly, you moron, if you'd been there she'd never have gotten away." Hollywood watched Vinny digest the insult.

He repressed the urge to laugh when Vinny swallowed hard, adjusted his glasses, and turned to look out the window. At least he had Vinny here to amuse him while he waited for Star to come out. He picked up his cell phone and tapped in Sig's number.

"Hey. Sig, what's up?" Hollywood snuck another peek at Vinny, who had tensed in the seat next to him. "I got some bad news, man. Yeah, Vinny took his eye off the ball and one of the girls did a runner."

"You fucking kidding me?" Sig spat out the words.

Hollywood knew it wasn't so much a question, as it was a threat, but he wasn't scared, at least not yet. He watched Vinny squeeze the steering wheel with both hands until his knuckles went white.

Holding the phone to his ear with one hand, and scratching his arm with the other, Hollywood said, "I know, I know, it's a mess, but Vinny's already on it, and I'm with him too, man. We've tracked the bitch down and should have her back at the motel shortly. I'll keep you posted."

"You do what you have to do." Sig's gravelly voice hinted at the unfiltered Camels he always kept in his front shirt pocket.

"Yeah, yeah, I got it." Hollywood disconnected the call and produced a low whistle.

"Got what, man? What did he say?" Vinny asked, frowning over at Hollywood.

Hollywood patted Vinny's shoulder. "Don't worry, bro, I've got your back. Always have, right?"

Vinny gave a slight, grudging nod, and Hollywood relaxed as he flipped down the sun visor and looked into the mirror, admiring his reflection. He stared into his own green eyes, brushing a strand of dark blonde hair back from his brow and smiling.

Looking good. Nothing to worry about.

He wasn't going to take the blame for passing out and allowing Star to slip past him. It wasn't his fault he'd gotten bored and needed a fix. The puny amount of smack Sig was passing around lately wasn't near enough for him.

He had needed more, so he'd shot up the junk that was meant for Star, as well as his own stash and had passed out. No big deal. Once he had Star back he'd teach her a lesson she wouldn't forget.

Hollywood looked down at his phone and watched the glowing dot on the screen. He glanced over at Vinny's worried face and chuckled, then turned up the volume of the radio and leaned his head back against the headrest. He wasn't sure how long they'd been sitting in the car, but he was beginning to feel itchy and restless.

Suddenly the dark street was illuminated by headlights as a bright red Mini Cooper sped by and stopped outside the big building. Hollywood watched as the wrought iron gate rolled open and the car pulled into a small parking lot on the left side of the building.

When no one emerged onto the front porch, Hollywood realized there must be a side entrance.

"I think you're gonna have to go up and check out the house. Maybe take a peek in the window," Hollywood said, scratching his arm again and wishing he'd brought his stash with him. If this was going to take much longer he would need a fix.

Vinny glared back, his glasses smudged and a lock of his normally slicked-back hair falling over his forehead but didn't reply.

Five minutes later the iron gate began to roll open again. This time a big, white Expedition pulled out and headed east on Shutter Street.

Hollywood saw a blonde woman in the driver's seat look both ways before she pulled into the road. The SUV's windows were tinted, and he couldn't see if anyone else was in the car, but the glowing dot on his phone had already begun to move.

"C'mon, dumbass, follow her," Hollywood barked, hitting Vinny on the shoulder and sitting up straight in his seat.

He pointed to the SUV's taillights and nodded his head in satisfaction as Vinny started the car and steered the silver sedan onto the street. His eyes gleamed as he watched the SUV turn left, heading toward downtown Willow Bay.

"Oh yeah, we're coming for you, Star; we're right behind you."

CHAPTER SEVEN

Detective Nessa Ainsley ran a weary hand through her tangle of auburn curls as she surveyed a growing pile of files that dominated her desk. She had planned to take the most urgent files home with her. Of course, that had been before the call came in about the missing girl.

Nessa often reviewed witness statements and finished the day's reports at her kitchen table once the kids were in bed and Jerry had drifted off in front of the television. She found that working in the familiar hush of her quiet house made reading and recording the disturbing details of violent crimes more bearable.

Late nights at home also helped Nessa manage her caseload without her partner, Detective Pete Barker, who had suffered a heart attack while mowing his front yard the previous month. Barker said the doctor had called it a myocardial infarction, which sounded less threatening. Kind of like a misdemeanor infraction, as opposed to the more felonious-sounding term, heart attack.

The last time Nessa saw Barker, he wasn't sure when he'd be able to return to work. But she had been determined to handle her cases efficiently on her own. She didn't want Chief Kramer to be tempted to assign her a new partner. She preferred to work the extra hours and wait for Barker; it would be too hard to break in someone new.

In any case, Nessa doubted the budget would allow for a new detective. The Violent Crimes unit she was in consisted of four dedicated detectives who handled homicides, sexual assaults, abductions, and robberies. Nessa knew that if Barker didn't return soon, Chief Kramer would likely move up a detective from another unit, such as Vice. Either that, or he'd have to add a headcount.

Adding a new headcount, even temporarily, would require Chief Kramer to approve a substantial increase for the unit's budget. The thought made her smile.

We'd have better odds playing the lottery than waiting for tightwad Kramer to cough up more money.

Nessa had been ten minutes away from packing up her worn leather laptop case and heading toward the exit when the switchboard of the Willow Bay Police Department patched a call through from the county jail.

"Detective Nessa Ainsley here, how can I help?" Her eyes involuntarily ticked to the clock.

"Hold on Detective and I'll connect you." She heard a click and then the faint sound of tinny music. She'd been put on hold.

Nessa took a calming breath and smiled. The ability to produce a smile of great forbearance at a moment of stress or irritation had been passed down to her from her mother, who had been, in Nessa's mind, a true southern lady.

Her irritation now under control, she made herself pick up a pen and prepare to jot down notes on a thick pad of paper.

Finally, the music stopped, and a tentative woman's voice said, "Uh, hello, is this the police?"

"Detective Nessa Ainsley here, how can I help?"

Nessa repeated her standard greeting, but this time her voice held a note of concern. The distress in the woman's voice was palpable even over the phone.

"This is Beth Carmichael. I'm an inmate at Willow Bay Women's Detention Center and I want to file a report about my daughter. She's missing. I think something bad must have happened to her."

Nessa felt the words vibrate in the pit of her stomach. Another missing girl. An unwelcome question popped into her mind.

Will we find this one in time?

A shiver coursed through her, despite the warmth of the room, but Nessa managed to keep her voice steady.

"Sorry to hear that, Ms. Carmichael. We'll need to fill out a report and get all the details. First of all, how old is your daughter?"

Over the next ten minutes, Nessa established that Beth Carmichael's sixteen-year-old daughter, Jessica Carmichael, had been staying with various friends and relatives while her mother was serving six months in the detention center that acted as the county's jail for all female inmates.

But no one, including Beth, had seen or heard from the teen for more than two weeks. Beth was beginning to panic. She'd reported her fears to one of the correction officers, who had suggested she file a missing person's report in hopes the police could track down the teenager.

"Do you have anybody in the area I can use as a point of contact? Someone who'll know Jessica's friends and such?" Nessa knew Beth wouldn't be able to help find her daughter from inside the jail, and she knew that Jessica wouldn't be able to communicate with her mother directly from the outside.

"My lawyer has offered to help me. I don't really have anyone else I can trust," Beth said, her voice cracking. She sniffled and continued, "Leo Steele is my court-appointed lawyer. He takes on cases for free, or pro bono, or whatever. He promised to help me find Jessica."

"Yes, I know Mr. Steele. He's a fine lawyer," Nessa replied, with mixed emotions. She was glad to hear Beth Carmichael had someone competent working for her, but then again Leo Steele had won more cases for his criminal clients than Nessa liked to think about. He'd ruined the last district attorney's conviction rate almost single-handedly.

Beth sounded more optimistic when she said, "Leo worked really hard to get my sentence reduced. The first lawyer I had was useless. She talked me into accepting a plea bargain that had me serving three years in the state prison. Luckily that lawyer quit, and I got Leo. He managed to get them to reduce my time to six months in county. I've only got four months to go, but now...now Jess is missing."

The words lingered in Nessa's mind as she sat at her desk five hours later still waiting for Leo Steele to arrive so that they could fill out an official form and discuss the game plan for trying to find Jessica.

Mr. Steele must be very busy and very important, Nessa thought with an elaborate roll of her pale blue eyes. *No need to worry about poor little me waiting here til all hours.*

She was tempted to give up and go home, but the despair she'd heard in Beth Carmichael's voice kept her in her chair. Another girl was missing. The last time Nessa had taken a report on a missing girl, the girl hadn't been found for more than three years, and Nessa had been the one that had to tell the girl's family that their daughter's remains had been found in the river.

"Nessa, someone's here to file a missing person's report." Dave Eddings, the uniformed officer manning the station's front desk, had stuck his head into the detective's office without her noticing. "I'll put 'em in room three."

* * *

Nessa was surprised to see an attractive woman with long, honey blonde hair sitting at the table when she entered the interrogation room. There was something familiar about the woman. She wore a white, tailored blouse and held a Macy's shopping bag on her lap. A golden retriever sat at attention next to her.

"I'm sorry, are you here to file a missing person's report?" Nessa asked the woman, thinking she must have mixed-up the room number. She buttoned her suit jacket and smoothed back her unruly hair, conscious that she must look a bit scruffy after the long day.

"Yes, well, I'm Eden Winthrop, and I need to report an...incident. I guess it *does* technically involve a missing person."

Eden placed a business card on the table that identified her as the founder and president of Mercy Harbor Foundation.

Nessa had heard of the organization; it had a solid reputation as far as she could remember. She tried not to stare at the dog. Was it a service dog? Would it be rude to ask? She decided to act like the dog wasn't there for the time being. She kept her eyes locked on Eden Winthrop's face.

"Okay, well, I'm Detective Vanessa Ainsley, but everyone around here just calls me Nessa."

She found that people seemed to share information more openly when they were on a first-name basis. She also hated the way most people mangled her last name. Nessa jotted down a few initial notes on her pad, looking up at Eden with an encouraging nod.

"I was hoping to speak to Detective Barker. He helped me years ago with another case." Eden swallowed hard, and Nessa tried to curb her impatience.

"Unfortunately, Detective Barker is on leave. He's a bit under the weather." Nessa poised her pen over her pad again. "But I'm his partner, and I'll be more than happy to help you."

Eden cleared her throat and began twisting her hands in her lap. Finally, she said, "Earlier tonight a teenage girl showed up at one of our residential shelters unannounced. She looked like she'd been beaten. She was scared and wanted a place to stay. She told me she was in fear for her life, and that a friend of hers is missing. I left her in one of the rooms to rest while I called the foundation's director. When I got back she had just ... disappeared."

"Disappeared? You mean she just up and left?" Nessa asked, writing down more notes.

"Yes, she ran out the back door without her shoes on. She left them behind. I've brought them with me."

Eden opened the shopping bag and pulled out a pair of small black tennis shoes with neon pink laces. She set the shoes on the scarred wooden table between them.

"She ran down to the river barefoot and disappeared into the shadows. It was dark, so I'm not sure, but I think she took the rowboat we had tied to the dock. I mean the boat is missing...and so is she."

Nessa tensed at the mention of the river; she mentally recoiled from the image it conjured. Bones, bleached white from the sun, strewn among torn, faded fabric and tangled in soft rush at the edge of the water. Some days she wondered if the image had been burned into her retinas. It seemed to always be there just waiting for her to close her eyes.

"Who's the girl?" Nessa asked, trying to ignore the irrational dread that had started in her belly. "How old is she?"

"Well, I don't know her real name. She said her name is Star, but I don't think that's true. I think maybe she stayed in the shelter before, but I'm not certain. And she says she's eighteen, but she's probably no more than sixteen, maybe younger."

Eden absently scratched the big dog's back, as if assuring herself he was still there.

"I run a foundation for women who have been abused. We provide safe housing; help them get on their feet. They're often hiding from violent partners."

Nessa nodded again, noticing the tremble in Eden's hand as she pushed back her long, blonde hair and took a deep breath.

She's wound tighter than a clock, Nessa realized with some sympathy. She knew from personal experience that some people never got used to confronting violence or its aftermath.

"Anonymity is extremely important to these women." Eden paused as if trying to come to a decision.

"I may have information on this girl...on Star...in the foundation's database, but I'd have to do some research. And what I find out would need to be kept strictly confidential."

"Well, we do have our fair share of crazies here in Willow Bay, so I understand what you're saying," Nessa replied, "but it'll be real hard to find someone if we don't have a clue who they are."

"You *have* to find her." Eden's glistening green eyes bore through Nessa. "She's in danger and I...well I know she needs help."

Nessa could see that Eden was becoming increasingly distressed. Her hands fluttered in her lap like frightened birds when they weren't stroking the dog's head.

She turned to the golden retriever. "And who are you then, big guy?"

The dog stared at Nessa with curious eyes. She liked the way he tilted his head as if waiting to hear what else she had to say.

"This is Duke," Eden said, her voice softening on his name. "He's my emotional support dog."

"Is that like a service dog?" Nessa asked, not daring to ask the more interesting questions that sprang to mind. She wondered about Eden Winthrop's past.

What had happened to her? And why did she need emotional support?

Eden looked at Duke and smiled for the first time. "No, he's not specially trained to perform tasks like a service dog, but he is a certified ESA, which stands for Emotional Support Animal. That just means he helps me cope with anxiety. I'd be lost without him."

A sudden, loud rap on the door was followed by the appearance of a man with disheveled blonde hair and a five o'clock shadow worthy of a GQ cover.

"I'm Detective Simon Jankowski with the WBPD, Special Investigations Unit," he said with a curt nod to Eden, before turning to Nessa. "You said you had a report about a missing teenage girl?"

"Hold your horses, Jankowski, slow down." Nessa held up her hands in mock surrender. "This isn't the missing person report I told you about earlier. This is Eden Winthrop, and she's here to report that a different girl may have gone missing."

"You mean there's been more than one girl reported missing in Willow Bay tonight?" Eden asked in dismay. "It may just be a coincidence, but Star did mention a friend of hers had disappeared a few days ago. Someone she called Jess."

* * *

Nessa wondered if the night would ever end. She rubbed her stiff shoulders and stretched her back as Jankowski fired questions at Eden Winthrop over the wooden table. The poor woman's chest was practically heaving in and out as she tried to explain again what she knew about the teenager called Star and her friend Jess.

"Did she give you a description of her friend? Did she tell you her last name?" Jankowski had asked the questions before, but he liked to throw out repeat questions during interviews to see if he could elicit a different answer.

Sometimes the tactic actually worked, but Nessa thought that tonight was not going to be one of those times. Eden had already provided all the information she knew. Further questioning could only be considered harassment.

Officer Eddington opened the door again and stuck his head in.

“Leo Steele is here wanting to see you, Nessa. He says it’s about a missing girl.”

“That’s fine, Dave, tell him I’ll be with him shortly.” She felt a small flash of satisfaction that now Leo Steele was the one waiting for her. *No need to be nasty, Nessa*, she scolded herself as she turned to Eden.

“Thanks for your statement, Ms. Winthrop. We appreciate you coming in and telling us about Star.”

She put her pen down and stood up to indicate the interview was over. Jankowski also rose and began moving toward the door.

“But what are you going to do about Star...and Jess?” Eden stammered, her brows furrowed in frustration.

“We’ll do what we can, Ms. Winthrop.” Jankowski jumped in before Nessa could respond. “And, hopefully, if these girls want to be found, we’ll find them. But if they make bad choices and associate with addicts and violent criminals, I’m not sure how much we can do.”

Eden’s face blanched at the words. "I see good kids involved in violent situations all the time. One day they’re living at home, and the next they are hiding in a domestic abuse shelter. After a crisis, life can tend to spiral out of control, especially for teenagers. They can end up making bad choices. Doesn't mean they're bad kids. They still deserve to be protected, Detective."

Nessa glared at Jankowski before placing a hand on Eden’s stiff shoulder. “We’ll do everything we can, I promise you that. Just let us know if you think of anything else, and we’ll be sure to update you as progress is made.”

Eden stayed seated at the table, her fists clenched in front of her. She looked up at Nessa, eyes blazing.

"That's what the police said when my sister's husband became abusive. They promised to *do what they could*. Well, it wasn't enough; he still managed to kill her."

Nessa stared at Eden in surprise, struggling to hold back the words that threatened to tumble out.

I thought I recognized you; Mercy Lancaster was your sister.

Everyone in the department knew about the violent murder of Mercy Lancaster, but Nessa had forgotten that Mercy's family name had been Winthrop. The connections slowly clicked into place inside Nessa's tired brain. Eden Winthrop was Mercy's older sister. The one that had found her sister's body.

No wonder Eden had asked for Barker. He'd worked the case, hadn't he? That had been before Nessa. Before they'd been partners. She made a mental note to ask him about the case the next time she checked in on him.

Jankowski froze with his hand on the doorknob, his belligerent expression falling from his face like a discarded Halloween mask, revealing a look that Nessa thought might be regret. At least she hoped it was.

Nessa noticed that Duke had moved closer to Eden and was nuzzling her hand. His eyes silently watched his owner, then flicked to Nessa. She looked away, feeling inexplicably guilty and useless. Just as she had when they'd found Tiffany Clarke's body.

Her stomach clenched, and she thought for one horrifying minute that she might actually throw up the dregs of the coffee she'd been drinking all night.

Eden sighed and stood up, and Nessa could see that she had curves in all the right places; curves she had tried unsuccessfully to hide underneath plain, tailored clothes.

Eden folded the now-empty Macy's bag and tucked it under her arm. Moving across the room with a ballerina's grace, she slipped past Jankowski's bulky frame and pushed open the door. Nessa noted that Eden was taller than she had appeared sitting down. Leather pumps added a few inches to her height, making her almost as tall as Jankowski.

"Come on, Duke," Eden said as she gave Nessa one last long look. "Let's go home."

Eden pushed the door closed behind her with a firm click, the cheap wood coming within inches of Jankowski's stony face.

Nessa folded her arms over her chest and said, "Before I get Mr. Steele and take his statement, I wanted to ask you something."

Jankowski cocked his eyebrow. "Sure, just hurry it up."

"Just wondering *why* you had to act like such a pig-headed ass to that poor woman. What's your problem tonight, Jankowski?" She cocked her head and kept her arms folded, wishing she were as tall as Eden so that she didn't have to look up to glare at him.

"I don't have time to waste on pleasantries," Jankowski responded, his eyes hard. "As I told you earlier, we've got a shitstorm brewing in Vice, and the chief is all over us to figure out what's going on before the press gets wind of it."

"Well, can you spend a few precious seconds and fill *me* in?" Nessa asked with a sugary sarcasm she usually refrained from at work. "You said this case of yours might have something to do with my missing person's reports?"

"Chief Kramer has created a special task force, operating on a strictly need-to-know basis only, even inside the department," Jankowski said, choosing to ignore her obvious irritation.

"I can only say that I'd like to sit in on the interviews related to the missing teenagers to see if there's a possible connection to our case."

"Goodness, you guys in Vice *are* very busy and important these days."

Nessa couldn't resist making the smartass comment even though she knew it was childish. Jankowski would be firmly on her naughty list going forward unless he had a major attitude adjustment. But as she opened the door to exit the room, she had a thought.

"You say your case may have a connection with these missing girls; Tiffany Clarke was a missing girl until she turned up dead in the river. Does your case have any connection to the open Tiffany Clarke investigation?"

Jankowski looked taken aback. "What? No, Ortiz and Ingram are still working that investigation as far as I know. And I'm sure you can put two and two together and realize our task force is tracking the type of illegal activity that Tiffany Clarke was not involved in. From what I heard she was a wholesome kid. No sign of troubles at home. Not a runaway junkie or a pro."

Nessa regarded the burly police detective with concern.

"So, you think these missing girls may be involved in some type of drug or prostitution ring? Maybe victims of sex trafficking?"

"Don't get ahead of yourself, Nessa," Jankowski replied, but he wouldn't make eye contact.

"You need to take Leo Steele's statement, and I need to collect information for the task force. That's as far as it goes for now. We have our hands full without looking for the psycho who killed Tiffany. Nothing to do with our case."

Nessa nodded and grew quiet. She was still angry that the Tiffany Clarke case had been turned over to Detectives Ingram and Ortiz after Barker's heart attack. It wasn't fair. But whatever was happening, she didn't like to work in a vacuum. Especially not in a small community like Willow Bay.

If there was a killer on the loose, and sex traffickers in the area, she wanted to be updated on both to make sure her missing girls weren't related to any other line of investigation. That just made sense.

"I'm wondering if someone in Vice knows anything about Star. Sounds like she's an addict, so maybe someone's encountered her while working undercover. What about your buddy, Reinhardt? You think he might know who her dealer could be?"

Jankowski's face reddened with what looked to Nessa like annoyance, but when he replied, his voice was calm.

"It's a stretch, but I'll see what Reinhardt knows. Now, can we get on with the next statement, please?"

"No need to have a conniption," Nessa muttered as she walked down the hall.

She'd get another coffee before calling Leo Steele back to the interview room. He'd taken his sweet time getting over to the station, so he obviously wasn't in too big of a hurry.

CHAPTER EIGHT

Leo Steele's phone buzzed in his pocket as he tried to feed a crumpled dollar bill into the only vending machine in the police station's lobby. He hadn't eaten since lunchtime when Pat Monahan had insisted that he take a break to eat the cheese and cucumber sandwich she'd brought back from Bay Subs and Grub. His empty stomach was now waging an all-out war. A bag of Sun Chips and a bottle of water would have to suffice for the time being.

"Hello?" Leo collected the bag of chips from the vending machine tray as he swiped his phone to answer the call. He already knew what the automated voice on the other end would say.

"This is a collect call from an inmate at the Willow Bay Women's Detention Center. All calls are recorded. To accept the call, please press 1. To decline the call, please press 2."

Leo accepted the call, settling his tall, lean frame into one of the hard-plastic chairs that lined the small waiting area. He stretched out his long legs, loosened his red power tie, and unbuttoned the top button of his white dress shirt. He heard a click, and then Beth Carmichael's worried voice.

"Leo, it's Beth. What did the police say? Are they looking for Jessica?"

"I'm waiting to talk to the police now, Beth. I got delayed, but I should be talking to them any minute." Leo tried to keep the exhaustion out of his voice. He'd been preparing the defense for a high-profile case all week and had been working twelve-hour days. The stress and lack of sleep were starting to catch up with him.

"Please do whatever you can, Leo," Beth implored, her voice thin and strained. "I know something has happened to Jessica; I can feel it."

"I'll make sure the police understand the urgency, and that it's crucial that they find Jessica right away. I won't let them shrug this off, believe me." Leo ran an impatient hand through his dark, unruly hair as he imagined the response he was likely to get from the police.

He'd had both personal and professional experience with police incompetence and indifference. That's why he'd initially asked to speak to Pete Barker, the only detective in Willow Bay that he trusted. The only one who had always treated Leo's father like a human being after he'd been arrested.

But the duty officer had informed Leo that Detective Barker was on leave and that Barker's partner, Detective Ainsley would meet with him. Leo didn't know much about Barker's latest partner, other than she was the first woman detective the city had ever hired, but he wouldn't be surprised if she was as cold and callous as the men she worked with.

It wouldn't matter to any of them that a mother was frantic about her missing daughter. Once they heard that Jessica's mother was in jail and that the girl didn't have a permanent address, they would assume she'd run off on her own accord. But Leo knew that Jessica was vulnerable and alone. She may have gotten herself into serious trouble. The kind she couldn't handle on her own.

He put a stack of three chips into his mouth and followed the bite with a long swig of water as Beth listed all the people the police should question. His eyes were trained on the door that led into the interrogation rooms. He'd been back in those rooms too many times to count over the years as he had tried to keep his clients out of jail.

He didn't usually ask the police for help, but this was different. A minor was missing, and the police needed to do something about it.

When the door finally opened, he saw a tall, blonde woman exit, followed by a golden retriever on a long black leash. The woman's fine, delicate features looked familiar, as did her gracefully curved figure. Did he know her? He certainly didn't see many women with her looks wandering around Willow Bay.

The small community had its fair share of attractive women, but a tall, curvy blonde that looked like she'd stepped off the cover of a men's magazine? That was a rare occurrence. And Leo had dated or slept with most of the eligible women in the town, or at least that's how it felt sometimes when he stopped working long enough to look around and wonder why he was still alone, and if there was anyone else out there for him.

The woman must have felt him watching her; she looked over at him with sad green eyes. Her eyes found his, and she recoiled, as if in shock, or was it anger? It certainly wasn't the look of interest he was used to receiving from an attractive woman. Turning her face away, she strode toward the door, urging the leashed dog to follow.

"Come on, Duke, let's go!" The woman's voice struck a chord in him, igniting unwanted emotions in his gut, and the niggle of a memory gnawed inside his brain, trying to escape.

Was it guilt, or perhaps shame? He'd seen those green eyes before. But when, and where? Beth's voice rose out of the phone and yanked him back to his primary purpose.

"Sorry, Beth, I'm here." He said into the phone, still watching the woman as she opened the door and stepped outside.

The dog trotted after her but wasn't fast enough. The door closed between them, trapping the golden retriever inside with his leash wedged between the door and the frame. "Hold on just a sec, Beth."

Leo walked to the door and pulled it open, careful to dislodge the leash and give the dog room to walk through.

"There you go, boy," Leo said, giving the dog a friendly smile. The dog looked back at him, his expression curious, but the woman didn't turn around or acknowledge Leo. He caught a flash of golden blonde hair as the dog and his owner disappeared into the dark night.

Behind him, a voice called out, "Leo Steele? Detective Ainsley is waiting for you in room three."

Leo ended his call. His pulse quickened, and his dark eyes took on a determined gleam as he followed the young officer into the back.

CHAPTER NINE

The blonde woman and her dog left the police station and hurried down the sidewalk toward the parking garage. Star wasn't with them. Hollywood looked at his phone and saw that the glowing dot on his app was still positioned directly over the WBPD on the digital map.

Was Star still in there? Had she even gone inside?

He was beginning to have doubts about the app's accuracy, and his cravings were getting stronger by the minute. He was also feeling nauseous and the itching had gotten worse. He needed a fix.

"Where's that bag she had?" Vinny asked as the woman and dog disappeared into the garage stairwell that would take them up to the second floor.

The parking garage was pretty much empty at this time of night, but the ground-level parking spaces were reserved for official police vehicles, so the woman had been forced to park on the second level. Hollywood had been too paranoid about getting trapped in a garage full of cops to follow the SUV into the garage, and he had yelled at Vinny to keep driving past the garage and circle back around.

They'd had to stop at two red lights and ended up driving by the police station again just in time to see the woman disappear inside. Neither he nor Vinny had seen Star, but the glowing dot had moved, hovering in place over the police station. Hollywood assumed that she'd already gone inside. Now he wasn't so sure.

"What bag?" Hollywood snapped, not taking his eyes off the garage exit.

"The Macy's bag she was carrying. She went in with the bag, and I didn't see it just now when she came out. She must have given something to the cops," Vinny said. He yawned and sat up straighter behind the wheel.

"You want to follow her when she pulls out?"

Hollywood was tempted to smash his fist into Vinny's big nose. How the hell was he supposed to know what to do? Who could think when all he wanted to do was shoot up or throw up.

And what will Sig do to me if he finds out I've lost that little bitch for good? Lost her at a fucking police station for Christ's sake. He won't be handing out smack if he's pissed at me.

Hollywood could feel his legs jittering, but he couldn't make them stop. His fingers tapped erratically against the dashboard as he tried to decide what to do.

He needed to get Star back to the motel fast. Otherwise, he'd have to find a new girl to take her place in the shipment to Miami next week. Sig was counting on that shipment to clear some of the debt they owed and get the crew from Miami off their backs.

"No, don't follow her," Hollywood muttered, knowing that finding out where Star was, and what she might have told the police, had to take priority over following the unknown blonde if Star wasn't with her.

"So, you think Star's inside?" Vinny asked, his glasses opaque in the dark car as he turned his head toward Hollywood.

"How the hell should I know?" Hollywood yelled, bashing his fist on the dashboard. Sweat had started to bead on his forehead, the drops trickling down his cheeks like tears as he stared out the window toward the police station.

"Calm down, man. Take it easy," Vinny muttered. He started the car and flipped on the air conditioning. "Take a chill."

Hollywood felt the cool air move over his clammy skin. He let his body relax back into the seat and tried to think. He needed a fix, and then he needed to find Star. And after that, he had to find another girl to meet the agreed quota for next week.

They still hadn't replaced Jess. She'd been questionable all along though. From the start, she hadn't been easy to control. Then once she'd gotten hooked, she'd been a mess. Always sick and whining. Probably better off that she was gone.

But they needed to provide ten girls or there would be hell to pay, and right now they only had nine at the motel. Well, nine if they found Star and brought her back. And that was looking like a big if.

"It's your fault, Vinny," Hollywood said in a cold, hard voice, all traces of amusement gone.

"You were supposed to watch the girls, keep 'em in line. You let 'em freak out about Jess, and now Star's gone, too. I vouched for you with Sig, and you're making me look bad. You're useless, bro."

"I told you I didn't want to get involved with this shit, man. This isn't my thing. This is all *your* fault." Vinny looked sullen and crossed his arms over his chest.

Hollywood lashed out as fast as a rattlesnake, grabbing Vinny's collar and twisting it tight around his neck. "You listen to me, moron, you better stop fucking up and start towing the damn line here. You're *in* now, and there's no way in hell Sig is gonna let you out."

He let go of Vinny's collar and settled back into his seat. "Star wouldn't have run if that shit with Jess hadn't gone down. I had the little girl wrapped around my finger."

Vinny clutched at his throat and smoothed out his shirt and collar. He didn't look over at Hollywood.

"No more mister nice-guy from me," Hollywood said, scratching his arm. "From now on, I'll show the girls who's the boss. You just watch and learn."

Vinny shook his head and looked out the window, his mouth closed in a tight line.

Hollywood decided he'd give it another ten minutes and then he'd go back to the motel to get high. He deserved it after everything he'd been through. After that, he'd figure out what to do next.

He looked over and saw that Vinny had a bright red mark around his neck and that his hands were trembling on the steering wheel.

What a wimp. Hollywood resisted the urge to scratch at his arm yet again and shook his head in disgust. *Once a loser, always a loser.*

CHAPTER TEN

The silvery light of the waxing crescent moon shimmered off the Diablo River, casting an ethereal glow on the man's pale face. He stood motionless in the night, transfixed by memories that had called him back again and again. He almost felt guilty. Almost felt like he'd defiled something sacred. The last girl had been a mistake. But the first one? The first one had been fate.

He looked around the clearing next to the riverbank. Everything seemed the same as the first time. The same weeping willow tree swooned against the sky. The same shadowy tangle of water hyacinth floated ominously in the black water, suffocating whatever lay beneath. The same all-consuming need coursed inside his veins screamed to be satisfied. The only thing that was missing was Tiffany.

He closed his eyes, trying to conjure the image of the long-gone girl, hoping to relive their last moments together.

Tiffany's golden hair shone in the moonlight, long and smooth against soft shoulders bared to the warm night air in a strapless yellow sundress. He watched her light a small camping lantern and spread out a blanket before taking two cups out of a wicker picnic basket.

She checked her watch and looked back at the dirt path that led up to Harrington Road. Her baby blue VW Bug was parked at the road's end, and the man imagined he could make out the Willow Bay High School Student

Parking Permit sticker on the windshield. She was still so young, so innocent. She had no business being there. No business meeting up with a man she hardly knew.

Well, he knew the man, and he knew exactly what the man wanted. Poor Tiffany had no idea what she had set herself up for. She'd be used and defiled like all the other girls before her. No, it was up to him to save her from her own foolishness.

The man stepped into the clearing. His heart raced as she turned her head, a smile starting to form before she saw that he wasn't the man she'd been expecting.

"What are you doing here?" she asked, her disappointment clear in her beautiful green eyes. "I'm waiting for someone."

"I know who you're waiting for," the man said. "And he won't be coming."

"I don't believe you." Tiffany's chin rose in defiance. "We're together now, you know. We meet here to be alone."

"You know he's come here before. Lots of times. With a bunch of different girls."

"Well, that's his business. I don't care what he used to do. Now he's with me. That's all I care about." Tiffany averted her eyes, searching the road, and when she saw that it was still empty, turned to the water.

"I would never leave you alone in the dark, waiting by yourself," the man said, his anger percolating at the thought of the danger she was in.

"You'd never have the chance," she replied, her mouth a cruel sneer.

"I wouldn't be waiting anywhere for you. Not in a million years. Now run along, before you ruin everything."

Her words seared through him, and he stepped closer to her, desperate to make her understand.

"You don't mean anything to him, Tiffany. He'll just use you and move on to the next girl. He'll laugh about it. Tell his friends that you were begging for it."

When she didn't look at him or speak, he continued. "But I'm different. I'd treat you right. I'd take care of you the way you deserve."

He reached out to touch her arm, and she jerked away. Tears stood in her eyes, shining like diamonds in the moonlight. His heart lurched at the sight.

"Don't touch me," she spat out, her fists clenching at her sides. "I'm going to tell him what you've said. No telling what he'll do once he knows you've tried to steal me away."

"Don't go, Tiffany," he called as she spun around and picked up the cups and blanket. "I don't want you to leave. Stay here with me."

"Stay away from me, you loser," she yelled over her shoulder as she picked up the lamp and stuffed the blanket back in the picnic basket.

Suddenly he felt as if he was watching himself from a distance. He saw his belt in his hands. He watched as his hands looped the belt around her throat and twisted. He observed as she dropped the lamp and collapsed onto the ground. Slowly, his hands loosened, and Tiffany rolled over. Her face was splotchy and red. An angry mark encircled her neck. She coughed and sputtered.

"I wanted to help you," the man said, touching her face, his hands shaking with need and excitement. "I wanted to keep you safe."

"Please," Tiffany said, coughing again and struggling to sit up. "Please, I just want to go home."

But the man knew it was a lie. The girl didn't want to go home. She wanted to leave him. Once she left, he'd never see her again. She'd let herself be used and degraded. She'd be ruined just as his mother had been.

He watched his hands tighten again on the belt with both regret and resolve. This is the way it had to be. The only way. This way, she'd be saved. She'd be pure. And he felt sure, a part of her would always be with him.

He gazed into the clear, green eyes, feeling the power of her emotion as she trembled against him. She couldn't speak, but her eyes told him everything he had wanted to hear for so long. She was with him. She would never leave him. As she closed her eyes and went limp beneath him, the rush of fulfillment took him by surprise. Her surrender had left him floating in a state of ecstasy, a feeling that no one could ever take away.

He stayed with her for a long time, holding her against him, relishing their last moments together, before he gently wrapped her in the blanket she'd laid out, and carried her to the water. He watched as the blanket sunk underneath the water hyacinth, glad that the bright blue flowers would adorn her resting place after he'd gone.

The man felt the tickle and sting of a mosquito on his arm, and he slapped at it, pulled back from his memories, cruelly recalled back into the humid night surrounding him. He looked into the water and felt a stab of loneliness.

She's gone now. They've taken her from me.

He knew he should feel lucky. She'd stayed with him for years, her memory carried deep within him, making the empty days and nights more bearable. But when they'd found her floating all the way down in the Willow River, he'd realized that her resting place had been desecrated. He'd watched with angry eyes as they took her bones away.

Then fate had intervened, had brought him back to the motel where it had all started. The birthplace of his rage. There he watched other men take what they wanted, degrading the girls around them without remorse. And the girls walked in willingly, like sheep to the slaughter, allowing themselves to be led dumbly into a life of depravity, realizing their mistake only after they'd already been ruined.

Then he'd seen Jess. He'd thought he might be able to save her, but something hadn't been right. He wasn't sure what. Maybe Jess had been too damaged, or maybe the motel was cursed. Whatever had gone wrong, he knew he couldn't give up. He needed to find a new girl to save, and he didn't know how much longer he could wait.

CHAPTER ELEVEN

Eden's nerves were, at last, starting to settle. Two full days had passed without further contact from Star or the police, and the acute anxiety Eden had suffered as she'd left the police station had since subsided into manageable concern for the missing girl. She thought she'd even gotten over her shock at seeing Leo Steele there.

Whatever he was doing had nothing to do with me.

Luckily, she'd managed to get a few hours of sleep the night before and had woken up with a renewed determination to find out if the police had made any progress.

But first, she needed to get Hope and Devon off to school. She slid cheesy omelets onto plates, poured orange juice into glasses, and called up the stairs, "Breakfast is ready, kids!"

She muted the sound of the small television on the kitchen counter just as eager footsteps clattered down the stairs. It was the last day of the school year, and both Hope and Devon were excited about the end-of-school parties and activities they had planned for the day.

"Morning, Aunt Eden," Hope called out as she hopped onto a stool at the breakfast bar. "Wow, real-live omelets, what's the occasion?"

"It's the last day of school, of course!" Devon answered as he, too, climbed onto a stool and picked up a fork. "I can't believe it; no homework for three whole months!"

Hope's bright blue eyes lit up as she looked over at Eden. "And this time next week we'll be flying toward the Bahamas!"

Eden nodded, and smiled at the joy in her niece's voice, glad that she had impulsively booked a week at an all-inclusive resort in Nassau. It would be their first real vacation together since the kids had come to live with her.

Eden knew it was going to be hard to pull herself away from the foundation for an entire week, but the kids deserved a chance to experience some of the normal family activities their classmates talked about at school.

The kitchen door swung open and Duke trotted in, pulling Sage Parsons behind him. The morning was already hot and humid, and Sage's pink tank top was damp and clinging to her smooth, tan shoulders. Her curly black hair had been pulled back into a ponytail under a Florida Gators baseball cap.

"Morning kids!" Sage called out as she knelt and unhooked Duke's leash from his collar. "Anything special going on today?"

Eden smiled over at Sage, grateful to have her help, along with her always cheerful attitude. She knew her own fluctuating moods could be hard for the kids to understand, so Sage's calm and happy demeanor meant a lot.

"It's only the last day of school," Hope responded with an exaggerated roll of her eyes.

"And the best day ever," Devon added, a smile splitting his face from ear to ear. He had just turned ten and hadn't quite reached the stage when it was considered uncool to show too much excitement.

"It may be the last day, but you still need to get there on time," Sage said, picking up the empty glasses and handing each of the kids a napkin. "Finish your breakfast and get those teeth brushed so we can get going."

Once Sage had herded the kids back upstairs, Eden's cell phone vibrated. She saw at a glance that the call was from Nathan Rush, her business partner. Or was he technically her ex-partner? She was tempted to let the call go to voicemail but knew she shouldn't avoid the inevitable. She needed to tell Nathan that she had decided to sell her shares in Giant Leap Data, the start-up company they had founded together after graduate school.

Giant Leap had been an almost immediate success, attracting the interest of several venture capitalist firms, and going public six years ago. Since then the shares had soared and both Eden and Nathan had reaped the financial benefits. But Eden hadn't participated in the day-to-day management of the company since Mercy had been killed.

Now, after more than four years, Nathan had asked her to rejoin the company's executive management team. But Eden knew she could never go back; it was time to make a clean break. She would sell her remaining shares to Nathan. She just had to figure out how to tell him.

"Nathan, what are you doing up so early?" Eden asked, realizing it wasn't quite six o'clock in the morning on the West Coast.

"I wanted to catch you before you head out to your office. Otherwise, I know you'll ignore my call, as usual," Nathan teased, his familiar voice making Eden smile.

Good old Nathan, he had always stayed in touch, despite everything that had happened. She knew that he had tried to be there for her, but in the end, he couldn't find a way through her grief and guilt, and she'd left San Francisco, left the company, left him. As she'd told him many times before: it wasn't him, it was her.

"You know I'd never ignore your calls, Nathan, but it's been crazy busy..." Eden's voice faded away as she saw a breaking news bulletin appear on the television's small screen.

The volume was still muted, but she could see a young, female reporter in a fitted, red dress holding a microphone. The reporter gestured toward a stark white crime scene tent that had been erected at the edge of a river. Tall cypress trees gave little shade to the people moving in and out of the tent. Some wore police uniforms, and a few had on white protective coveralls complete with hoods and booties.

The headline displayed in capital letters across the bottom of the screen prompted Eden to disconnect the call without another word. Her knees threatened to buckle as she grabbed the granite kitchen counter for support.

She stared at the words, knowing her worst fears may have come true: BODY OF TEEN GIRL FOUND IN WILLOW RIVER.

Could the girl in the river be Star? Eden closed her eyes, wanting to pray, but knowing from experience that the most fervent prayers wouldn't make the dead come back to life. *Of course, it could be Star. She disappeared by the same river two nights ago. Who else would it be?*

She flinched at the shrill ring of her cell phone.

"Sorry, Nathan, I can't talk now," she said into the phone, her eyes still on the television screen.

"This is Detective Nessa Ainsley calling, Ms. Winthrop." Eden recognized the southern drawl immediately, but she looked down at the phone in confusion, her mind reeling, struggling to make connections.

"Ms. Winthrop are you there?" The kindness in Nessa's voice terrified Eden. It was the sympathetic tone that people tended to use when delivering bad news.

"I'm here, Detective," Eden said, walking to the kitchen table and sinking into an oak-backed chair. "Is it Star? Is the girl in the river Star?"

"That's what we're trying to figure out," Nessa replied. "We haven't identified the, um...the body yet. As you've probably already seen on the news, it's a female. A teenager from the looks of it. Blonde hair, visible track marks."

"Oh God, I knew she needed help," Eden cried, her raised voice waking up Duke who had been napping near the backdoor. He scrambled over to sit next to her, one paw lifting to rest on her leg.

"Ms. Winthrop, um, Eden...can I call you Eden?" Nessa interjected.

"What, oh, well, yes, of course," Eden responded, leaning down and hugging Duke to her.

"Eden, we're hoping you can come down to the Medical Examiner's Office to see if you can identify the body. We need to know if it's the same girl you reported missing two days ago."

Nessa's voice sounded far away. Eden realized she was getting dizzy. She closed her eyes to stop the room from spinning. Mercy's lifeless face, her eyes bruised and swollen shut, flashed in her mind. The medical examiner had needed her to identify the body then, too. It had been the worst day of her life. Nothing had ever been the same since.

"I don't think I can do that," Eden whispered into the phone. She cleared her throat and tried again. "I'm not sure that's possible."

"Eden, we need to know who this poor girl was...so we can find out what happened to her. I know it's hard, but we need you to help us."

When Eden didn't respond, Nessa spoke again. "Isn't that what your foundation is all about? Helping women? Isn't that why Star came to you? She was seeking help. Now you just might have a chance to help her."

"I'll...I'll try," Eden said, her hand groping for Duke's soft head, her eyes still closed against the reality of what had happened. "I've got to take care of the kids, make some arrangements, but I'll try to come down later this morning."

"Thank you, Eden." Nessa sounded relieved. "You can go straight to the M.E.'s office. It's a stone's throw from the police station. Can't miss it. Just ask for Iris Nguyen. She's the Chief Medical Examiner for Willow Bay."

Eden disconnected the call and rested her head on the table. What had she agreed to do? The last time she'd seen a dead body she'd ended up in the emergency room. She was convinced that finding her sister's battered body had been the catalyst of her subsequent anxiety disorder, although she still couldn't remember everything that had happened that day.

Reggie had ultimately diagnosed her with dissociate amnesia. She said the condition had been caused by emotional trauma, and that Eden's memory would return once she had time to come to terms with what had happened.

After struggling for years to overcome the frequent panic attacks and bouts of worry and depression, Eden felt that she was finally getting better. She'd been hopeful, even arranging the vacation away with the kids. Now the world seemed to be folding back in on her.

Footsteps on the stairs reminded her that the kids needed to leave for school. It was their last day, and she didn't want anything to ruin it for them. Pulling herself upright into a sitting position, she called over her shoulder, "Hope and Devon, you guys had better get going or you'll be late." She waved as they carried backpacks out the door.

Sage stopped at the door and looked back. A rare frown appeared on her perpetually cheerful face. "Everything okay, Eden?"

"Yes, everything's okay. I've got to go to Reggie's, so I won't be here when you get back. I'll take Duke with me."

She watched the young woman leave, grateful she had someone reliable to help with the kids. She had a feeling she was going to need all the help she could get to make it through the rest of the day.

"Reggie," she said in a small voice. Duke looked up at her with worried eyes. "I need to talk to Reggie."

* * *

The renovated farmhouse sat on a five-acre plot alongside Little Gator Creek. An ancient wooden bridge that spanned the shallow creek groaned under the weight of the big Expedition. Heart thumping, Eden avoided looking down into the slow-moving water.

She knew it would eventually merge with the muddy water of the Willow River on its hundred-mile journey to the Gulf of Mexico, and she fought back a sudden, irrational fear that if she looked down, she would see Star's body floating there, bruised and bloated.

Breath in...breath out...breath in...breath out.

She just needed to get to Reggie. Once inside the safety of Reggie's house she would be able to relax. She looked in the rearview mirror at Duke, who was enjoying the open window and the warm but steady breeze that ruffled his fur and swept his ears back from his grinning face. The sight made Eden smile despite herself.

As the Expedition rounded the bend, she could see the two-story house nestled among the wide-spreading branches of flowering dogwood trees. Pink blossoms, the color of cotton candy, sprinkled the ground, giving the house a fairytale feel.

Reggie was already standing on the front porch, clad in a royal blue wrap dress, holding a huge cup of what Eden assumed would be herbal tea.

I need something stronger than Chamomile today, Eden thought as she brought the SUV to a lumbering stop in the circular drive. *I'm going to need caffeine and lots of it.*

CHAPTER TWELVE

Reggie watched Eden and Duke climb out of the silver SUV and walk toward her. Her heart broke a little as she saw the all-too-familiar slump of Eden's shoulders.

Always one step forward, two-steps back, Reggie thought, fixing a smile on her face. *Will this fragile woman ever get the chance to fully heal?*

Duke trotted up the steps and greeted Reggie with a few licks of her hand. She crouched next to the big dog and hugged him to her.

"Hey Duke, how are you? You taking care of our girl?"

Reggie watched Eden mount the steps more slowly.

"I've seen the news, dear," Reggie said, the smile slipping from her face. "Do they know if the girl in the river is the same girl? The girl that came to Shutter Street?"

"Oh Reggie, it's so awful." Eden's voice was thick with emotion. "They don't know who she is, not yet. They want me to come down and try to identify the body. Tell them if it's the same girl I reported missing."

This was worse than Reggie had feared when Eden called that morning sounding desperate to see her. Asking a woman with an anxiety disorder and a history of panic attacks to view a dead body? Not a good idea.

"Let's go inside and sit down. I'll put on a pot of coffee and we can talk this through." She opened the door and let Duke and Eden walked past her into the cool foyer, before following them down a long hall, walls adorned with framed photos of Reggie and her late husband, Wayne.

Most of the pictures had been taken as Reggie and Wayne traveled the world together during their twenty-year marriage. In the early days following Wayne's unexpected death, it had been impossible for Reggie to walk past the photos without feeling physical pain. But she couldn't bear to pack them away, and so they had stayed.

Now the photos reminded her of how lucky she was to have found Wayne, to have found her soulmate, even if he had left her far too soon. Her work at the foundation during the last four years had shown her just how rare that was.

Eden sank into a white wicker chair, cradling her head in her hands, while Reggie filled a coffee pot with water and turned on the brewer. Duke settled in on the floor close to Eden's feet.

"I don't know if I can do this, Reggie," Eden said softly, looking down at her hands as they twisted on the polished wood of the kitchen table. "I don't think I'm strong enough."

"It's not about being strong, Eden," Reggie said, taking a seat at the table. "Most people would be fearful of having to view a dead body. Especially the body of someone they met recently. Someone they tried to help."

Eden's hands clenched into fists as she dropped her head to her chest in frustration. "If only I hadn't left her in the room alone! If only I'd been there to stop her from leaving. She'd be alive, safe somewhere, instead of dead in the morgue."

"First of all, we don't know for sure if it *is* the same girl." Reggie rose and moved across to Eden, wrapping a thin, firm arm around her shoulders. "And second of all, even if it is Star, what happened to her isn't your fault. You can't do this to yourself again, honey."

Reggie looked down at Duke, who sat with both his paws touching Eden's topsiders. She'd taken in the golden retriever as a puppy after hearing success stories about ESAs helping patients with anxiety disorders. She thought having a dog in the office of her private practice could have a positive impact on her patients.

Duke's worried eyes now matched her own concern and stirred up memories of the first counseling session they'd had after Eden had suffered a full-blown panic attack and ended up in the emergency room.

Duke had been drawn to Eden immediately, somehow sensing that the nervous, trembling, shadow of a woman needed him. When Eden stood to leave after their hour was up, Duke had followed her to the door and then trotted over to the window to watch her drive away.

That day he'd looked back at Reggie with those same serious eyes, and she'd known just what to do. Duke and Eden had been inseparable ever since.

"I shouldn't be complaining, I guess," Eden sniffed and raised red-rimmed eyes.

"I wanted to help women in need. I wanted Mercy Harbor to be the place abused women could come to when things got bad. Deadly even. That's what I signed up for. But now that it's so...real...I don't know if I can handle it."

Reggie opened her mouth to offer further reassurance, but then closed it again. She was suddenly torn between her feelings of friendship for Eden and her responsibility as the director of Mercy Harbor.

In her role as director, how could she not ask Eden to assist in identifying a girl that had been on the foundation's premises before possibly turning up dead in the river? Wasn't the foundation now involved, whether voluntarily or not?

But then again, as a friend, how could she ask Eden to put herself in a situation that might instigate an acute relapse of her anxiety disorder? What if the stress caused her to suffer a major panic attack? It had been over a year since Eden's last episode. Was it fair to ask her to risk her emotional health?

Eden was no longer officially Reggie's patient; they had agreed it would no longer be appropriate once they'd started working together at the foundation. But Reggie still tried to help Eden manage her anxiety and prevent a reoccurrence of the panic attacks she'd suffered after Mercy's murder.

For the first time, Reggie felt as if her professional and personal interests may be at odds.

"Before Mercy died, I was always frustrated with people who were indecisive, or who saw everything in gray, instead of black and white," Eden said, her voice trembling. "It seemed so easy back then to decide what was right, to know what to do."

Eden rose from the table and began pacing around the big kitchen. "Now there are so many questions I can't answer. Should I spend my time helping the women at the shelter, or taking care of Mercy's children? Should I help an unknown girl in distress, or protect the women that are already in our care? Should I save my own sanity, or try to identify a young girl's body, and perhaps provide her family with closure?"

Reggie also stood up and faced Eden. "Take a deep breath, honey. Don't get yourself worked up. That's the last thing you need."

"I know, Reggie. But I'm scared, and I don't know what to do."

Eden stopped pacing, standing in front of the French doors that led out to the back garden. She folded her arms around her body.

Reggie joined her, looking through the glass panes as if an answer could be found in the bright day beyond. The June sun sizzled down onto an explosion of red, pink, and white perennials. A monarch butterfly lazily dipped in and out of a huge purple blossom.

"The butterflies always seem to prefer the Lily of the Nile for some reason," she said to Eden. "They must want to spend the little time they have surrounded by the biggest, most beautiful thing they can see."

Eden nodded, contemplating the flowers outside. "Can't blame them for that. The world can be a very ugly place."

"Which is the very reason you started the foundation in the first place," Reggie gently chided. "To try and make the world a better place. And we've just got to keep on trying."

"I knew there was a reason I came over here," Eden said, squeezing Reggie's small, delicate hand. "You can always make me feel brave. Or at least feel like I should be brave. I don't know what I'd do without you."

Reggie squeezed back. "Well, you're going to have to do without me for a little while at least. Our last room at Shutter Street will be occupied later this afternoon. I got a call this morning from social services. So, I've got to get over there now and make sure everything's ready. You and Duke can stay here for as long as you want, of course."

"Thanks, Reggie," Eden said, her eyes returning to the garden outside. "I think I know what I've got to do. I just have to work up the courage first."

CHAPTER THIRTEEN

The Willow Bay Medical Examiner's Office occupied the first two floors of a bulky concrete building that sat across the street from the police station. The building's gray exterior matched Nessa's mood as she pushed her way into the lobby and nodded at the sleepy-looking clerk sitting behind a reception window.

"Mornin', Maddie. Awful hot out there today," Nessa said, the lingering warmth of the June sun on her skin starting to fade as the heavy, frigid air inside the building surrounded her. "Iris should be expecting me."

Maddie nodded and heaved herself out of the chair. "I'll let the chief know you're here."

As Maddie shuffled away, Nessa wrinkled her nose against an unpleasant smell hanging in the air: an underlying hint of decomposition mixed with pineapple air freshener. She tried to breathe through her mouth as she waited for Maddie Simpson to return.

Maddie had worked for the city for close to thirty years, recently moving to the Medical Examiner's Office after a ten-year stint clerking at the county courthouse. Nessa knew from experience that she wasn't the type to hurry.

Her stomach clenched, and Nessa wondered if the upset was a reaction to what she had seen that morning by the river or dread of what she was about to see in the rooms beyond. Her phone vibrated in her suit pocket just as Maddie's round face reappeared in the window.

"Iris is ready for you, Detective. She's still in the autopsy room, so you'll need to suit up. You know where to go?"

Maddie was already settling back into her chair, sipping muddy-brown liquid from a Styrofoam coffee cup, as Nessa ignored the incessant buzzing of her phone and headed toward the door marked, *Restricted – Authorized Personnel Only.*

The bitter aroma of Maddie's coffee rose to mingle with the smell of decay and air freshener as Nessa slipped through the door and let it close behind her.

The last time she'd had reason to visit the autopsy room had been close to six months ago when a father and his six-year-old son had discovered the remains of a body in the Willow River. It had been an unusually chilly January morning, and Nessa had been the first detective to arrive at the scene, her nervous breath coming quickly, fragile white clouds of condensation proceeding her as she approached the water's edge.

She'd found the responding uniformed officers shaken and pale, stunned by their first exposure to skeletonized remains, and she'd quickly taken control, helping them cordon off the area and coordinating efforts with the four officers that made up Willow Bay's only dedicated crime scene unit.

Pete Barker had eventually pulled up to the scene in an unmarked police car, the department's standard, a black Dodge Charger, and they'd stayed at the scene until Iris Nguyen, Willow Bay's Chief Medical Examiner, arrived to examine the body in situ.

Hours later, they'd watched as an unmarked white van pulled away from the riverbank, its generic exterior concealing the horror of the desecrated remains within. And she and Barker had been in the autopsy room that evening when Iris had tentatively identified the body as that of Tiffany Clarke. That day had been one of the longest of her life, and one she had never been able to forget.

Nessa felt a sense of déjà vu as she donned the protective clothing and pushed open the door to the autopsy suite. The unmistakable smell of death rushed to greet her.

Is this really happening again?

"Oh, Nessa, good morning, I'll be right with you," Iris called from across the room, where she stood talking to a tall, broad-shouldered forensic technician.

Her voice was muffled by the protective mask she wore, but her friendly greeting acted as a balm on Nessa's frazzled nerves. Nessa didn't like to be around death. That was one of the reasons she'd accepted the job in Willow Bay after seven years on the force in Atlanta.

As a young uniformed officer, she'd seen too much blood, dealt with too much violence, but then, after she'd made detective, it had gotten much worse. Within weeks of her promotion, she'd been assigned to a task force investigating the homicides of two young women that seemed to be connected.

Both victims were in their early twenties, attended the same community college, and lived alone near campus. They had both been attacked in their own beds in the middle of the night with no sign of forced entry. They'd both been beaten and raped, before being strangled.

Nessa had been sure that the profiles were too similar not to be connected. But, in the end, they'd discovered the murders had been committed by two different killers. Somehow the knowledge that there were two different men capable of such sadistic acts operating in the same city, at the same time, had shocked her to her core. How many killers were out there prowling the city streets, just waiting to strike?

She had never been able to detach herself from the horror of each new murder, never been able to forget the image of each tragic body she'd recovered. The dead haunted her dreams. So, when she'd gotten the opportunity to move to Willow Bay, she had jumped at the chance, hoping a smaller town would mean less crime.

She'd wanted a safe place to raise Cole and Cooper. Now, looking at the small, naked body on the metal examination table in front of Iris, Nessa had to accept that, even here in Willow Bay, she hadn't escaped the specter of death or the monsters that lurked in the shadows.

"Nessa?" Iris Nguyen's gentle voice pulled Nessa back into the present. She'd removed the face mask and was looking up at Nessa with inquisitive brown eyes.

"Sorry to make you wait. I was writing up the toxicology request, but Wesley can finish it from here."

Nessa smiled at the young man dressed in protective gear, his hair covered by a blue paper cap. He'd been down at the river's edge with Iris early that morning, and Nessa had been impressed with his quick, professional handling of the body. He'd kept his composure for such a young man.

"Hey, Wesley, how's it going? You ever get that cup of coffee you were looking for?" Nessa called over, knowing her stomach would never let her digest anything within the walls of the autopsy suite.

Wesley waved a gloved hand at her and grimaced. "I wish that was all it'd take to wake me up. I'm dragging, and I still got tons to do."

Iris cleared her throat. "I'm all yours now, Nessa...if you have time."

"Of course, I have time. Although I sure didn't think I'd be back here so soon...and for another body pulled out of the river." Nessa rubbed the back of her neck, averting her eyes from the sight of the brawny forensic technician packaging up specimen containers and vials. She felt a headache coming on, and the cloying smells in the room weren't helping.

"Yes, that's right, it's only been six months since you and Detective Barker were here to view the Clarke autopsy. How is Detective Barker doing?" Iris asked.

"He's a tough one; he'll pull through. Not back on the job yet, though," Nessa replied, glad to have an excuse to look away from the small body on the table. She pulled out her little recorder.

"You mind if I record our conversation? I don't wanna miss any of the details."

"No problem," Iris agreed, stepping away from the examination table and moving toward a standing desk situated in the corner of the room.

"Let's review the findings so far over here. I remember from last time...you don't like to be too close to the body."

"Well my goodness, does anyone?" Nessa exclaimed before she could help herself. "I mean, well, I can handle it if I have to, but I'd rather not."

Iris smiled and shrugged her narrow shoulders. "I think it can be pretty interesting, actually. But I guess most people feel the way you do. No shame in that."

But Nessa *was* ashamed; she felt that after all these years she should have grown a thicker skin, but she'd come to realize that there was nothing she could do to change the way she reacted to death.

She knew the pitiful remains she'd seen that morning would haunt her dreams, like all the others. When she closed her eyes tonight she would still see the shimmer of the sun on the water and hear the vibrating buzz of the cicadas that had added a surreal twist to the morning's crime scene.

"Any progress in identifying the victim?" Iris asked, her eyebrows lifting in hope. "I took prints but as far as I know nothing came back."

"No, nothing at the scene to suggest who she is, but we did get reports on two missing girls that meet her basic description. We'll be asking the folks that filed the reports to come in and see if they can make an identification. Should be here later this afternoon."

Iris nodded and sighed, obviously not relishing the idea of arranging a viewing for two distraught relatives.

"Okay, I'll ask Wesley to make the arrangements as soon as we're done here."

"So, what have you found?" Nessa asked. "Is there a clear cause of death? Call it a hunch, but I'm guessing it wasn't an accidental drowning?"

A frown creased the brow of the diminutive forensic pathologist.

"No, my findings are inconsistent with drowning. The pattern of contusions and abrasions around her neck were caused by some type of ligature. I'm still writing up the details, but I'd say it's clearly a homicide by ligature strangulation."

Nessa recoiled at the image the words invoked. She tried to calm her mind. "Was the hyoid bone broken?"

"Well, no, the hyoid wasn't fractured, but it often isn't with ligature strangulations," Iris said, seeming to find the question interesting.

"A broken hyoid bone more often results from manual strangulation. But I did observe petechia in the eyes, which corroborates the strangulation theory."

Nessa had seen the tiny red spots in the eyes of other strangulation victims and knew they were a sign of broken blood vessels. She tried to hide her involuntary wince at the vision Iris' words conjured by dropping her head to check the status of her little recorder.

"Luckily this Jane Doe hadn't been in the water long enough to attract many fish or turtles yet," Iris continued. "But she's probably been submerged at least two or three days based on the condition of the body."

Nessa mulled over the information, not surprised that the timing Iris had calculated meant that the Jane Doe could very well be one of the two girls reported missing.

"The girl had obviously been an intravenous drug user, although from the track marks I'd say that her habit started recently." Iris looked down at her notes.

"She hadn't sustained any serious damage to the veins in her arms yet, and I don't see signs that she had moved on to injecting into other veins."

Nessa's head reflexively turned to look at the small figure on the table. Her eyes rested on the stiff, white feet, the toes still bearing traces of pink toenail polish.

What had the poor girl gotten involved with? What, or who had driven her to stick drug-filled needles in her arm?

"Of course, we won't know what she had in her system for sure until the toxicology reports come back from the state lab," Iris said, tucking a wayward strand of dark, shiny hair behind her ear.

"However, whatever she may have taken or injected, I don't believe it was a direct cause of death."

"If this does ever go to court, you can bet some defense attorney is going to imply it was an accidental overdose," Nessa murmured, speaking more to herself than to Iris.

"Well, the cause of death will be recorded as homicide by ligature strangulation on the death certificate, unless the toxicology report comes back with a big surprise." Iris raised her eyebrows in concern as she looked up.

"Are you okay, Nessa? Do you need to take a break?"

"No, I'm fine." Nessa cleared her throat and wished she'd remembered to bring her water bottle.

Now that the summer heat had settled in, she'd been trying to drink more water, had started carrying an enormous refillable bottle to work with her, but had forgotten it this morning in her rush to arrive at the scene before the reporters or gawkers.

"There are also bruises and lacerations that are indicators of physical and sexual abuse, although I found no semen or other biological evidence during my examination that could be linked to the perpetrator." Iris' voice betrayed her disappointment.

"The body was emerged in river water, which is fairly warm and acidic, so any biological or trace evidence on the outside of the body was likely lost in the river."

"You think this homicide could be linked to the Tiffany Clarke case?" Nessa finally asked the question that had nagged at her since she'd seen the small, battered body on the river bank that morning. She didn't want to turn the case over to Ortiz and Ingram, but if the cases were connected, she'd have no choice.

"Yes, I think it's possible," Iris said, with no hesitation in her soft voice. "The cause of death for both girls appears to be the same, and both were found in the same river."

Nessa nodded and felt her already dry throat tighten as Iris seemed to confirm her worst fears. The tests on Tiffany Clarke's remains had indicated that her body was first submerged in one of many tributaries that fed into the Willow River.

The dark water initially concealed the decomposing remains until the slow-moving currents finally carried them into the larger river, where they had been caught in the rush near the shore.

"Right, and the killer targeted victims with a similar profile: white, teenage girls, both blondes," Nessa added, her voice tense as anger started to simmer in her chest at the thought of the person who had chosen the girls.

What kind of monster had dumped the bodies of the two young girls into the river for the fish and turtles to eat?

Iris held up a hand of caution. "Of course, there had been an extended amount of time between the deaths - almost three years - which could indicate the murders may be completely unrelated."

Nessa paused, before nodding in agreement. "It sure does seem like they had very different lifestyles. Tiffany was an honor student in a good home, with no history of drug use. This Jane Doe is obviously a victim of abuse with visible track marks. I don't imagine they moved in the same social circles."

"No, I don't imagine so." Iris offered up a pained smile. "Wesley grew up in Willow Bay and knew the Clarke family. He was torn up when we identified Tiffany's remains last winter. He said she had been a good kid, always involved in the community."

Iris put a hand on Nessa's arm. "Best to be cautious and not jump to any conclusions. We'd have to be very sure to verify a link before announcing a serial killer may be operating in Willow Bay."

"Absolutely," Nessa agreed, not ready to call in Ortiz and Ingram just yet.

She was anxious to head back to the crime scene to help with the canvassing. She also wanted to stop by and see Barker. Maybe the thought of catching a killer would motivate him to heal faster. She pressed the button to stop the recorder and pulled out a folder.

"Eden Winthrop and Leo Steele are the folks I mentioned earlier. They'll be coming by later to try to identify the remains. As you'll see in these reports, they both reported a different teenage girl missing two days ago."

Iris accepted the folder, her sad brown eyes silently acknowledging what they both knew: one of the girls reported missing was very likely the girl on the table behind them.

* * *

As Nessa left the Medical Examiner's Office, she fell into step behind a man walking toward the police station's parking garage. His faded blue jeans, black t-shirt, and scruffy boots helped him blend in with the other pedestrians on the sidewalk, but Nessa recognized the long, confident stride of Kirk Reinhardt.

Now in his fifties, Reinhardt had started his career with the WBPD as a uniformed patrol officer. He'd worked his way onto the city's Major Crimes Unit, before being promoted up to the rank of Lieutenant, reporting directly to the chief of police. But after a few years in the high-profile role, he was unexpectedly reassigned to the vice squad and began working within a special task force.

Nessa wasn't sure exactly what the task force did on a daily basis; she knew they handled undercover work and had organized several covert sting operations that had resulted in numerous arrests. She didn't see Reinhardt in the station very often, but they occasionally passed each other in the halls. Hopefully, he wouldn't mind if she asked for his help.

"Lieutenant Reinhardt?" Nessa jogged toward the garage, feeling drops of sweat already trickling down her back under her silk blouse and suit jacket.

Reinhardt swung around and faced Nessa just as she reached him. Her breath coming in short gasps, she promised herself she'd start back at the gym as soon as this case was solved. "Sorry to bother you, Lieutenant. You got a minute?"

"Sure, but I'm no longer a Lieutenant. I'm just plain-old Detective Reinhardt, now."

Reinhardt's voice was low and deep. Nessa wondered if the move back into the field had been his idea. She could see deep lines around his eyes and mouth, but his graying hair was still thick, and his body seemed solid and strong.

"How can I help you, Detective Ainsley?"

"Well, you can start by calling me Nessa. All my friends do." She flashed her sweetest southern belle smile. Reinhardt didn't smile in response, but he nodded and raised his eyebrows, indicating Nessa should continue.

"Detective Jankowski may have already followed up. About a missing person case? A teenage girl that we suspect may be using drugs?" Nessa searched his face, hoping for a flash of recognition.

"No, I haven't seen Detective Jankowski lately. Haven't heard from him either." Reinhardt's brow creased, and he tilted his head. "Why was he supposed to follow up with me?"

"Well, I'd asked him to see if you had any information that could help us track down the missing girl," Nessa said, trying to suppress irritation at Jankowski's lack of follow-through.

"Why would I know anything about a missing girl? Is she connected to one of our operations?" Reinhardt looked wary. "What information has Jankowski shared with you?"

"Well, nothing, really, but I have heard a little about the undercover work your team does, and I was wondering if you had any informers or contacts that may help us track her down."

Nessa's tone and expression had cooled. She didn't like being questioned and treated as an outsider. "She's only sixteen. Her mother's pretty worried."

Reinhardt's face softened, the wrinkles becoming even more pronounced. He looked around to see who else may be within hearing, his gray eyes anxious. "Sorry, I've been working an intense caseload. Guess I'm on edge. I think we all are."

Nessa nodded, her affront at being questioned morphing into concern for the department. Seemed like Jankowski had been right; there really must be a shitstorm brewing.

"I'll try to catch up with Jankowski so he can fill me in. In the meantime, send me over the details. I'll see if there's any way I can help." Reinhardt's phone began to ring in his pocket. He looked at the display and grimaced, already heading toward the parking garage.

"Okay, I'll email you the reports," Nessa called as she watched Reinhardt disappear into the stairwell.

She turned away with an empty feeling in her stomach, suspecting she had little hope of getting help from the stressed-out detective. As she walked back toward the station, she caught sight of her reflection in the window across the street.

The hulking building that housed the Medical Examiner's Office loomed behind her, and, despite the thermometer hovering just under triple digits, a chill rippled through her.

CHAPTER FOURTEEN

Eden cleared her throat and fidgeted with her keys as she waited for the receptionist to look up from the computer. The woman's badge identified her as Maddie Simpson and contained a photo that appeared to have been taken when she'd been twenty years younger and fifty pounds lighter.

"Sorry," Maddie said, craning her neck and adjusting gold-rimmed glasses so that she could peer over the counter at Duke, "but animals aren't permitted inside the Medical Examiner's Office."

"Actually, this is my support dog," Eden replied, her already frazzled nerves adding an edge to her voice. "And he *is* allowed to accompany me in here. I confirmed that directly with the M.E. before I agreed to come down to make an identification."

Eden's tone of defiance prompted Maddie to roll her eyes and let out an audible huff as she pushed a clipboard and pen across the counter. "Log your name and time of arrival. I'll let Chief Nguyen know you're here."

Eden jotted her name and noted the time, before adding Duke's name to the line underneath hers. She looked down and gave Duke a reassuring smile, feeling better just to have the dog's warm body nestled against her leg. When she heard someone open the door behind her, she absently moved toward the waiting area and took a seat on a green vinyl chair, closing her eyes and trying not to think about what could be causing the sweetly putrid smell that cloaked the room.

The sound of a deep, masculine voice behind her made her catch her breath. Her body stiffened as she listened to soft-spoken words. She knew that voice; she knew the slickly handsome man that owned that voice. Anger stirred inside her as she listened to the warm, persuasive tone that she suspected had been used to sway countless judges and juries.

Keeping her head still, Eden opened her eyes and looked sideways to confirm her suspicions. She saw Leo Steele leaning against the reception counter, an iPhone held to his ear with one hand, his other handwriting something on the sign-in sheet.

He was clean-shaven and, as usual, perfectly groomed. But he looked tired, and his expression was tense. He hadn't seemed to notice that she or Duke were in the room.

Still oblivious to what's going on around him, she thought as she reached out to scratch Duke's head, her unsteady hand seeking comfort in his soft fur. Her pulse quickened in anger as she remembered the first time she'd seen Leo Steele.

It had been almost five years now, but it still felt disturbingly clear in her mind. He'd been wearing the same type of power suit he had on today: well-tailored, expensive, and accented with a bold tie that couldn't fail to draw attention. He'd been sitting next to Preston Lancaster at the defense table in the county courthouse, representing her brother-in-law who'd been charged with violating a restraining order.

Eden's eyes watered as she thought of Mercy that long-ago day. Her sister had been so young and scared, so heartbreakingly beautiful, torn by the conflicting feelings of love and fear she had for the man who had been her high-school sweetheart before they'd gotten married.

Her grief turned to rage at the thought of the quiet young man her sister had fallen in love with. He'd been plagued by jealousy and self-doubt, obsessed by the fear that his lovely wife was going to leave him. Over time he'd become possessive and abusive until finally, Mercy had no choice but to move out in order to protect herself and her children.

But Preston hadn't been able to accept Mercy's departure, and thanks to Leo Steele, he been free to leave the courthouse that day, only to hunt down and kill Mercy five days later. Eden pushed the thought of Preston Lancaster out of her mind. It made her head hurt to think of him and the devastation he'd caused.

Leo turned toward the window, cupping his hands around the phone, seeming to shield his conversation from prying ears. With his back turned, Eden took the opportunity to stare at him. Her green eyes blazed with fury as they silently reproached him.

If you hadn't gotten the charges dropped, then Preston would have been locked up. He'd have been in jail the night Mercy died. My sister would still be alive. Hope and Devon would still have a mother.

She bent to give Duke a hug, resisting the rush of painful memories. She couldn't let herself slide back into the abyss of anxiety she had only recently escaped.

"Do you have any idea where she may have met Hollywood?" Leo kept his voice low, but Eden was sure she hadn't misunderstood the words he'd murmured into the phone.

Could he be talking about the same guy that had abused Star? Could there possibly be two different guys in Willow Bay called Hollywood?

An abrupt tap on her shoulder brought Eden's attention back into the room. Maddie Simpson was standing over her, aggravation written all over her face.

"Ms. Winthrop, are you okay?" Maddie crossed her arms over her substantial chest and looked down at Duke in suspicion as if he was responsible for Eden's failure to respond when her name had been called.

"The M.E. is ready for you now. Please come with me."

Maddie opened the door to the restricted area and motioned for Eden to follow her. Eden stood up, then hesitated, looking back to see if Leo had finished his call. Regardless of her distaste for the smooth-talking lawyer, she needed to ask him if he knew where she could find Hollywood. Star might be with him, that is if she wasn't laying on the autopsy table in the room beyond.

But Leo was still clutching the phone to his ear, too caught up in the conversation to notice her intense stare.

"Ms. Winthrop?" Maddie said, not bothering to hide her impatience. "The M.E. has a very busy schedule today as I'm sure you can understand."

Eden sighed and followed Maddie, her fear at what she was about to see returning in full force. As she walked through the doorway, a chill slithered up her spine. Wrapping her arms around herself, Eden looked over her shoulder and caught a glimpse of Leo's brooding face. His dark eyes rose to meet hers as the door closed between them with a soft click.

CHAPTER FIFTEEN

Maddie escorted Eden and Duke down a brightly-lit corridor into a narrow room. She motioned for Eden to take a seat in one of several matching chairs positioned against the far wall. The only other furniture in the room was a polished wooden table that held a box of tissues, a pitcher of ice-water, and a stack of Styrofoam cups.

Eden poured water into a cup and let Duke lap it up, knowing the hot weather was even harder for the dog to endure with his thick, golden coat. She tried not to look at the wide glass window that dominated the left wall.

She knew from her previous visit to this same room that a gurney with the dead girl's body would be positioned on the other side of the window, and that the forensic technician would open the blinds to allow her to view the body when the time came.

The technician had explained to her last time that this method was the most practical approach since she wouldn't be required to don protective clothing and wouldn't be exposed to the often-upsetting sights and smells of the autopsy suite.

Eden swallowed and tried to force back the terrifying onslaught of memories that were crashing in on her: Mercy's battered face, the hot blood on her hands, her own wail of despair when the grief had proven too much to bear.

A light rap on the door frame brought Eden back into the present and announced the entry of a petite woman wearing a white lab coat over black pants. Her dark, shoulder-length hair framed an elfin face and kind brown eyes that crinkled at the corners when she smiled.

"Nice to meet you. Ms. Winthrop. I'm the Medical Examiner, Iris Nguyen."

Eden reached out to shake the offered hand, not trusting herself to speak. She noted that Iris was very different than the medical examiner that had performed Mercy's autopsy. The older man had been cold and stiffly professional, his bedside manner seemingly better suited to dealing with the dead rather than the living.

"I know this is difficult for you, and I appreciate you coming here today." Iris opened a file folder and pulled out a copy of the missing person's report Eden had filled in at the police station.

"I understand that the girl you've reported missing isn't your relative, but that you have an interest in locating her since she turned to your foundation for assistance?"

When Eden nodded but didn't respond, Iris continued. "I've read through the description you provided, and I have to say the girl found in the river does seem to be a possible match, but I need you to view the deceased and let us know if you think she is in fact the same girl."

"Okay," Eden croaked out. She cleared her voice and tried again. "Okay, I'm...I'm ready when you are."

Frown lines appeared between Iris' brows. "Are you going to be all right, Ms. Winthrop? Are you feeling okay?"

"I'll be fine," Eden said, hoping it wasn't a lie. "I've got Duke here to help me. He's my emotional support dog."

"And he's a very cute dog at that." Iris knelt next to Duke and looked into his big, brown eyes. "Hi there, boy."

Duke wagged his tail and sniffed the hand Iris offered, but his body was rigid, and Eden wondered if the smell and feel of the place were spooking the sensitive dog.

Can he smell the chemicals and decay through the walls and glass? Can he sense death next door?

Iris stood up and walked to the window. "When you're ready, let me know and I'll open the blinds. You'll see a metal gurney covered in a white sheet. A nice young man named Wesley will be there as well. He's one of our forensic technicians. You won't see the deceased until you indicate that you are ready for Wesley to pull the sheet down. He'll reveal just the face and shoulders."

Eden clutched at Duke's collar. Panic clawed in her stomach.

I have to do this. I have to be strong.

After taking several long, deep breaths, Eden nodded at Iris and stood up, inching her way over to stand next to the window. She towered over Iris, who was now holding the cord to the blinds and looking at Eden with an encouraging smile.

"There's no rush," Iris said. "Just let me know when you're ready for me to open the blinds."

A wave of dizziness washed over Eden as she stood next to the window. She reached out with a shaky hand and steadied herself against the cold, concrete wall.

"I'm ready," she whispered.

Iris pulled the cord and the blinds rolled up, revealing a metal gurney covered in a crisp white sheet. A young man stood next to the gurney, dressed in green scrubs. His hair was covered by some type of cap, and his face mask had been pulled down around his chin.

"That's Wesley," Iris said, putting a hand on Eden's shoulder. Eden pulled away, not wanting the forensic pathologist to feel her trembling. She could see Wesley looking anxiously at Iris, waiting for her signal.

"I'm ready...please, just let me see if it's her." Eden covered her mouth with both hands as Iris nodded at Wesley.

She held her breath as the sheet was pulled down to reveal a thin, waxen face; a large purplish bruise stained one cheek. Dark roots along the hairline contrasted with the strands of limp, blonde hair that had been smooth back from the discolored face. Angry red bruises and abrasions encircled a frail neck.

Eden felt a rush of air leave her lungs as her knees threatened to buckle. She leaned against the window and closed her eyes.

"It isn't her," she managed to say. "It isn't Star."

"So, you feel sure this girl is not the same girl you reported missing?" Iris asked, her voice calm.

"Yes, I'm...I'm sure. Star's hair was different. It was much lighter and curly, and she didn't have dark roots. I would have noticed."

Eden had a vivid picture of Star in her mind; she could still see the mass of platinum curls and swollen eye clearly. "And she had a black eye. It was pretty bad. That was just two days ago. There's no way it healed that quickly."

Eden looked through the glass at the ruined girl. Another senseless death that she couldn't prevent. The girl wasn't Star, but she *was* somebody's daughter. Someone out there must be wondering where she is. A disturbing thought crossed Eden's mind.

Maybe she's Star's friend. Maybe that poor, dead girl is Jess.

Iris nodded to Wesley and he pulled up the sheet as she closed the blinds. She turned to look at Eden with a worried smile.

"Have a seat, Ms. Winthrop, while I pour you some water. You look a bit pale."

"I'm fine," Eden whispered as she squeezed her eyes shut against the image of the dead body on the gurney.

But with her eyes closed, she saw Mercy's face on the other side of the glass, Mercy's battered body under the sheet. Time seemed to stop and reverse, the room spun, and Eden's legs felt unbearably weak. She sank onto a chair, her head slumping forward into her hands.

Suffocated by the heavy air and the sickly smell, Eden's breath began to hitch, and she put a hand to her throat. Panic set in, and she was sure when she drew her hand away it would be coated in blood. She looked down with wide eyes. Her hand was shaky but clean. She clutched at the medical examiner's coat sleeve and struggled to draw in air.

Duke stood and nudged Eden's face, one pawing rising to rest on her knee. He whined softly in his throat and looked up at Iris as if waiting for her to do something.

Iris strode to the door and opened it, calling out in a brusque voice, "Wesley, I need your help. Ms. Winthrop is feeling faint."

Quick footsteps were heard in the hall, and the young man hustled into the room, putting two strong hands gently on Eden's shoulders, holding her steady.

"I've got you," he said in a soft voice. He looked over at Iris and motioned to the wooden table.

"There's a vial of lavender oil in the drawer. That will usually do the trick."

Iris opened the drawer, picked up a small glass container, and handed it to Wesley. He pulled out the stopper and wafted the vial near Eden's head, the sweet scent of the essential oil immediately filling the room.

"Breathe in slowly, ma'am," Wesley urged. "Slow breaths in and out."

Duke nudged his head onto Eden's lap, and she sucked in a deep breath, before loudly exhaling. After several more inhalations and exhalations, her head started to clear but she could still feel her heart racing.

My pills...I need my pills.

She always carried her anti-anxiety medicine in her purse, but today she'd left her purse in her car, taking just her keys and an ID into the office. She needed to get to her car, needed to take one of her pills before her panic attack escalated any further.

Feeling an overwhelming impulse to get out of the room as fast as possible, Eden lifted her head and squared her shoulders.

"I'm all right now." Her voice was thin but firm. "I just needed to catch my breath. And now I need to go. I have...I have an appointment."

Eden rose to her feet, knees still weak. She cleared her throat and spoke to Duke. "Come on, boy. Let's get going."

"The police may have more questions for you, Ms. Winthrop," Iris said, for the first time looking rattled. "And you shouldn't be on your own if you've been feeling faint."

"Detective Ainsley knows where to find me," Eden replied as she shuffled toward the door. Wesley stood in the doorway, his sturdy figure blocking her exit. He looked wary, and for a minute Eden thought he might try to stop her, but then he stepped aside.

"Please, take it easy for the rest of the day, Ms. Winthrop," Iris called, as Eden and Duke made their way back down the corridor and pushed out into the reception area.

Maddie Simpson had her back turned behind the reception window as Eden hurried Duke toward the exit. The harsh sunlight blinded her momentarily as she stepped onto the sidewalk, and it took a minute for her eyes to adjust.

"I've got to go, Beth," she heard Leo Steele's voice behind her before she saw him. He was leaning against the building, his cell phone once again held to his ear.

"I'll come by and see you as soon as I'm done here. It probably isn't Jess. Try to stay positive."

Eden's breath caught in her throat as Leo strode back into the building, leaving her standing on the hot pavement staring after him.

She had needed to talk to him, had wanted to ask him about Hollywood.

Her head spun, the glare of the sun causing lights to flash and swirl in front of her eyes. Fighting back the dizziness and gripping Duke's leash, she knew she had to make it back to her car. She had to take one of her pills and have a chance to regain control of her emotions.

Once inside the parking garage, she located her SUV and pulled her purse from the back seat, digging for the pill bottle that she hadn't opened in months. She studied the bottle containing the benzodiazepine that had ruled her life for the first two years after Mercy's death.

The tranquilizer had allowed her to sleep. Allowed her to function without jumping at every loud noise. It had taken the edge off the feeling that the world was caving in on top of her.

But the pills had taken control, and at Reggie's urging, she had slowly weaned herself off regular usage. For the last year, she'd only had the fast-acting pills on hand for emergency use in the event of a panic attack, and just the feel of the bottle in her hand was usually enough to take the edge off her anxiety.

"I don't need this anymore. I can handle this on my own," she said to her reflection in the rearview mirror. She caught sight of Duke's worried eyes and sighed.

"Well, not all on my own then, Duke. But I can handle it without the pills."

Eden put the bottle back in her purse. She looked out the window at the quiet rows of cars. It would be so easy to start her car and drive home. But her hands remained in her lap, and she leaned her head back against the headrest. Now that her anxiety had faded, Eden's mind seemed clearer, and the situation was impossible to ignore. The dead girl she'd seen *had* to be Jess, and that meant that

Star was still out there and that someone, maybe the man Star called Hollywood, was a killer.

Leo Steele's dark eyes flashed through her mind. He had mentioned both Hollywood and Jess to someone on the phone. How was he involved? Could he tell her something about what was going on?

Eden clenched her fists at the thought of asking Leo Steele for help. But she knew she would have to do whatever it would take to prevent Star from being the next girl to wash up on the river bank.

CHAPTER SIXTEEN

Hollywood clutched the small package, trying to estimate how much smack Sig had dropped off. He suspected the bag was lighter than usual as he stuffed it into the pocket of his baggy jeans and watched Sig's car exit the parking lot of the Old Canal Motel.

Stingy old bastard. You think this tiny-ass bag is enough for me and all the girls?

Still shaking his head in disgust, Hollywood turned and headed toward the rear of the motel. Faded asphalt baked underneath his worn-in topsiders as he approached Building D, which faced the narrow canal that had given the motel its name. Graffiti covered the canal walls as they cut through the east side of the city before feeding into the Willow River.

In addition to boasting a canal view, Building D was set back from the interstate, providing a measure of privacy for those entering and exiting the rooms. It was the ideal set-up to secure the eight remaining girls that Hollywood and Sig were preparing for the next shipment through Miami.

Hollywood greeted a sullen-faced man sitting on the stairwell with a curt nod. The man had been assigned look-out duty for the afternoon, and he didn't seem to be very happy about it. Hollywood took in the man's ponytail and wrinkled clothes and shook his head, wondering again why Sig had to involve the losers from Miami in their operation.

Can't take a piss around here without someone from Miami looking over my shoulder.

Hollywood rounded the corner and slowed his steps as he saw the hulking figure of the motel's night manager hovering outside the window of Room D-101. He crept up behind the mountain of a man.

"What's up, Big Red?" Hollywood bellowed as he stopped directly behind the big man, causing him to jump and twist around in fright. Hollywood greeted him with a sardonic grin.

"See anything you like in that window?"

Big Red's face flushed a fiery-red that matched his full head of hair and long, bushy beard.

"I was just seeing if anyone was home, you know?"

"I know what you were trying to see, fat boy," Hollywood replied with a wink.

"I don't blame you. You got to get your rocks off somehow."

Big Red's face flushed an even deeper shade of scarlet, but this time Hollywood thought the rush of blood may be a sign of anger rather than embarrassment. The motel manager might be dumb, but he could also be mean, and he knew too much about the operation for Hollywood's comfort.

Best not to piss off the jolly red giant just yet.

"Just kidding, my man," Hollywood said, reaching out and slapping one of Red's hefty shoulders. "You come back later and I'll let you party with us, okay? But I've got a few things I gotta take care of now."

"I saw the news," Big Red said, his small, close-set eyes gleaming. "They had a special report about the girl they found in the river. Had one of them sketches and everything. She sure looks like one of them girls you had in there last week. The skinny blonde one. The one that was sick all over the parking lot."

"Have you been smoking crack, my friend?" Hollywood issued a hollow chuckle, fighting the urge to slam Big Red's head into the window. "My girls are all safe and accounted for."

"Don't worry, I can keep a secret," Big Red said, moving his head so that he could see through the gap in the curtain. He looked over at Hollywood and licked his meaty lips. "I'll be back later to party."

Shit, could the girl in the river really be Jess? What am I gonna tell Sig? He'll go apeshit.

Hollywood clenched his teeth as he watched Big Red waddle away.

I'll think of something. I always do. But first I need a hit.

"Good afternoon, ladies," Hollywood called out as he entered the room, his hand cupping the bag in his pocket, reassuring himself that it was still there.

Two girls lay dozing on one of the double beds. Vinny sat in a straight-backed chair by the window playing solitaire on his phone.

"You sound happy. Did you find Star?" Vinny asked, still tapping away on the screen.

"No, I didn't find Star," Hollywood said, his mood instantly turning sour. "But I bet somebody in this room knows where she is."

"I don't have a clue, man," Vinny said without looking up, his brow furrowed as he peered at the little screen.

"I don't mean you, you dumbass. But Mia or Brandi here probably knows where Star went. They probably have plans to meet up with her."

Hollywood kicked the bed, but the soft topsider didn't do much to rouse the girls from their stupor. He wished he had worn his combat boots.

That would wake them the hell up.

"Hey, Brandi," Hollywood barked. "Look at me."

He bent over the girl closest to him and grabbed a thin arm, dragging her up into a sitting position. The strap of her thin tank top slipped off her shoulder, revealing a purple butterfly tattoo hovering above a soft, round breast. She didn't bother adjusting the strap.

"What do you what?" Brandi's voice was hoarse, but she sounded coherent. She hadn't shot up since the day before, and Hollywood could tell she was starting to sober up. He gritted his teeth at the thought of his precious stash.

No way I'm going to waste it all on these whores.

"I wanna know where Star's hiding out," Hollywood replied, his hand tightening on her arm. "I wanna know where you're planning to meet up with her."

"I told you, I don't know where she is," Brandi muttered, her eyes hard as they glared up at Hollywood. "She didn't tell me anything."

"Star *was* freaking out," Mia offered as she too sat up and stretched her arms over her head. Her long, dark hair fell in tangled waves over plump shoulders. "She was going mental, saying something bad happened to Jess."

"She's not the only one," Brandi said. She twisted out of Hollywood's grasp, pulled her knees to her chest, and wrapped her arms around them.

"Jess was really sick; she was way too sick to run off. And why would she just leave all her stuff here?"

Hollywood's hand shot out, knocking Brandi's head back against the wooden headboard before she could react. "I already told you, I don't wanna hear that bitch's name again."

"What the hell, man?" Vinny stood up and approached the bed, but Hollywood swung around and pointed a finger in Vinny's face. "And I don't wanna hear one word from you, bro. I'm not in the mood for your bullshit."

Vinny raised his hands and took a step back. "Calm down, man. Take it easy."

Hollywood felt his arms starting to itch. He reached down and traced the outline of the bag that rested in his pocket. He needed to find a place to shoot up. Somewhere he could be on his own.

"You got some smack, baby?" Mia watched Hollywood's hand clench the bulge in his pocket, ignoring his outburst. Beads of sweat had formed on her forehead and her fingers scratched at her arms, both of which were peppered with reddish sores. "I need something soon."

"You want to party?" Hollywood asked, his voice deadly calm. "Then you better tell me where that bitch Star is hiding. Maybe then I'll hook you up real good."

Hollywood strode over and sat on the chair Vinny had vacated. "Get dressed; we're going to a party."

"But I need a fix, baby," Mia whined from the bed.

"Shut up and get dressed," Hollywood snapped. "I treated you both real good, gave you everything, and how did you repay me? You let Star run off and didn't even try to stop her."

Ungrateful bitches, always whining for a hit. When I'm done with them they'll wish they'd kept their big mouths shut.

"I'm gonna check on the other rooms," Vinny said to Hollywood, before turning back to Brandi and Mia. "You girls watch yourselves around Hollywood. He's been acting a little crazy."

"What's that supposed to mean?" Hollywood asked, but his voice was distracted. No longer worried about telling Sig that Jess might be the girl in the river, or that the police might trace her back to them. He was instead focused on his plans to divide up the drugs so that he had enough to keep him going.

No need to waste too much shit on the girls. They'll do what I say in any case. Got 'em all wrapped around my little finger.

Vinny opened the door and looked back, his eyes darted from Hollywood to the girls, who were rifling through a pile of clothes on the floor. "I'll be back," he said.

Hollywood took out his phone and started typing in a text to Sig, while Brandi crossed to the bathroom. She looked after Vinny with angry eyes, before closing the door behind her.

Mia knelt in front of Hollywood and pushed his phone to the side. "I know you've got some candy for me, baby," she murmured, her hands sliding to the pocket she'd seen him rubbing earlier. "And I've got some candy for you."

Hollywood heard the door click behind Vinny as he leaned back and allowed Mia to work her magic. Sure, he'd give her a little bump, but that was all. He smiled as he felt the rush begin.

CHAPTER SEVENTEEN

Leo Steele stared in horror at the body on the gurney. Little Jessica Carmichael lay battered and bruised, her lustrous brown hair had been cut short and dyed a harsh, brassy blonde. Her beautiful gray eyes now closed forever. But he knew it was her. He recognized the fine cheekbones and the cupid's bow mouth that turned up at the corners when she smiled. Not that he'd seen her smiling often during her mother's trial.

His stomach churned at the thought of Jessica's mother, and he struggled not to retch.

How the hell am I going to tell Beth that her daughter is gone?

"It's her," he told Iris Nguyen. "That's Jessica Carmichael. She grew up here in town, so I'm sure one of the local dentists will be able to verify her identity as well through her dental records."

"Right, that sounds like a good idea," Iris said and motioned for Wesley to pull up the sheet as she lowered the blinds.

"I want to be the one to tell her mother," Leo said, forcing the words out.

The thought of telling Beth that her daughter had been murdered produced a familiar ache in his chest. It was the same kind of ache he'd felt when he'd found out his mother had been killed. The kind of ache that never truly went away, no matter how long you lived, or how hard you tried to forget.

"You're free to tell your client what you've seen here today, of course," Iris agreed, biting her lip as if trying to find the right words.

"But I'll need to give the next of kin the official notification once we've confirmed the findings. I see from the missing person's report that the deceased mother's name is Beth Carmichael and that she's currently incarcerated at the Willow Bay Women's Detention Center. I'll work through the proper channels to contact Ms. Carmichael once I've got everything in order."

Leo frowned down at Iris, his jaw clenched. She made it all seem so very official. As usual, the city officials would try to break down the anguish and horror of murder into neat procedures and processes.

It made him sick to think Jessica's death was now just a case to be handled. A procedure to be followed by cold-eyed bureaucrats. Just as they'd done with his mother's murder. Just as they'd done when they wrongly convicted his father. It was all just another day of work for them.

Leo spun on his heels and pushed past Wesley who had been standing by the door. He didn't look back as he strode out of the Medical Examiner's Office and headed toward the parking garage where he'd left his car. He tried to imagine the right words to say when he saw Beth.

I'm sorry, Beth, but Jessica is gone...Jessica is dead. Some sick bastard strangled Jess...it isn't fair...I'm so very sorry.

Nothing sounded right. All the words he thought of would still tear out Beth's heart. There was no way to take away the pain.

Before he reached the stairwell to the second level of the garage, Leo saw the tall blonde woman he'd noticed at the police station the night he'd reported Jessica missing. He thought he'd caught a glimpse of her earlier today at the Medical Examiner's Office as well.

The woman was sitting on a bench, shaded by an ancient elm tree. The golden retriever he had opened the door for the other evening was sitting at her feet. Both the woman and the dog stared at Leo as he approached, and he nodded.

"Hi," he said with a forced smile. She was a stunner, but he wasn't in the right frame of mind to start a conversation. He needed to get to Beth.

"You really don't know who I am, do you?" the woman asked, her voice cool. She didn't smile as Leo slowed his stride and looked more closely.

"I'm sorry," he said, though at the moment he didn't much care if he offended some past fling. "I'm actually having a rough day, and I have somewhere I need to be. Perhaps we can catch up some other time."

"Does the name Mercy Lancaster ring a bell?" the woman said, ignoring his words and standing up.

She was tall, and she squared her shoulders as if to try to face him on equal terms. He knew he had at least six inches on her, but her words made him feel suddenly small. A trickle of shame worked its way down his back as he searched for a response.

"You're her sister, aren't you?" he said, his voice filled with sympathy. "You're Preston Lancaster's sister-in-law."

"Yes, I'm Eden Winthrop, Mercy's sister, but I prefer not to think of myself related to her murderer in any way. He killed my sister, killed the mother of his own children." Eden gulped in air, her cheeks flushed.

"And you're the one who got him released on bail so that he was free to kill her."

"Everyone deserves a fair defense," Leo said, his eyes dropping.

He noticed the dog staring at him and forced himself to raise his head and meet Eden's icy gaze.

"That's what they all say." Eden's eyes glistened with unshed tears. "That's always the excuse used by people who aren't impacted by the outcome. The people who consider it *just a job* to defend wife beaters and murderers."

Leo winced at her words, which so closely echoed his own recent thoughts about Iris Nguyen and the officials who would be following up on Jessica's murder.

Am I just as guilty as the bureaucrats I claim to despise?

"I'm sorry, Ms. Winthrop. I'm truly sorry for your loss. I know that doesn't help, but it's true." Leo's shoulders sagged, and he ran a hand through his dark hair just as his phone began to vibrate with an incoming call. He pulled the phone from his suit pocket and recognized the number. It was Beth Carmichael.

It can't be over the phone. I have to tell her about Jessica in person.

"Another client needing your help getting away with murder?" Eden said, but the fire had gone out of her voice.

He thought she now looked more tired than angry. She slumped back down on the bench, and the golden retriever flopped down at her feet.

"Yes, it is a client needing help, but in this case, her daughter is the victim." Leo looked around, making sure no one was nearby.

The street behind him was deserted. He wasn't sure why he was confiding in a woman who obviously hated him, but he found himself saying, "I just identified her daughter's body. She's the girl they found in the river this morning. Now I need to go tell her mother. Oh, Christ, what am I going to say?"

Leo turned toward the stairwell, knowing he had to get to the jail as soon as possible. He didn't want some stranger telling Beth that her only child was dead.

"I wondered why you were there," Eden called after him, her voice shaky. "I overheard you mention the name Jess and thought you might have information about a missing girl I met. A girl who told me that someone named Hollywood had killed her friend. Her friend's name was Jess."

Leo stopped and closed his eyes, trying to process the information she'd thrown at him. He turned around with his head cocked to one side. "What are you saying?"

"A girl named Star told me she was afraid her friend Jess had been killed by some guy she called Hollywood." Eden looked into Leo's eyes, and he saw fear in the emerald depths.

"But then Star disappeared, and I've been looking for her. I thought the girl they found was Star...until I viewed the body."

"You saw...Jessica?" Leo asked. Eden nodded, and Leo felt a flicker of anger that a stranger had witnessed the dead girl's violated body.

"Now I'm the one who's sorry," Eden said, the words sounding stiff in her mouth. "I can tell she meant something to you."

"Her mother is a client of mine. Admittedly a client that made some bad choices, and ended up in jail, but she loves her daughter. When Jessica went missing, she was desperate to find her."

Leo recalled the worry in Beth's eyes the last time he'd seen her. "She's going to be devastated."

"Do you always get so emotionally invested in your client's lives?" Eden asked, and Leo thought the question sounded sincere.

"Sometimes it's impossible not to, I guess," he admitted. "I know how lonely it can feel to be accused and locked up. I saw my father go through hell trying to prove his innocence until it finally broke him. I can't just stand by and let others go through that without at least trying to help."

A rumble of thunder sounded in the distance. Leo looked up to see dark clouds brewing toward the east. Another storm was about to hit the city, and the traffic would be a mess. "Look, I've got to go. I want to get to the jail before...well, before anyone else tells Beth what's happened."

"Star's still missing," Eden said, her voice sounded small against the background of more thunder. "She may be the next one to turn up in the river. It may already be too late."

"You need to tell the police what you've told me. They'll follow up I'm sure." Even as he said the words, he felt like a fraud and a liar. Since when did he believe the police in Willow Bay would do the right thing and find the right killer? They'd screwed up cases before. Just look at what had happened to his father.

"Oh, I've told them, but I'm not sure that will be enough to save Star and to find the monster that killed Jessica. The police in this town weren't able to save Mercy," Eden said, her chin held high and her mouth set in a flat line. "How can I trust them to save Star?"

Leo opened his mouth to respond, but then closed it again. Eden was right. It was highly unlikely that the police would figure out who was behind Jessica's murder in time to save her missing friend. And what exactly would he tell Beth when she asked him who had killed her daughter? Would she ever know what had happened to her only child?

Leo had grown accustomed to living with the pain of not knowing who had killed the person he had loved above all others. The knowledge that the killer was still out there living his life, free to kill again, haunted him. Would Beth have to learn to live with that same pain?

"Come with me," Leo said, surprising himself with the curt command. "There's someone that may be able to help us find out what happened to Jessica. If we know what happened to her, we may be able to find Star."

"You mean, now?" Eden asked, her eyes wide at the thought of going anywhere with Leo Steele.

"Yes, now," Leo said, already taking the stairs two at a time. "But I'll need to stop off at the jail first."

CHAPTER EIGHTEEN

Bruised storm clouds threatened in the distance, but the rain hadn't yet started to fall when they arrived at the Willow Bay Women's Detention Center in Leo Steele's BMW. Eden looked up at the barbed wire that ran along the concrete fence and noted the guard towers positioned above each corner.

It's a full-fledged prison, not a detention center, she thought, bemused. *Why sugar-coat it? Why not just call it what it is?*

They had driven the five miles to the detention center in silence, and Eden told Leo she and Duke would wait for him on a bench outside the visitor's reception area while he met with Beth.

She almost felt sorry for him as he walked inside, his face pale and his eyes downcast.

Maybe he isn't completely heartless, after all.

The thought made Eden feel disloyal to Mercy, and, needing a distraction, she pulled out her phone to check her email. She was still reading through her messages twenty minutes later when Leo stepped out.

"Let's go," he said, not waiting to see if she would follow him as he made his way back to the car. She let Duke slip into the back and then climbed into the passenger seat, the leather seat hot beneath her legs as she secured her seat belt.

"So, where exactly are we going?" Eden asked, determined not to inquire how Beth Carmichael had taken the news of Jessica's death. Leo's clenched jaw didn't invite questions, and besides, she wasn't ready to bear the weight of any more sorrow just yet, even if it wasn't her own.

"We're going to my office," Leo replied, his eyes fixed on the road ahead, his voice distracted. "I've arranged to meet someone who has been looking into Jessica's whereabouts. Hopefully, he can tell us where she was before this all happened."

After ten minutes of weaving through heavy traffic, Leo nosed the BMW off the interstate and drove toward the modest cluster of modern, glass, and metal buildings that formed downtown Willow Bay.

Eden was surprised when he turned onto a shady street lined with older homes that had been converted into businesses and offices. She'd pegged him for someone who would have offices on the top floor of the tallest, shiniest building in town.

The BMW pulled into a small, paved lot next to a two-story house that appeared to be newly renovated. The wooden walls were painted a crisp white in contrast to the dark, forest green of the shutters and trim. A porch swing added a homey touch to the wide front porch.

Eden and Duke followed Leo up the stairs and into a cozy waiting room just as the first fat drops of rain began to fall.

"Looks like you all just beat the storm," a cheerful voice called.

Eden turned to see the owner of the voice. Perhaps in her late fifties or early sixties, the woman's gray curls and rimless glasses gave her a grandmotherly appearance. She stood and offered a soft, plump hand to Eden, her gray eyes bright and curious.

"I'm Pat Monahan, Leo's secretary."

"No, she's actually a paralegal for this law firm," Leo corrected as he looked around the room. "I guess Frankie Dawson hasn't arrived yet?"

"Well, you can call me what you want, Leo, but I think *paralegal* sounds a bit depressing."

Pat rolled her eyes and winked at Eden, before releasing her hand and turning to face Leo.

"And yes, Frankie has arrived. Unfortunately, he isn't afraid of an early death from lung cancer. He's smoking a cigarette on the back porch."

Pat turned to Eden and raised her eyebrows. "And you are?"

"Oh, sorry, I'm Eden Winthrop, I'm here to meet someone with Mr. Steele. I guess Frankie?"

"Yes, I've asked Frankie Dawson to join us," Leo confirmed. "Let's go on out back. We don't have time to wait while he blackens his lungs."

Leo strode down the hall, but Pat reached out and put a hand on Eden's arm. She looked down at Duke, who was sitting politely by the door.

"Does this big guy want to stay with me and have some water and a snack? I have some doggie biscuits in my bag. My little pug, Tinkerbell, has a hollow leg, so I never leave home without a snack."

"That would be very nice. I'm sure Duke would appreciate that," Eden said, guilt tinting her cheeks pink as she remembered that the dog hadn't had access to water for several hours. She bent down and hugged Duke to her, glad to feel his warm, solid body against her.

"You stay here with Pat, now. I'll be back for you soon."

As Eden stepped onto the raised wooden porch, an angry flash of lightning cracked the sky open, and the deluge of rain that had been threatening finally arrived. The porch was covered by a sturdy awning, but the rain blew in sideways, splattering Eden's leather flats. She hovered by the back door as Leo spoke to a tall, lanky man with limp brown hair and puffy, bloodshot eyes.

"Frankie, this is Eden, she's trying to find a runaway, too. Someone who may have known Jess." Leo glanced at Eden but didn't give her or Frankie a chance to respond.

"So, what did you find out, Frankie? Where was Jess staying?" Leo fired the words at the man as if he were questioning a hostile witness in a courtroom. "Who was she with?"

"Slow down, man," Frankie muttered, throwing down the smoking remains of his cigarette and smashing it into the deck with a grubby tennis shoe.

"My boy took the picture you gave me and showed it around. Some dude told him that Jess had been stayin' with another girl at a sober house on the east side. Dude said she split a few weeks ago. I was plannin' to check out his story, but I've been busy, ya know."

"Yeah? Well, it looks like you've been busy getting wasted, Frankie." Leo shook his head, his fists clenching at his sides. "I thought you were staying clean."

"I am clean, bro! I've been clean for months." Frankie's thin face settled into a scowl. "It was a late night. I wasn't plannin' to come all the way out here today, ya know."

"And I didn't plan for Jessica's body to be pulled out of the river, but there it is," Leo snarled, turning away from Frankie and Eden, staring out into the gray curtain of rain that had descended all around them.

"Oh shit, man, I'm sorry," Frankie groaned. "Was that girl on the news Jess? That's fucked up."

"Tell me something I don't know," Leo said. "Where's this sober house? Who was the friend she was supposed to be with? Give me something to work with."

"The place is called Clear Horizons. It's on Baymont, past the old Blockbuster building. I'll text you the address. From what the guy said, the old lady that runs the place is a real piece of work."

Frankie stopped talking while he plucked a single cigarette out of his shirt pocket and held a grimy Bic lighter to the tip.

After taking a deep drag, he put the lighter away and cleared his throat. "So, this broad takes in all these addicts fresh out of rehab. Most of 'em are real young. Their parents don't want 'em back in the house. They pretty much pay her to provide Junior a place to stay until the next relapse."

"How noble," Leo said, eyes narrowed against the smoke that hung in the air.

"From what this guy said, the old lady drives a Beamer or a Jag or some shit." Frankie looked impressed. He puffed out another cloud of smoke.

Grabbing the cigarette from Frankie and throwing it on the ground, Leo used an expensive-looking leather shoe to grind the cigarette into the wet wood. "I didn't get you out of prison so you could kill yourself with that crap."

"Hey, man, not cool. That was my last one," Frankie whined, the scowl back on his face.

Leo turned to Eden and narrowed his eyes. "You want to pay a visit to this so-called sober house? Maybe they can tell us if Jessica really was there, and if she was, who she left with."

* * *

Eden braced herself for a possible impact as Leo sped down rain-slicked streets and weaved in and out of traffic, not seeming to notice the torrential rain that beat against the windshield. Duke whined from the backseat.

"You mind slowing down?" Eden asked, her tone cold. "Duke doesn't like being thrown around like a stuffed animal."

"Sorry," Leo said, his eyes flicking to the rearview mirror. "Sorry, Duke, didn't mean to scare you."

"Do you think we should let the police know what we've found out?" Eden asked, her heart slowing along with the car's speed. "Maybe we should let them handle this?"

"We've gone through this before," Leo said with exaggerated patience. "The police will act on what they want to when they want to. I want to know what happened to Jess *now*."

Eden sighed and sat back in the seat, staring out the rain-streaked window. She had to agree with Leo. If they waited for the police to act, and something happened to Star in the meantime, she'd be the only one to blame.

The BMW made a quick turn onto Baymont Court. The street was lined with a mix of small businesses and modest apartment buildings. Halfway down the block, she saw a small sign in front of a two-story apartment building that identified it only as Clear Horizons.

"I guess they don't advertise this as being a sober house," Eden murmured, her eyes searching the windows as Leo pulled alongside the curb and turned off the engine. "Neighbors would probably object."

"Actually, recovering addicts and alcoholics are protected by federal law. They can't be kept out of a neighborhood just because they're in recovery. Plenty of people are ready to sue if you try."

"Oh, I didn't realize," Eden said. "I guess I'm a bit ignorant about addiction. I've never personally known an addict or an alcoholic. At least not that I'm aware of." A vivid image of her pill bottle sitting next to a large glass of red wine flashed in her mind; she pushed it away. *I'm not addicted. Those pills have been prescribed to treat my anxiety. And I haven't used any for ages. And red wine is full of antioxidants. Besides, it helps with my insomnia.*

"Well, Florida is full of recovery facilities and sober houses, and I've personally had plenty of clients who have been railroaded because they suffer from addiction." Leo gripped the steering wheel as he spoke.

"It's easy to pin something on someone who has lost credibility. It's an easy out for the police or a prosecutor who wants a quick conviction."

Eden looked over at Leo, curious for the first time about what had made the man so angry with the police and the court system.

Something terrible must have happened to make him this full of rage.

Leo looked past Eden, seeming to size up the building. "From my quick search online, I believe a woman named Denise Bane runs the place. She founded it in the nineties."

"Seems rather run down to me," Eden said, not liking the way weeds sprouted from the broken sidewalk and years of dirt clung to the faded concrete walls.

"Looks like the rain's letting up. Let's see what we can find." He reached back and let Duke out on his side, and the dog walked next to him toward the sidewalk without hesitation, unbothered by the light drizzle. Eden opened her umbrella and watched the dog, chagrined that he didn't seem to notice she was still standing by the car.

You little traitor.

By the time Eden had caught up with Leo, he had knocked on a ground floor door. Eden saw a weathered *House Manager* nameplate just as the door opened to reveal a tall woman with short, white hair. Her wide, plain face was tan and leathery, and to Eden, it looked like the face of a lifelong smoker.

"Yes?" The woman's cool expression matched her tone. She had on a crisp, blue cotton blouse, fitted black pants, and canvas ballet flats. The only accessories she wore were small diamond stud earrings and a silver wedding band.

"Denise Bane?" Leo asked, his voice smooth and pleasant. "I'm Leo Steele, and this is Eden Winthrop. We're wondering if you may have information regarding a former resident of yours."

"Which resident?" Denise asked, her pale blue eyes narrowed, her mouth set in a hard line.

"Jessica Carmichael," Leo said, holding out a color photo. In the photo, Jessica still had long, dark hair. She was smiling but her big gray eyes looked pensive.

"I haven't seen her in weeks," Denise said, her expression unchanged. "She was never really a resident here in any case. Couldn't find a sponsor."

"What do you mean by sponsor?" Eden asked, her heart dropping with the knowledge that Jessica hadn't been at the sober house since the night Star said she'd disappeared.

"She means that Jessica didn't have someone to pay her way, isn't that right Ms. Bane?" Leo's dark eyes filled with anger, and he seemed oblivious to the raindrops that continued to fall and glisten in his thick hair.

"She didn't have money to cover her stay, no. And she was a minor and didn't have an adult to give their consent for her to live here." A frown furrowed the older woman's leathery brow.

"She tried to sneak in at night and stay with one of the girls. I had to chase her out more than a few times."

"Do you have any idea where she may have stayed when she wasn't here? Where she could have been staying in the last two weeks?" Leo asked. "Do you think the girl she knew here would know?"

"All our residents are guaranteed complete confidentiality and discretion." A satisfied gleam entered her eyes. "Unless you're with the police, and have a warrant, I can't allow you to speak to any of my residents."

A slim, young man appeared behind Denise. "What seems to be the problem?"

A flash of annoyance crossed Denise's face. "Nothing I can't handle, Trevor. I've got this under control."

"Do you work here, too?" Eden called out, ignoring the woman blocking the door, knowing they had no hope to get any more information from Denise Bane.

"Yes, I'm the assistant manager, Trevor Bane," the young man said with a curious smile. "Who are you?"

"I'm a lawyer, my name is Leo Steele, and this is Eden Winthrop, she runs a foundation in the area," Leo said. "We're trying to find out what happened to the daughter of one of my clients."

"They're looking for Jessica. You know, the girl that was always hanging around." Denise glared back at Trevor. "I already told them she wasn't a resident and we don't know where she is."

"I think you misunderstand, Ms. Bane," Leo said. "We know exactly where Jessica is now. We're trying to find out where she's been."

"Why don't you ask her, then?" Trevor looked confused.

"Because she's dead, that's why," Leo said, anger oozing out with each word. "And we are trying to understand the circumstances leading up to her death."

Eden watched Denise Bane's face and thought she saw the woman register genuine shock. Her mouth opened, then shut. After a pause, she said, "Let's all step inside, out of the rain."

Leo followed Denise into the office, but Eden hesitated, seeing the wet mud on Duke's feet. She didn't want to leave him outside in an unfamiliar neighborhood.

Trevor stood at the door and motioned her in. "Don't worry about getting the floors wet, they're already a mess."

Eden nodded and ushered Duke into the small room. An empty desk stood in a corner, and several office chairs were positioned around the stark room. The bare walls were a dingy white, matching the scuffed white tiles on the floor.

"I guess I shouldn't be shocked that she's dead." Denise sat at the desk and sighed, the lines in her face cruelly exposed by the overhead fluorescent light. "I'm assuming it was an overdose of some kind? These young girls treat their bodies like garbage nowadays. It's a real shame."

Eden recoiled at the lack of sympathy in the woman's tone. While the older woman was definitely taken aback by the news of Jessica's death, she didn't seem to find it particularly sad.

"She seemed like a nice kid," Trevor said, his face somber.

"She *was* a nice kid," Leo replied. "And she *didn't* die of an overdose. She was murdered."

Trevor gaped at Leo, his eyes wide with disbelief. "You aren't serious? She was...killed?"

"I'm sure you've heard about the girl they found," Eden said. "She was strangled and dumped in the river. It's been all over the news."

"That was...Jessica?" Trevor whispered. "Oh my god! Do the police know who did it? Do they know who killed her?"

"I'm sure they're working on it," Leo said, "but we're trying to find out what we can for Jessica's mother, who is a client of mine. She reported Jessica missing before her body was found. We think she was missing a few weeks before she was killed."

"Well, she hasn't been here for weeks," Trevor said, running a slim hand through his thick blonde hair. "I don't know where she went once Mom...I mean, um, Denise, told her she couldn't come back or we'd call the police."

"She was a runaway and a minor. I have liability insurance to consider." Denise stood up and squared her shoulders. "I wish we could help, but there's nothing we can do."

"Can we at least speak to the resident that knew her? The girl she stayed with?" Eden pleaded. "Please...another girl may also be in danger. A girl named Star. Young and blonde. Do you know her? Could she be a resident here?"

Eden saw Trevor and Denise exchange a long look.

"No one named Star has ever stayed here as far as I remember. And, as I already said, our residents are guaranteed privacy. However, in this case, I couldn't let you speak to the resident even if I was willing to break my client's trust, since the girl no longer lives here."

Denise paused as if thinking. "I guess she completed her stay around the same time as Jessica stopping hanging around."

"Fine, then just give us her contact details and we'll be on our way," Leo said, crossing his arms across his wide chest.

"You know I can't do that, Mr. Steele. If I give you the name of my minor resident her parents would likely sue me for everything I'm worth." Denise didn't seem bothered by the prospect.

"I wish I could help," Trevor said, his eyes worried. "I knew Jessica had a drug habit, I mean, that's one of the reasons we didn't want her hanging around here, but I never thought she was in danger of anything other than an overdose. I can't believe she was killed. And strangled? It doesn't make sense."

The young man looked genuinely puzzled, and Eden felt her hopes drain away. It was unlikely he knew anything that could help them.

Leo seemed to come to the same conclusion, and he grasped Eden by the elbow and guided her toward the door. The shock of his warm skin on hers made her inhale sharply, but Leo didn't seem to notice her discomfiture.

"Someone just killed a girl who stayed in your facility, and other young girls in similar circumstances could be in danger. I hope you'll have enough sense to warn your residents accordingly."

Leo opened the door and let Eden and Duke pass through. Trevor followed them out.

The rain had stopped, and a weak sun was shining through the remaining clouds as Eden walked toward Leo's car.

"Cool car," Trevor said, looking at the rain-splattered BMW with a half-hearted smile. "My mother was going to get a beamer, but then she decided on an Audi."

"Taking in recovering addicts must pay well," Leo said, his eyes on Trevor's face. "You like working for your mother? It can't be easy."

"Yeah, she can be a bit hard to take, but I like it here," Trevor said, looking over his shoulder. In the sun Eden could see he was younger than she had thought. Maybe early twenties. A thought popped into her mind.

"Trevor, did you know Tiffany Clarke?"

Trevor considered the question. "The name sounds familiar somehow. Who is she?"

"She's a girl that went missing a few years ago. Her body was found in the same river as Jessica's. Just wondering if there could be a connection. For example, could she ever have stayed here?"

"Oh yeah, now I remember. There were all those posters everywhere with her name and picture. That must be why I recognized the name. But no, I never knew her. She definitely didn't stay here."

"Okay, just thought I'd ask," Eden said, handing Trevor her card. "If you think of anything that could help us, please contact me."

"Sure, will do," Trevor said and turned on his heel to walk back inside.

Eden watched him walk back to the office and noticed Denise Bane staring out of the window. She looked back at Eden with hard eyes, before the curtain dropped back into place.

CHAPTER NINETEEN

Leo stood next to his car but didn't open the door. He surveyed the surrounding buildings. He knew someone in the neighborhood must have seen Jessica coming and going. She didn't have a car, so it's likely she was on foot.

Someone must have noticed a pretty, young girl hanging around.

"We need to talk to some of the neighbors," Leo said as Eden approached.

"Let's take Duke for a little walk. He'll get a chance to stretch his legs while we scope out the area. I might even knock on a few doors and show Jessica's photo."

Eden looked over her shoulder. "Do you think Ms. Bane will have a problem with us leaving the car here?"

"If she does, then it's her problem, not ours." Leo was already walking down the sidewalk toward the corner. "Let her call the cops if she has an issue."

Eden shrugged and dug in her purse for Duke's leash. She clipped it onto his collar and they set out after Leo.

On foot, the neighborhood appeared more neglected than Leo had noticed as they'd arrived. Of course, he'd been in a rush and hadn't paid much attention, but now that he was walking down the block, he could see that the area was in serious decline. Rundown apartment blocks shared the road with several small shops that had gone out of business, the dirty windows displaying only empty shelves. Parking lots were cluttered with overflowing trashcans and stacks of empty boxes and crates.

As they approached the corner, Leo saw a small park set back from the road. A woman was walking out of the park pushing a toddler in a stroller, and a few young men were leaning on a bicycle rack on the sidewalk outside the park entrance.

"Let's take Duke over there," he said, pointing to the Baymont Neighborhood Park sign. "He can run around a bit."

Leo crossed the street and saw that the park consisted of a fenced-in square of weedy grass outfitted with a rusty metal jungle gym and a few concrete benches. He waited for Eden and Duke to pass through the gate before turning to face the three young men on the sidewalk.

Two of the men seemed to be having a heated conversation, while a third was pacing while talking on his cell phone. They all wore jeans and t-shirts. Leo looked down at his suit and tie with a grimace, wishing he followed the casual Friday tradition most companies had adopted.

So much for fitting in with the local vibe.

"Hey guys, you live around here?" Leo asked, already reaching into his suit pocket and pulling out Jessica's photo. "I'm hoping you can look at a picture for me."

The two men stopped in mid-conversation and stared over at Leo with suspicious eyes. They both had their dark hair gelled up into tousled quiffs, although one was tall and skinny while the other was short and stocky.

"Have you seen this girl around here?" Leo asked.

"You a cop?" the short man said, ignoring the picture, keeping his eyes on Leo's face.

"No, I'm a lawyer, and this girl is missing. Her mother is my client." Leo waited for the man to react. When he didn't move, Leo said, "You know how mothers worry."

"Stop being such a dick," the taller man said, jabbing a long finger into the shorter man's arm. He turned to Leo. "Let us see the picture."

After a quick look, both men shook their heads.

"Never seen that girl around here," the tall man said with confidence.

The shorter man agreed. "No, never seen her. I'd remember her if I had. She in trouble?"

"Yes, you could say that," Leo said, trying to reign in his disappointment as the men walked away.

"Who are you looking for?"

Leo heard a deep voice from behind him and turned to see that the third man had ended his phone call. He was a tall, muscular black man with close-cropped hair and a strong jaw.

"I'm looking for information about a girl named Jessica," Leo said, holding out the picture.

"Jess? Yeah, I know a girl named Jess," the man said, taking the picture from Leo and studying it. "That's her all right, but she didn't look like that when I saw her."

Leo's heart beat faster. "What did she look like...um, sorry, what's your name?"

"I'm Charles. Charles Wyatt." He held out a big hand and Leo shook it, noting the man's strong grip.

"I'm Leo Steele. I'm a lawyer for Jessica's mother." He stopped himself from saying more. He wanted to hear what Charles knew before telling him that the girl was dead. Murder tended to scare people away.

"So, you said Jessica looked different?"

"She had short, blondish hair. Kind of punk, I guess. I met her a few times...right there," Charles said, nodding toward the bench inside the park gate where Eden was sitting as she watched Duke explore. "She said she knew a girl staying at Clear Horizons. It's just around the corner."

"We've just come from there, but they couldn't tell us anything. Confidentiality and all that." Leo motioned over to Eden to join them.

Eden stood and walked toward him, eyebrows raised.

"Eden, this is Charles Wyatt," Leo said. "He met Jessica here a few times...and he's familiar with Clear Horizons."

"Yeah, I live a few houses down from there. I went to school with Trevor. His mother owns the place."

"When did you last see Jessica?" Eden asked, her eyes hopeful.

"It's probably been a few weeks. She was pretty excited. Said she'd found a boyfriend and had a new place to stay." Charles frowned and shook his head.

"Trevor's witch of a mother had been giving her a hard time about trying to stay there, so she'd been roughing it. I was glad for her to get off the street."

"Did she tell you the name of her new boyfriend?" Leo asked, his pulse racing as he imagined tracking down whatever miscreant Charles named.

"No, she didn't say. Acted like it was a secret or something." Charles looked down and Leo had the feeling he was holding something back.

"Can you tell us anything else?" Leo asked, his voice pleading. "Anything you can tell us would be helpful."

"Well, I don't like to talk bad about people, but...well, I'm pretty sure Jess was high on something the last time I saw her. She was acting...different."

"So, you think that was the first time you saw her under the influence of drugs?" Leo asked. "She always seemed straight to you before that?"

"Yeah, she seemed like a really smart girl. We talked a few times, mainly just killing time, but she didn't seem like a druggie. Not until that last night," Charles said, his brow furrowed with the memory.

"Something was different that night. I haven't seen her since then. To be honest, I didn't expect to, based on what she'd said about getting a new place with her boyfriend."

"Have you met anyone named Star?" Eden asked. "She's a friend of Jessica's."

Charles looked as if he were thinking. "No, that name doesn't ring a bell. But there are always a few girls from Clear Horizons hanging around the park. Most of them are too young to drive or have lost their license, so they get bored."

Eden looked crestfallen, and Leo sighed, putting his hand on her shoulder. "It's okay, we're just getting started. We'll find her."

"Yeah, I'm sure Jess is okay," Charles said. "She'll turn up."

Leo felt guilt stir in his stomach. He may as well come clean. "Charles, I'm sorry, I should have told you before...but it's not really my place to say. Not until the police make it public."

"What are you talking about? What should you have told me?" Charles asked, his eyes worried.

Eden stepped forward and said in a quiet voice, "Jessica is dead, Charles. She was the girl they found strangled in the Willow River."

Charles' face registered shock and then anger. "What game are you playing? Why did you let me say all that stuff, believing she was...was still alive?"

"We're just trying to find out what might have happened to Jessica. As well as find her friend, Star, who is still missing," Eden said, stepping closer to Leo, her voice soft but firm. "Leo and I are just trying to do the right thing."

Leo looked over at Eden, noticing how green her eyes were in the dappled sunlight. He felt a warm rush of emotion. He hadn't had many beautiful women jumping to his defense lately.

Too bad she'll hate me again when she comes to her senses.

Charles clenched his jaw and shook his head. "I can't believe it. Why would someone kill her? She was just a messed-up kid."

"Charles, do you have any idea who could have done this to her?" Leo asked, worried by the look of anger growing on the young man's face.

"No, but I know whose fault it is that she's dead. That witch that runs Clear Horizons could have saved her. Could at least have given her a place to stay. She's an evil woman. She always has been from what I've heard. And her son isn't much better." Charles clutched his head and released a shout of frustration.

Both Eden and Leo stepped back, and Duke ran over to Eden, the fur on his back standing on end.

"Take it easy, Charles," Leo said, stepping in front of Eden, shielding her. "There's nothing to be gained by acting out."

"I tried to warn Jessica...and the other girls. Tried to tell them something bad could happen," Charles said, ignoring Leo's plea.

"What other girls?" Leo asked, confused. "Who did you warn?"

"Does it matter?" Charles cried. "Jessica is dead, and Brandi is gone. It's too late now."

"Who is Brandi?" Eden asked, her eyes wide with fear, her voice shaky. "What do you mean by *gone*? Do you know another girl that's disappeared?"

"Charles, you need to go to the police station and make a report," Leo said, knowing they couldn't handle this on their own any longer. "You've got to tell them what you know. So they can try to help."

But Charles wasn't listening. He was already jogging down the street, his hands fisted at his sides. Leo felt a tug on his arm and turned to see Eden gasping for breath, one hand on his sleeve, the other hand clutching her throat. Leo looked over his shoulder just in time to see Charles disappear around the corner.

CHAPTER TWENTY

Eden sat in Leo's car, still shaky in the aftermath of her panic attack. She looked over at Leo, her cheeks red with embarrassment.

He probably thinks I'm crazy. Just another hysterical woman.

But she had to admit he didn't look exasperated; he looked worried. Once he realized she was having a panic attack, he'd practically carried her to the car and then talked her through breathing exercises until her breathing had slowed, and her heartbeat returned to normal. And when he had insisted that they put a halt to their inquiries, for the time being, Eden hadn't argued.

She wanted to go home, hug the kids, and never leave her house again. The temptation to open her purse and pull out her pill bottle was strong, but the thought of Leo watching her give in to her weakness stopped her.

Her phone buzzed in her pocket, and she quickly pulled it out and looked at the display. It wasn't a number she recognized. Not Sage or one of the kids. Not Reggie or Nathan. She almost decided to ignore the call, but then she thought perhaps it was someone she'd given her card to. Someone who might have information on Star.

"Hello?" she said, her voice wary, half expecting a telemarketer to start pitching her the best deal ever.

"Ms. Winthrop? Is this Ms. Eden Winthrop?" The deep male voice had the clip of authority. "This is Detective Reinhardt, with the Willow Bay Police Department.

"Yes," Eden stammered, scared now that something bad had happened to Hope or Devon. "I'm Eden Winthrop."

"I'm calling because Detective Nessa Ainsley asked me to assist her with a missing person investigation that you submitted. I've gone through the report and have some questions. Do you have a few minutes now?"

"Yes, of course." Eden tapped the mute icon and turned to Leo. "It's a policeman calling about Star."

Leo nodded and motioned to her to continue.

"Ms. Winthrop, I see on the report that you feel you've met the missing juvenile female at your foundation on a previous occasion. Says here you may be able to uncover the girl's legal name and last known address?" The detective paused, waiting for Eden's response.

Something about the man's tone, and the formality of his words, rankled Eden. She didn't hear even a shred of compassion or emotion in his voice.

Star is just another case to this guy. Just another missing drug-addict.

"Well, Ms. Winthrop, will you be able to help me, or not?" Reinhardt's voice was curt, and Eden suspected he wasn't used to being kept waiting. "As you can imagine, this is a time-sensitive situation. The sooner we have the information, the better."

"I'm sure you also read in the report that the possible information on the missing teenager would be contained within Mercy Harbor's confidential database, Detective Reinhardt," Eden said, a slight tremble in her voice the only sign of the distress she was under.

"The foundation helps scared, abused women escape from violent, even murderous, partners. In many cases these men will go to any lengths to find the women they feel have betrayed them. So, you can understand why I can't just distribute their names and addresses without proper assurances and precautions."

"Of course, Ms. Winthrop, I understand and can assure you that any information you provide will be kept confidential," Reinhardt said, his tone impatient.

"I'm aware that information in police reports can be accessed by the public in most cases," Eden insisted, her eyes turning to Leo for confirmation. He nodded at her, his brow furrowing as he listened to her side of the conversation.

"Ms. Winthrop, do you want us to try to find this girl or not?" Reinhardt snapped. "We've got serious investigations going on in Willow Bay right now that need our attention. If you are no longer interested in pursuing your missing person's report, I can move on to more pressing matters."

Eden gasped at the callousness behind his words. Before she could utter a reply, the detective's voice continued.

"But maybe I should tell you something before you decide how to proceed." The man's voice dropped lower as if he didn't want to be overheard.

"One of our CIs – an informant we use regularly - said some pretty bad characters are looking for a girl named Star. Apparently, she's pissed off somebody and disappeared. Probably in hiding. But she won't be able to hide forever. She needs help."

Eden's head swam with the harsh words and the detective's implications. She knew he was right about Star needing help, but she wasn't sure she could even find Star's family in the database. And if she did find the family's name and last known address, would they still be there? Would Star have run home? Would she want to be found?

"I'll try to find the information as soon as possible, Detective Reinhardt. If I manage to find it, I'll be in touch." She disconnected the call with a distracted swipe and looked out the window at the now deserted street. She wasn't sure what she should do, but she wanted to get back to her car, and then back to her house; she needed time to think.

* * *

Leo remained silent on the drive back to the parking garage where Eden had left her car. He looked pensive and ignored the frequent vibrations that rattled his phone in the cup holder where he'd dropped it after helping Eden inside. The radio was tuned to a local station that mixed eighties music with a few more contemporary hits. She sank back in the seat and listen to a song by Tom Petty that she couldn't name, but somehow knew the words to anyway.

"I don't know what to do," Eden blurted as they pulled up to the curb outside the garage. She wasn't sure if she'd meant to say it out loud, but she had, and now Leo was looking at her with raised eyebrows.

"I'm sorry you're having to deal with all this. I can see it's hard for you," Leo said, his words coming out slowly as if he were picking out his words carefully, perhaps not wanting to upset her again.

"No, I'm the one who should be sorry...about what happened back there." Eden inhaled deeply. Could she really tell this man the whole uncomfortable truth? *Why should I trust him, after everything he's done?*

"So, what exactly did happen?" Leo asked, his dark, curious eyes resting on her face. "Has that happened to you before?"

"I have some...issues with anxiety." Eden could feel her cheeks redden. "The doctors call it a disorder, but I prefer to think of it as a temporary reaction to certain stressful events."

"Okay, that sounds reasonable based on what I know you've been through," Leo said.

Eden studied his face, trying to judge if he was being sarcastic, or even worse, pitied her. But he just looked interested. He appeared to be waiting for her to say more.

"I wasn't always this way," Eden said, looking behind her to see Duke curled up and dozing on the backseat. "I used to be fearless. Probably a bit like you. A driven, high-achiever. Nothing I couldn't do."

Leo smiled and nodded. "I suspect you still are, Eden. Running the foundation can't be easy."

"It isn't," Eden said, feeling her eyes water, and hating herself for it. "But I didn't have a choice really. If I was going to make it past Mercy's death without going crazy...well, going even more crazy than I am now."

She gulped for air and Leo reached out and put a warm, strong hand on her arm. "Hey, you definitely are not crazy. I'm sure you have your reasons for the anxiety. Don't be so hard on yourself."

"I'm sure it's hard for others to understand, but Mercy was...very special. She was just a newborn when Mom died, and I was five. Mercy was like a perfect little doll, but she was always delicate...fragile. And I was the strong one. At least I thought I was."

Eden's earliest memories centered around her younger sister; taking care of Mercy had eclipsed everything else, even grieving for her mother. Their father had been so protective, perhaps overprotective, always putting Mercy first. Eden tried to forget her childhood feelings of resentment. They shamed her even now. Eden's frustration at always being the afterthought in their family, the one who could take care of herself, now seemed petty. Mercy *had* needed extra protection, and Eden had failed her.

"She sounds lucky to have had you," Leo said, his voice quiet. He reached over and turned down the volume on the opening strains of another eighties hit. Something slow and dramatic.

Journey or Foreigner, maybe? I need a refresher on my eighties music, Eden thought.

"We were lucky to have each other. And when my father died, we were alone. Just the two of us against the world."

Her voice broke at that, and she looked out the window and cleared her throat.

"Luckily, I had already graduated college, and Mercy had just turned eighteen, so we managed."

Mercy's heart hurt as she remembered her father's overriding concern for his younger daughter when he found out his diagnosis was fatal.

Take care of her, Eden, he had pleaded, his eyes clouded over with pain, each word an effort. *Mercy isn't as strong as you. She's so innocent; she'll need you. Protect her.*

Eden knew now that her father had been wrong to trust her. She hadn't been the strong one at all. She blinked hard, erasing the images that refused to fade. Anxiety grew and throbbed in her chest, and she gave in to the impulse to unburden herself to the stranger beside her.

"When Mercy met Preston, I had a feeling something was off, but I didn't know what. He was so polite, so attentive at first. I thought I was just being overly protective like my father had been."

"And when I moved to San Francisco and founded my start-up, Mercy said she wanted to stay behind. She wanted to stay in college here. She didn't want to leave Preston. I thought she was finally growing up."

Eden clasped her hands, her nerves instantly on edge as she uttered the hated name. Guilt edged her words with regret.

"I was so involved in the start-up, and Mercy seemed happy. She was ecstatic when she found out she was pregnant with Hope." Eden imagined she could still hear her sister's happy voice after all these years.

"But after that, she quit college. Preston wanted her to be a stay-at-home mom, she'd said. By the time she had Devon years later, she was miserable, but still trying to make it work."

Eden looked at Leo, suddenly self-conscious at her rambling. "Sorry, I know you need to go, and here I am blabbing away."

"I'm interested," Leo said. "There's nothing that can't wait."

Eden looked doubtful, but she had to admit that sharing her story with Leo was somehow cathartic. She didn't have to pretend to be strong with him. Not like she had to with the kids, or with the volunteers at the foundation.

"Well, you know how the story goes, or at least how it ended," Eden said, fighting back the sudden wave of sadness that threatened to suffocate her. She gulped in a breath of air before continuing.

"Preston isolated Mercy. He became possessive and controlling. Once Mercy started protesting, his behavior turned physically abusive. I helped her get an apartment, helped her work up the courage to leave." Eden had pleaded with Mercy to get out before it was too late. She blinked back angry tears at the memory.

Why did she wait so long to leave? Why didn't she listen to me sooner?

Eden cleared her throat, knowing the hardest words were ahead.

"After she left him, he went crazy. She was so scared. Then she won a restraining order and thought it would be okay."

"But then he violated the order by showing up on her doorstep," Leo said, his voice grim. "And I helped him get out on bail."

Eden nodded, her eyes downcast as she remembered. "After the trial, I made arrangements to go back to San Francisco. I was sure Preston wouldn't be reckless enough to break the order again. The judge said that if he did, he would definitely go to jail."

Leo's jaw clenched. "I warned him to stay away from Mercy. I told him...well, I told him not to do anything stupid."

"I went to Mercy's apartment the night before she was killed. I was scheduled to fly out to San Francisco the next day. I begged her to bring the kids and come with me. She told me she was going to meet Preston the following morning to talk things through. Try to make the break-up amicable for the sake of the kids."

Eden had been enraged by Mercy's naïve decision to try to smooth things over with her abusive husband.

"I told her she was putting herself and the kids in danger. I was angry. I said that I couldn't be responsible for what might happen and wouldn't be around to pick up the pieces."

Eden's eyes were bright with unshed tears as she looked over at Leo. "But she just smiled. You know what she said?"

Leo shook his head slightly and waited.

"She said, 'I know you'll always be there for me, Eden. You always have been. And if anything happens to me, I know you'll be there for Hope and Devon, too.'"

Eden had stared at her sister in resignation. How could she deny the one thing that had been a constant in her life? She was her sister's keeper. And nothing would change that. Not an abusive husband, or the three thousand miles that would separate them once Eden was back in San Francisco.

"The next morning, I stopped by her apartment to try to talk some sense into her one last time." Eden's throat constricted with the memory.

"Preston's car was outside when I pulled up. I got out of my car, but I can't really remember everything that happened after that."

She closed her eyes against the pain, oblivious to Leo sitting beside her, the words spilling out like blood from a fresh wound.

"The next thing I knew I was in an ambulance and I heard someone screaming Mercy's name, over and over."

Eden could still hear her own voice wailing her sister's name. It was a voice that would echo through many of her nightmares in the following years. Somehow, she'd known Mercy was gone, even though she couldn't remember what had happened. She had looked at her hands and seen blood. So much blood.

Eden sniffled and dug for a tissue in her purse. She wiped her nose and dabbed under her eyes.

"They told me I had called 911. They said my sister had been shot, and that her husband had been shot, too. They said it was an apparent murder-suicide."

Eden shivered as a vivid image flashed in front of her eyes: a room cruelly lit by the morning sun; two blood-spattered bodies sprawled on the floor.

Leo's big, warm hand closed over her trembling fist. She didn't pull away. It felt too good. It made her feel alive again. She'd been numb for so long.

"I had to identify Mercy's body. She'd been beaten, her face was...ruined. And she wasn't there anymore. It was her body, but it wasn't *her*. I panicked. I couldn't breathe. I thought I was going to die. Part of me wanted to die."

She'd never said those words aloud before to anyone, not even to Reggie. The truth of it shamed her. Leo squeezed her hand but didn't speak. She looked up and saw her own pain reflected in his dark eyes and turned away.

Looking out the window, she said, "I couldn't bear to face what lay ahead. I just wanted to give up. But I knew I was going to have to tell my sister's children that their mother had died and that their father had killed her. After that, I was going to have to live in a world without my sister. A world where terrible things could and did happen. The fear...it...just took over for a while. Sometimes it still does."

"So, you stayed in Willow Bay after that? To take care of your sister's children?" Leo asked, keeping his hand on hers.

Eden nodded as she raised the tissue to her eyes again.

"Why not take the kids to San Francisco? Start a new life?" Leo asked.

"I knew Mercy wanted Hope and Devon to grow up in her hometown, surrounded by friends and familiar faces. She'd have hated for them to grow up in a big city full of strangers," Eden said, her voice sounding defensive to her own ears.

The other reasons were harder to explain. *I wanted to be close to home, too. I wanted to feel close to Mercy. Everything had changed. I had changed.*

"I'm sure your sister would be proud of what you've accomplished," Leo said. "Raising the kids and starting up a foundation in her name? I don't know how you managed."

"With counseling and a few friends," Eden said, looking back at Duke, who was still curled up in the back of the car. "Hope and Devon make it all worthwhile, They're great kids. Truly special. And so like their mother. I don't know what I'd do without them."

CHAPTER TWENTY-ONE

Eden's words hung in the chilled air of the car. Outside the sun was shining again as if the rain had never come at all. Leo wished he could ease the pain he heard in Eden's voice, but he knew better than anyone else what losing someone felt like. Nothing he said could make that kind of pain go away.

"Sounds like you made the right decision, then," Leo said. "Sounds like you're doing pretty good despite it all."

But, did I make the right decisions?

Leo wondered. The only thing that had gotten him through the darkest times had been his focus on law school and then building up his law practice.

For the last twelve years, he'd been on a quest to fight back against the injustices he saw all around him. The hours of work and study had required all his attention and energy; the effort had consumed him. It had left no time for a personal life, no time to form relationships. Looking over at Eden he admired her strength, and also envied her for having a family that brought her joy.

Eden sighed and pulled her hand away, before tucking her tissue back into her purse. Leo could see her straighten her spine, preparing to go back out into the world where she had to appear strong, no matter how much she was hurting. His hand felt empty, and he realized with sudden clarity that he didn't want her to leave. He didn't want her to open the door and end the intimacy they'd shared. It was an all too rare occurrence for him, and he didn't want it to end.

"Before you go..." he said, not quite sure what he was going to say next. "I...I wanted to say again how sorry I am for what happened with Preston. I mean, I'm sorry that I'm the one who represented him. That I got him out on bail. And I hate what happened because of it."

Eden grew still and then stared over at him with an expression of dismay.

Finally, she ran a slender hand through her still-damp hair and said, "No, it isn't your fault, Leo. I know that. Of course, I do. Sometimes it's just easier to feel anger than sadness. It hurts less. And it helps to have something or someone to be angry with...other than me."

"I can understand that," Leo said, relieved she'd exonerated him, but not ready to excuse himself so easily. "But I do regret it. It's one of many things that I feel guilty about."

"What do you have to feel guilty about? And why do you distrust the police so much?" Eden asked, turning toward him. "I've shared my deep, dark secrets...so what's your story?"

Leo watched Eden's face, not fully convinced she had shared everything. Her green eyes still looked guarded. He wondered what secrets lurked behind them. If he was lucky, he would get a chance to find out. Although he knew some things were just too painful to speak about.

He rarely talked about his past, because when he did, he usually ended up feeling angry and resentful. He needed all his energy to be focused on his mission. He couldn't afford to waste energy on negativity that wouldn't get him anywhere. His father had let the anger eat away at him until he couldn't take it anymore. Leo wouldn't let that happen to him.

"It's a depressing story," Leo said, forcing the words to come out. Something inside him wanted to share his story with the damaged woman next to him. He felt a pull that he didn't understand.

"When I was in college my mother was murdered. Someone came into our house one night and...killed her."

He couldn't bring himself to say the words he would need to use to describe what had been done to his mother. The knife. The blood. The gaping wound in the slender, pale throat that only a few years before had worn pearls to his high-school graduation.

"The police immediately focused in on my father, who had been working a double-shift." Leo stopped, surprised to find a lump in his throat. He had thought there were no more tears left. But he needed to say this. Needed to let Eden, and whoever else would listen, know what a good man his father had been.

"My father had been working double shifts a lot. He was saving up money to send me to law school," Leo cleared his throat.

"He and my mother had married young, just out of high-school. They never had great jobs, but they both worked hard. Their dream was to help me achieve my dream of becoming a lawyer."

"That night he got home and found my mother in their bed. He screamed and tried to save her. He tried to put pressure on the wound, tried to do CPR. Of course, it was useless, but he was desperate with grief. By the time the police and ambulance arrived, he was covered in her blood," Leo said, not looking at Eden.

"And the neighbor said she had heard him yelling. Calling out my mother's name. She thought he sounded angry. That's all the police needed to decide my dad was the killer."

"Oh, Leo," Eden said, her voice soft and low. "And they convicted him?'

"Yes, the District Attorney thought it was an open and shut case," Leo spat out. "He didn't care that my father's fingerprints weren't on the knife. He didn't care that the M.E. said the time of death could have been up to two hours before my father got home. He didn't even look at any other suspects."

Leo paused and waited for Eden to ask the inevitable questions. They always came, anytime he told someone about the case.

How do you know your father didn't really kill her? Are you sure it wasn't your dad? Why didn't his lawyer raise these issues during the trial? Was there any solid evidence that someone else killed her?

These were questions that Leo hated to hear because the truth was, he didn't have any irrefutable proof, but he *knew*. He just knew that his dad would never kill anyone, especially not his mom. His dad had loved his mother more than anyone in the world. Of that, he was sure.

"It must have been horrible to have your dad accused that way, and not to be able to save him," Eden said. "You must have felt so alone and helpless."

Leo felt his eyes prickle at her kind words. She didn't ask the questions. She believed him. He took a deep breath and continued.

"Yes, I felt helpless, and my father was so grief-stricken he couldn't help with his own defense. After they sentenced him to life in prison, he didn't even want to see me. He'd tell me not to come to visiting hours. To get on with my life."

Leo pictured his once virile father as he sat across from him in the visiting room. His thin stooped shoulders. His dark hair suddenly streaked with gray.

"Then one day my father called me. He wanted to see me. I was relieved." Leo allowed himself a sad smile at the memory.

"I told him I'd been saving up money to hire someone to review his case. I was going to use the money I'd saved for law school. I knew he couldn't wait for me to become a lawyer to get him out, so I was going to pay someone else to do it. I would also find the person who had killed Mom. Maybe hire a private investigator. I told him everything would work out."

Leo felt Eden's hand on his arm, and the lump returned to his throat.

"But that night, once I'd gotten home from the prison, I got a call. They told me my father had hung himself. He'd done it as soon as he'd returned to his cell after my visit."

Eden gasped, and her hand tightened on his arm. "I'm so sorry, Leo. God, I'm so sorry."

"He left a note," Leo said. "Said he loved me, and it wasn't my fault, but he didn't want to get out. Didn't want to be free to start a new life. He just wanted to be with Mom."

Leo turned to Eden and saw a tear slide down her cheek. He lifted a long finger and touched the tear, feeling the warm drop on his fingertip. Eden dropped her head into her hands and sniffled.

"I'm sorry," she said, her voice muffled. "This is your story and I'm the one crying. Not fair of me I know."

"Well, I think we both have plenty of reasons to cry, but that doesn't help anything." Leo felt a lessening of his sadness. *Maybe this is what they mean by sharing a burden*, he thought.

"So, you became a defense attorney to help other people avoid your father's fate?" Eden asked. "Has it worked out?"

"Mostly," Leo said, thinking back about the people he'd tried to help. "Not everyone's innocent, of course. But I've gotten off quite a few people who were. Frankie Dawson, for example. He was my first case. He'd been convicted of an armed robbery that he didn't commit. Was sentenced to ten years in state prison. I helped him win a new trial and proved he couldn't have been there when the robbery occurred."

"That must have felt good," Eden said, her eyes now dry.

"Actually, it made me even madder," Leo said. "To know that other people were going through the same thing my dad did. That his case wasn't an anomaly. It made me even more determined to fight the system that was ruining the lives of innocent people."

"I can relate," Eden said, gazing up at him, her eyes the color of emeralds as the setting sun shone softly in the window.

"Once I started the foundation in Mercy's name and saw just how many women suffered the same type of abuse she had, it made me even more determined to help. More determined to do something about it."

Leo nodded just as his phone vibrated again.

"Time to get back to the real world," Eden said, and Leo thought he heard a hint of regret in her voice.

"Yes, I guess it is. But I'm glad we got a chance to talk today and clear the air. If we're going to work together to find out what happened to Jessica and Star, it's best to be on good terms. And it looks like we actually have some things in common, so maybe we don't have to be enemies after all?"

Leo smiled at Eden, and as she turned to wake-up Duke, she smiled back. It was the first real smile he'd seen on her face, and it took his breath away.

CHAPTER TWENTY-TWO

The man stood by the canal in the darkening shadows, watching dusk fade into night. Muggy air clung to him as he listened to the distant whoosh of the interstate that lay to the west behind a small grove of pine trees. A mosquito buzzed around his head, and he waved it away with a distracted hand. He heard a splash in the water below but didn't take his eyes off the motel.

Probably just a frog, or maybe a fish that had worked its way up the canal from the river.

A car's headlights appeared in the distance, but the car drove past the motel entrance without turning in. It was a slow night so far. Of course, it was still early. Most johns wouldn't show up until later, once tired wives and noisy kids were safely in bed.

The man kept his eyes trained on the stairwell. They only had one lookout posted tonight, a short man who had his long, dark hair pulled back into a messy ponytail and wore tight chinos and a wrinkled Polo shirt. The look-out held a cell phone to his ear as he sat on the steps looking bored.

The man's fists clenched with tension as he watched the lookout begin to pace in front of Building D. There were lights on in some of the rooms, but his gaze stayed focused on room D-407, even though the windows were dark and the curtains drawn. That was the room where it had all started. No matter how many times he had come to the motel, he'd never been able to see D-407 as just a room. It was a portal. A portal into the nightmare that had become his life.

He kept his eyes on the dark window and remembered.

The boy looked over his shoulder into the gloom behind him. He knew he was being silly. No way his foster mother would be out here in the muddy darkness following him. If she knew he had snuck out she would just close and lock the windows and doors, and he'd be out on the street. He shivered as he pictured her grim face. She wasn't the kind to give second chances, so he needed to find his real mother fast, and get her out of here. He looked at the neon sign of the motel and sighed.

This wasn't the kind of place Mama should be if she wanted to get better. He may only be twelve, but he knew that much. He waited for a tractor-trailer to exit the lot and then scurried through the parking lot and around the back to Building D. He stayed off the concrete corridor, concealing himself in the darkness beyond the harsh, artificial lights that buzzed overhead. If anyone saw him, they might ask questions. Might even call Child Services. Then he'd be in all kinds of trouble.

As he approached room D-407, he saw the lights were on behind the curtains. He practiced what he was going to say. "Mama, you've gotta come with me, now. You can go back to rehab and then once you finish we'll get a place together. Like we used to have."

Suddenly the door to D-407 swung open without warning, and a man stepped out and looked around as if worried he'd be seen. He didn't see the boy standing in the shadows, watching him with hate-filled eyes. Why was this man in his mother's room? The boy waited until the man had walked down the corridor and turned the corner before he ran to his mother's door and knocked. No sound came from the room.

The boy reached for the knob and saw that the latch hadn't fully closed. He pushed on the door and it swung open, the lights within revealing an unmade bed. A bundle of sheets covered a sleeping figure.

"Mama?" the boy called out, knowing already that something wasn't right. He could picture the man's glassy eyes. Had the man done something to his mother?

"Mama!"

The boy ran to the bed and pulled down the sheets. His mother's face was swollen and bruised, and her eyes were open and staring at him. He saw angry red splotches. He gagged, before backing away, his fist still gripping the sheet. The sheet fell aside, and he could see a thick rope had been wound around his mother's throat. Bloody scratches circled her neck, and her fingers were covered in blood.

The boy realized she must have fought. She must have tried to live. But she hadn't made it. She hadn't been strong enough. She was gone. She had made her choice, and she had left him all alone.

Rage and sorrow simmered in the boy's chest as he stared at the ruined body that had been his mother. She was the only family he had ever had. Ever would have. The woman that he lived with was nothing like a mother. But she would have to do. He had nowhere else to go. He couldn't let anyone know he'd been here. Couldn't let anyone know what he'd seen.

As he turned to leave, he saw his mother's purse laying on the table, and he walked over and dumped out the contents. An empty wallet, a lighter and a tube of pale pink lipstick fell out. Nothing of value. He noticed something sticking out of the inside pocket. It was a picture. His school picture from first-grade. He stared at his own, unsmiling face and dead eyes.

He put the picture back in the purse and looked over at his mother's lifeless body.

"I tried to save you, Mama," the boy whispered into the silent room. "But it will be okay. They can't hurt you anymore."

The boy turned and ran back the way he came, sneaking back into his foster home before anyone knew he'd been gone.

The man was startled back into the present when the door to Room D-403 slowly swung open, and a slender girl slipped out, pulling the door closed behind her.

He could see by the careful way she moved that she was trying to leave without anyone hearing her. His gaze flicked to the stairwell and he saw that the lookout with the ponytail was nowhere in sight. The girl must have been watching and waiting, too. He smiled slowly, frustration turning to anticipation.

His eyes followed her as she jogged toward him, seeking cover in the shadows by the canal, getting closer and closer. He held his breath as she passed by, worried she would see him lurking by the water and scream. Her scream might alert someone at the motel that she was gone, and he didn't want that. That would ruin everything.

But the girl didn't see him in the dark. Her eyes were wide and glassy with fright. Or maybe she was just high. She slowed her pace as she trudged alongside the canal, her plastic flip-flops squishing through the muddy scrub as he tailed her.

She hesitated when she reached the river, looking in one direction and then the other, before turning west. The man felt a surge of satisfaction.

She's heading in the right direction, he thought as the girl emerged into a patch of moonlight and then scurried across a barren muddy stretch of riverbank.

The smaller Diablo River lay just ahead, past the lights of the interstate overpass. Suddenly, the man realized where she was going.

She's trying to make it to the highway. If she does, who knows what kind of pervert might pick her up.

He'd have to make his move soon before she made it far enough to be seen by passing cars. Increasing his pace, he tried to calculate a plan as he closed in on her. If he took her by the Willow River, she would likely be found as quickly as Jess had been. He'd seen the news report only days after he'd put her in the water.

It had taken them three years to find Tiffany, but of course, he'd left her in the more secluded Diablo River. Water hyacinth covered much of the Diablo's surface, suffocating the dark waters with its lush green leaves and bright-blue blossoms. The aggressive weeds had hidden Tiffany's remains until they'd eventually washed further downstream.

Yes, the Diablo River would be the safest place. And maybe there, where he'd saved Tiffany, the act would be more satisfying.

Before he had time to think through his plan, the girl started jogging ahead, perhaps motivated by the glare of headlights on the highway that were getting closer with each step. The man reached out and impulsively put a hand on her shoulder.

The girl whirled around, her scream already piercing the still night, and gaped at the man in terror.

"Sssh! You'll let them know where you are," the man said, putting a finger to his lips and speaking in an exaggerated whisper.

"They know you're gone and are trying to track you down."

The girl's face twisted with confusion and fear, and she looked over his shoulder, her eyes searching the darkness behind him. "What are you doing here? Did you follow me?"

"Yes, I saw you leave the motel," the man whispered, also looking back over his shoulder as if he expected something to jump out at him at any minute. "I can help you get away."

"Why would you do that?" the girl questioned, her glassy eyes trying to focus.

"Because you don't belong there. It's not right, what's happening to you girls." The man looked toward the highway, gauging the distance. Could the drivers see them?

"You want to help?" She looked doubtful, then seemed to think of something. "Hey, did you help the other girls get away...did you help Star and Jess?"

The man nodded, trying not to let the relief he felt show on his face. She hadn't seen the news. She'd probably been too high to remember anything if she had seen it.

"Yes, but you can't tell anyone it was me. I don't want to get on anybody's shit list. I'm just trying to do a good deed here, not get myself killed."

"I won't say anything." The girl's shoulders relaxed. "So, how do we get out of here? You have a place to go?"

"I can take you where I took Star and Jess if you want. You'll be safe there, just like them. Come on."

He started walking toward the interstate and the girl fell into step behind him. They walked under the interstate overpass, and the girl looked up expectantly, but the man put his finger to his lips and motioned for her to keep walking. Twenty minutes later they reached the confluence of the Willow and Diablo Rivers and turned south to follow the smaller tributary.

"Just a little further," he said over his shoulder. He saw the sprawling outline of a weeping willow tree. This was the spot. "Let's stop under this tree and catch our breath."

The girl stopped under the tree's drooping branches and stared out over the black water of the river.

"It's scary around here," she said, wrapping her arms around herself. A splash close by startled her and she spun around, eyes wide.

"Over there!" The man pointed toward the opposite shore of the river. "I think something's moving."

As soon as she turned her head, the man slid his belt off and looped it around her neck, the strength of his grip momentarily pulling the girl off her feet. He maintained his hold on the belt even as the girl clawed at the belt, digging her fingernails into her own skin, drawing blood.

He waited patiently, arms shaking with the effort, knowing that as long as he kept up the pressure, the lack of oxygen would do the rest of the work.

The girl made a last, weak attempt to grab at his hands, desperate to pry the belt from her throat. When her hands finally fell away, the man released the pressure on the belt and she crumbled to the ground. He pushed her onto her back and straddled her. He could see her face now, illuminated by the sliver of moon that hung in the summer sky. He watched her eyes flutter as she tried to focus on his face, only inches above hers.

Her voice was soft and hoarse. "Why?"

He watched the butterfly tattoo on her shoulder. The wings trembled.

"Because I'm...the only one...who can save you," he gasped out, his hands tightening on the belt, the rage and need inside him drowning out the sights and sounds of the night around him. Then he heard something nearby. A splashing and thrashing sound that felt *wrong.*

He stilled, momentarily ignoring the limp girl underneath him. For a second the only sound was the huffing of his own labored breathing. Then the sound of something scuttling through the grass. Something big.

The man turned his head as if in slow motion just as a long, rounded snout appeared above a thick tangle of tall grass and weeds. Two red eyes glowed in the dark. Panic flared in the man's chest as the alligator lunged forward, its huge tail slicing through the grass.

The man rolled off the prostrate girl and ran without hesitation toward the dirt path that wound its way toward Harrington Road. He'd run down that same road many times as a boy, and his feet knew the way even as his brain issued the same command over and over.

Run, run, run!

He didn't risk a look over his shoulder, just pumped his arms and legs at top speed. Behind him, the alligator's muscular body thrashed briefly, its sharp teeth and strong jaws ripping at the heap of wet clothes and soft flesh before dragging its prize backward toward the safety of the water. Before the man had reached Harrington Road, the gator had disappeared into the depths of the river.

CHAPTER TWENTY-THREE

Hollywood was floating on a tranquil lake, a soft breeze ruffled his hair and cooled his skin. He watched wispy clouds drift by in a sapphire sky and noticed a plump bumblebee hovering overhead. The bee buzzed and circled, coming closer. The buzzing grew louder and more insistent, prompting Hollywood to swat at the bee.

"What the hell, ya' dumb bee," Hollywood muttered as he opened one eye and saw with disgust that he was not floating on a lake, but instead was laying on a saggy unmade bed in a dingy motel room. The artificial light from the bedside lamp hurt his eyes as he peered around. The buzzing was coming from his cell phone, which had fallen out of his hand and onto the worn, discolored carpet.

He sat up, wincing at a sudden, stabbing pain in his head. Tempted to lay back down and curl into a fetal position, he forced himself to swing his legs off the side of the bed.

His stomach lurched, and he retched out a loose string of bile that hung suspended in the stagnant air, before dropping onto the ground beside his still buzzing phone. His mind swam as he tried to remember what had happened.

Did I shoot up that whole bag? Nah, I'd be dead. But I must have done a shitload.

Kicking his phone out of his way, Hollywood stood and staggered to the bathroom. He flipped on the light and stared at the man in the mirror, noting the bloodshot eyes, matted hair, and hollow cheeks.

He bent over the sink and splashed cold water into his face and mouth, before cupping his hands and pouring a few handfuls over his head. Raising his dark eyes back to the mirror, he winked at his reflection, flashing his straight, white teeth in a smile despite the persistent pain in his head. *High as shit, and still handsome as hell.*

The buzzing began again, and Hollywood looked over his shoulder at the phone, still laying on the floor.

Who the hell keeps calling? And where is everyone?

Hollywood looked around, a nagging suspicion beginning to form in his mind as he surveyed the empty room. It seemed deserted somehow. Brandi and Mia had been getting ready for work when he'd passed out, but there was no sign of them now.

The clock showed ten-thirty, so he estimated he'd been out of it for at least three or four hours. He tried to assure himself that the girls were already working and making money, but his gut still felt queasy and nervous.

Sig will flip out if another girl goes missing. The guys in Miami won't be too fucking pleased either.

Hollywood picked up his phone. He'd missed twenty-four calls. He thumbed through the names and numbers, seeing that most of the calls had been from his mother or Vinny. The last few calls had been from Sig. He scrolled through his text messages and saw Sig's last message: *Where are you? I'm on my way.*

He knew all the girls were supposed to be taking clients. After all, it was Friday night. They should be able to do big business before the girls were moved next week. No way would Sig want to give up the earnings from a busy Friday night. Hollywood wondered if he had time to check the other rooms on the ground floor before Sig arrived.

The girls slept in the ground floor rooms of Building D, bunking two or three girls to a room. The two adjoining rooms at the far end of the second floor acted as holding pens for the girls on duty as they waited for the next john to show up.

All business was then transacted in the remaining rooms on the second floor. The two stairwells were strategically positioned to allow the lookouts to deny or allow access to the johns who were coming and going.

A thought stopped Hollywood just as he headed for the door. He jabbed a finger at his tracking app and the map screen popped up. Seven dots hovered above the Old Canal Motel. The yellow dot for Mia was there, as were dots for six other girls. There was no purple dot. Brandi was not showing on the map. Hollywood navigated to the search screen and selected a name from the dropdown list. A message appeared on the screen: *Tracking device not found.*

The stabbing pain started again in Hollywood's head just as Sig unlocked the door and stepped inside, his wide shoulders filling the doorway as he entered. The older man was wearing a black baseball cap and dark glasses. He scanned the room without removing his glasses.

"Where have you been? Why haven't you answered your phone?" Sig's voice was quiet and steady.

Hollywood knew that Sig didn't need to shout or lose his temper; he had other ways of making Hollywood do whatever he wanted. Hollywood thought of the little bag of dope that had been in his pocket but that was now gone and gritted his teeth.

The old bastard has me by the balls.

"I had business to take care of," Hollywood said, cocking his head and narrowing his eyes. "*Personal* business."

"Cut the shit, kid." Sig slammed the door behind him and walked toward Hollywood.

"I've got that scumbag from Miami all over my ass about the deteriorating situation here. The numbers are moving in the wrong direction. We had ten girls last week, and now we're down to eight. I need you bringing in more girls fast, and you're off screwing around. What's the fucking problem?"

"There's no problem, Sig," Hollywood said, deciding to change tactics. "I've been working on the next target. A real beauty. Young and fresh, just like they asked for. But it takes time, man. I got to have a little time to lure her in, you know."

"Well, we haven't got time. We're scheduled to send a shipment of ten girls out next week. There are buyers waiting. This isn't small-time shit like you're used to. These guys are serious. If we don't send the shipment, there will be consequences...for both of us." Sig leaned over and parted the curtains and motioned for Hollywood to look outside.

A man stood in the circle of light outside the window. He was tall and muscular, his bulky arms and chest straining the material of his gray blazer. Like Sig, the big man wore dark sunglasses, even though the sun had set hours before.

"What's that meathead doing here again?"

"Rick's here to check on the shipment. What do you think he's doing, stopping by for tea?" Sig spat out the words and adjusted his cap. Sweat shone on his forehead as he removed his glasses and stared at Hollywood. "They're worried we can't handle our end of the deal. Can't say I blame 'em."

"Don't panic, man. I've got it under control." Hollywood produced the million-dollar smile that had seduced countless gullible teenage girls. The smile didn't work as well on old men.

"Well, you better, or the goodies are gonna dry up real quick," Sig said, pulling out a few baggies stuffed full of white powder.

"You want some of this dope? Well, you're gonna have to bring in some money to pay for it. And that means you need to find some more girls to earn you that money."

Anger flashed in Hollywood's eyes as he watched Sig stuff the baggies back into his pocket. He fought the urge to jump on the big man and wrestle the bags from him.

Too bad the old guy is always packing that big-ass pistol. Otherwise, I'd jump his ass right here and now.

His anger evaporated as he remembered Brandi's purple dot was missing. Could the app be wrong? Did the little device break? Or did she run off like Star and Jess? His thoughts swirled as he pulled out his phone and tapped on the app's icon again.

No fucking purple dot. And definitely not the right time to tell Sig that Brandi might be gone, too.

"Listen, Sig," Hollywood said, remembering Big Red's earlier visit.

"We may have bigger things to worry about anyway. Big Red was snooping around earlier asking questions about Jess and about the girl they found in the river. He said the sketch of the girl on the news looks like Jess. What if he goes to the cops?"

"Big Red isn't going to the cops, no matter who they find in the river. As long as he's getting a piece of the action, he'll keep his mouth shut." Sig looked at Hollywood with hard eyes.

"But I'm pretty curious about Jess, too. She runs from here without anyone seeing her and is pulled out of the river a few days later? You know anything about that?"

"Hell no, I don't know what happened to that crazy bitch," Hollywood said, raising his hands in protest.

"If that girl they found in the river is Jess, then she probably threw herself in. She was always getting sick and whining about going home. When she left I just thought she'd run off."

Hollywood didn't admit that he had been glad to be rid of her. She'd been using up too much of the smack for his liking, and she'd been too sick to make any real money off the johns.

Sig considered the stubborn look on Hollywood's face and then shrugged. "Well, the fuss about some dead druggie won't last long. Just lay low and make sure not to let any of the other girls run off."

"No way, man. I got these girls wrapped around my little finger," Hollywood said, wiggling a long, thin finger in the air.

"That's what you said about Star, and she's still in the wind," Sig said, putting his sunglasses back on and taking another peek between the curtains. "Just stay focused on finding replacements for Star and Jess. The guys in Miami aren't going to be happy if they don't have a full shipment to send next week as planned."

The big man walked to the door and grabbed the knob, then paused and looked around. "I'm gonna text you an address. It's the home address of the nosy bitch that reported Star missing to the police. Stake out her house. See if she has Star holed up there."

Hollywood raised his eyebrows in mock respect. "How'd you manage to find out who she is and where she lives? You got friends at the DMV, man?"

"I got friends everywhere, smart-ass," Sig said, tapping out a cigarette and sticking it between his teeth as he talked.

"Speaking of friends...where's Vinny? You take Vinny with you on the stakeout. He'll watch your back and keep you out of trouble." Sig lit the cigarette and blew a puff of smoke in Hollywood's face. "And lighten up on the dope. You're starting to go off the rails again. We can't afford any more of your screw-ups right now."

As the door shut behind the man's broad back, Hollywood clenched his fists and shook his head, imagining how good it would feel to slam the fist into Sig's sturdy gut.

Who the hell does he think he is? Vinny's not my damn babysitter.

The thought of Vinny brought a new surge of resentment.

I'll break that little ass-kisser's glasses next time I see him.

The thought brought a tight smile to Hollywood's face. He began to whistle as he picked up his phone and dialed Vinny's number.

CHAPTER TWENTY-FOUR

The sun was low in the eastern sky over the Diablo River, but it shone with a cruel intensity that made Nessa's headache. After five sweltering summers in Florida, she still hadn't gotten used to the heat and humidity. She had already taken off her jacket and rolled up her shirt sleeves, and it was only nine a.m.

Nessa closed her eyes against the glare and sighed. "If it's already this darn hot, noon is gonna be a real you-know-what."

"Let's hope we'll be done and out of here by then," Iris said, her voice muffled by a protective mouthguard.

The chief medical examiner was dressed in white hooded coveralls, PVC boot covers, and latex gloves. Nessa knew the small woman was probably baking underneath all the Tyvek and latex. They'd been at the crime scene for over an hour, and Nessa suspected that noon would come and go long before they could collect all the evidence and release the scene.

Alma Garcia, Willow Bay's senior crime scene technician, called over to Nessa. "Detective, we've got some footprints here that lead out toward Harrington Road. Looks like we need to expand the crime scene area at least that far."

Nessa nodded and held up a thumb. "You got it, Alma!" she called and turned to Officer Dave Eddings, who was standing at the edge of the scene, staring with wide eyes at the tent that had been erected at the river's edge.

Nessa noticed a light spray of freckles on the uniformed officer's chubby, unlined face and wondered exactly how old he was.

"Dave, you go move the outer cordons back. Get everybody to move out of the way. I don't want anyone contaminating my scene."

Eddings gave a nervous nod and turned to follow orders. The morning had been difficult for everyone, but for an inexperienced officer like Dave Eddings, the grisly aftermath of the crime was hard to comprehend. Nessa was finding it a little hard to get her mind around it as well. She'd thought she'd been exposed to almost every type of horror one human could inflict on another, but she hadn't counted on what she'd seen that morning.

The morning had started off as usual, with a mad dash to get Cole and Cooper ready for school and onto the big yellow bus that stopped outside their house at eight a.m. sharp. She'd kissed Jerry good-bye, enjoying the soft scratch of his beard against her cheek, just as her phone started ringing.

"Right on cue," Jerry had groaned, pulling her rounded figure tight against his long, lean frame. "I miss you, you know."

But the moment of intimacy had ended when Nessa answered her phone. It was WBPD dispatch. They'd had a call from an official with Willow Bay's Fish and Wildlife Conservation Commission. One of their trackers had responded to a reported incident at the Diablo River and had requested police assistance.

"I think you'd better get down there pretty quick," the dispatch operator advised.

When Nessa had arrived at the scene twenty minutes later, Officers Dave Eddings and Andy Ford were standing outside the cordoned area talking to a middle-aged woman with two small dogs straining against their leashes.

"The girls saw it first," the woman said, her voice high-pitched with emotion.

"The girls?" Nessa asked, looking around for other witnesses.

"Sugar and Spice, my Yorkies." The woman nodded at the two dogs that circled her, yapping at her ankles.

"Oh, how...cute," Nessa said, regretting the question. "Sorry to interrupt, go right ahead."

"Well, the girls started barking like crazy. They ran right up to the edge. I thought they were going to jump in. When I looked out across the water I saw it." The woman shuddered and turned her head away. "It was like something out of a horror movie."

"What exactly did you see?" Nessa asked, impatient to get to the tent, but wanting to hear what the witness had to say. She preferred to hear the details firsthand as opposed to reading them in a police report.

"I saw *that*!" The woman pointed further down the river's edge. Nessa squinted at a group of officers wearing orange and brown Fish and Wildlife uniforms. They gathered around a long, dark form on the ground. Nessa blinked and then squinted. "Is that a...a...*gator*?"

"Yes, ma'am." Eddings nodded. "It's a twelve-footer."

"Holy cow," Nessa said, not liking where the story was headed. "But what does that gator have to do with us...I mean why call in Major Crimes for an animal attack?"

"Well, when I saw the gator swimming around I noticed he had something sticking out of his mouth," the witness said, pulling her dogs closer to her. "I wasn't sure at first, but then I saw what it was. It was an...an arm."

"A human arm," Eddings added helpfully.

"Oh." Nessa opened and closed her mouth a few times, but before she could ask whose arm it was, the woman continued.

"So, I called 911. Told them I'd seen a big alligator. They sent over those men, who caught the gator." The woman paused to take a breath.

"When they confirmed the arm in the gator's mouth was human, they cut the gator open," Eddings said, looking over at the men gathered around the alligator's massive carcass. "But there wasn't anything, or anyone, inside. That's when they called us."

Officer Ford finally spoke up. "When we arrived, we surveyed the area and located the site where we think the initial gator attack happened."

He pointed to a clearing under a sprawling weeping willow tree where another technician was taking pictures.

"We cordoned off the area and called the crime scene techs to come out."

"That's when the trappers saw something in the rush and called us over," Eddings added, but Nessa had already begun moving toward the white tent that had been erected at the edge of the river.

Alma Garcia had stopped her and advised her to walk along the common approach path they'd laid out. When the tech handed her a pair of coveralls, mask, and shoe covers, Nessa had known she would be seeing a body or at least body parts.

Brace yourself, Nessa. Don't lose your breakfast in front of everyone.

She had hesitated at the tent's opening, the smell of decay ripe in the hot, still air. Alma and the other techs stepped aside to give the detective a clear view.

The girl lay on her back in a sodden tangle of tall grass and water hyacinth. Her face was partially covered by a spill of dark hair, and she was bare from the waist up, although what looked like the remains of a tank top lay in shreds around her. One stiff arm lay in a puddle of muddy river water; track marks scarred the pale flesh. The other arm was gone, her shoulder ending unexpectedly in a torn stump of blood and bone.

Near the bloody shoulder, Nessa could see a delicate butterfly tattoo. But what made Nessa's pulse race was the leather belt looped tightly around the girl's thin neck.

Solid, physical evidence. Maybe the killer has finally made a mistake.

Nessa had escaped the tent as quickly as she could, pulling off the suffocating protective gear as soon as she'd reached the outer cordon. Sweat drenched her cotton shirt, but she still shivered in reaction to the grisly sight of the girl with the butterfly tattoo.

The girl had been attacked by two different, but equally vicious, monsters. The trackers had managed to hunt down and kill the reptilian monster that lay defeated on the shore. Nessa knew the human monster was still out there, lurking and waiting for his next victim.

Nessa had watched Iris Nguyen pull up to the scene in the white Medical Examiner's van, Wesley Knox riding shotgun next to her, and waited for them to pull the protective clothing over their street clothes.

Now, they stood together waiting for the crime scene technicians to finish recording the scene. The video could be used later as a reference for the detectives, as well as evidence during any trial. Nessa hoped there would be a trial. The maniac that did this was still out there, and she had a sinking feeling that he wouldn't stop until he was caught and locked up. And right now, she was the only one even looking for him.

Alma approached, her brown eyes serious. She removed her face mask, revealing a pert nose and round cheeks.

"Good to see you, guys," she said, nodding at Iris and Wesley. "We got a real bad scene down there. We've tried to protect the body by putting up the tent, but she's half in the water and the sun's only gonna get hotter. I'm thinking you'll want to conduct your initial examination pretty quickly and get the body back to your office for the postmortem."

"Sounds about right, Alma." Iris pulled out her camera and adjusted her bag over her shoulder. "Wesley, you get the stretcher out and make sure the van's ready. Hopefully, I won't be down there long."

"I'm on it, boss," Wesley said, walking toward the back of the van. "Just give a shout if you need help down there."

"We've already taken lots of photos, Iris," Alma said. "And we've got the video done, so she's all yours for now. Once you're done we'll collect and document any remaining evidence."

Nessa turned to Alma. "What about the belt? Have you tried to get any prints from it?"

"No, not yet." Alma looked over at Iris, eyebrows raised. "We wanted to wait until Iris examined the scene before removing the belt or disturbing the body."

"Of course, that's good," Iris reassured Alma. She turned to Nessa. "I'll be as quick as I can, so we can check for prints right away. I know you want to find out who did this as soon as possible. So do I."

Nessa watched Iris hurry toward the tent. She knew she should put her coveralls back on and follow after the medical examiner, but she didn't think her stomach would be able to handle the heat and the smell again so soon. She would need her energy for what lay ahead. The race to find the killer was just beginning.

A black Dodge Charger nosed its way onto the grass and parked inches from a barricade that had been positioned to block cars from entering the area. Detective Simon Jankowski stepped out, his jaw already sporting a shadow of stubble, and his tie loosened at his neck. He approached Nessa, and she saw her own distorted reflection in his mirrored aviator sunglasses.

"Morning, Jankowski. I'm surprised to see you. I know how busy and important you are," Nessa said, still smarting from their last encounter. "Were you just passing by, or are you here to gawk?"

"I'm here because Chief Kramer called me," Jankowski said, his tone flat. "Took me off the case I was working on for Vice and re-assigned me. I'm now officially part of the Major Crimes Unit. And for the time being, I'm your new partner."

"Well, I'll be goddamned," Nessa sputtered before she could stop herself. "Would have been nice for him to let me know."

"Check your messages, Nessa,' Simon said, a sarcastic smile emerging. "I'm pretty sure he's been trying to get you on the phone most of the morning."

Nessa didn't take her phone out of her pocket. She'd turned the ringer off before she'd walked the scene and hadn't thought to turn it back on. But she wasn't going to let Jankowski see her fumbling with her phone now.

"Maybe Kramer forgot I already have a partner." Pete Barker's worn face flashed through Nessa's tired mind. "Barker will be back on the job soon, so your *partnership* won't be needed."

"Well, that's not the way Kramer sees it," Jankowski said, crossing muscular arms over his bulky chest. "The way he sees it, we've found two dead girls in the space of a week, and you're in way over your head on your own."

"Is that what he said?" Nessa asked, then regretted saying the words out loud. Before Jankowski could reply, Iris approached them, removing her mouth guard and pulling off a pair of latex gloves. Nessa could see the medical examiner wore yet another pair of latex gloves underneath them.

Sweat beaded on Iris' forehead and her cheeks were flushed. She didn't waste time greeting Jankowski. "I've completed my initial examination and taken photos of the body in situ. The crime scene techs are collecting and tagging the evidence now. I'd like to get her back to my office for the autopsy. The sooner the better, of course."

"Can you determine the time and cause of death?" Jankowski asked.

"Her body temperature indicates she's probably been dead between twelve and fourteen hours, but it's hot out here so it's hard to say for sure at this stage. But she's in full rigor now, so I'd say death occurred at least ten hours ago." Iris sighed and bit her lip.

"Lividity also indicates the body has been in the same position for at least ten hours. And based on the lividity patterns on her back, it looks like she's been laying in the same spot as well."

"So, late last night then," Jankowski said, taking off his glasses as he gazed down at Iris. "What about cause?"

"It's difficult to say at this stage whether death was ultimately caused by the ligature strangulation or from the blood loss sustained from the alligator attack. It doesn't look like she was fully submerged in water, so we can probably rule out drowning, although once I perform the autopsy and can observe her internal organs we'll know more."

Jankowski looked over at Nessa. "Alligator attack?"

"I guess Kramer couldn't tell you everything, could he, Jankowski?" Nessa said, but her tone was softer. She didn't have the energy to be mad at Jankowski and try to find a killer at the same time.

"There's a dead girl down there that has a belt wrapped around her throat and track marks on one arm. The other arm was torn off by a twelve-foot gator. Now we gotta find out who killed her, and why."

"A belt?" Jankowski asked, absorbing the situation without showing signs of shock or surprise. "You get any prints?"

"I want to remove the belt and check for trace evidence and latent prints once we get back to our facilities. The conditions here are less than ideal," Iris said, waving over Wesley. "You going to attend the postmortem, Nessa?"

"We both will," Jankowski interjected before Nessa could respond. "We need to expedite the entire process. I want any fingerprints from the belt to be the top priority. He's already killed two girls in one week. If we can I.D. this freak, we may be able to stop him before he kills a third."

"So, you're assuming this homicide was committed by the same person that killed Jessica Carmichael?" Iris asked, glancing at Nessa.

Nessa wanted to argue. After all, she knew from her first homicide case in Atlanta that similar crimes weren't necessarily committed by the same perp. And she hated to agree with Jankowski's theory when he'd only been brought into the investigation five minutes ago, but she nodded.

"Of course, we've got to keep an open mind, but I'd be surprised if this isn't the same guy. Looks like we just may have a serial killer in Willow Bay after all."

Nessa watched Wesley and Iris wheel the stretcher toward the tent. She turned to Jankowski and saw he'd put his sunglasses back on. She looked into his mirrored gaze. "I'm still waiting to hear back from Reinhardt. Last time I talked to him he said you never followed up to ask about the missing girls."

"I've been a little busy," Jankowski said, then grinned. "But, I guess that excuse is getting a little old."

Nessa sighed and fished in her pocket for a tissue. She wiped the sweat off her forehead and stuck the tissue back in her pocket.

"We need to know if these girls got their drugs from the same guy who killed them. If Reinhardt can find out who's supplying them, we may actually have a lead."

"It's a long shot," Jankowski said and hesitated.

He took off the aviators again to wipe the sweat from his forehead, and Nessa saw his eyes were tired and bloodshot. His brow furrowed, and he looked as if he wanted to say something but wasn't sure he should.

Shaking his head, he said, "Okay, I'll reach out to Reinhardt. It's worth a try."

Nessa studied him, trying to get a read on the man that was going to be her partner, at least until Barker returned. He was a handsome man under the glasses and stubble. His hazel eyes seemed worried, and she thought maybe a bit sad.

Simon Jankowski is not a happy man. I wonder why.

"You have some sort of problem with Reinhardt?" she asked, thinking maybe Jankowski's reluctance to reach out to the older detective was caused by a personal dislike between the two alpha males.

The engine of the medical examiner's van roared to life, and Nessa looked around and waved at Iris and Wesley as they pulled slowly away.

When she turned back, Jankowski was already climbing back into his Charger. He gave Nessa a mock salute and then slammed the door shut. Within seconds he was on the road behind the van, headed toward downtown. Nessa stared at the road until the vehicles disappeared around the bend, a thoughtful look on her face.

You're hiding something, Jankowski. I'm sure of it. And I'm sure as hell going to find out what it is.

CHAPTER TWENTY-FIVE

Eden stood at the granite-topped kitchen island, the ingredients needed to make Hope and Devon's favorite lunch, grilled cheese and tomato sandwiches, spread out around her. She held up a container of spicy yellow mustard.

"My secret ingredient," she told Reggie, who sat on a stool across from her. "Don't tell anyone or I may have to kill you."

The words were out of her mouth before she could stop them.

Not really the right time to be making jokes about killing people, Eden thought with a grimace.

"Don't look so worried." Reggie winked. "Your secrets are safe with me."

"Yes, I know you are great at keeping secrets, which is why I trust you with all of mine. But that's not what I'm worried about."

Eden felt guilt tug at her heart as she spread a light layer of mustard over thick slices of bread. She had kept a secret from Reggie. It wasn't that she didn't trust her friend, it was more that she didn't trust her own memory.

Eden still wasn't sure what had happened the night Mercy died, but lately, her nightmares had been disturbingly realistic. She was beginning to suspect her nightmares might actually be flashbacks.

"I told the police I'd try to find out Star's real name and last known address from the Mercy Harbor database. I was up all night stewing it over."

"Oh," Reggie said, her forehead creasing into a rare frown. "That *is* a dilemma. I can see why you're worried."

"I take Mercy Harbor's pact of confidentiality seriously. If we share the resident's details, we could put their lives and their children in danger."

Eden knew that estranged husbands and boyfriends could stalk their ex-partners for years, trying to win them back, determined to stop them from meeting anyone else. These obsessed men could turn up months or years later with the intent to kill. It happened more often than most people wanted to acknowledge.

Most women who had been the target of a violent ex-partner wanted to stay as far away from their ex as possible, and often went to great lengths to hide where they lived. Some changed their names and their appearance, desperate to live a life free of fear and harassment.

"It's a shame we can't count on the police to keep the information from getting out if we do provide it to them," Reggie said, absently tapping her long, red fingernails against the granite countertop.

"The detective that called, Detective Reinhardt, said he would keep the information confidential, but I didn't get warm and fuzzy feelings from him. He sounded pretty callous about the whole situation." Eden stacked swiss and cheddar cheese onto the bread along with generous slices of tomato.

"But if we can find out Star's real name, and where her mother lives, we might be able to find her. And she may be able to tell the police where to find the guy she said killed her friend, Jess."

The pan sizzled as Eden lowered in the two sandwiches.

"That smells delicious." Reggie inhaled deeply. "Wish I could join you all, but I've got a group session starting in twenty minutes. You give the kids a hug from me."

"I will, and thanks for stopping by, Reggie." Eden adjusted the heat of the stovetop and moved around the island to give the small woman a hug.

Reggie's thin body felt fragile in Eden's arms, and she wondered, not for the first time, how such a little woman made her feel so safe. "I'll let you know what I decide to do."

"It isn't an easy decision, but whatever you decide, don't let yourself get too emotionally invested. This situation isn't your fault. You're trying to help the best way you know how. That's all anyone can ask of you, and it should be all that you ask of yourself."

"I got it, Reggie," Eden said, a rueful smile appearing. "No negative self-talk. No worrying. No guilt. I'll do my best to follow your advice."

Once Reggie's Mini Cooper had sped away, Eden picked up her cell phone and tapped on Nathan Rush's name in her favorite's list. He picked up on the first ring.

"Well, this is a pleasant surprise," Nathan said, the smile in his voice making Eden feel guilty for not calling him back sooner. "I thought you were officially avoiding me."

"Sorry Nathan, but you can't imagine what has been going on here," Eden said, not knowing where to start. "I don't have time to go into all the details, but I need your help."

"Oh, I see," Nathan teased, "you've suddenly found time for me now that I can be of service."

"Nathan, this is serious," Eden said, talking fast, impatient to find out if Nathan was going to be able to help her.

"I'm trying to track down a girl who showed up at one of our safe houses and said her friend may have been killed. Then, two days later, her friend's body was pulled out of the Willow River. And the girl I talked to ran away, so I need to find her to make sure she's safe, and to find out what she knows about the guy who may have killed her friend."

"Wow, that sounds dangerous, Eden. Are you sure you should be involved in this?" Nathan's concern was palpable, and Eden's guilt returned.

Nathan still worried about her. If she was honest with herself, she knew he still loved her. She shouldn't be stringing him along. She should leave him alone to find someone who could make him happy.

"Nathan, you don't have to worry about me anymore. I'm a big girl, and I've been doing really well," Eden said, not sure she was convincing anyone, including herself.

"But I am running a foundation for battered women, so it's part of the job to get involved in helping these women even when the situation may be unpleasant."

"And hunting down a killer? Is that also part of the job?" Nathan asked, his voice serious. "You've got Hope and Devon to consider. What happens to them if you become the target of some psycho?"

"You know I would never put Hope and Devon in danger," Eden replied, indignation making her voice shake. "And if you don't want to help me, then I have to go. I don't have time to waste."

"Of course, I'll help you, Eden," Nathan said. His voice was resigned, almost sad. "There's nothing I wouldn't do to help you."

Eden felt a lump in her throat and forced herself to swallow it and take a deep breath.

"I need to find someone who stayed in one of our shelters. We keep certain information about the residents in our database. Names, ages, names of their children, history of their interaction with the foundation. It's all confidential and used only by the foundation's staff. But now I need to search the database for a girl that might have stayed at a shelter in the last few years. I don't have many details, but I was hoping you may be able to build a query I could run against the data?"

"What kind of query?" Nathan asked, his interest peaked. "What kind of database is it?"

Eden knew that if anyone could help her sort and filter data, it was Nathan, the technical genius behind Giant Leap, their data-mining start-up. He'd been the brains behind the products and services that had earned the company rave reviews and a steady stream of new clients, while Eden had handled the business and finance side of things, coming up with strategies that had helped make the company one of the few start-ups that was actually profitable in its first year of operation.

"I need a list of the women who stayed at the 1408 Shutter Street location within the last three years, and who had a daughter between twelve and seventeen years old at the time," Eden said.

"I'm hoping the query results can list out all possible matches. The list should include the name of the resident, the name of the resident's daughter, and the daughter's photo. We keep a photo of all residents in their files for security reasons."

"As long as you have collected the data to support the query, it should be simple to create and run it," Nathan said. "Of course, I'll need access to the database, and I'll need a login with the necessary permissions to create and run queries."

"No problem, you can remotely access my work computer and use my login." Eden looked toward the side counter where her work laptop usually sat. The counter was empty.

"Oh, great. With everything going on, I forgot my laptop at the office. I'll need to go to the office before we can try to build the query."

"No problem," Nathan said. "You get to the office and then call me. I'll be waiting by the phone."

"Okay, it'll probably be about an hour." Eden looked at her watch as she put down her phone. Sage had taken the kids and Duke out shopping for supplies for their upcoming trip to Nassau. They should be home any minute. Eden reached for the spatula. The sandwiches were golden brown, with a few drips of melted cheese oozing down the sides. She arranged the sandwiches on plates and set them on the counter.

She looked at her watch again and felt her stomach rumble. She was too nervous to eat anything now, but with any luck, she'd be able to find the information on Star and decide what to do in time to come back and enjoy dinner with the kids. But the feeling of unease wouldn't go away.

She replayed Nathan's comment in her head.

You've got Hope and Devon to consider. What happens to them if you become the target of some psycho?

Eden's heart started to beat faster as anxiety rose in her chest. She had known that sharing the information might put Star's entire family at risk, which is why she'd been so torn about what to do. But she hadn't thought about her own risk. By getting involved, was she putting herself in danger, as well? What about Hope and Devon?

Mercy, if you're there, please tell me what to do, Eden silently begged. But no answer came as Eden sat and waited in the silent room.

CHAPTER TWENTY-SIX

The air conditioning in Vinny's little silver sedan was no match for high noon in south Florida. Hollywood's white cotton t-shirt clung to him, damp with sweat, as they drove along the wide, tree-shaded street looking for the address Sig had texted to him yesterday.

Did Sig really think some rich lady was going to let a runaway druggie like Star stay at her house? Hollywood didn't think so.

This is the real world, Sig, and women like that stuck-up busybody don't like to get their hands dirty.

"So, this must be how the rich folks live," Hollywood said, putting on a high-pitched country accent. He watched the luxurious homes roll by, unimpressed with their three-car garages and overly manicured yards.

Vinny didn't respond, so Hollywood tried again. "I'd die of fucking boredom if I had to live around here."

But Vinny just kept eyes on the road, looking up only to check the house numbers. Hollywood scratched his arm and jiggled his leg, annoyed that he was driving around on one of Sig's pointless missions when he should still be in bed. He wasn't used to waking up before one or two in the afternoon, and he hadn't had time for a hit to keep him going.

This is a waste of time, Hollywood thought, his irritation rising. And Vinny is a waste of space.

"There it is," Vinny said, pointing to a white, two-story house set back from the road. "8156 Briar Rose Lane."

Hollywood noted the long, curving driveway that led around to the side of the house. A stone footpath led from the driveway to the front stoop. The house number was prominently displayed over an imposing wooden door.

"Bitch must be loaded," Hollywood said, shaking his head at the idea that Star would be hiding out in the exclusive neighborhood, "or at least her daddy is."

But Vinny had gone back to staring at the big house, his hand hovering over the gearshift, as if unsure whether he should park on the road or keep driving.

"Over there," Hollywood said, pointing toward a luxuriant oak tree. Several thick branches stretched out over the road, providing a dark patch of shade. "Go to the end of the block, do a U-turn, and park under that tree."

Vinny nodded and put his foot on the gas. The little car accelerated just as a black Jeep Cherokee approached from the opposite direction and passed them. Hollywood looked back to see the Jeep slow down and turn into the driveway they had been watching.

"Hurry, up, man," Hollywood said. "Turn the fuck around so we can see who's in the damn car."

Vinny swung the car around in a wide U-turn and pulled over beneath the tree. Both men watched the Jeep park in the driveway. A boy jumped out of the backseat first, carrying a shopping bag and holding the leash of a golden retriever, who hopped out of the car after him.

The boy was jumping around in excitement, and soon he was joined by a slim teenage girl with long, light brown hair, wearing faded jeans and a pink t-shirt. She climbed out of the passenger seat and walked around to the driver's side, laughing and motioning for the driver to get out.

"I don't see Star," Vinny said, his voice tight. "Just some dumb kids and a dog."

Hollywood glanced at him and narrowed his eyes. "You got someplace to be, Vinny? You'd rather be at home jerking off than here, helping me fix the mess *you* made?"

Before Vinny could reply, the driver's side door of the Jeep opened, and a young woman stepped down, then turned to lift out several full shopping bags. Her dark, curly hair was pulled back in a ponytail, and she wore sunglasses and a Gators baseball cap. Slim, tan legs were topped off by denim shorts and a loose, white t-shirt.

"Not bad," Hollywood said, leering at the young woman. Something about her made Hollywood take a longer look as she started walking toward the front door. "She looks familiar."

"Yeah, in your dreams," Vinny said. "That chick wouldn't give you the time of day. Look where she lives. She doesn't need to go slumming."

"That's just it, my man. That's exactly what they do want. All these sluts. They don't want some prissy, rich guy scared to hold their hand. They want it rough and dirty. They want someone who'll make 'em scream." Hollywood grinned at Vinny. "But then, you wouldn't know anything about that, would you?"

The girl in the pink shirt opened the front door and hurried the boy and the dog inside. The woman followed them, depositing the shopping bags inside the entryway while the boy darted back to the Jeep. He opened the tailgate and picked up two small cardboard boxes that had been stacked in the rear. The woman stood by the front door, waiting as the boy carried the boxes toward her.

Hollywood and Vinny could see her remove her cap and sunglasses as she called out to the boy. The boy laughed and disappeared into the house, while the young woman leaned out and pressed the lock button on the car's remote key, revealing a wide smile on a pretty face.

"Holy shit...did you just see that?" Hollywood stammered, doubting his own eyes.

"Yeah, I saw it," Vinny said, his voice calm and low. "And I think we better call Sig. Now."

CHAPTER TWENTY-SEVEN

Nessa watched the four detectives file into the briefing room. She leaned against a whiteboard that spanned the length of one wall, anxious for the men to settle in.

Detectives Marc Ingram and Ruben Ortiz sat together at a metal table near the front of the room. They arranged their mugs of coffee, laptops, tablets, cell phones, and a selection of power supplies around them, before nodding to Detective Reinhardt who had arrived empty-handed. The older detective leaned against the back wall and folded his arms across his chest.

Detective Jankowski came in last and sat down at a table by himself. He removed his black leather backpack and began unpacking files, a notepad, and a variety of electronic gadgets.

"I see you guys like to travel light," Nessa said, taking a sip of coffee from her own big mug. "Can we get started, or does anyone need to use the little boy's room first?"

None of the men cracked a smile. Nessa raised her eyebrows and sighed to herself.

This is going to be a rough crowd, Nessa. Don't let them get to you.

"Okay, well thanks everyone for getting over here so quickly," Nessa said, using her all-business voice.

"As y'all know, Chief Kramer has asked me to head up a task force to investigate the murders of the two girls found in the river this week. Based on the short time span between the two killings, we're worried the offender won't waste time picking his next victim."

"I'm partnering with Nessa on this one," Jankowski said in a loud voice as he leaned back in his chair and looked around the room. "We appreciate your help."

Nessa stared at him for a few seconds, trying to decide if she should waste time on a sarcastic remark about alpha males feeling the need to mark their territory, or if she should just grit her teeth and move on. She turned to the whiteboard where she had taped up two photos and took a deep breath. She had to keep herself calm and detached.

You're a professional, she reminded herself, then began to speak without looking around.

"The first victim was Jessica Carmichael. A sixteen-year-old white female. She'd been a student at Holy Cross High School up until her mother was incarcerated in March, at which time the victim was displaced, moving between friends and family. She hadn't been seen by any of her acquaintances for over two weeks but was only officially reported missing on Wednesday. Her body was then found in the Willow River on Thursday."

Nessa stopped to take a breath, staring at the photos. Jessica Carmichael's tenth-grade school picture showed a girl with big, gray eyes and long brown hair parted on the side. High cheekbones and rosebud lips transformed her from plain to pretty. The other photo was a mugshot.

Jankowski stood and strode to the whiteboard, tapping a long finger on the mugshot.

"The second victim has just been identified as Brandi Long. She'd been arrested in Tallahassee last year on a drug charge, so her prints were in the FDLE database when the M.E. scanned her during the postmortem. We don't know too much about her yet. Still trying to find her next of kin for notification."

Reinhardt spoke in a quiet voice from the back of the room. “And what about the girl that’s been reported missing? The one you asked me about the other day, Nessa. Is she considered a possible third victim?’

“She’s definitely a person of interest to this investigation.” Nessa turned toward Ingram and Ortiz.

“You two haven’t had a chance to look through the files, of course, but you’ll see we’ve received a missing person’s report on a teenage girl that goes by the street name Star. This girl suspected a friend of hers named Jess had been killed. We believe she was referring to Jessica Carmichael.”

“Yesterday I called Eden Winthrop. She said she’d call me back, but I still haven’t heard anything,” Reinhart said.

“Eden Winthrop?” Ingram asked, his voice hard. “How’s she involved with this?”

“She’s the woman who filed the missing person’s report,” Nessa responded, surprised by the hostility in Ingram’s voice. “Is there something you want to say? You got a problem with her?”

Ingram opened his mouth, then snapped it shut. After a beat, he said, “Nah, I don’t have any problem with anyone. But you might want to ask your partner about Ms. Winthrop. Maybe he’d have something to say.”

Nessa hesitated, then decided to file the comment away for later consideration. She needed to stay focused on the case at hand. She turned back to Reinhart.

“So, you called her?”

“Yeah. But I don’t think she’ll be much help,” Reinhart said, his face expressionless, “but I’ll keep trying.”

“Good. We should keep in contact with Ms. Winthrop in case she gets more information or has further contact with the missing girl.”

Nessa wondered what it would take to get a rise out of the stone-faced detective. Kirk Reinhardt must be around Pete Barker's age, she realized.

Maybe all detectives burn out in the end. Maybe the exposure to death and violence kills whatever passion for the job they once had.

But doubt swirled as she looked into Reinhardt's impassive face. She got the feeling that Reinhardt had always been indifferent. That this was just a job to him.

"I'm sure you know the question Ortiz and I want answered," Marc Ingram said, his thin face somber, his pale blue eyes intense under a severe blond crew cut.

"Yeah, we want to know if these new homicides can be linked to Tiffany Clarke's murder," Ortiz added, his expression eager. "Could be the lead we've been waiting for."

Nessa had already decided she liked Ortiz. He was young and handsome, earning the nickname Don Juan based on his dark good looks and ever-changing succession of girlfriends, but she'd found him to be down-to-earth and approachable. He seemed to care more about solving crimes than getting credit or showing off.

She couldn't say the same about his partner, Ingram. She didn't think the high-strung, wiry detective had earned a nickname yet, but if it was up to her, she could think of a few uncharitable names that would fit. He always looked cagey to Nessa, like he was up to something, or wanted to be. He reminded her of a weasel, and she wasn't sure she could trust him. Not yet.

"I agree," Nessa said, glad that they were all thinking along the same lines. "We need to review the Clarke case against these new ones. See if we can establish a connection between the victims or a pattern of behavior that could help us identify any overlapping suspects."

"In the meantime, I think we should add both Tiffany and Star to our board, so we can factor them in when assessing the victimology of the girls our killer is choosing," Nessa said, making the sudden decision. She turned to Ortiz. "You have a photo of Tiffany Clarke we can use?"

Ortiz opened his briefcase and pulled out a thick file. He rifled through and found a color photo that had been used on all the flyers posted up around town after Tiffany had gone missing.

"This should do," Ortiz said, handing the photo to Nessa who taped it on the board.

She thought for a minute, wishing she'd had Eden Winthrop work with a sketch artist to create a sketch of Star. Another task for her growing list.

Nessa tore a blank piece of paper off her notepad and, in big letters, she wrote *Star - missing white female minor.*

She taped the paper on the whiteboard beside the three photos and noticed with unease that she had instinctively positioned the photos to one side, leaving a blank space for the photos of additional victims to be added.

A sense of foreboding settled in her chest as she turned to face the four detectives. Before she could speak Jankowski was up again and standing beside her holding what looked like a rolled-up poster.

"This is a map of Willow Bay and the surrounding area," Jankowski explained as he unrolled the map and held it over a poster-sized map of Florida that hung on the far wall. The state map had been mounted on a foam core board, and a cup of pushpins sat on the nearby ledge. Jankowski pinned the Willow Bay map to the board and looked back at Nessa, obviously pleased with himself.

"Why, thank you, Detective Jankowski," Nessa said, chagrined that she hadn't thought to bring the Willow Bay map she kept in her cubicle.

"That's very helpful. Of course, we'll want to plot the relevant locations. Unfortunately, except for Tiffany, we know very little about the victims' whereabouts during the days leading up to the murders. That'll make it hard."

"Well, we can stick a pin in the body disposal sites," Ingram offered. "At least we know where he dumped them."

As Nessa picked up three pins and began positioning them on the sites along the river where the girls had been found, she fumed at the way Ingram talked about bodies and disposal sites. She knew the words were often used by detectives, but she didn't like his callous tone, or the implication that the victims hadn't been thinking, feeling people, but were just bodies that had been dumped like garbage.

"But we don't know where he picked them up or grabbed them," Ortiz added.

Reinhardt spoke up. "We don't know if he grabbed them at all. Maybe he knew all these girls. But until we know where the victims lived and who they associated with, it'll be impossible to tell."

"We found out yesterday that Jessica Carmichael had been intermittently staying at a local sober house called Clear Horizons, although she hasn't been seen there for several weeks," Nessa said, picking up another pin and sticking it into the map along a thin line listed as Baymont Court.

"We can start by using that as her last known address."

They continued placing pins in the areas around town that seemed relevant until they felt they'd covered all the locations they had identified so far in the investigation. It wasn't much to go on, and the results were no surprise. The one linking factor was the river.

"Our guy definitely is drawn to the river," Ortiz said. "All these girls pulled out of the river couldn't be a coincidence, could it?"

"The river does seem to link them," Nessa agreed, "but is that because he takes them there, or because he finds them there? I mean, does he find them somewhere near the river? Is there a place by the river where people go to buy drugs or sex?"

"Sounds like a question for you, Reinhardt," Jankowski said, not looking back at the detective still leaning against the back wall. "You know of a place by the river where druggies and pros hang out? Or you got any CIs that could help us find out?"

"I could make some calls, but that'll take some time," Reinhardt said without enthusiasm. "And if we're thinking these girls have been picked up off the street by a stranger, maybe a john or a dealer, then Tiffany Clarke doesn't fit the pattern."

"I know you're already working several other cases, and that you need to keep your informants' trust," Nessa said, turning to Reinhardt, "so how about you make a list of people in the Willow Bay drug scene that might know where the girls are getting their supply? We can assign some uniformed officers to find them and show them the girls' pictures. Act like it's a routine canvas of the area. They'll never know you were involved."

Reinhardt stared at Nessa as if she'd slapped him. He shifted his weight against the wall but didn't stand up. Finally, he said. "I'll see what I can pull together."

"I need the list today...before you leave," Nessa said, her voice firm. "We don't have time to waste. We can't afford you getting pulled into another case once you leave here."

She didn't wait for Reinhardt to respond but instead faced Ortiz and Ingram.

"And I need you guys to go through the Tiffany Clarke files again, this time alongside the information we have on the new cases. Try to identify any connections. We already have substantial indications the cases are linked. Similar cause of death, forensic results, and geographic location of the disposal sites. See if you can come up with anything else."

"Jankowski, you and I will start working up a summary of the investigation status, and write up an initial profile of the offender," Nessa said, her blue eyes trained on his, waiting for a reaction. "Chief

Kramer wants an update by end of day. He wants to know if we need an assist from the FBI on this one."

Jankowski's phone buzzed on the table in front of him, and he peered down at a text message that had popped up on the screen. He straightened in his chair and picked up the phone, scrolling down to see the entire message.

"It's Alma Garcia from the CSI team. She says she has news on the river girl investigation."

"Good name," Ortiz said, as everyone else in the room stared at Jankowski. "The River Girls Investigation. I like it,"

Jankowski ignored the comment. "They've lifted a latent print from the belt used to strangle Brandi Long. Looks like they already got a hit in IAFIS."

Adrenaline raced through Nessa's veins. She'd had little hope they could even obtain a usable print from the murder weapon, much less a print that would find a match in the FBI's Integrated Automated Fingerprint Identification System.

"Well, who matched the print? Who's the perp?" Ingram demanded. "Don't keep us in suspense, Jankowski."

"She didn't say." Jankowski started to repack his backpack. He looked up at Nessa's flushed face. "She wants to see us in the CSI lab. *Now*."

CHAPTER TWENTY-EIGHT

The WBPD crime scene lab was modest compared to the polished, high-tech laboratories depicted on prime-time crime dramas, but Alma Garcia kept it immaculately cleaned and organized.

Jankowski could see that the white counters and cabinets held a bewildering range of equipment and supplies. He could identify the laboratory microscope, mass spectrometer, and fingerprint development chamber, but was clueless as to the function of several complex-looking machines that had been added since the last time he'd had reason to visit Alma.

"So, Alma, we're dying to know what you've found," Jankowski said, looking around the small lab as if the identified perpetrator might be in the room.

Nessa hovered at his right shoulder, her eyes wide with anticipation. But Alma's expression made Jankowski's heart drop. He could see in the technician's downcast eyes that the news wasn't going to be all good.

"Well, we managed to lift several really good latent prints off the buckle," Alma said, moving to a computer monitor in the corner.

"The results came back from IAFIS pretty quickly. They found one potential match, and I've done the comparison."

She stepped aside so that Jankowski and Nessa could see the screen. Two fingerprints were positioned side by side, and various points had been plotted on the whorls, arches, and loops.

"It looks like the latent print from the belt buckle matches a print found at another crime scene." Alma held her hand up as if to stop the questions she knew were coming.

"Before you ask, I don't have all the details of the scene, but I was able to look up the basics because the file was stored in our system. It's a Willow Bay case. An unsolved homicide from 2006."

Jankowski felt the breath leave his lungs and was having a hard time drawing in another one. "A cold case homicide in Willow Bay from twelve years ago? Linked to these new homicides?"

"Who was the victim?" Nessa asked. "Please tell me it wasn't a Jane Doe."

"No, it wasn't a Jane Doe." Alma's voice was somber. "The victim was a woman named Natalie Lorenzo. You'll see pretty quickly in the file that she was known to the police as a drug user. She'd also been picked up for solicitation."

"Where was she found?" Jankowski asked. "Where was the disposal site?"

"A motel down by the old canal," Alma said. "It's all in the report, but it looks like one of the motel rooms was the scene of the homicide. The body was left at the site. No attempt to move the body or cover up the crime. The M.E. estimated that the victim died about twenty-four hours before being discovered by the cleaners."

"I think I know the motel. I'm not real familiar with the place, but something does strike me as coincidental," Nessa said, and Jankowski wondered if she was thinking the same thing that had come to his mind.

"That canal leads out to the Willow River," Jankowski said, raising his eyebrows at Nessa. "Is that what you were thinking?"

"Bingo, Jankowski," Nessa said, flashing a sarcastic smile. "Guess we're both real detectives now."

"There's another coincidence that's even more significant," Alma said, pulling up a digital image of Natalie Lorenzo's death certificate on the computer.

Jankowski scanned the document. "I'll be damned," he whispered, as Nessa gasped beside him. The cause of death had been listed as homicide by ligature strangulation.

* * *

Jankowski arranged the files on the table, making room beside him for Nessa's laptop. She'd been quiet ever since they'd left the crime lab and headed back to the briefing room to work on the offender profile and case status report for Chief Kramer.

Jankowski wasn't sure if she was pissed off with him again for some reason, or if she was just busy mentally processing the information Alma had shared. It was a lot to take in. Two murders and a missing girl in one week that were linked to not one but two cold homicide cases? Not a usual occurrence in Willow Bay.

"You okay, Nessa?" Jankowski asked. He braced himself for her usual sarcastic comeback.

He knew Nessa didn't like him, but he wasn't sure why. Perhaps she thought all the detectives resented having a woman in the previously all-male department. Or maybe it was just him. Maybe it was personal.

"Sure, I'm swell," Nessa said, her tone distracted. "Just trying to figure out what the hell has been going on in Willow Bay these last twelve years. Cause someone has been killing young women and we didn't even know about it."

"We don't know that for sure. The print at the motel is an unexpected piece of evidence but it isn't proof that the same person who killed Natalie Lorenzo killed Tiffany Clarke or these other girls." Jankowski gestured to the pictures on the wall.

Nessa walked to the board and taped up a fifth photo. It was another mug shot. Natalie Lorenzo stared out of the photo with miserable, bloodshot eyes.

Limp brown hair fell past her thin shoulders. According to the date, the mugshot had been taken only weeks before Natalie had been killed. Jankowski imagined he could see the shadow of death in her eyes.

Nessa picked up a dry-erase marker and began writing on the whiteboard above the row of photos. She stepped back to let Jankowski read what she had written.

"The River Girls Task Force," he said, nodding slightly. "I guess that name will do as good as any other."

"Ortiz came up with it, but I think it fits. It puts the girls at the heart of the investigation, not the killer. I prefer it that way."

Jankowski narrowed his eyes at the mention of Ortiz. All the women at the police station swooned over the young detective, who fancied himself a real lady's man. Maybe Nessa had the hots for him, too. Maybe all women were liars and cheats like Gabby. His mood darkened at the thought of his estranged wife.

I'm sure Nessa's husband would love to know she's got a thing for hunky Detective Don Juan.

He watched Nessa write *River Girls Task Force: Do Not Disturb* on a piece of paper. She walked over to the door to the briefing room, stuck the sign on the door, and closed it, then walked back into the room and sat down next to Jankowski.

"Okay, let's work on the profile first," she said. "You type, and I'll talk."

Jankowski smothered the spark of indignation that her words aroused. He wondered what Nessa would do if *he* tried to order *her* around like that. Probably file a sexual harassment complaint with

Internal Affairs. No, he'd just have to take her attitude in stride. He wasn't sure what she was trying to prove, but he didn't have time to get involved in a pissing contest with Nessa.

Between this investigation, which was heating up fast, and the personal problems he had been dealing with out of the office, he couldn't afford it. He needed to stay focused and keep his emotions in check.

"So, let's document what we know so far about the offender," Nessa said, standing and pacing around the room.

"We know that he targets young, white females, possibly intravenous drug users, and dumps his victims by the river, most likely trying to conceal them in water," Jankowski said as he typed.

"But what about Natalie Lorenzo?" Nessa asked. "She wasn't dumped."

"I just don't get the feeling that Natalie was a victim of the same killer," Jankowski said, "The M.O. doesn't match."

"Okay, what are the differences? What's bugging you?" The words didn't seem like a challenge. Nessa looked genuinely interested.

"Well, Natalie was found naked inside a motel room. The others were found outside or in the water, and they all had clothes on. So, either the killer didn't undress them or decided to redress them."

Jankowski opened the file on Natalie Lorenzo and flipped a few pages. He saw from the copious notes in the file that the lead detective on the case had been Nessa's previous partner, Pete Barker. Back then he'd been partnered up with Ingram.

"Yes, it says here she was sexually assaulted. Semen was recovered, but they didn't get a hit on CODIS when they ran it through in 2006. From what Iris has reported on the other cases, there was no evidence of recent sexual assault on the victims, and no semen or biological evidence has been found."

Nessa cocked her head as in thought. "Sure, there are some differences, but maybe Natalie was his first victim, and maybe he changed his M.O in the meantime to better hide his crimes."

"I guess it's possible it's the same guy, but the evidence we have so far doesn't support it," Jankowski said, wishing he could add that his gut also didn't buy it, but he knew that would sound ridiculous.

He'd always believed that only detectives that didn't want to take the time to collect and evaluate evidence relied on their guts or their instincts. Now wasn't the time to change his mind.

Just follow the leads. Work the evidence, he told himself.

"I hear you," Nessa said, rubbing the back of her neck as if in pain. "But what else do we know? Any idea on a motive for this guy?"

"Well, if we could establish that there had been a relationship between the offender and one or more of the victims, we may be able to figure out his motive," Jankowski said. "Although if this perp is a true serial killer, there may not be any relationship or link between him and his victims at all."

"I went to a conference a few years back in Tampa. One of the FBI profilers gave a presentation on the motives behind serial killings. It was creepy, but I did learn a lot. Some of it kept me up at night for weeks after." Nessa continued pacing as she spoke.

"According to the presenter, most serial killers have a sexual motive."

"Well, if we leave Natalie out of the equation, there's no evidence of sexual interaction between the offender and the victim," Jankowski pointed out.

"No, we have no evidence of sexual penetration," Nessa agreed, "but that doesn't necessarily mean the motivation isn't sexual. His drive to kill could be based on sexual fantasies or inclinations that don't involve penetration."

"Of course, there are other types of motivation. Anger. Jealousy. Revenge," Nessa continued, sitting in the chair opposite Jankowski.

"We had a case up in Atlanta where the serial offender was killing people that worked at the hospital where his father had died. He believed the hospital staff were all responsible for his dad's death, so he was hunting down doctors and nurses and shooting them execution-style. Four people died and two were wounded before we figured out what was happening and why."

"So maybe our offender hates drug addicts or prostitutes?" Jankowski suggested, considering the idea. "Maybe he had a bad experience with a pro? Maybe she laughed at his...well, his lack of size? Or maybe he was turned down by some teenage girl?"

Nessa rolled her eyes and snorted.

"Most men have had bad experiences with teenage girls when they were in high school, but, yes, maybe something like that is driving him. Making him mad enough to hunt down and kill girls that live a certain lifestyle or girls found in certain locations."

"Or maybe the guy is just downright crazy," Jankowski said, his head starting to pound. "Maybe our perp is mentally ill."

"The FBI guy at the conference said that very few serial killers are actually diagnosed as mentally ill or psychotic."

"Okay, so what about the oldest reason in the book. That is other than a sexual motive," Jankowski said, thinking of the adage they always brought out in investigative training courses.

"And what's that exactly?" Nessa asked, eyebrows furrowed.

"Greed," Jankowski said, rubbing his forefinger and thumb together in front of Nessa's face. "Follow the money...isn't that what they always say? Maybe what our guy is doing is based on a financial motive."

"Like what...he's a hitman? He gets paid for killing helpless teenage drug addicts?" Nessa's voice was heavy with skepticism.

"Well, no. More like, maybe these girls threatened the guy's income. Maybe he's the supplier or the pimp, and they have put his income stream at risk."

As he was saying the words, Jankowski thought of the special investigation he had been working before he'd been pulled off and assigned to the River Girls Task Force. The feds were sure that a drug and human trafficking ring was trying to expand its Miami operations. They believed that police departments in various small towns in south Florida had been infiltrated and were helping the traffickers move their products.

And they aren't wrong there, Jankowski thought. *But that's nothing I can tell Nessa. And it can't have anything to do with the river girl killings, can it?* Suddenly, he wasn't so sure.

Nessa opened her mouth to offer a rebuttal, but then closed it. She shrugged and sighed again. "So, we tell Kramer we need an FBI assist? Maybe ask for a profiler to help us figure out who we should be looking for?"

Jankowski hesitated.

What exactly will the feds find once they start poking around?

He needed time to think this through, and in the meantime, he definitely needed a cup of black coffee and some ibuprofen.

"Let's wait until we've had time to properly go through Natalie Lorenzo's file," he said, not meeting Nessa's eyes.

"See what Ortiz and Ingram can find to link Tiffany Clarke to the other victims. See what leads Reinhardt may be able to give us. I think we need to give our team at least another day before we ask Kramer to get us some help from the feds."

He lifted his gaze to Nessa's face. She seemed to be considering his words, her head cocked as she looked at him. Finally, she nodded and picked up a file.

"Okay, then let's get to work. We have a lot to do in the next twenty-four hours."

CHAPTER TWENTY-NINE

Hope and Devon had devoured the grilled sandwiches, washing the food down with gulps of freshly-squeezed lemonade. Their excitement about the end of school and the start of summer was contagious, and Eden was drawn into their chatter, momentarily forgetting her worry about Star and the task that lay ahead.

"Why did school start to be fun just before summer vacation?" Hope asked, turning the pages of her yearbook, and reading the end-of-year messages written by friends in playful, looping handwriting. Eden could see that several messages had smiley faces or hearts next to them.

"Will you miss all your friends?" she asked, liking the shy smile that played around the girl's mouth. "Or is there someone special you'll miss the most?"

"She's gonna miss Luke Adams the most," Devon offered up with a laugh. "She's got a major crush on him."

"I do *not* have a crush on Luke." A pink flush spread over Hope's cheeks as she looked down, still wearing the shy smile. "He's just a...friend."

"Yeah, a *boyfriend*," Devon teased and began dancing around the kitchen singing, "Hope has a boyfriend! Hope has a boyfriend!"

"Devon!" Eden admonished. "Don't tease your sister."

But Devon had already reached the stairs and was bounding up toward his room, still singing loudly.

"So, is it true, Hope?" Eden asked, her voice soft. "Is this boy Luke your boyfriend now?"

Hope looked down at the table, biting her bottom lip, a habit she'd gotten from her mother. Mercy had always done the same when she'd been embarrassed or unsure what to say, and Eden's heart ached at the sight. The girl's innocent young face was so like Mercy's had been at that age.

Mercy had possessed a fragile, almost ethereal beauty that had drawn attention wherever she'd gone. And as a teenager, she'd been just as sweet and shy as Hope was now. Eden felt tears prickle as she put her hand over her niece's hand and squeezed.

If only you could be here now, Mercy, to see your beautiful girl growing up.

"Well, I do like him," Hope finally said, still staring at the table. "And he said he likes me."

"He did? When did he tell you that? What did you say?" Eden asked, her eyes wide.

"It was after school on Friday, when he signed my yearbook. I said I liked him, too. But now that it's summer and all, I don't know if I'll even get a chance to see him for ages. I mean I want to but..." her voice faded as she glanced up at Eden.

"Do you think he'll still like me once summer's over? Do you think he'll meet some other girl?"

Eden paused, not sure what to say. She knew that Mercy had cared too much about what Preston Lancaster had thought, had sacrificed too much for what he had wanted. The magnitude of what she'd sacrifice for him still infuriated Eden, and it made her scared for her young niece. She feared giving the impressionable young girl the wrong message.

Eden didn't want Hope to follow in Mercy's tragic footsteps when it came to men. But she had fiercely protected and insulated her niece for so long, she now wondered if she'd inadvertently prevented the girl from gaining the experience and confidence she would need to navigate the trials and tribulations of romance that lay ahead.

"I don't think you should worry about what might happen months from now," Eden said, reaching out to push a silky strand of hair off Hope's face.

"If Luke is sincere and really likes you, then he'll still like you in the fall. And, if he doesn't, then you'll know it wasn't meant to be. Either way, you'll be just fine. With or without Luke Adams."

Hope nodded and sighed. "But he's just so cute. And I want him to like me so much. I know I should play hard to get, but when he's around I forget all that. I forget everything but him."

The look of longing in Hope's eyes startled Eden. She wasn't a child any longer. Her niece was becoming a woman. And Eden knew she was doing so in a world that had proven to be treacherous for the trusting and the innocent.

Eden had seen her fair share of women that had made decisions by listening to their hearts rather than their heads and had suffered for it. She had seen the same longing in their eyes that she saw now in Hope's. The women just wanted to be loved.

But sometimes, for reasons Eden couldn't fully understand, love morphed into something evil and dangerous. The love and happiness the women had hoped to receive from a partner turned into hate and fear. How could she tell her fifteen-year-old niece that sometimes following your heart proved fatal?

"Just be sure you don't forget to be safe," Eden said, using a light tone. She didn't want to discourage Hope from sharing her feelings in future.

"Remember to protect yourself and use your head. It may be tempting to surrender to the emotions, but I know you're smarter than that. No boy is worth risking your future or your safety."

Hope rubbed the silver locket at her neck. She'd received it as a present on her tenth birthday. It had been the last gift she'd gotten from her mother. Whenever she was pensive, she would reach for the locket.

"Thanks, Aunt Eden, I'll be careful," Hope said, her mood quiet now. "I'm going to go upstairs and try on the clothes I bought for the trip. Sage talked me into buying tropical colors, but I'm not sure they are really my style."

"I'd love to stay and play stylist, but I have to go to the office. There's something I need to do on my laptop and I left it on my desk." Eden stood up and followed Hope toward the stairs. She pulled Hope into a hug, squeezing a little too tight before letting go.

"What's that for?" Hope asked, frowning up at Eden. "Is everything all right? Has something happened?"

"No, nothing you need to worry about," Eden said, her chest swelling at the concern and love she heard in the girl's soft voice. "Everything is going to be fine."

But as Eden climbed into the Expedition and waited for Duke to get settled in the back seat, she wasn't so sure. Would she be able to help the police find Star? And if she did, would she be putting herself or her family in danger? Questions swirled in her mind as she backed out of the garage onto Briar Rose Lane and headed downtown.

Eden's talk with Hope had reminded her about the other young girl out there, alone and scared. She knew she had no choice but to try to find Star. And she wanted to help Leo Steele find the man who had killed Jessica. She wouldn't be able to forgive herself if her inaction led to another girl suffering Jessica's fate.

CHAPTER THIRTY

Hollywood waited until he was sure the Expedition had driven past before sitting up in his seat and looking around.

"Coast is clear, man," he said to Vinny, who was crouched over the gear shift with his head turned at an awkward angle to avoid being seen. "Don't think she saw us."

He looked back at the driveway. The black Jeep was still there. *She* was still there. Hollywood smiled as he imagined what her reaction would be when she saw him.

But, first things first. Vinny was nervous about going along with Hollywood's new plan without Sig giving them the okay. He said that Sig didn't like surprises. He wanted approval from the old man before he would agree to join in. So, thanks to Vinny, Hollywood needed to get in touch with Sig and explain his idea. Hollywood gritted his teeth.

The little wimp is always scared about something. His whining is getting on my last nerve.

Sig's phone rang twice and then a gruff voice answered. "Yeah?"

"Hey, I got some good news." Hollywood knew better than to say anything too specific over the phone. "I've got a new, um, *product* for our shipment. A real fine one. I'll bring her, I mean *it*, to the home base tonight. I think you'll be happy."

"You think so?" Sig's voice was deep, almost a growl. "Well, the *product* you have, had better be young and fresh. No more spoiled goods, if you know what I mean. No more fuck-ups."

"Right, right," Hollywood said, his tone casual even as rage simmered, heating the blood in his veins. "Only the youngest, freshest products for our partners in Miami. No sweat. Just make sure you bring lots of candy."

"You'll get your *candy* when you've delivered the expected quota, kid," Sig said, and Hollywood heard a hint of panic under the bluster in the old man's voice. "Otherwise, our partners in Miami might decide to have a little word with you. And I don't think you're gonna like what they have to say."

"Stop sweating, man, everything is fine. Just wait. You'll see. Now we gotta go."

Hollywood disconnected the call before he lost control of his temper and said something to Sig that would disrupt the stream of dope the old man supplied. Hollywood wasn't scared of Sig; he wasn't scared of anyone. But he was very scared of having his supply cut off. He needed the smack now, couldn't last long without it. No, he couldn't do anything to jeopardize his source.

"So, you didn't exactly tell him what you're planning to do." Vinny's voice cut through Hollywood's fog of anger. "You didn't say you were planning to knock on the door and introduce yourself."

"The old fuck doesn't need to know everything," Hollywood spit out, glad to have Vinny there, glad to have a target for his rage.

"He's freaking out about those Miami dirtbags and their stupid shipment. They must have something big on his ass. They must *own* his ass."

"But what if she calls somebody before we can tell her what we want?" Vinny asked, ignoring Hollywood's rant about Sig.

"Who the hell would she call? She won't call the cops, I know that." Hollywood put his hand on the car door handle. "Now come on. Quit screwing around before it's too late."

Hollywood stepped out of the car and scurried across the road. He looked back to see Vinny slide out of the driver's side and reluctantly trot after him. Hollywood grinned as he crossed the wide, green lawn.

I knew he'd cave. The dumbass has no backbone.

"Just look like you belong here," Hollywood said over his shoulder as he rapped on the door, "in case one of the neighbors gets curious."

Vinny stood behind him on the porch, and Hollywood could hear his heavy breathing.

Probably scared shitless, Hollywood thought and felt a ripple of anticipation in his stomach as he heard footsteps approach.

The door opened, and Sage Parker stood in the doorway staring at him as if she'd seen a ghost.

"Well, well, well...look who we have here. Just the girl I was looking for," Hollywood said, his tone cheerful, as he pushed his way past Sage. "And I got Vinny with me, too, ain't that great? We can all have a friendly little reunion."

Sage gaped at Hollywood, fear shining in her eyes as if she already knew what his sudden appearance could mean for her.

"Looks like you got a cushy little set-up here." Hollywood grabbed her arm and pulled her down the hall towards the living room. "Aren't you gonna offer to show us around?"

"Come on, Hollywood, this isn't cool," Vinny said, then closed his mouth at the angry look Hollywood aimed at him.

"Hollywood? Is that the name you're using now? I thought that was just some dumb joke," Sage said, seeming to have gotten her voice back. "And what the hell are you doing here? I'm not using anymore. I'm clean now, so I don't need whatever it is you're dealing."

"That's good, Sage, since you still haven't coughed over what you owe me for the last bag you begged off me." Hollywood's tone had gone from cheerful to nasty. "I've come to get what you owe me. Plus interest."

"Look, I'm sorry I didn't come back," Sage said, looking over her shoulder. The stairs that led to the second floor were empty.

"I was messed up. I needed to get help. By the time I'd gotten through rehab, I figured it wasn't a good idea to hang out with the same crowd anymore."

"How convenient," Hollywood said, grabbing her arm again and dragging her toward him. "So, you decided to just screw me over? Now you're too good for me and my boy here?"

"Sage?" A soft voice called from upstairs, and footsteps could be heard overhead. "Who was at the door?"

Sage flinched and pulled away. "Please, they don't know about my past. You can't say anything."

Hollywood grinned and turned toward the stairs, watching as slim legs, clad in faded jeans, began descending. Soon he could see a pink t-shirt and then a fresh-faced girl with long, brown hair and big blue eyes. Nice. From a distance, she had looked like a kid, but up close he could see she had already started to develop in all the right places.

You asked for young and fresh, Sig, and look what shows up. This just may be my lucky day.

"Hope, go back up to your room, everything is okay here," Sage said, her voice shaky. "I used to know these guys. They stopped by to say hello, but they aren't able to stay. They're just leaving."

Hope looked at Hollywood with friendly, curious eyes. He could see she was something special. A real knock-out. He thought that once the Miami guys got a load of her, they'd be drooling at the thought of all the money she'd bring in.

Maybe they'll even be willing to take her in place of both Star and Jess. This innocent young piece is worth more than both those druggie whores.

"What's your name?" Hollywood asked the teenager, cocking his head and looking at her from under hooded eyes. His dirty-blonde hair fell over one eye and he pushed it back without taking his eyes off Hope. "You sure are a pretty, little thing."

Hope blushed and smiled, before looking down at her feet in confusion.

Hollywood felt a surge of adrenaline. He liked the challenge of seducing a new girl. It was almost as good as the high he got from shooting up. Almost. Mainly he enjoyed the power kick when he sensed a girl was interested. And almost all of them were interested.

He knew if he focused his charm on a female, young or old, the chances were high he could persuade them to give in to him, at least physically. The men around him never understood what it was about Hollywood that always seemed to intrigue any female between fifteen and fifty.

Of course, the more experienced women soon lost interest once they'd gotten past the stimulating exterior and initial sexual high. But it took longer for the young girls, the innocent or vulnerable ones, to become disillusioned. He fascinated them, made them desperate to earn his desire.

Maybe it was his broody, dark blue eyes or the full, almost-feminine mouth, framed by chiseled cheekbones and a sculpted jaw, that transfixed them. Perhaps they sensed he was ultimately unattainable, and they longed to possess what they could never have.

Whatever it was, he had used it to destroy too many girls over the years to count. And now, another lovely conquest stood before him, waiting for her turn to surrender. Too bad he would have to forgo the seduction routine. There wasn't enough time. He'd have to get her back to the motel and ready to pass on to the Miami gang within days.

Hollywood sighed at the thought of what he was going to be missing. She would have been fun to have around for a few weeks. But business was business, and he was already craving a hit. He needed to earn some credit with Sig after the recent screw-ups with Star and Jess so that he could get more dope. No time for fun and games now.

"Hope, how'd you like to go for a ride with us?" Hollywood asked, reaching back to draw out the little black handgun he'd stuck into the back pocket of his pants when they'd gotten out of the car. Sage screamed and pulled Hope backward, eyes wide.

Hollywood aimed the .38 Special at Sage and cocked the hammer. The sound sent a thrill through his body. He'd never killed anyone before, and he suddenly wondered what it would feel like to pull the trigger and take a life. What a rush to have the power of life and death over the girls in front of him.

But then the thought of the blood and the resulting mess made him recoil. He wasn't the type for violence. At least not the messy kind. Best to use his smarts instead, as he always had done. The gun was just a way to intimidate the girls. Besides, it was his mother's gun, and he wasn't even sure it was loaded. He'd stolen it from a box under her bed before he'd forced Vinny to hide it.

Hollywood looked up to see Vinny staring at him. He was blinking rapidly behind his glasses, as if unsure what he was seeing. The gun had been in the silver car's glove compartment ever since Sig had pulled them into the operation at the Old Canal Motel. Vinny hadn't liked it, but he knew the crew from Miami were armed and dangerous. If something went south, Hollywood had insisted they have some protection.

"Vinny, go upstairs and get Hope's purse and cell phone. Bring anything she'd take with her if she ran away." Hollywood waved the gun towards the stairs and Vinny turned as if in a trance and ascended to the second floor.

Hollywood turned back to Sage and Hope, who were huddled together. Their terror-filled eyes trained on the little revolver. He lowered the gun to scratch at his arm. The itching was getting worse, and the jitters were starting to come back, too. He needed to get back to the motel.

For his plan to work, he'd need enough dope to keep Hope drugged up and compliant for the next few days. And he'd need a fix for himself soon. His stomach was already feeling the effects of withdrawal. Queasy waves of nausea lapped at him, and he knew it would only get worse if he didn't shoot up soon.

"Hope is coming with us," he said, once again raising the gun. "And you, Sage, are going to say she ran away. You're going to make sure no one comes looking for us."

"Why would I do that?" Sage asked, anger starting to spark in her eyes along with the fear.

"Because if you don't, we'll tell them the truth. That you're a druggie and a thief. That you lied about your past and invited us into this house." Hollywood smirked, liking the look of doubt that had entered Hope's eyes.

"Yeah, that's right, Hope. Your nanny is a drug addict who steals money and drugs from her friends. Or should I say, ex-friends? And now to pay off her debts, she's going to betray you, like she has everyone else." Hollywood turned to see Vinny hurrying back down the stairs.

"Get the car and pull it around to the garage," Hollywood barked at Vinny, as the nausea in his stomach began to worsen. "I'll bring the girl out that way."

Vinny paused as if he were thinking about refusing, but then he shrugged, opened the door, and stepped outside.

"I don't care what happens to me," Sage said, her voice shaking. "If you take Hope I'll tell the police everything I know about you. They'll find you and you'll go to jail."

"I don't think so," Hollywood said, tempted again to aim the gun at Sage and pull the trigger.

But he knew he couldn't do it. If he did, the police would know for sure Hope had been taken. His plan was much simpler. Make everyone think the teenager had run away to meet up with some guy. Some pimply kid at school. When she never came home, they wouldn't know what had happened to her.

Teenagers ran away from home all the time, right? She'd be in some motel in the next city, maybe even the next state, before they suspected foul play was involved.

"Go to the garage," Hollywood said, waving the gun at Sage and Hope. "Walk slowly and don't make any quick moves, or I might get jumpy and pull the trigger."

Sage walked toward a door off to the left of the kitchen. It led into a two-car garage. One side held a collection of bikes, scooters, and sporting gear. The other side was empty. Hollywood inspected the panel by the door and pushed a button that activated the garage door opener. The big door rolled up, and Vinny's little silver car pulled inside.

Hollywood grabbed Hope by the arm and pushed her toward Vinny, who had already opened the door to the backseat. As Vinny bundled Hope inside, Hollywood grabbed a jump rope coiled against the wall and threw it in after them.

"Tie her up so she doesn't try to jump out once we're on the road," Hollywood said, before turning back to Sage.

"You'll never get away with this, you know," Sage said, tears shining in her big, brown eyes.

"I better get away," Hollywood growled, trying to keep down the meager contents in his stomach.

"Because I've seen the woman and boy that live here, and if you tell them or the cops anything about me, I'll come back and kill both of them. But before I do that, I'll stop by your mother's house to give her a little surprise. I haven't seen her in a while. I'm sure she'd be glad to find out what I've been up to."

Sage choked out a sob. "Why are you doing this?"

"Let's just say that there are some very bad men that won't be happy if I show up empty-handed. Once they have Hope maybe they'll leave *me* alone. So, you're gonna tell everyone that Hope ran away. Say you don't know where she is, but that she was talking about some guy at school. And you better make it sound believable. The life of everyone you love depends on it."

CHAPTER THIRTY-ONE

The administration offices of the Mercy Harbor Foundation were located on the tenth floor of Riverview Tower, an elegant glass and steel building that soared two hundred and fifty feet over the Willow Bay Riverwalk, a promenade full of boutique shops and cafes with views of the river. The Riverwalk was always busy on Saturdays, and Eden had to wait for scores of pedestrians to pass through the crosswalk before she could turn into the building's dedicated garage and pull into one of the spaces on the ground floor reserved for the Mercy Harbor staff.

The empty, dimly lit garage contrasted sharply with the sunny, crowded street outside. Eden stepped out of the SUV and looked around the empty space. Ash gray walls supported a low, concrete roof that made Eden feel instantly claustrophobic. A shiver of unease rippled down her spine.

A strong sense of foreboding washed over her, and she stood still, fighting the urge to panic.

This is just my anxiety acting up. There's nothing wrong. Everything's going to be fine.

Duke whined from the backseat and Eden forced herself to step back and open the rear door. The dog jumped down and stood next to Eden, his ears pricked up and his tail down. A rumbling sound echoed above, somewhere out of sight, and the garage seemed to tremble around them.

"Just a plane flying overhead," Eden said to Duke, her voice thin in the still, heavy air. "Let's get inside, boy. It's creepy in here."

They walked out of the garage and followed the sidewalk to the building's lobby. The front doors were locked, the sparkling glass panes revealing the empty, dark interior beyond. Eden had a keycard that unlocked an employee entrance on the side of the building.

As she approached the door, it swung open and a white-haired man in a blue security uniform stepped out. He smiled at Eden and waited for her to reach him.

"How are you today, Ms. Winthrop?" the man asked, his voice hoarse but friendly.

"Hi, Edgar, I'm doing fine. And please, I keep telling you, call me Eden."

The older man had worked on the security team since she'd leased out the office space more than four years previously, but he still treated her with a respectful formality that was rarely used in business anymore.

"Hi there, Duke," Edgar said, reaching down to scratch behind the dog's silky ears. "You staying out of trouble?"

Duke sniffed the security guard's hand politely and looked back at Eden. She was glad to see that he appeared to be more relaxed now. The gloomy garage had spooked him as well.

"What are you doing here today, Edgar? Have they started manning the place all weekend now?' Eden asked, surprised that the building needed security on the weekend when all the businesses within were closed.

"No, I was called in to work a special shift." The man looked around as if someone might overhear, then turned back to Eden with an excited gleam in his eye.

"We had some suspicious activity here last night. Someone managed to bypass the security on the employee entrance and made it all the way to the tenth floor before they set off an alarm system in one of the office suites. By the time the police arrived, the intruder was gone. So, until we find out how they got in, we'll be manning the place the old-fashioned way."

Eden felt a tingle of fright. *Could someone have been trying to break into our office? Could they be searching for information on one of the residents?* A disturbing thought took hold. *Or maybe someone is trying to find Star before we do.*

She knew it was farfetched. How would anyone know the foundation even had information on the missing girl? The only people besides her that knew she suspected Star had stayed at the shelter were Reggie, Leo, and the police. And they all were waiting on Eden to find the information. Weren't they? Eden wasn't so sure.

Has someone else found out that Star's real name and family's address might be contained in the foundation's database?

Thunder rumbled in the distance, although the sun still shone high in the sky. Eden looked to the west and saw storm clouds gathering. The hot, heavy air felt electric around her. Something felt *wrong.* A sense of doom hung in the air. She recognized the feeling from her bout with anxiety and depression. She'd suffered through months of worry and panic that something terrible was about to happen.

But I'm better, now, aren't I? Or am I having a relapse? Is my anxiety getting worse?

"You all better get inside," Edgar said, opening the door wide so they could pass through. "There's a big storm coming. Weatherman said it is going to be a doozy."

Eden walked down the hall and into the building's lobby. She stood by the bank of elevators and pushed the up button. The doors slid open immediately, and she and Duke stepped inside. As she pushed the button for the tenth floor, she wondered if she was doing the right thing. She'd already been worried about giving out Star's information. Now she was worried that whoever broke in before might decide to come back.

Could kindly old Edgar hold off an intruder that was determined to get in? She looked down at Duke's furry head, glad that she wasn't alone. Good old Duke always seemed to be there when she needed moral support.

The elevator doors slid open and Eden half expected someone to emerge from the shadowy corridor beyond and jump at her. But all was quiet, and she soon had unlocked the door to the Mercy Harbor suite and turned on the lights.

She crossed to her office and saw her laptop was still there, right where she'd left it. She sat at her desk and booted up the laptop. Digging in her purse, she found her cell phone and tapped on Nathan's name in her list of recent calls.

"I thought you'd forgotten about me." Nathan's voice sounded far away, and Eden imagined him sitting at his big glass desk, ignoring the million-dollar view of the San Francisco Bay splayed out behind him. He seemed to be a world away. And it was a world where she no longer belonged.

Fifteen minutes later Nathan had remotely logged in to the system, created a simple query, and produced a short list of records that met the criteria Eden had stipulated. It took only moments for Eden to skim through the names and click to view the photos that had been linked to the files.

"Here it is," Eden said into the phone. "Trisha Moore stayed at 1408 Shutter Street two years ago. Her daughter Stacey and son Zane stayed with her."

The photo she was staring at showed a somber young girl with curly brown hair held back by a red bandana. Eden stared at the girl's pale skin and sad brown eyes.

"It's her. It's Star. The daughter...Stacey...she's the girl that came to the house. She's bleached her hair since then, but it's definitely her. Stacey Moore is Star." Eden glanced at the data in the file and groaned. "She's only *sixteen*. I mean I knew she wasn't eighteen. But now that I know she's only sixteen I feel sick. The poor girl."

Nathan cleared his throat and sighed. "I don't think I'm supposed to be seeing this stuff, am I? I'll drop the query on your desktop and log out of your computer."

Eden watched as he closed several files and exited the screens he'd been working in.

"I guess you're done with me for now."

Eden detected a note of bitterness in his voice for the first time. She wasn't being fair to him, and she knew it.

"I'm sorry, Nathan. I don't want to take advantage of you, or of the feelings you have for me."

She inhaled deeply, dreading the words she knew she had to say. "That's why I'm going to sell my shares of Giant Leap. You need to get on with your life...and I can't be a part of that life anymore."

"Please don't say that, Eden." His voice was little more than a whisper. "I know you're going through a hard time now, and I'm patient. I can wait for you to figure it all out."

"That's just it, Nathan. You've already been *too* patient. You've been waiting for four years...and...well, I've decided not to move back to San Francisco. I've made a new life for myself here in Willow Bay and I need to spend all my energy on the kids and on Mercy Harbor. So, I won't be returning to Giant Leap."

The next words stuck in her throat. "And I won't be coming back to *you*, Nathan."

Eden listened to the silence on the other end of the phone, pain and regret radiating through her as she braced for Nathan's response.

"It isn't me I'm worried about right now," Nathan finally said, his voice achingly kind and familiar, "I'm your friend, Eden, if nothing else. And I'll always be here for you, wherever you live."

"Good-bye, Nathan," she managed to say, but he'd already disconnected the call. Duke stirred at her feet and Eden made herself sit up and look again at Stacey Moore's file, which was still displayed on her screen.

The intake notes detailed the situation that had brought Trisha Moore and her two children, Stacey and Zane, to Mercy Harbor. It was a heartbreakingly common story. The single mother had started dating a man named Buddy Jones several months before, and he had eventually moved into the family's apartment. Buddy soon began verbally and physically abusing Trisha, but she was unsure how to get him out of the apartment.

The notes in the file went on to describe Buddy as being possessive and suspicious. He would follow Trisha to work and even tried to attach a GPS device to her car to track where she went. Finally, after a particularly ugly fight, she'd asked him to leave, and he'd waved around a kitchen knife, threatening to kill her and her kids.

That episode had scared her enough to call the police, and social services had arrived as well. The counselor assigned to Trisha's case had convinced her to seek shelter at a safe house until Buddy had been prosecuted on the pending domestic battery charge.

Further in the file, Eden could see that the Moores had stayed at the Shutter Street house for two weeks before they'd been placed in a new apartment that the foundation had secured for them. The apartment address was listed, along with the standard note that the new address should be kept strictly confidential.

Additional notes had named Trisha's ex-boyfriend, Buddy Jones, as a potential security risk, and recommended that all necessary precautions should be taken to prevent Mr. Jones from discovering Trisha Moore's new address.

A brief follow-up note had been added to the record several months later. Buddy Jones had been sentenced to two years in prison. Eden knew that meant Trisha Moore's abuser could already be back on the streets by now. She shuddered at the image of an angry, knife-wielding man stepping out of the shadows, demanding to know where Trisha Moore had gone.

Could Buddy Jones have been the one that had entered the building last night? And could he somehow be involved with Star's disappearance?

Eden shook her head, eager to dislodge the irrational thoughts that were swirling around, causing her pulse to race. She opened the notepad on her desk and wrote down Trisha Moore's new address. She looked back at the record on the screen and saw that no phone number had been listed.

She moved the mouse to close the file but hesitated. Something in the file was bothering her. She felt as if she was missing something.

She read through the intake notes again and paused. So, Buddy Jones had tried to track Trisha Moore by attaching a GPS tracker to her car. Why was that fact bothering her?

Many residents at Mercy Harbor's shelters had been the victims of stalking, with ex-partners that went to all means, including electronic surveillance, to follow them or hunt them down if they attempted to hide. That's why Mercy Harbor security staff always performed a search on the residents' personal items and vehicles before they were brought to the safehouse.

The image of Star's shoes lying by the bed flashed into her mind. She remembered what Star had said that night. *Why would Jess leave her shoes? They were the only shoes she had.*

Eden gasped with sudden understanding. Star's personal items hadn't been checked for tracking devices. Star had arrived directly at the safe house; she hadn't gone through the normal screening. If the man who had abused Star wanted to track her, he just might have stuck a device into her shoe. Especially if they were the only shoes she wore. The next thought made Eden's stomach drop.

Could the man have tracked Star back to Shutter Street? Did he think she might still be there? Were the women there in danger right now?

Eden fumbled in her purse for the card Nessa had given her two nights previously. She tapped in the number and held the phone to her ear. After four rings the call went to voicemail.

"Detective Ainsley...um, Nessa...I need you to check the shoes I dropped off the other night. I think they might have a GPS tracking device or chip or whatever in them." She swallowed hard, willing the rising dread to go away. She couldn't afford to have a panic attack now.

"I didn't check her shoes or anything, and I'm worried Star may have been tracked to our safe house. Please, have them checked out and let me know as soon as possible."

Eden looked at the screen in front of her, Star's real name and address still displayed.

"And, I found out some information about Star. Please, call me back." Eden recited her number and then disconnected the call.

She wondered if she should alert Reggie that they may need to activate the emergency relocation plan for Shutter Street.

Great job, Eden, she berated herself. *You've put the whole houseful of residents in danger.*

Duke suddenly sprang to his feet, his hackles raised. Eden was surprised to hear a low growl begin in his throat. He ran around the desk and into the suite's reception area, stopping in front of the closed glass doors. He barked at the dark corridor beyond. Eden had rarely seen Duke get agitated, and his low-pitched bark made her flinch. She grabbed her phone and hurried toward Duke, her mouth dry and heart pounding so loud in her ears she thought she might faint.

A figure could be seen in the shadows beyond. It was moving closer to them and Eden opened her mouth to scream when she saw Edgar step into the small square of light that spilled out into the corridor beyond the door.

"Sorry to bother you, Ms. Winthrop," the man said as he opened the door and stepped in. "My manager asked if you could do us a favor."

Eden slumped her shoulders in relief and produced a weak laugh. "You startled me and Duke, Edgar. We thought you were an intruder."

"Oh, dear. I'm sorry, Ms. Winthrop. I should have known better than to just appear unannounced." He looked back down the dark corridor. "I forget that it can be a little spooky out there when the lights are off and no one else is around.

"So, what favor did you need?" Eden was anxious to get out of the building. She wanted to tell someone what she'd discovered.

I need to tell someone I can trust, like Reggie or Leo.

Her heart skipped a beat at the thought of the dark-haired lawyer. If someone had told her two days ago that she'd trust Leo Steel with top-secret information, she would have called them insane.

"We're hoping you can take a look at a clip from the security camera. The camera caught the intruder walking up to the panel by the door. It's not much, but we thought maybe you would recognize him."

"Sure," Eden said, intrigued. "It's definitely worth a shot."

"My manager said he's already emailed it to the listed contact for Mercy Harbor. That you?"

"It should be me. Let me check." Eden went back into her office with Edgar trailing behind her.

She clicked on the mail icon on her laptop. Her inbox showed over fifty unread emails, but she could see that the latest had been sent from the security company.

She clicked on the email and opened the attachment. A movie clip popped open and Eden could see grainy footage of the sidewalk outside the employee entrance. Within seconds a broad-shouldered man appeared and walked toward the door. He was wearing a baseball cap and dark glasses. He took a black handkerchief out of his back pocket and reached toward the camera. The picture went black.

"He used that to block the camera," Edgar said. "The police that responded to the alarm found it, but it's just a regular black bandana. Nothing special about it."

The old man looked at Eden, then asked, "So, you recognize him?"

"No," Eden said, watching the clip again. "Sorry, but I've never seen that man before."

As Edgar walked her downstairs and escorted her and Duke to her car, Eden felt as if she were being watched.

"Be careful, Ms. Winthrop," Edgar said as he waved her off. "It's a crazy world out there."

CHAPTER THIRTY-TWO

Eden's eyes flicked to the rearview mirror again, sure she would see a man in dark glasses and a baseball cap in the car behind her. But it was hard to get a clear view of the driver, and the traffic was unusually heavy with cars weaving in and out of the lanes around her. She couldn't even be sure if the white car in the rearview mirror was the same one she'd seen pulling out of Delancey's after she'd crossed South Street, or if it was the car she'd seen merging into traffic off the interstate exit ramp.

She swiveled her head to watch as the white car accelerated and passed the Expedition. The elderly couple within seemed oblivious to Eden's stare.

Her head began to ache as she wondered for the hundredth time, *Am I being paranoid, or am I being followed? And why hasn't Nessa called me back?*

Her anxiety was growing faster than the brewing storm clouds ahead. She needed someone to talk to. Breaking her own strict rule about texting and driving, Eden picked up her phone and tapped in a message to Reggie. *Please call me as soon as possible.*

The light ahead turned red, and Eden stopped and waited for the green light, wishing she knew what she should do next. She noticed the empty building that had once housed the only Blockbuster store in Willow Bay.

Isn't Clear Horizons just down that street?

The thought of the sober house conjured the image of Leo Steele's handsome face as he'd stood talking to Denise Bane. Should she call Leo? Wouldn't he want to know she'd found out Star's real name? The thought of Leo and the intimate talk they'd shared the previous day triggered a strange mix of guilt and excitement.

Eden had just broken Nathan's heart, and she knew she should feel terrible about keeping him in limbo for so long. Would it be wise to begin another relationship so soon?

And of course, Leo had played a key role in securing Preston's bond so that he had been free to kill Mercy. Although Eden sympathized with Leo's past and understood his commitment to defending his clients against a wrongful conviction, could she really fully forgive the man who had represented her sister's killer? She wasn't sure.

There's no denying Leo Steele is a very attractive man.

She felt a flush of something she hadn't felt for a long time. The sensation was too close to desire for her comfort.

Perhaps he's a bit too attractive.

When the light turned green, Eden impulsively turned onto Baymont Court and drew her car up to the curb in front of Clear Horizons. She tried to reassure herself that it was daylight and that she was perfectly safe. She checked her rearview mirror. *See, Eden, no one is following you. You'll be fine. You're just going to ask them if the name Stacey Moore rings a bell.*

Duke followed Eden to the same door she'd entered the last time she'd been there. She knocked softly, tempted to forget the whole thing and scurry back to the car before the stern-faced manager could open the door. But it was too late. The door was pulled open and Denise Bane glared out at Eden, her expression accusatory.

"I've just told the police everything I know about Jessica Carmichael," the woman said, her brow furrowing into a deep scowl. "And I'm not about to waste more time talking to *you*."

"Sorry to bother you, Ms. Bane," Eden said, ignoring her urge to tell the hateful woman what she really thought. She forced herself to keep her tone polite and even. "I was just wondering if the name Stacey Moore means anything to you or Trevor?"

"If it did, I wouldn't tell you," the woman sneered, forcing the leathery skin around her mouth to fall into deep wrinkles. "Now, leave us alone."

A flash of long, blonde hair passed behind Denise in the dim office. Eden looked over the woman's shoulder and saw several girls sitting on folding chairs as if they were having a meeting.

"Again, I'm sorry to interrupt, but perhaps some of your residents may have met Stacey Moore. Could I speak to them and ask?"

Eden raised her voice, hoping to catch the attention of the girls beyond. "Or can I talk to Trevor?"

"Trevor isn't here. And as I told you before, I don't give out information about our residents. Now leave before I call the police back here and tell them you've been harassing me."

Eden caught a look of fear in Denise Bane's icy blue eyes just before the door was slammed shut in her face.

Why is she afraid to speak to me? What is she hiding?

She looked down at Duke and shrugged. "At least we tried, boy. I guess that's all we can do for now. You want to take a walk over to the park and stretch your legs?"

Duke looked up at Eden as if in agreement, and they walked toward the small park around the corner. The sidewalk in front of the gate was empty and she couldn't hear the sounds of children playing on the rusty equipment. She began to hope they'd have the dilapidated park all to themselves.

But as they got closer, she saw Charles Wyatt sitting on one of the concrete benches inside the fence. He looked up just as they walked through the gate.

"Can't stay away, huh," Charles said, leaning back against the bench and stretching his long legs in front of him. "You here to make up some more stories?"

"I'm sorry about yesterday, Charles. We shouldn't have waited to tell you about Jess. It wasn't fair." She took the leash off Duke's collar, so he could explore the park. "I came back to Clear Horizons to talk to Denise and Trevor Bane."

"So, how'd that go?" The big man cocked his head, his expression telling her he knew it hadn't gone very well.

"Denise wouldn't even let me come in. She slammed the door in my face," Eden admitted. "And Trevor wasn't there."

"Doesn't surprise me. He's gone a lot. If he does show his face it'll be later in the afternoon."

Eden considered the words as she watched Duke roam around the overgrown stretch of grass beyond the swings. "Doesn't sound like you're Trevor's biggest fan."

"You're right, I'm not a fan at all. You catch on fast."

"So why not? What's wrong with him?" Eden kept her eyes on Duke, but she could see Charles clenching his fists as he sat up straight in response to her question.

The man had a temper, as she'd seen the day before. She needed to be ready to call Duke back and get out of the park quickly if he started to lose it.

"Trevor's got a pretty big ego and a cocky attitude to match. Thinks he's some big stud."

He leaned forward and propped his elbows on his knees. "I wouldn't care if he didn't mess with those little girl's heads so much."

"You mean the girls that stay at Clear Horizons?" Eden asked. "Trevor messes with the female residents?"

"Yeah, he likes the young ones from what I can tell. Gets them to think he's their boyfriend and shit. Then just dumps them when the next one comes along. It's like a game to him."

"Charles, do you think he might have been involved with Jess when she hung around here? That he might have been the one…that…" Eden's voice faded as she realized what she was asking.

She couldn't go around asking people if they thought their neighbors could be murderers. She might end up making the wrong person angry, and she was here on her own.

"I warned Jess about Trevor," Charles said, clenching his jaw. "I told her that guy was bad news. But you never know. The girls all seem to like him. He seems like a little weasel to me, but they fall all over the guy."

"Do you know if a girl named Stacy Moore was staying at Clear Horizons? She used the name Star sometimes."

"Yeah, I knew Stacy," Charles said, nodding slowly. "She was cool, just a little messed up. Got hooked on something, so her mother wanted her out of the house until she got clean. Arranged for her to live at Clear Horizons. I think there was a little brother or sister at home and she didn't want them seeing Stacey high and shit."

"I can understand that." Eden felt a flicker of hope. She wanted to keep Charles talking. "When did Stacey leave Clear Horizons?"

"She stayed there up until a few weeks ago. I'm not sure where she was headed, but she seemed happy enough the last time I saw her." Charles cocked his head. "And you know, she was one of Trevor's favorites. At least that's what Brandi told me before she disappeared."

"What do you mean *disappeared*?" Eden asked.

"I mean one day Brandi was just *gone*. She was older than most, maybe eighteen or nineteen, so I guess she was free to leave whenever she wanted. No obligation to let me know. But she'd been really friendly. We hung out a few times and she'd even come back to my place to chill."

Charles wouldn't meet Eden's eyes, and she wondered what *chilling* consisted of.

"She'd been in rehab up in Tallahassee," he continued. "When she got out her parents told her she had to live at a sober house for a few months before going home. She thought they just wanted her out of the house, but she didn't really blame them. Said she'd put them through hell."

"So, she was friends with Stacey?" Eden asked. "Is there a way you can help me get in touch with Brandi?'

"I wish...but, like I said, she's gone. Seemed pretty depressed for a while and then one day she was just gone. Never said good-bye or anything." Charles leaned back against the bench again and scratched his head. "Kind of hurt my feelings, you know? I thought we'd gotten close."

Eden's heart dropped. It seemed that both Star and this other girl were missing. Could Brandi be one of the other girls Star had mentioned that lived with her and Hollywood?

She needed to get Nessa the information she'd discovered right away. Just then thunder rumbled, prompting Duke to trot back over and sit at her feet. He didn't like storms. A flash of lightning lit up the sky in the distance.

"Looks like it's going to be a bad one today," Charles said, nodding toward the angry clouds that were swiftly moving overhead.

He stood and stretched his arms before walking toward the gate. Eden watched him, feeling as if she'd missed something. Perhaps had let some vital information slip by her.

Charles stopped and turned toward her. "You know that girl that went missing a few years back...Tiffany Clarke?"

Eden nodded, surprised by the sudden question. Her heart beat faster. Had she been right to wonder if Tiffany Clarke's disappearance was connected to what had been happening to the girls in Willow Bay?

"She went to school with me and Trevor. She was younger than us, just a freshman when I was a Junior, and Trevor was a senior." Charles looked thoughtful, perhaps picturing a long-ago day.

"She was beautiful, popular." He shook his head as if to clear an unwanted image. "Of course, she hung out with a different group than me and Trevor. But back in high school, all the girls liked Trevor. I doubt Tiffany was an exception."

Eden tried to make sense of what he was telling her about Tiffany and Trevor. What was he suggesting?

"You know, I thought I saw them together once, right before she went missing. I never said anything, but I always wondered. Once her body was found, I thought about going to the police. Thought about telling them I'd seen her with Trevor, but I figured they'd probably try to pin it on me. A young black guy steps out of nowhere saying he may know what happened to a murdered white chick? Nah, that'd been suicide around here."

Eden frowned. "What do you mean by *around here*?"

"Everyone knows WBPD has some crooked cops on the payroll. And the ones that aren't crooked are probably looking for a fall guy to pin Tiffany's murder on."

"I doubt that's the case," Eden said, but her voice sounded unsure.

"Well, she's been missing for years, and they haven't found the killer even though it's been six months since they found her body." Charles smiled, but his eyes looked angry. "Someone's bound to be getting their ass chewed out on a daily basis over that."

"So, you're just going to stay quiet?" Eden asked, still reeling over the implications of what Charles had suggested.

"You don't need to pull a guilt trip on me; I feel bad enough already." Charles raised a big hand and balled it into a fist. He pointed a long finger to the sky. "I've got to look out for number one. You know what I mean?"

Eden stared at him in dismay. When she didn't answer, he turned and walked away without looking back. Eden didn't try to stop him. She attached Duke's leash and hurried down the sidewalk. She was frantic to get back to her car.

Now that Charles had raised questions about Trevor Bane, she felt her anxiety rising. She didn't dare look over at the sober house as she approached the car. As she got nearer, she saw that her right front tire was flat. Her mind raced.

Could I just have run over a nail? Or is this a threat? Or worse, is someone trying to keep me here?

She climbed into her car and locked the doors, then got Duke settled into the back. She'd have to call for roadside assistance. No way was she going to stand in front of Trevor Bane's house trying to fix a flat tire. But she needed to get the air on, the car was baking.

She stuck her key into the ignition and started the car just as someone rapped loudly on the driver's side window. Letting out a high-pitched scream, she turned with wide eyes to see Leo Steele.

Rolling down the window, her breath coming in gasps, she said, "God, you scared me, Leo! What are you doing here?"

"I came to speak to Denise Bane again. Wanted to try to talk some sense into her," he said, his warm voice instantly calming Eden's nerves. "What are *you* doing here?"

Eden hesitated, not sure how to explain all that had happened. She decided to keep it short. "I think I might know who killed Jessica."

CHAPTER THIRTY-THREE

Leo covered Eden's tightly clenched fist with a big, warm hand and gave a reassuring squeeze. She stiffened, and he pulled back, knowing they hadn't quite reached the holding hands stage of their tentative new friendship. Wrapping both hands around the steering wheel, the unsettling urge to comfort her grew. He wanted to make her feel safe. He just wished he knew how.

"It's going to be okay," he said, although his mind was full of questions and doubts.

Is she really being followed by a mystery man who broke into her office and flattened her tire? If so, why? And is Trevor Bane a killer? Or could Eden's anxiety disorder cause paranoia?

He struggled to keep his eyes on the road, even as they were drawn to the fear clearly evident in Eden's stricken face. He had to think logically. Needed time to review everything she'd told him.

But Eden had insisted they drive straight to the police department, and so they'd left her Expedition sitting at the curb with a flat tire, settled Duke into the back of the BMW, and headed toward downtown. Leo wondered what the police would think when they reported the strange series of events.

"I hope Nessa is on duty," Eden said, her head turned toward the window. "She might listen. The other detectives will think I'm overreacting and dismiss me as a hysterical woman.

"I'm sure when you explain the situation, they'll take you seriously." Leo knew he wasn't being honest with her.

He actually had little hope that the cynical Willow Bay detectives would investigate her claims once they found out she suffered from anxiety and panic attacks. In his experience, only Pete Barker could be trusted, and he was now out of commission. The other men on the force weren't prone to hunting down clues and untangling sophisticated plots. They usually jumped on the easiest and most convenient suspect.

"Well, Charles seems to think the WBPD will try to pin the murders on *him* if he comes forward and tells them what he saw." Eden sounded defeated.

"Based on what happened to my father, I'd have to say he may just have a point," Leo said. "Unless, of course, Charles is trying to point the investigation away from himself."

Eden looked startled. "You mean, maybe Charles is the killer and he's trying to make it look like Trevor did it?"

"Well, Charles is the only one that admits having known all the girls missing...or dead."

Leo thought about Charles, trying to recall the big man's face.

Could Charles be the killer? Could he be trying to manipulate Eden into accusing Trevor?

Leo wasn't sure. He had believed the surprise and grief Charles expressed when he'd found out Jessica had been killed.

Eden's purse buzzed in her lap. She reached in and pulled out her phone, swiping to answer as soon as she saw the number calling.

She held the phone to her ear. "Hi, Sage."

Leo heard a gasp and saw the phone drop from Eden's hand. She immediately scrambled to find the phone on the car's floor, shouting, "Oh my god, no...no!"

Leo saw a gas station on his right and instinctively pulled in and stopped the car. He reached down and found the phone and handed it to Eden, who pressed the speaker icon.

"Sage, what happened? Where's Hope?" Eden cried out, her voice raw.

"They took her," Sage said through tears. "Two men burst in. They had a gun, and they...they took Hope."

Leo gently took the phone from Eden's shaking grasp.

"Sage, I'm a friend of Eden's, have you called 911? Did the police say they were on their way?"

"Yes, I...I called them as...as soon as the men left," Sage stammered. "They said they'd be here right away but aren't here yet."

"And Devon, what about Devon?" Eden cried. "Where's Devon?"

"He's here with me," Sage said. "He was upstairs when they burst in. He's okay, I think. Just upset about Hope."

Police sirens sounded in the background. "The police are here," Sage said in a wobbly voice.

Leo looked over at Eden, but her eyes were unfocused and glassy. Was she in shock? He spoke into the phone, straining to maintain a calm tone.

"Sage, go let the police in. We'll be there within minutes. Stay with Devon and make sure he knows we're on our way."

The call disconnected, and Leo lay the phone in Eden's lap.

"What's the quickest route to your house?" he asked. When she didn't answer he shook her shoulder. "Eden, come on!"

He was scared for her but knew the only thing that could help her now was to find her niece. "Tell me your address. We need to get to your house. Hope needs you to stay focused!"

Eden blinked and croaked out, "8156 Briar Rose Lane."

Leo entered the address in his satnav and pulled back out into traffic. Eden picked up the phone and pressed redial. She activated the speaker and waited. Nessa answered on the third ring.

Nessa's voice was tired. "Hello, Eden. Sorry I missed your call earlier. It's been a hell of a day."

"My niece has...been...taken," Eden's voice cracked on the words. She tried again. "Two men with a gun broke in and...and, they kidnapped my niece. Hope is gone."

"What? When did this happen?" Nessa asked, all traces of fatigue in her voice gone. "Did you call 911? Are they on the way?"

"My nanny called 911, and the police just got to the house. I'm on my way..." Eden's voice broke off as she looked over at Leo. "We're on our way. Leo Steele is with me."

"We'll be there in seven minutes according to the satnav," Leo said, his eyes scanning the traffic ahead for an opening.

"I'll head over there right now," Nessa said, and Leo could hear the rustle of paper. "What's the address?"

Leo recited the address and said they would see her shortly. He dared a glance at Eden and saw tears streaming down her face. The guilt and pain in her eyes as she looked back at him broke his heart.

"Oh god, Leo...this can't be happening. What am I going to do?"

Leo didn't know what to say. Would the police be able to track down and rescue the missing girl? Doubt seeped in.

The police hadn't saved his mother, and they had never found her real killer. But he couldn't let his bitterness show. Eden was hurting, and she needed him. He had to stay strong, had to keep the faith. As the rain began to fall, he pressed his foot harder on the gas and raced toward the heart of the storm.

CHAPTER THIRTY-FOUR

Hope listened to the rain pounding down on the pavement outside the motel. She wondered again if this was all a dream. Just a terrible nightmare that would end soon. But the coarse rope had already rubbed a raw, red circle around her wrists, and she shivered as the stale air blasted from the dusty wall unit under the window making goosebumps appear on her damp skin. No, it all felt too frighteningly real to be a dream.

She'd been too scared to scream or try to escape as they'd driven out of her neighborhood. She'd huddled in the backseat, her hands tied behind her, with Vinny driving and Hollywood pointing the gun back at her. She could tell that he liked to aim the gun and wave it around. He seemed to enjoy her fear.

Hope knew it would only take one careless move on his part and she could end up dead. She had tried to stay still, tried not to make any sudden movements.

They'd come to a stop outside an old, rundown motel that Hope had never seen before. She knew they hadn't been driving very long, not more than twenty minutes, but as she stared out of the car window, it looked like they were in a whole different town.

The motel's dirty walls and trash-strewn parking lot didn't look like the Willow Bay she knew. An angry-looking man with a ponytail sat on the stairwell. He saw Hollywood step out, and got up and walked over to the car, leaning to stare into the backseat. He raised his eyebrows and then frowned, before turning to talk to Hollywood. They talked in low, angry voices for a few minutes and then the man reached into his pocket and pulled out something that he handed to Hollywood.

Hollywood had then opened the door and motioned for her to get out. She tried to memorize the surroundings as Vinny guided her toward a room on the ground floor. In the distance, she saw a dock and graffiti-covered walls that seemed to lead to some sort of a canal. She would have to find a way to escape, but she needed a plan.

If I can get away, which way should I go? Is there anywhere to run? Could I follow the canal back to the river and into downtown?

Before she could see anything else, she'd been pushed inside, and Hollywood had stepped in behind her, closing the door in Vinny's face. It was now just the two of them in the dim room.

"You try to scream or run away, and I'll use this," he said, brandishing the gun.

The dark eyes she had thought dreamy when she'd first met him now seemed crazed. His face glistened with a sheen of sweat, and he scratched at the inside of his arm over and over.

"What do you want with me?" Hope asked, keeping her voice small.

He looked as if he could erupt in a rage at any minute and she didn't want to give him any reason to do so.

"I want to introduce you to some friends of mine, little girl." Hollywood produced a nasty smile. "I think you'll like them. And I know they're gonna like you."

"Please, I just want to go home." Hope felt her eyes fill with tears and blinked hard to stop them from falling.

"Don't start that crap already," Hollywood snapped. "And stop trying to play the innocent routine. I know how you rich girls get around. I've had my share of rich bitches, you know, and you're all the same. Whining all the time. But you aren't going home any time soon, so just relax and enjoy the ride."

Hope recoiled as Hollywood approached, noticing the red marks on his arms as he reached toward her. He spun her around and began to untie her hands.

"I've got something that'll make you relax all right," Hollywood muttered as he led her toward the bed, unbuckling his belt. Her knees buckled under her as he pulled the belt through the loops, and she sat back heavily onto the scratchy, blue bedspread, fear coursing through her at the thought of what lay ahead.

"Watch me," Hollywood said, pulling out a bag of white powder. "I'm gonna ride the dragon, baby. And once I'm done, you can go for a ride, too. It'll rock your world, little girl. You'll never want to go home again."

Hope stared as Hollywood reached under the bed and pulled out a plastic bag. He waved the gun again and cocked his head. "Now you stay right there while I work my magic. I'd hate to have to use this on you before you get a chance to party."

He dumped the contents of the plastic bag on the small, round table under the window. Hope felt a flash of relief. He wasn't going to touch her, at least not yet. Then her horror returned as she saw him take out a syringe with a needle, a spoon, and a lighter before he sat down and blocked her view.

After a few minutes of preparation, he picked up the belt and wrapped it around his arm, securing it tightly. She turned her head away in disgust when he picked up the needle and jabbed it into his arm. She had to get away. She couldn't let him stick that needle in her.

Hope saw Hollywood throw his head back and take a deep breath. Slowly rising off the bed, her legs weak and shaking, she crept behind him, thinking she might be able to make it to the door before he noticed her. She saw his eyes were closed, and she slipped around him, grasping the doorknob with her hand, planning to dash toward the canal if she made it clear of the motel corridor. She thought her heart would burst out of her chest as she twisted and pulled. The door was locked.

She heard a lazy laugh behind her, and she turned to see Hollywood holding a metal key in one hand, and the little .38 in the other. The belt was loose around his arm now, and his eyes looked heavy but dreadfully aware.

"Now it's your turn, baby." He picked up the needle again and grinned. "Go on now. Sit next to me and I'll fix you up. You're gonna love it."

The room wavered in front of Hope, and she thought she might faint. She forced her feet to walk toward the offered chair, but instead of sitting down, she rushed into the bathroom and slammed the door closed behind her.

She reached for the knob and realized with dismay that it didn't have a lock. But as she looked up she saw that a rusty barrel bolt lock had been installed at eye level. She threw the bolt and turned to look around the small room.

Her heart sank. There was no window, just a pedestal sink, a toilet, and a small, dingy white bathtub that lined the right wall. She was trapped. But at least she had escaped the needle for now. If she just could stay in the bathroom until someone came to rescue her. Fear flooded through her.

They will come to find me, won't they? Sage will tell Aunt Eden and the police I was kidnapped, right? She won't say I ran away?

Doubt settled in her stomach as Hollywood began to beat on the door. How could Sage have lied to her and Aunt Eden about everything?

"Open up, Hope!" Hollywood called out, but he didn't seem mad anymore. The drugs must have calmed him down. "Okay, stay in there if you want, but you don't know what you're missing. If you don't want to party, then I guess I'll enjoy it all by myself."

Hope listened by the thin door, her mind swirling.

Is he really going to give up that easily? Maybe he's trying to trick me; maybe he's planning to shoot the door down. But then why should he? I can't stay in this little room forever. He knows I'll have to come out eventually.

Hope sat on the edge of the tub and pulled a towel around her shoulders. She hugged herself and tried to hear what was going on in the room outside. It was quiet for a few minutes and then there was a hard rap on the motel room door, and she could hear voices. It sounded like Vinny. She crept to the door and put her ear against it.

"Just make sure you don't damage the goods, man," Vinny was saying. "Sig'll be here soon, and you'll have some explaining to do."

"She's not cooperating," Hollywood's voice was slurred. "She doesn't want to party."

"Don't worry, I'll look after her," Vinny said. Then the television was turned on and she had to strain to hear what he said next. "I'll get her to play along. Just leave her alone for now. You stay here and chill, and I'll be back in a minute."

Hope listened to the drone of the television. She couldn't hear any other sound. She bit her lip and contemplated her next move.

Maybe Hollywood passed out. Maybe Vinny left the door to the room unlocked. Maybe I can get away before anyone comes back.

Taking a deep breath, she slowly pulled the barrel back and opened the door an inch. She could see Hollywood sitting slumped on the chair, his head rolled back at an awkward angle, and his hands limp at his sides. She couldn't see the gun. Where was the gun? Had Vinny taken it?

Opening the door just wide enough for her to slip through, she tiptoed a few feet and paused, thinking she heard footsteps outside. The door to the room swung open and two hulking men stepped inside. Hope froze and stared in horror at the guns hanging from their belts. She wasn't sure if they had come to kill her or to save her.

Both of the men were wearing dark glasses. The older man had wide shoulders and wore a black baseball cap. The other man had dark, slicked-back hair and wore a shiny, gray suit.

The man in the suit frowned over at Hollywood. "What the hell's wrong with him, Sig?"

"He's a fucking addict," the man named Sig replied, and grabbed Hope's arm. He pulled her toward him.

"So, you're the new girl, huh?" He inspected her, eyes lingering over her delicate face. "Hollywood was right, Rick. She's fresh."

The other man nodded. "Yeah, she's not too bad. As long as she doesn't cause any trouble."

"Where'd Hollywood find you, anyway," Sig asked, his voice hard. "You seem too fresh to be a druggie. And too clean to be a street kid."

Hope watched as Rick adjusted his jacket to cover the gun on his hip. She swallowed and tried to speak but couldn't find her voice.

Sig's pocket beeped. He reached in and pulled out a pack of Camel cigarettes and a cell phone. He glanced at the message displayed on the screen.

"Shit!" He walked to the door and flung it open. "Vinny! Get in here."

Vinny must have been standing guard outside. He stepped inside and nodded at the two big men. "What's up, Sig?"

"Watch the new girl. Rick and I have to go. We've got major problems."

"You got it, man," Vinny said, waiting for Sig and Rick to rush out before closing the door. He turned a metal key in the lock and dropped the key into his front pocket. He looked over at Hope and smiled.

"Don't worry, Hope. I'm not like them. I'm not a druggie, and I'm not a thug."

"Then why are you doing this?" Hope asked, her voice wary.

"It's a long story, but I owe Hollywood. He's been like a brother to me, I guess." Vinny's smile faded. "Although with a brother like him, who needs enemies?"

Hope wasn't sure if he was kidding, but she knew she had to try to win Vinny over. He seemed like the only one that might be willing to help her. If she was nice to Vinny, maybe he'd help her escape. She smiled up at him, about to ask for something to drink when someone knocked on the door.

A look of anger flashed over Vinny's face, making Hope step back. Then, just as quickly, the look was gone, replaced by a reassuring smile.

"Hold on just a minute," he said, crossing to the window and pulling the curtain back a little to peer out into the corridor.

"It's just Big Red, the motel manager. I'll get rid of him and be back." He looked over at Hope and hesitated, before saying, "I'll be right outside, so don't do anything stupid."

Hope nodded and wrapped her arms around herself, trying to look agreeable.

I've got to make him trust me. I've got to convince him to help me.

Vinny stopped at the door and looked back. He motioned to Hollywood's slumped form. He put his finger to his lips and whispered, "And don't wake him up. He can get pretty nasty if he doesn't get his beauty sleep."

Hope nodded again and waited until the door had closed, then walked over to Hollywood and looked down at him. She knew he had a phone in his back pocket. If only she could get hold of it before he woke up. She could call 911 and tell them where she was.

She could even try to call Aunt Eden. Aunt Eden had saved her before, and she would save her again if only Hope could let her know where she was.

But as she stood there thinking, Hollywood murmured in his sleep and adjusted his body over the pocket that held his phone.

Hope sighed and crossed over to the old television set, changing the station to the local news. Maybe they were already looking for her. The screen showed a young, female reporter in a navy-blue raincoat standing in front of a Channel 10 news van. The reporter held an umbrella in one hand and a microphone in the other. Hope turned up the volume, straining to hear the reporter, who was visibly excited.

"...the body of a teenage girl was found in the Diablo River earlier today. Although we are still waiting for an official briefing from the WBPD, if the reports are true, this would be the second victim found in the town of Willow Bay this week. Our sources tell us that the gruesome discovery was made by a local dog walker..."

Hope stared in horror as the cameras panned out and showed the trees that surrounded the river's edge. Crime scene tape blocked the reporters and camera crew from getting any closer, but she caught glimpses of the dark water as it lapped hungrily at the soggy riverbank.

Hope looked toward the closed curtains, imagining the canal beyond. A terrible certainty grew in her mind.

Those girls had been at this motel, too. Somehow, they ended up dead in the river, and if I don't find a way out of here, I'll be next.

CHAPTER THIRTY-FIVE

Nessa jumped out of her unmarked Dodge and splashed toward the front door of Eden's house, just as a brilliant bolt of lightning lit up the sky. Yellow crime scene tape blocked her progress, and she looked up to see Officer Andy Fordham waving her around to the side of the house.

"Over here, Detective," the young officer called, his face pale and wet under a dark rain jacket. "We had to cordon off the front entrance and the garage until the CSI team arrives, but we've set up a path in through the back."

"Good job, Andy," Nessa said, glad she hadn't contaminated the crime scene by tramping her wet shoes through any evidence that may have been left behind.

She followed Andy, passing through a wooden fence before reaching the back deck, which led into the house. Leo Steele's tall, lean frame filled the doorway.

"Evening, Detective."

Nessa considered hiding her surprise at seeing the lawyer, but then decided she didn't have time to act coy. "What are *you* doing here, Mr. Steele? Has Ms. Winthrop retained your services?"

"No, I'm here to support Eden as a friend, not as her lawyer."

"Friends, huh? I'm amazed she'll even speak to you after you represented her sister's killer," Nessa said, pushing her way past Leo and stepping into the big, brightly lit kitchen.

"Eden and I have made our peace." After a pause, he added, "And I'm also here to try to find out who killed Jessica. I don't think it's just a coincidence that Eden's teenage niece has been kidnapped the same week two girls have gone missing, and my client's daughter has turned up dead."

Nessa cringed at his words. Not one but two girls had turned up dead, actually. She knew she'd have to tell both Leo and Eden about Brandi Long, and soon.

She'd tried to keep the scene off-limits to news crews for as long as possible, to avoid the crime scene being compromised, but the local stations wouldn't hesitate to interrupt their regular broadcast with this type of breaking news. After all, a dead body could be used to help drive their ratings.

"Where's Ms. Winthrop?" Nessa asked Officer Fordham, who had followed her inside. "And the woman who called it in?"

"They're in the living room talking to Detective Jankowski," Fordham responded.

"Based on Sage Parker's initial statement we cordoned off the front entrance and the area leading out to the garage. She said two men came up the front walk, stood inside the foyer, and then walked the girl over to the garage. They pulled a car into the garage, put the girl in the car, and drove away."

"Was she able to identify the car?" Nessa asked, anxious to send out an APB as soon as possible.

"She just said it was an old silver sedan. Couldn't give a make, model, or license tag number," Fordham said, frustration obvious in his voice. "Officer Eddings is out canvassing the neighbors to see if anyone may have seen the car."

"Good. Let me know right away if you find a witness." She moved toward the hall and Leo followed her into the living room. She needed to talk to Sage Parker to uncover more details. Nessa realized they had a chance to get an Amber Alert issued if they could provide enough information.

Eden huddled on a plush, white sofa beside Duke and a boy that looked to be only a few years older than Cole. Nessa realized he must be Eden's nephew, Devon. She noticed the boy's eyes were glassy. He didn't seem to hear Eden's soft voice as she soothed him, and Nessa decided he must be in shock.

Can hardly blame him. God forbid one of my boys ever has to face something like this.

Eden raised her eyes to see Nessa approach, and the raw hopefulness that filled them unnerved her.

She thinks I'm the one who can find her niece. She's counting on me to bring the girl home.

Nessa perched on the edge of the sofa and took Eden's hand. "I'm so sorry, Eden. I know you're going through hell right now. But believe me, I'm going to do everything in my power to find your girl."

She looked around the room, wondering where Jankowski had gone. Fordham had said he was in the living room, interviewing the witnesses, but as far as she could see he was nowhere in sight.

"Has Detective Jankowski spoken to you yet?" Nessa asked Eden.

She knew they needed to be patient and methodical, take the necessary time to gather all the relevant facts so they wouldn't go charging off in the wrong direction, but her nerves shouted at her to hurry. Precious minutes and seconds were slipping away, and the probability of bringing Hope back alive was slipping away with them.

"No, we haven't had a chance to speak yet, but I just talked to Sage Parker, the children's nanny," Jankowski said from behind her, making her jump. He must have come down the carpeted stairs.

So much for my cat-like instincts, Nessa thought as she turned to stare up at him.

"Let's go in the kitchen and talk in private with Ms. Winthrop," Nessa said, looking at Devon with concern. "Officer Fordham, can you be sure to watch over Devon while we're talking?"

"Sure," Fordham said, summoning a friendly smile for the boy. "We'll be fine."

But Devon didn't look fine. He kept his eyes cast downward, looking at the floor and rocking back and forth. Duke sat next to him, the big golden retriever a familiar presence that should provide comfort, but the boy seemed oblivious to anything around him.

Nessa was worried Devon may be permanently traumatized, but there was little she could do to comfort him now. The best thing for him was to get his sister back. That had to be her only focus.

"Andy, make sure you watch out for the nanny, too. She's still upstairs and is pretty upset," Jankowski ordered.

Then Nessa heard him say something in a low voice. "And don't let her go anywhere. Whatever happens, don't let her leave."

Nessa raised her eyebrows as they walked toward the kitchen behind Eden. "What was that all about?"

Jankowski leaned so close she could smell his musky cologne. "The nanny can't remember much, but what she does remember just doesn't add up. There's something about her story that bothers me."

Nessa frowned back at him, wanting to ask more, but deciding she needed to give her full attention to Eden for the time being. They needed to tell her about the second body that had been found that morning before she saw it on the news.

Leo Steele was sitting at the table with a notepad and pencil. He had been making notes and looked impatient as the detectives followed Eden into the room.

"We need to figure out where they may be taking her," Leo said, tearing the top sheet of paper off his notebook and crumpling it into a ball.

Jankowski put up his hand in a placating gesture. "Hold on now, Leo. I know you're anxious to find out who killed Jessica Carmichael, but we can't jump to conclusions. We can't assume the men who took Hope had anything to do with Jessica's murder."

"Of course, they're related," Leo fumed. "Eden reports that Jessica's friend is missing, and she tries to identify Jessica's body, and then her own niece is kidnapped days later? Do you seriously expect me to believe it's just coincidental timing?"

Jankowski looked ready to fire back at Leo, but Nessa stepped between the two men and raised her voice. "A fifteen-year-old girl is missing and needs our help. So, just stop the macho bullshit!"

She looked Eden in the eyes, making sure she had her attention. "Before we go on we need to give you an update. You see, the body of another teenage girl was found in the Diablo River this morning. She'd been strangled."

Eden gasped and sank into the chair next to Leo. Nessa could see the horror dawn on Eden's face as she realized what this might mean.

"Did the same person who killed Jessica kill this other girl?" Eden asked, her voice strained. "Is this the work of some kind of serial killer?"

Nessa nodded. "There are similarities that make us think the homicides are most likely the work of the same perpetrator. Both girls were strangled and left in or by the river. Both girls had visible signs of drug use."

Jankowski cleared his throat and loosened his tie. "The story on the latest river girl just broke on the news. And, well, some of the gorier details have been leaked."

"What do you mean?" Leo asked.

"An alligator got to the poor girl before we did." Nessa decided to just say what needed to be said and get it over with. "The gator was swimming around with the girl's arm in his mouth. A woman walking her dogs saw and called it in."

Nessa could see the panic rising in Eden's eyes. Her chest was heaving in and out, and Leo put his arm around her.

"Eden, just breathe," Leo said, immediately coaching the distressed woman as if they were in a Lamaze class. "Try not to think about anything. Just concentrate on breathing."

"I'm okay," Eden said, shrugging off Leo's arm, but her breathing was still heavy, and her eyes were wet. She turned to Nessa.

"Do you think Hope's kidnapping is related to these murders, and to Star's disappearance? Is that why you're telling me this now?'

"We can't be sure, yet," Nessa said. "We need to find out more...but, we do need to consider the possibility."

"The victim found today has already been identified through fingerprints. She had an arrest record for drug possession." Nessa hesitated, knowing she shouldn't be sharing this type of confidential information with a civilian. "We can't release her name yet pending notification of her next of kin."

"Let me guess," Eden said, her voice thick. "Was the girl's name Brandi?"

Nessa and Jankowski stared at each other in shock.

"Why would you say that?" Jankowski demanded. "What do you know about the girl in the river?"

"I know that a girl named Brandi went missing from Clear Horizons, the same place that Star was staying before she came to Mercy Harbor asking for help," Eden said, raising her chin to glare at Jankowski.

"And I know that Star's real name is Stacey Moore and that she was friends with Jessica Carmichael before she disappeared."

"We sent officers to check out Clear Horizons earlier today based on the tip we got from Leo yesterday," Jankowski said, frowning down at Eden. "I haven't had a chance to review the report yet."

"Well, I went by there today and one of the neighbors said that the assistant manager, Trevor Bane, likes to hang out with the young female residents. The neighbor claims that Trevor singled out Star, or Stacey as he called her, before she suddenly moved out. He said another girl named Brandi had gone missing as well."

"So, who is this neighbor that knows so much?" Jankowski asked, "We can send someone over to interview him right away."

"His name is Charles. I don't remember his last name."

"Wyatt," Leo muttered. "His name is Charles Wyatt."

Jankowski narrowed his eyes. "Have you talked to this guy, too?"

"I met him the other day," Leo admitted. "Seemed like he had some anger issues."

"What's his address?" Jankowski was typing in a message on his phone as he spoke.

"I don't know." Eden clasped her hands together in her lap. "He just said he lived near Clear Horizons. That he'd gone to school with Trevor. Oh, and he said they both had gone to school with Tiffany Clarke."

Nessa's heart jumped at the words. Could they finally have found a solid connection between the Clarke case and the new murders?

"We need a description of this man right away," Nessa said, trying to keep her voice even. "We'll send Ingram and Ortiz over to talk to Trevor Bane and to find out more about Charles."

Eden's voice trembled as she gave Jankowski a description of the big man she'd seen in the park. She then crossed to the counter and pulled out a sheet of paper from her purse.

"This is the information I found out about Star. Her real name's Stacey Moore, and she stayed with her mother and little brother at one of our shelters two years ago."

Eden took a deep breath as she handed the paper to Nessa. "Their new address is in there. Please keep the information confidential. As you'll see, the family was trying to escape the mother's ex-boyfriend. A real lowlife named Buddy Jones. He may still be trying to track them down."

Nessa remembered the call she'd gotten earlier from the crime lab.

"The techs checked those shoes you turned in. The ones Star was wearing. A common GPS tracking device had been tucked into the lining. The techs are going to see if they can trace the source, but it's doubtful."

Eden exhaled a tortured moan. "That must be how these guys found out where Star had gone. It must be how they found *me*. They must have followed me home, must have seen Hope."

Nessa strained to make sense of it all. She needed to think fast and figure out what was going on before another girl ended up dead.

Her eyes rested on a picture of Hope displayed on the refrigerator. It showed a strikingly pretty young girl holding up an honor roll ribbon. An image flashed into her mind of the photo taped to the whiteboard next to the other pictures in the River Girl's Investigation room.

Her stomach lurched, and she had to fight off a wave of nausea. She couldn't let another young girl die. She couldn't tape yet another picture on that whiteboard. She had to piece together the information in time to save Hope.

* * *

After Leo had followed Eden back into the living room to check on Devon, Jankowski took out his cell phone and called Ingram.

"I hear you guys got called out. What's the status?" Ingram asked, his voice tense.

"A fifteen-year-old female was abducted from her house at gunpoint. We're still at the scene. Based on what we've uncovered so far, we figure the abduction might be linked to the River Girls Investigation."

Jankowski filled Ingram in on their suspicions, and they agreed that Ingram and Ortiz would track down Trevor Bane and bring him in for formal questioning. They would also attempt to locate Charles Wyatt and get a statement.

"Hey man, before you go, can you do me a favor?" Jankowski asked. By the time he turned back to Nessa he'd gotten Ingram to run initial checks on Buddy Jones and Trevor Bane.

"Ingram verified the information Eden Winthrop gave us," he said, jotting some notes on a small pad of paper. "Buddy Jones was sentenced to two years for domestic battery, aggravated assault, and violation of a restraining order. The victim was one Trisha Moore."

"He get out recently?" Nessa asked.

"He was released over a year ago, but he's still on probation." Jankowski checked his notes. "According to the latest probation report, he's unemployed and lives with his brother in a trailer park off Good Shephard Highway."

Nessa looked at the paper that Eden had handed her. She studied Trisha Moore's name and address.

Is this where Stacey Moore has been these last few days? Did she run back home after dumping the tracker on her shoes? Or is she already dead and waiting for us to find her in the river? Nessa knew there was only one way to find out.

"Jankowski, why don't you drive over to Trisha Moore's place? See if she's heard from Stacey. She may not even know the girl moved out of Clear Horizons. If that doesn't lead to anything, you can go by and see what Buddy Jones has been up to."

"I should stay here and try to get more information out of Sage Parker or Devon," Jankowski said. "They're the best leads we have. They have to be able to provide something more useful."

"You go and try to find Star. Let me see if I can get more information from Sage." Nessa hoped the young nanny would be more comfortable talking to a woman.

Jankowski could be intimidating when he questioned witnesses, and Nessa liked to use a gentler approach. Did that make them the stereotypical good cop, bad cop team?

"Okay, then, I'll go by Trisha Moore's first," Jankowski agreed.

"You shouldn't go on your own," Nessa said, standing up. "There's been too many dead bodies and people running around with guns in Willow Bay lately for you to be out there on your own. Call Reinhardt and see if he'll back you up."

Jankowski seemed ready to object, but Nessa raised her hand. "Don't bother arguing. I'm heading up this investigation and I can't let you go on your own. Reinhardt's the only other detective that knows what's going on, and Chief Kramer already gave the okay for him to work with us."

"Fine," Jankowski said, gathering his notepad, papers, and pen and stuffing everything into his black leather backpack. "I'll call Reinhardt on the way back to the station. I'll ask him to meet me there."

Nessa watched the paper with Trisha Moore's address on it disappear into Jankowski's bag. She felt a pang of worry.

"Oh, and Jankowski? Remember not to give the Moore's address to anyone. Trisha Moore is most likely still in hiding from Buddy Jones. And make sure you tell Reinhardt to keep it under wraps, too."

"Yes, boss," Jankowski shot back with more than a little sarcasm as he opened the back door. "Whatever you say."

Nessa watched the door close behind him, a frown marring her forehead. She thought again about Jankowski's reaction to working with Reinhardt. She knew the older detective wasn't exactly a barrel of laughs, but he seemed competent. So, what was Jankowski's problem? With two new murders, an abduction, and a missing girl, they didn't have time for internal politics.

See why I need you back here, Barker, she thought, knowing even as she did, that her old partner may not ever come back.

A wave of loneliness washed over her, and she thought of Jerry and the boys at home, probably having dinner by now. She picked up the phone and waited for the voice that always seemed to calm her down, no matter how bad things got.

"You holding up, babe?" Jerry asked, sounding concerned. "I've seen the news, about the second girl found in the river. It's horrible."

"Yeah, it's bad." Nessa felt tears sting her eyes. She blinked hard and cleared her throat. "The day has been a nightmare, and I'm not sure when it'll be over. You go ahead and give the boys a goodnight kiss from me. And, Jerry? Don't wait up. It's gonna be a late night."

CHAPTER THIRTY-SIX

Reggie's Mini-Cooper slid to a stop inches from the black and white police cruiser blocking Eden Winthrop's driveway. Flashing blue lights illuminated a torrent of raindrops spewing from the cloud-darkened sky.

Reggie stepped out of the car, popped open a bright red umbrella to shield her silk dress, and refused to think about the damage the relentless downpour would cause to her eye-wateringly expensive pumps.

Eden needs me, she told herself, wincing as she stepped into a puddle. *Shoes are replaceable - friends are not.*

"I'm Reggie..." she started to say to a young police officer standing beside the cruiser. Then she paused; the jarring sight of the yellow crime scene tape along Eden's front walk had taken her breath away. The whole scene felt surreal, like she'd walked onto the set of a horror movie.

The officer stared at her with raised eyebrows. After an awkward silence, Reggie regained her composure.

"Um, sorry. I'm Dr. Reggie Horn and Eden Winthrop is expecting me."

"Oh, yes, Dr. Horn. Detective Ainsley told me you'd be coming. Follow me."

The officer turned and led Reggie around the side of the house. She followed muddy shoe prints onto the back deck and into the kitchen.

As Reggie entered through the back door, Eden was talking in hushed tones to a woman in a wrinkled black suit. The woman's disheveled auburn curls and short, softly rounded frame contrasted sharply with Eden's golden hair and tall, striking figure.

Earth mother meets Greek goddess, Reggie thought distractedly as she approached the women, not wanting to interrupt, but anxious to let Eden know she was there.

"The crime scene technicians will be working for a few more hours I'm sure," Nessa said to Eden as Reggie approached.

"They are searching inch by inch to try and find any trace evidence the abductors may have left behind in the house, and they'll be searching the immediate vicinity of the neighborhood as well."

Reggie met Eden's eyes over the woman's shoulder.

"Reggie, what am I going to do?" Eden cried out as Reggie hurried to wrap her arms around Eden's trembling shoulders. "Hope is gone, Reggie. They took her."

"I know, honey, I know," Reggie soothed as she patted Eden's back. "But we're gonna find her and bring her home. She's gonna be fine."

Reggie turned her eyes toward the woman in the wrinkled black suit. "Are you with the police?"

"Yes, I'm Detective Ainsley." Nessa held out a firm hand, but her voice revealed fatigue. "You can call me Nessa."

"And I'm Dr. Horn, but please call me Reggie." She felt a flash of sympathy for the disheveled detective as she took the offered hand.

The woman looked drained, and Reggie wondered how she coped with such a stressful job. Did the responsibilities listed in her job description include finding missing children and hunting down killers? She imagined that very few people would be willing to take on the life-and-death role.

"I was just telling Eden she should take Devon to stay somewhere else for the night. Our crime scene techs are still working, and the poor boy looks knackered." Nessa met her eyes, and her worried expression scared Reggie.

"Is Devon okay? Can I see him?" Reggie asked, moving toward the living room.

"Oh Reggie, he won't say a word," Eden said as tears filled her eyes. "I don't know what to say to him. What can I tell him?"

"Let's take him to my house and see if, away from all this, he'll talk to me," Reggie said.

She'd counseled both Hope and Devon in the year following their parents' deaths, and she'd come to know them and love them. So much so that when Eden had requested that Reggie become the children's guardian in the event of Eden's death, Reggie had instantly agreed.

They were family now, and it was up to her to make sure Devon was taken care of while they searched for Hope. If his sister wasn't found safely, Reggie wasn't sure how Devon would cope.

"That sounds like a good idea," Nessa said, adding, "I can have one of our officers escort you and stand guard if that would make you feel better."

Reggie jumped when a strong voice spoke up behind her, and she turned to see Leo Steele.

"No need for a guard. I'll go with them and make sure they get settled in. If Eden's okay with it, I can even stay overnight to make sure they're safe."

Reggie watched as Leo searched Eden's eyes for her answer and was surprised by the intimacy she detected between them. She had assumed Eden would hate Preston Lancaster's lawyer. She felt a spark of indignation.

He's not nearly good enough for her. If rumors are true, he's already dated and dumped half the women in town.

"Thanks, Leo, I'd appreciate that," Eden said, her voice trembling on the words. "I don't know how I'll make it through the night not knowing where Hope is and what might be happening to her."

Reggie moved to embrace Eden, but Leo beat her to it. His big arms enveloped Eden, pulling her against his broad chest and making her tall form seem small and delicate against him.

Nessa watched with an expression of disbelief as the defense attorney comforted Eden, and Reggie realized the detective was just as stunned as she was.

Was the whole town going crazy?

As Eden left the room to pack an overnight bag, Reggie turned to Leo. "It may not be my place to say this, but I can't help myself. I love that woman like a sister, and she is vulnerable at the best of times. But now? In the middle of this nightmare? She's not ready to make any important decisions. And she certainly doesn't need anyone taking advantage of her."

Leo's face darkened at her words. "I'm offering her support and comfort. That's all. I'd never hurt her or take advantage of her. She needs all the friends she can get right now, so that's what I'm trying to be. Just a *friend*."

Reggie narrowed her eyes and tilted her head as she returned his gaze. "Make sure you keep it that way, Mr. Steele. That woman has already been through enough heartache and has experienced enough pain for two lifetimes. She doesn't need the likes of you rolling in and causing more."

Nessa stood to the side, averting her eyes. When Leo turned away, the detective offered Reggie a quick thumbs-up, before stepping onto the back deck. Reggie watched as Nessa spoke with a tall, hunky man in suit pants and a dress shirt with the sleeves rolled up. He had tousled blondish hair and a shadow of a beard.

One of WBPD's finest? she wondered, straining to catch what he was discussing with Nessa.

She could hear Nessa's voice grow more heated. "Look, Jankowski. I talked to Sage Parker and she doesn't know anything else. Sure, she's flustered, but that's to be expected. The girl she was supposed to protect got abducted on her watch. She feels terrible. But what good will it do to detain her at this point?'

"I don't like the idea of her going off with the family. Something feels wrong," the man said, running a big hand through his hair.

"Wow, you sure have a lot of feelings all of a sudden," Nessa said, the fatigue clear in her voice.

"First you have a feeling that Natalie Lorenzo's murder isn't connected to the River Girls case, and now you have a feeling that Sage Parker is hiding something? With all these sudden feelings I might start to think you're turning soft on me, Jankowski."

"Yeah, real funny, Nessa." Jankowski shook his head in frustration. "But don't blame me if you fail to follow up on something that just might have saved Hope Lancaster's life."

Before Reggie could hear more, Leo pushed past her with an overnight bag in each hand. Eden followed him through the kitchen, guiding Devon and Sage toward the back door. Duke scurried through as well, his golden tail disappearing into the dark night beyond the deck.

Reggie watched as Leo helped Sage, Devon, and Duke get settled in the backseat of his BMW, while Eden strapped herself into the front passenger seat. Opening the umbrella against the persistent rain, she motioned for Eden to roll down the window.

"I'll follow right behind you, dear," she said, glancing over at Leo with a stern expression. "You don't drive too fast, Mr. Steele. And don't stop for anyone."

Leo looked over at her, the lights from the dashboard reflected in his dark eyes. He reached over and opened his glove compartment and took out a sleek, gray gun.

"If anyone tries to stop us," he said in a hard voice, "they'll have to get past this first."

Eden shrank against the seat, her terrified eyes glued to the gun, as Leo pushed the button to roll up the window. He kept his eyes on Reggie for a long beat before the car began to roll away from the curb.

Heart pounding, Reggie hurried to the Mini Cooper, jumped in, and smashed her foot on the accelerator.

* * *

The rain had slowed to a soft drizzle by the time they'd all settled into Reggie's comfortable farmhouse. They had decided that Eden and Devon would share the guest bedroom while Sage would sleep on the pull-out sofa in Reggie's study. Leo said he preferred to sleep on the big sectional in the front room. That way he'd hear any unusual sounds and would be ready to confront any intruders that might try to enter.

Reggie was waiting to get Leo alone to tell him that she didn't want his gun in her house. She hated guns and refused to own one. Her alarm system would have to suffice as protection tonight. Then tomorrow they'd have to talk to the police about getting an official guard assigned to watch over Eden. Having a hot-headed lawyer waving a gun at every creak and groan of the old house just wasn't safe for any of them.

"I'm going to take Duke for a walk," Sage announced as she entered the kitchen where Reggie was making a pot of coffee. Reggie had figured Eden would want to stay awake as late as possible in case there was any news on Hope. Coffee would help.

"Okay, but you'd better take an umbrella," Reggie advised, pointing to a rack by the door. "There's a spare one there."

Leo entered just as the door closed behind Sage and Duke. "Where's she going?"

"Just taking Duke for a walk. He needs to get outside and take care of business." Reggie opened her mouth to voice her concern about the gun when Eden walked in and stared at her in dismay.

"Devon still won't talk to me, and he refuses to eat the soup you made," Eden said, her eyes beseeching Reggie for help.

"Let me talk to him," Reggie offered, stirring cream into a cup of coffee and sitting it on the table for Eden. "You sit down and drink this."

But Eden ignored the coffee and followed Reggie into the dining room with Leo close behind her. Devon was sitting at the table, his hands in his lap and a blank expression on his face. Reggie sat in the chair next to him and took his small hand in hers. His hand was cold, and she could feel a slight tremor.

"Oh Devon, my sweet boy," she soothed, suddenly remembering the way he'd clung to her and cried as a frightened five-year-old who missed his mother. She would never forget his sad blue eyes when he'd asked where his mommy had gone, and could he go there too.

Seeing him like this again, facing yet another family tragedy, broke her heart. She smoothed a lock of silky hair back from his forehead and put a gentle hand under his chin, turning his face toward her.

"I'm here now, Devon, and Aunt Eden is here, too. You're safe, and we're not going to let anything happen to you. Everything's going to be all right." Reggie looked into his eyes, speaking in a calm, slow voice.

She squeezed his hand and pulled him closer until his small head lay against her thin shoulder. Slowly she rocked back and forth, murmuring the same words of comfort over and over. She could hear Eden's soft sobs behind her but didn't turn her head. Devon needed her full attention. He needed to know he was safe.

"It's okay, Aunt Eden," Devon's small voice broke the stillness in the room. "Please don't cry anymore."

Eden hurried to Devon and knelt in front of him, taking his hands in hers and holding them to her cheek. "I won't cry anymore, Devon. Not if you're with me. We can be strong and get through this together."

Reggie felt Devon relax against her, the trembling gone for the time being. She caught Leo's gaze over the top of Eden's head, but then looked away when she saw the glimmer of tears in his eyes. The hard-boiled lawyer wouldn't want her to see that he actually had a heart.

"Aunt Eden? I need to tell you something," Devon whispered, looking down at his hands. "But you might be mad at me."

"I could never be mad at you, honey," Eden reassured him. "Whatever it is, you can tell me."

"I...I saw the men who took Hope," Devon said, his eyes welling with tears. "I saw them and...and...I saw the gun...and I hid. I ran back to my room and I hid under the bed. I let them take Hope. I didn't even try to stop them."

Guilty sobs wracked Devon's small frame and Reggie hugged him to her again, starting to understand why he'd been so reluctant to talk. He must be terrified they would blame him for not saving Hope. He must think it was his fault she had been taken.

"Oh Devon, it isn't your fault, baby," Reggie reassured him, holding him even tighter. "You couldn't have stopped two grown strangers with a gun from taking Hope. You were right to hide and save yourself. It was the only choice you could make."

"But...they weren't really strangers," Devon said, biting his lip. "Sage knew them; they said they were her friends."

Reggie and Eden stared at each other in disbelief. Determined not to scare the boy even more, Reggie kept her expression neutral, kept her voice measured and quiet. "Are you sure, Devon? Did you hear anything else they said?"

"The mean one...I think his name was Hollywood...said that Sage owed him money." Devon's eyes widened at the memory. "He's the one that had the gun."

At Devon's words, Leo hurried over and grasped one of the boy's thin arms. "Are you sure that was his name? Are you sure he was called Hollywood?"

Devon shrank back in fear, pulling back to hide his face against Reggie's shoulder. Reggie scowled up at Leo, but before she could say anything, the back door opened, and Sage's voice could be heard in the kitchen urging Duke to come in from the rain.

Devon clutched at Reggie and lifted his anguished face to stare back at Eden, as he cried out, "Sage let her friends take Hope. She let them drive away, and she didn't stop them. She didn't even call 911 until I came down and begged her to call."

A gasp came from the doorway, and Reggie turned to see Sage, wet and disheveled from the rain, her face pale in the dim light. She stood still as if frozen in place, and then sunk to the ground in uncontrollable sobs.

"I'm sorry," she gasped out, her face hidden in her hands. "I'm so sorry."

Leo turned to stare at the crumpled figure, his face a mask of rage, and Reggie wondered where he'd put the gun. He looked ready to use it as he stalked toward Sage and dragged her to her feet.

"You tell us who has Hope, and where she is, now!" Leo demanded, his voice loud but under control. Reggie saw him glancing over at Devon, who was now cowering in her arms, and she realized Leo was trying to keep himself in check for the boy's sake. He wasn't going to do anything to further upset Devon.

"I don't know where they took her," Sage moaned, wiping the tears from her face. "And they *aren't* my friends. But I do know them. Or, I used to know them. But that was when I was an addict."

"An addict?" Eden asked, her voice incredulous. "You're a drug addict?"

"I used to be, but not anymore. I'm clean now. I have been since way before I started working for you," Sage insisted, her eyes pleading with Eden.

"You brought these drug dealers into my home? You let them take Hope?" The hurt and anger in Eden's voice were palpable in the room. Reggie knew heightened emotions could bring on a full-fledged panic attack at any minute. She had to calm things down.

"We don't have time to talk about that," Reggie urged. "We need to find Hope *now*. Sage, who are these guys? What are their names and where can we find them?"

Leo broke in, his voice impatient. "Who's this Hollywood guy? Is he a drug dealer? Where does he live?"

"His name isn't Hollywood," Sage swallowed hard. "He just uses that name because he thinks he's good-looking enough to be a movie star."

"What's his real name?" Leo demanded, his voice hard.

"His real name is Trevor," Sage whispered, her eyes filling again with tears. "Trevor Bane. I met him at the sober house where I stayed last year."

Eden moaned and clutched Leo's arm. "He's the one that Jessica and Star talked about. He's the one that knew Brandi, the girl they found in the river today."

Sage looked confused. "Who are Jessica and Star? And what do you mean, they found someone in the river?"

Reggie jumped up, pulling Devon with her. "I need to take Devon into the other room to lay down."

She couldn't let Devon hear about the girls who had been found in the river. He couldn't know that Hope had been taken by someone who may be a killer. Leo nodded in understanding. He gripped Sage by the arm, leading her toward the kitchen.

"Yes, you take care of Devon, Reggie. Make sure he rests and stays inside. I'll call and request police protection." Leo looked down at Sage with hard eyes. "We'll need someone here before I can leave to escort Sage to the police station."

"Okay, I'll get Devon settled into the guest room, and Duke can keep us company."

Reggie led Devon toward the hall, but she looked back, not liking the way Eden was struggling to catch her breath. Was this the beginning of a panic attack? Could this terrible night get any worse?

CHAPTER THIRTY-SEVEN

Leo waited for Reggie to disappear into the other room with Devon and Duke before turning back to Eden. She was slumped in a chair, her head in her hands. She was in no shape to call anyone. He would have to call the phone number listed on Nessa's card.

The detective had said to call if Eden changed her mind about needing police protection. He took out his cell phone and dialed the number. No answer. He left an urgent message, then decided to call the station. They couldn't afford to sit on the information Sage had given them about Trevor Bane.

"Willow Bay Police Department, may I help you?" a perky voice asked.

"I'm trying to reach Detective Nessa Ainsley or Detective Simon Jankowski. It's about an abduction they're working on," Leo said, impatient to talk to someone who could help him.

"Oh, yes, the whole department is on alert. The switchboard has been crazy. I'll transfer you to the hotline that's handling the case." Before Leo could reply, he heard an automated voice telling him that all lines were busy, but that his call was important.

Leo disconnected the call and dialed 911. Within minutes he'd arranged for a police car to be sent out to the house to guard Devon and Reggie. He was assured that Nessa or Jankowski would return his call as soon as they were available.

He stuck his phone back in his pocket and turned to Sage. It was all he could do not to shake the young woman. His anger simmered as he thought of the hours wasted by her silence.

If only she had told them who had taken Hope immediately, they might have had a chance to catch the abductors before they could hole up somewhere. Now, hours later, the men were surely laying low. And who knew what they would have done with Hope by now.

"Sit down and stop the *poor little me* routine," Leo demanded, gesturing to the sofa.

"You're no victim in all this. You deliberately withheld information and obstructed an active investigation into the abduction of a minor. That alone should earn you a trip to prison. And who knows what else you've done with your drug-dealing boyfriend."

"Trevor wasn't my boyfriend. He's the son of the lady that runs this place called Clear Horizons. It's supposed to be a sober house, and my mom knew the woman who runs it."

Sage looked sad at the mention of her mother, but Leo wasn't going to fall for her sob story.

"Anyway, my mom thought I could kick my habit by living there, instead of paying for rehab."

"So, what do you know about Trevor?" Leo asked, anxious to hear something that could be a lead. Even the smallest piece of information might be the clue they needed to track down Trevor.

"He called himself the assistant manager but that was a joke. He wasn't there much, and when he was, he was trying to hook up with the younger girls. I heard he gave drugs to some of them and I asked him to get me some. I hadn't quite kicked the habit I guess."

Sage cast a quick glance over at Eden, but Eden still had her head in her hands.

"I stayed there about a month getting high regularly before my mom wised up and got her insurance to pay for a real rehab program," Sage said. "When I left I owed Trevor some money that I couldn't pay, so I just skipped out. But I don't know how he found me here."

"Do you know who he got the drugs from?" Leo asked. "Did you know his supplier?"

"Trevor always acted cagey about how he got the drugs, but by the time I moved out I'd seen this old guy stop by a few times and drop off a bag of something. I assumed it was drugs."

Eden's head raised at Sage's words. Her voice was faint as she asked, "Was it an older guy wearing a black baseball cap and dark glasses?"

"Yeah, that sounds right. I heard Trevor call him Sig once, but I'm not sure if that was his real name," Sage said, nodding.

Eden stood up and walked into the kitchen without explanation. She was back within minutes carrying her laptop. She set the laptop on the table and turned it on. She clicked on an email and opened the attached file. A grainy video started to play. Eden turned the laptop toward Sage so that she could view the screen.

"Is that the man who had come by Clear Horizons?" Eden asked. "Does he look like the man Trevor called Sig?"

Sage studied the video for a second then nodded again. "Yeah, that's him. Or it looks exactly like him."

Eden put her hand to her throat, as if she was struggling to breathe. "That's the man who broke into my office last night. And he's likely the same man Star mentioned to me when she came to Shutter Street. She was scared someone named Sig would come after her. He's one of the men she was running from, and now he might have Hope."

Leo stared at Sage, trying to decide if he believed her story. *Was she one of Trevor's victims, or his accomplice? Was the man called Sig in on it, too?*

"So, was Sig with Trevor when he took Hope?" Leo asked, watching Sage carefully for her reaction.

"No, Trevor came here with Vinny," Sage said. "Vinny used to hang around Clear Horizons all the time. He told me once that he was like a brother to Trevor, but I don't think they were related. He doesn't look anything like Trevor. And he always seemed pretty quiet. A decent guy. Not a hustler like Trevor."

"You can give the police a full description of this Vinny when we get there," Leo said, wondering how soon the police officer would arrive to watch the house.

He wanted to get Sage to the station, and then start looking for Hope himself. He couldn't just sit around while Jessica's killer took the life of another innocent girl.

Eden spoke up, her voice shaky. "Leo, do you think Trisha Moore's ex, Buddy Jones, could have anything to do with all this? Could he possibly be calling himself Sig to hide his identity? Could he be Star's connection to Clear Horizons?"

Leo considered the question.

Was Buddy Jones a serial killer and drug dealer as well as an abusive creep?

From what Eden had found out in Mercy Harbor's database, Buddy Jones had likely been released from prison within the last year, so the timing made it possible, if unlikely. But it was impossible to know for sure based on the limited information they had.

The police had jumped to the wrong conclusion about his father, and Leo knew the tragic consequences all too well. He refused to make the same foolish mistake himself. They would need more information before they could determine if Buddy Jones was a viable suspect.

"I just don't know," Leo admitted, his mood darkening with his growing frustration. He turned to Sage.

"Why didn't you tell us about Trevor and Vinny before? Why didn't you tell the police when they showed up?"

"I know it was wrong, but I was scared," Sage said, recoiling at the hostility in his voice.

"Trevor threatened me with a gun. He told me to say that Hope had run away. He said if I didn't, he would kill my mother, then come back and kill Eden and Devon. I didn't know what to do."

Leo prepared to fire back a response, but then he heard panicked wheezing behind him. He turned to see Eden struggling to catch her breath.

"They threatened to kill Devon?" she gasped, her eyes wide. Beads of sweat had formed on her forehead, and she swayed on her feet. Leo rushed to her side, putting strong arms around her and leading her to the nearest chair.

"Sit down, Eden, you'll be okay," he told her, trying to decide if he should call out to Reggie for help.

Can someone die of a panic attack? Can this level of anxiety be dangerous?

"Her pills," Sage said, eyes huge with fear. "She told me she has the pills in case the anxiety gets too bad. They're in her purse."

She charged into the kitchen and returned seconds later carrying a small prescription bottle. Leo took the bottle and read the label. He opened the child-proof cap and shook out two pills.

"Take these, Eden," he said, taking her hand and pressing the pills into her palm.

Sage appeared beside him with a glass of water and set it on the table in front of Eden.

"Please, Eden, please take the pills," Sage urged. "I'm so sorry. I'm so sorry about all of this."

Eden's hand clenched around the pills and then opened, spilling them onto the floor. She inhaled and wheezed, over and over, clutching out at Leo and Sage as she fought for air.

"It's all...my...fault..." Eden gasped out, just loud enough for Leo to make out. "Hope's been...taken, and...it's all my fault."

Leo's jaw clenched in frustration. He knew she must be blaming herself for bringing a recovering drug addict into her home, and for not vetting Star before letting her into the shelter. The knowledge that she'd put her niece's life in danger, and may have failed her sister after all, must be killing her.

"Eden, this isn't your fault," Leo said, bringing his face close to hers. "You've got to be strong. You can fix this. *We* can fix this. But only if you stay calm. Now breathe..."

Leo inhaled deeply, placing Eden's hand on his warm chest. He held her hand against him as he breathed in and out slowly and smoothly, murmuring instructions.

"Breathe in and breathe out. That's it, you've got this. You're going to be just fine."

After a few minutes, Eden's breathing slowed. She leaned her head forward, resting it on Leo's chest, and he placed a strong hand on her shoulder.

"I'm here for you, Eden. I'm here and I'm going to help you," he said, his voice soft but firm. "Now open your eyes. The police are here to watch Devon, and we need to go find Hope."

CHAPTER THIRTY-EIGHT

Jankowski checked the black tactical watch strapped to his wrist again, even though only minutes had passed since he'd left the last voice mail on Detective Reinhardt's phone.

Where could the old guy be? Jankowski wondered. *And why isn't he calling me back?*

The likelihood that they would find Hope Lancaster alive and well diminished with each minute that passed since she'd been taken. He had to do something. He couldn't just stand around the station and wait for Reinhardt to show his craggy face, could he?

Jankowski hadn't been happy when Nessa had asked him to take Reinhardt with him to Trisha Moore's house, but he hadn't been able to refuse without raising suspicions as to why he didn't want to partner with the old detective. For now, he had to play it cool and stay focused on the case at hand.

Unable to control his impatience, he pressed the last number in the recently called list on his phone. Voice mail again. He decided he couldn't wait any longer as he listened to the recording.

"Reinhardt, I'm not sure where the hell you are," Jankowski said, digging in his pocket to pull out the piece of paper with Trisha Moore's address, "but I'm heading over to question Trisha Moore, the mother of the girl that Eden Winthrop reported missing. We think there's a connection between the girl and Jessica Carmichael. Nessa requested that you back me up, so meet me over there when you get this. I'll text you the address."

He disconnected the call and typed Trisha Moore's address into a text message to Reinhardt before pressing send. He felt a twinge of guilt but then quashed it. He'd tried to follow Nessa's request. It wasn't his fault Reinhardt hadn't responded, but he had to admit he was relieved he wouldn't have to take Reinhardt with him.

He downed the last gulp of cold coffee in his mug and reached for the keys to his Charger. Just then a text alert beeped on his phone. It was a text from Reinhardt: *Just got your message. On my way now.*

Jankowski sighed and sat back down at his desk, wishing he'd just gone without sending the text. Now he was obliged to wait. He clenched his fist and allowed himself to pound on the desk just once. Enough wasted energy.

He pulled out the file on Trisha Moore's case against Buddy Jones and began to read. Best be prepared before he showed up to question the poor woman. He looked at the mugshot stapled to the file. An angry man with dark, shaggy hair and a bushy mustache looked back at him. Jankowski wondered why the man had felt the need to beat up Trisha Moore.

He's got those small, mean eyes you see on some men, Jankowski thought. *Maybe he was just born mean.*

After he'd gone through the entire file, Jankowski looked at his watch again. Shaking his head in frustration, he grabbed his backpack and headed out of his cubicle. Officer Dave Eddings was standing in the lobby by the vending machine as Jankowski passed by.

"Detective Jankowski?" Eddings asked, his voice tentative. "Any progress on finding the girl?"

Jankowski noted the distress on the face of the young officer. Eddings had joined the force almost two years ago, but Jankowski still considered him a rookie, and he knew the events of the last few days must be upsetting to the whole department. Homicides and kidnappings weren't everyday occurrences in Willow Bay. Or at least they hadn't been until recently.

"Nothing solid yet, but I'm following up on a promising lead now. I'd hoped Detective Reinhardt would be able to join me, but I can't reach him," Jankowski said, rubbing the stubble on his jaw that was starting to look more like a full beard than his usual five o'clock shadow.

"If you see him, let him know I'm looking for him, will you?"

"Well, sure, but I can come along and back you up if you can't find Detective Reinhardt," Eddings said, sounding hopeful. "The Chief asked all available personnel to work overtime tonight since that Amber Alert has gone out. In case we get lots of calls. But I'm just waiting around now."

Jankowski paused. Maybe taking Eddings along would save him from Nessa's wrath. After all, she *had* specifically warned him to take along back up. It would also give the baby-faced officer some much-needed experience.

Jankowski knew he should spend more time mentoring the younger officers trying to work their way up. He'd had a few good mentors when he'd been in uniform. Maybe it was his turn to be the mentor now. He'd been on the force since he'd been a hot-headed twenty-two-year-old. Now he was a hot-headed thirty-six-year-old. Had it really been almost fifteen years?

"Okay, sounds good, thanks," Jankowski said. "Let's get going."

"You mean, like, right now?" Eddings asked, a deer-in-headlights look appearing on his smooth, round face.

Jankowski raised his eyebrows and nodded. "Yeah, we gotta go now. Go tell the duty officer that you're going with me to question a lead, and then meet me out front."

"Okay, I guess you'll brief me in the car?" Eddings asked, a look of apprehension overriding the earlier eagerness.

"Sure," Jankowski said. "I'll fill you in on the way."

* * *

The Paradise Palms Residential Community was nestled into a wooded area on the corner of Channel Drive and Surrey Way. A collection of modest two-story duplexes lined the narrow streets of the neighborhood. True to its name, large palm trees swayed overhead as the Charger pulled onto Palm Drive. Night had fallen, and the rain had picked up again, making it difficult for Jankowski to make out the house numbers.

Eddings peered out the window, squinting into the dark, before pointing to a duplex ahead.

"Over there, at the end of the street, Detective. That should be 1066 Palm Drive."

The unit on the right appeared to be unoccupied. The driveway was empty, and all the windows were dark. But the unit on the left had a little Honda parked in the driveway, and a light could be seen in an upstairs window.

Jankowski parked against the curb and stepped out of the car, feeling for the gun on his hip to make sure it was holstered securely. He hurried through the drizzle without an umbrella, and waited for Eddings, who had worn a yellow rain jacket, to join him on the front porch.

"I'll do the talking," Jankowski said.

"Of course," Eddings responded, just as a scream sounded from inside, followed by a gunshot, then an angry shout. Jankowski tried the doorknob, but it was locked. He hesitated, tempted to try to force the door open, but reluctant to announce their presence before he knew what was going on.

He motioned to Eddings to stay quiet and follow him around the side of the house. The young officer fell in behind Jankowski without hesitation, although the expression on his face was strained.

You never knew how someone would react to gunfire and the threat of imminent death until they were faced with it in real life. Jankowski cursed his decision to bring along the inexperienced officer.

If baby-faced Eddings panics or decides to cut and run, this could end up being the worst decision of my life. Other than marrying Gabby, of course.

As Jankowski circled around to the back, he saw that the sliding glass door was open, and a light in the living room beyond was on. He crept closer, his pulse beating fast and hard.

He strained to see into the room. As he moved closer he saw the body of a man sprawled on the floor. A bullet had blown the back of the man's head off. Blood splatter covered part of the wall. Eddings crept up behind him, and Jankowski could feel Eddings first recoil and then begin to shake.

This could be bad, Jankowski thought, as he calculated his options. He turned to face Eddings, putting a finger to his lips and looking directly in the young man's wide eyes.

"Go to the car and call for back-up," Jankowski whispered, his lips almost touching Eddings' ear. "Tell them we have an active shooter. Stay in the car with the doors locked until I come out."

Eddings frowned and shook his head, his eyes narrowing. "I'm not gonna do that," he hissed back. "I'm not going to leave you to deal with this on your own."

Jankowski started to protest, but this time it was Eddings that raised his finger to his lips.

"I'll go back and call for backup," the young officer whispered, "and then I'll circle around the other way and cover you while you get closer to see what's going on. You wait for me to give you a signal from behind that tree over there."

Jankowski saw the large Elm tree that stood at the corner of the building and nodded his agreement at Eddings. He watched as Eddings' yellow raincoat disappeared back into the rainy night.

Jankowski inched forward, his suit and shoes soaked through from the rain, and peered into the room. A large mirror hung on the far wall. It reflected a clear image of a large man in a gray suit holding a gun to the head of a slim, blonde girl.

Even at a distance, Jankowski recognized Stacey Moore from the picture in Eden's file. But who was the man holding the gun?

Could that be Buddy Jones?

Jankowski pictured the mugshot he'd looked at only thirty minutes before, and knew the man holding Stacey was not Buddy Jones. His eyes flicked to the man lying in a pool of blood on the floor.

While the bullet had done considerable damage, Jankowski could see the dead man had dark shaggy hair and sported a bushy mustache. Somehow, he knew that the man on the floor, and not the shooter in the gray suit, was Trisha Moore's abusive ex. He tried to make sense of what he was seeing, but his mind reeled.

Just what the hell is going on here?

Creeping even closer, stopping only a few feet back from the door, Jankowski watched from the cover of night as a small woman emerged from the hallway and stepped into the room. She held out a big handgun in front of her, aiming it directly at the shooter. Jankowski thought the pistol looked like a Ruger, but he wasn't sure.

Sweat dripped from the woman's face, and her thin brown hair lay slick against her head. She was shaking so hard that the gun she held appeared to be jumping up and down, but she kept her eyes trained on the gun pointing back at her.

“Put the gun down or I'll put a bullet through both your heads," the big man called out in a deep voice. “If you put the gun down we can talk, and no one else has to get hurt.”

"Mom, don’t listen to him,” Stacey cried out. “He already killed Buddy. He’ll kill both of us no matter what he says. Just shoot him, Mom! Shoot him now!”

The shooter ducked behind Stacey and pushed her toward the sliding glass door. Jankowski realized the man was going to try to escape using the girl as a shield. He had to make a move before he was seen and lost the advantage of surprise.

As the man stepped backward, putting one foot out of the sliding glass door, Jankowski lunged forward and delivered a quick, sharp kick. The gun flew from the shooter’s hand, falling onto the carpet just inside the door.

Jankowski jumped onto the big man’s back, pulling him outside onto the grass and wrapping a rock-hard arm around his thick throat. He squeezed until he felt the man’s struggles start to fade. Only then did he look up to see Officer Eddings standing behind the Elm tree, a dazed look on his face.

“Stay there, Eddings” Jankowski called out. “We’ve still got a loose firearm in the house.”

Stacey ran to her mother and hugged her, then gently took the gun from her hand.

“Drop the gun,” Jankowski shouted, tensing his muscles, ready to dive for cover if the girl pointed the gun in his direction. But Stacey placed the gun on the floor, then used her foot to slide it under the sofa.

“Okay, Eddings, come help me cuff this bastard,” Jankowski called. He pulled back the man’s meaty arms as Eddings hurried over and snapped on metal handcuffs. “You watch him. If he makes a move, shoot him. I’m going to check inside to see if it’s all clear.”

Jankowski peered into the room and saw that Trisha Moore was still standing in the same spot, but Stacey was nowhere to be seen.

"Ms. Moore? Where's your daughter? Where'd Stacey go?" Jankowski demanded, his nerves on edge as he glanced around the room.

He hadn't pulled his gun yet, but he reached down and put his hand on his holster, knowing he may still need it after all.

Trisha Moore stared at him with a blank expression, before saying, "He killed Buddy. That man killed Buddy."

"Yes, I know that, ma'am," Jankowski said, "but Officer Eddings will make sure he can't hurt anyone else. Now, I need to know where Stacey is. Did she leave the house, or is she hiding somewhere?"

"She's upstairs," Trisha Moore said. "She's probably checking to make sure Zane's okay."

"Who's Zane?" Jankowski barked, looking at the stairs as he pulled his gun out of the holster. "Who else is in the house?"

"Zane's my son. He's only six," Trisha said, her eyes narrowing as she saw the gun in his hand. "Are you that dirty cop Stacey warned me about? Are you Sig?"

Jankowski frowned, moving further into the room. He called up the stairs, "Stacey, come on down here. Everything is okay now. We're here to help you."

CHAPTER THIRTY-NINE

The old-fashioned television set had been bolted onto the wooden table in Room D-407 a decade before Hope had been born. But, with the help of a slightly bent antenna, it still managed to display a grainy image, and provided the only light in the motel room.

Hope huddled on the edge of the bed, her arms wrapped tightly around herself, and watched the local news. The shock of seeing that another girl's body had been found that morning had faded somewhat, and she watched the coverage with a growing determination not to be the next body pulled out of the river. She would find a way out of this. She just needed time to figure out how.

Hope focused all her energy on finding a way to escape the little room, and it took her several seconds to realize she was staring at her own face on the small, fuzzy screen. Although Vinny had turned down the sound, she could see from the headline that an Amber Alert had been issued.

The alert showed a school picture taken earlier that year and listed her name, age, and the warning that she had been abducted by two men in an older model silver sedan. Hope's heart jumped, and she glanced over to where Hollywood sat slumped in the chair. He was motionless. Still out of it.

She then looked over at Vinny, who was sitting very still on the chair across from Hollywood. He was watching her, and as she caught his eye, he smiled. Hope wasn't sure she liked the smile. Something was off about it.

But he didn't appear to have seen the screen, so that was good. It was much safer for her if he didn't know an Amber Alert had been issued, and that everyone in the state would be looking for his silver sedan. If she just waited, surely someone would see the car in the parking lot and call the police.

Vinny kept his eyes on her as if transfixed, and Hope recoiled from the expression on his face. He looked like a feral wolf watching a deer lost in the woods. The skin on her neck felt tight and tingly, and an impulse to run and hide grew as she saw Vinny stand and walk over to Hollywood.

"Hey, Hollywood? You awake, man?" Vinny asked in a soft voice. "You feeling okay?"

Hollywood didn't react. If his chest hadn't been moving up and down, Hope would have believed he'd taken a fatal overdose. But no such luck. He had just passed out, and she was sure he'd regain consciousness soon.

Vinny turned toward her and walked the few steps to the edge of the bed. He was close enough now for her to smell the faint odor of sweat and soap that surrounded him. She felt the urge to gag as he reached out a hand and wrapped a finger around a lock of her hair. He caressed the hair before letting it fall back across her shoulder.

"You're a pretty girl," Vinny said, his voice low and husky. "The prettiest I've seen in a long time."

"Oh, thanks," Hope replied, turning her head away to hide her distaste, worried that perhaps her plan to get him to help her had backfired.

Maybe he thinks I like him. Maybe he's going to try something.

"I want to help you." Vinny's fingers encircled Hope's arm and began pulling her toward him. "You don't belong here. And you certainly don't belong where these guys are going to send you."

"Where are they going to send me?"

"Somewhere worse than hell for a girl like you." Vinny spoke in a voice barely above a whisper, as if talking to himself. "A nice girl like you would be ruined."

Hope tried to resist Vinny's grip, but his hand tightened, and she felt herself slide off the bed, her feet landing only inches from his. She still wore the light-weight sandals she'd been wearing at home, and she suddenly wished she had on her thick-soled running shoes.

If she was going to get away from this place, and all the predators that lurked within, she'd need to be fast and tough. Taking a deep breath, Hope turned her face up to Vinny and tried to look him in the eyes. But the glow from the television reflected off his glasses, and she could see only a blur of lights and shadows. She summoned all her strength and produced a small smile.

"You won't let them take me there, will you?" Hope asked, her voice steady in spite of the trembling that had begun inside her.

"No, I won't let them have you," Vinny agreed, and his head dropped toward her, his hot, sour breath only inches away. "I'll save you, I promise."

Without thinking of the possible consequences, Hope jerked her knee up hard, connecting with Vinny's crotch in a sickening thud. She didn't wait to see what he would do, but instead ran to the door and pulled. She screamed out in frustration. Still locked.

Shaking now with adrenaline and fear, Hope turned to see Vinny writhing on the floor, his face a mask of pain and rage. She wondered if she could risk getting close enough to see if he had the key to the room on him but then decided not to take the chance.

She hurried back to the bathroom and closed the door. Once again, she looked around the windowless room in despair.

What am I going to do now? Now Vinny will never help me.

As if Vinny had read her thoughts from the other side of the door, he called out to her in a strained voice. "Why'd you have to do that? I just want to help you."

Hope didn't respond. She tried to listen for sounds from the other room, but for several minutes there was only silence. Then she jumped as Vinny's fist or foot connected with the door. Hope backed away, wondering if the thin door would withstand a kick, or worse yet, a blast from Hollywood's little gun.

"Please, Hope, you don't know what they're going to do to you. I just want to help," Vinny pleaded. "If you don't want me to kiss you, then I won't. I thought maybe that's what you wanted. I'm sorry. Please open up before it's too late."

Hope looked around in frustration. If she waited here any longer, the other men would show up and possibly take her to somewhere even worse than the shabby motel room. And who knows what they'd do to her then. She *had* acted friendly to Vinny, so maybe it was her fault he'd tried to get close to her. Maybe he was sorry, and really would help her get away. What other choice did she have?

Hope turned on the faucet in the rusty sink and splashed water into her dry mouth. Her throat tightened, and she could barely swallow. As she faced the door, she knew she had no choice but to open it and face the man waiting outside.

Her hand shook as she grasped the barrel on the lock and inched it back. She twisted the knob and opened the door, half expecting Vinny to jump at her. But she was still taken off guard when he grabbed her and twisted her around so that her back was against his chest. Before she could utter a scream, he had looped a belt over her head and tightened it around her throat.

Panic set in as Hope felt her breath leave her body in a sudden whoosh of air. The pressure on her neck was unbearable, and her chest was jerking with the need for air. She reached up to grab Vinny's arms, desperate to make him release his excruciating grip when the doorknob rattled, and a deep voice sounded from the corridor.

"Open up, Hollywood!"

"Oh, shit, it's Sig," Vinny gasped, and the pressure fell away from Hope's neck as he removed the belt and hurried toward the door. Before he could retrieve the key from his pocket, Hope drew in a deep, ragged breath and issued an ear-piercing scream. She turned back towards the bathroom, but her legs wobbled and then collapsed beneath her.

Vinny ran to kneel beside her, pulling her hands behind her back and strapping them together with the still-looped belt. He looked around frantically, then grabbed a pillow from the bed and stripped off the thin pillowcase, tying it tightly around Hope's jaw as a makeshift gag.

Hope strained to pull her arms free. The room seemed to vibrate with each bang on the thin door, and she watched in dismay as Hollywood sat up in dazed confusion, looking around for the source of the commotion. Her chance to escape was gone. Tears trickled down Hope's face and onto the cheap pillowcase as Vinny unlocked the door and flung it open,

"What the hell is going on in here?' Sig demanded, removing his glasses, and giving Hope a view of rage-filled eyes surrounded by deep wrinkles.

"We've got you a new girl, Sig," Hollywood said in a groggy voice and looked around. His eyes widened at the sight of Hope tied and gagged on the floor, but he didn't say anything, just looked back at Sig as if waiting to gauge his reaction.

"Yeah, I know that. I came by here before and saw this *new girl* you got. But at that time, I didn't know who she was." Sig's voice was rough, perhaps from the yelling, or maybe from the decades of unfiltered cigarettes.

"She's Eden Winthrop's niece," Hollywood said, sounding proud. "That'll show that bitch to mess around in my business."

"Oh, I know who she is *now*, you idiot," Sig growled. "The whole fucking state knows who she is now. Just look at the damn TV and you can see exactly who she is, and who took her."

Hope turned her eyes back to the television screen and saw that the news was rerunning the report on the Amber Alert.

"Oh, shit," Hollywood murmured, his eyes wide.

Hope saw Vinny shrink back against the wall as if hoping the mad old man would forget he was in the room.

"Oh, shit is right," Sig agreed, lowering his voice, and stepping further into the room. "You two have made a big mistake, and you're gonna have to take care of it...*now*."

"What do you mean?" Hollywood asked, looking over at Vinny for the first time. "What do you want us to do?"

"I want you to get rid of the problem," Sig said, his eyes hard. He looked over at Hope on the floor, and she recoiled at the look of pure hatred on his face. "She's seen all of our faces."

Hollywood frowned and tilted his head as if trying to understand. "So, you're telling us to..."

"I'm telling you to get rid of her," Sig spat out. "She's a witness that could take us all down."

Sig's phone began to buzz, and he looked down, then jabbed at the screen to reject the call. Sweat stood on his forehead, and Hope could see the vein in his temple throbbing from all the way across the room.

"I've gotta take care of something. Make sure she's gone before I get back."

"But, Sig, man, you can't mean you want us to...to...kill her?" Hollywood's voice was no longer groggy as he stared straight at the old man. Hope felt the room spin around her.

"That's exactly what I mean." Sig nodded toward Vinny standing against the wall. "But if you don't have the balls, I'm sure your boy over there can help you."

Vinny looked down at the floor, his hands clenching into fists at his side, and the old man looked as if he were going to say more, but then he shoved his glasses back on and turned to leave.

"Just do it," Sig barked, and slammed the door behind him.

The words sent a wave of terror through Hope; she renewed the futile struggle to free her hands.

This is just a dream, she told herself. *I'll wake up any minute and it will all be over.*

But she knew in her heart the situation was unspeakably, horribly real. She had lost her mother on a similarly nightmarish day; she had thought then that the day would be the worst day of her life. Now she was finding out she'd been wrong.

Her mother's face flashed through her mind, and she suddenly remembered how young and beautiful her mother had been, and how fragile. But that fatal day, as Hope had watched from her hiding place, her mother's anguished face had been bruised and bleeding, the face of a stranger. And with the blast of a single gunshot, her mother was gone.

Hope forced herself back into the present, not allowing herself to think about what had happened next. She'd managed to stay alive then, and that was all that mattered. Now she had to stay strong and alert. She might still get one last chance to escape, and if so, she may be able to cheat death a second time.

CHAPTER FORTY

Fatigue clung to Nessa like a sodden blanket, making her arms and legs unbearably heavy as she climbed back into her car. She'd stayed at Eden Winthrop's house until the crime scene technicians had called it a night.

The continuous rain had made it difficult to properly search the area outside the house and along the road where the abductors had likely parked, but Alma Garcia had been adamant that they complete the job before the rain and the elements destroyed any evidence left behind.

Alma's diligence had paid off when they'd found tire tread imprints in the mud under a towering oak tree across the street. A huge branch hung over the curb, protecting the print enough to allow Alma's team to make a cast of the tread using dental stone. Nessa knew the cast of the tire tread might prove to be key evidence if they ever located the silver car, but she was becoming more and more discouraged as the hours passed.

Hope had been gone for more than six hours now. That was more than enough time for motivated and efficient serial killers to satisfy their sick desires and then dispose of the victim's body in the nearest river.

Glancing at her watch, Nessa wondered if she could make it home before the kids fell asleep. They'd likely be getting ready for bed. Maybe brushing their teeth and whining to Jerry that they wanted to stay up late since it was Saturday. She could almost smell the baby shampoo they both still used. Even though they were now much too old for baby products, she loved the familiar scent and wasn't ready to give it up just yet.

Maybe I can get home in time to tuck them in, and then take a nice, long, hot shower, she mused, knowing it was an impossible dream, but relishing the idea just the same. *Maybe Jerry would be willing to give me a little backrub, along with a little something else.*

The sound of her phone ringing interrupted her wishful thinking. She needed to get back to the station and find out what the other detectives had discovered. Looking down at her phone, she saw a number that was rapidly becoming familiar. She swiped to answer and tapped on the speaker icon.

"Hello, Jankowski," she said, just as a huge yawn washed over her. "I'm just heading toward the station now. You got an update?"

"I guess you could say that," Jankowski replied, sounding wired. "I can update you on the dead body I found and the killer I caught."

Nessa blinked and looked at the phone, trying to decide if he was messing with her or being serious.

"Okay, update me then," she said, deciding even Jankowski wouldn't play pranks on a day like this.

"Well, I did as you asked and called Reinhardt, but he never showed. I ended up taking Dave Eddings along for the ride. When we got to Trisha Moore's house we immediately heard a gunshot from inside. We circled around and saw that a man had been shot in the head. Another man was holding Stacey at gunpoint."

"You're making this up," Nessa said, shaking her head. "Tell me this is a sick joke."

"Nope, it's as real as all this rain," Jankowski shot back, and Nessa felt a ripple of irritation at the jovial tone in his voice.

What exactly was so funny about a man dying?

"Anyway, Trisha Moore also pulled out a gun and the big guy that was holding Stacey tried to leave, but I managed to disarm him." Jankowski gave a satisfied laugh. "He's in the county jail as we speak."

"And the Moore family? Are they all okay?"

"Yep, they're fine. A little shaken, of course, but not physically harmed." Jankowski sobered at the words. "The little boy, Stacey's brother, he was a real trooper. A real cute kid."

"What about the victim?" Nessa asked. "Who got shot? Who's the dead guy?"

"You're not going to believe this," Jankowski stalled.

"Try me." Nessa's patience was running low.

"It was Buddy Jones. He'd been hanging around again. I guess Trisha Moore thought he'd been rehabilitated while in prison. Although the bruises on her arms make me think she was mistaken."

"Well, I'll be damned." Nessa exhaled a disgusted breath. "Why are some women so darn gullible when it comes to this kind of lowlife?"

"Yeah, I kinda wondered what she was smoking that would make her let that scumbag back in the house. And with her kids there, too."

"I guess we'll have to ask her when we take her statement," Nessa said. "Maybe it's more complicated than we think."

"Yeah, sure. It always is." Jankowski's voice had reverted to a cheerful tone. "But look on the bright side. At least we got a killer off the streets of Willow Bay today."

"Does this killer have a name?" Nessa asked.

"According to his ID, his name is Richard Serrano and he lives in Miami."

"What's a killer from Miami doing in Willow Bay?" Nessa didn't like the idea of hardened criminals coming to their small town. They weren't equipped to deal with the type of organized crime and gang violence that bigger cities had to face.

"Stacey recognized the dead man," Jankowski said. "She says he's one of the men that held her at the Old Canal Motel."

"That old motel? I didn't even know it was still open." Nessa tried to make sense of what she was hearing. "She's saying she was kidnapped and held there against her will?"

"Well, she went willingly at first, I think, but then they wouldn't let her leave. It's the classic con of these kinds of traffickers. Make a vulnerable young girl think she's your girlfriend. Get her hooked on drugs. Then persuade her to support her new habit by selling herself."

"Yeah, that sounds about right. Sick bastards." Nessa heard a beep on the line. She looked down at the display but didn't recognize the number of the incoming call.

"Look, Jankowski, I have another call coming in," Nessa said as she prepared to make a right turn toward the river. "I'm heading over to the Old Canal Motel. Maybe the creeps who held Stacey Moore there are the same ones who took Hope."

"You can't go on your own, Nessa," Jankowski warned, his voice suddenly serious.

"So, I'll meet you there," Nessa said and tapped the option to switch to the incoming call. "This is Detective Ainsley."

"Nessa? It's Eden. Sage Parker says she knows who took Hope. She says Trevor Bane was one of the men who came to the house."

"Why didn't she tell us this earlier?" Nessa asked, pressing her foot down hard on the gas despite the slick road. "Is she sure?"

"She's right here with me and Leo Steele," Eden said. "She seems pretty sure."

"Okay, I'll radio the detectives that have gone to question Trevor Bane," Nessa reassured Eden. "They're already looking for him. We're planning to bring him in for formal questioning. I'll let them know he's been identified as one of the men that abducted Hope. And we can try to get Trevor's name added to the Amber Alert."

Nessa saw the faded sign for the Old Canal Motel directly ahead. She would park in the lot and call in the new information on Trevor Bane to Ingram and Ortiz. Then she'd wait for Jankowski to arrive.

But as she pulled into the dark parking lot, she saw a black Dodge Charger sitting under a flickering lamppost. A man was standing by the car, seemingly oblivious to the rain.

"I've got to go now, Eden," Nessa said, her eyes trained on the figure in the rain.

"We located Star...I mean Stacey Moore, and she's told us that she was held at the Old Canal Motel. I'm approaching the motel now, to see what I can find. You and Leo should head over to the station and wait for me there. I'll update you as soon as I know anything."

Nessa didn't wait for Eden to respond. She disconnected the call and pulled up beside the Charger. Reinhardt stood in the rain, his black baseball cap the only protection he had against the storm. Nessa shrugged on her navy-blue rain jacket and stepped out of the car.

"Hey there, Detective," she called out, blinking against the drizzle that refused to stop. "Did Jankowski get a hold of you? Did he tell you to meet me here?"

Reinhardt stared at Nessa for a long beat, then shook his head as if already regretting what he was about to say. "I think there's something you need to know about Jankowski."

CHAPTER FORTY-ONE

Eden stared down at the phone in her hand, wondering if she should call Nessa back and ask more questions. Did Nessa think Hope could be at the Old Canal Motel? Had the kidnappers taken her niece to the same place they'd kept Stacey Moore before she'd managed to run away?

She turned to Leo, who was driving his BMW at full speed toward the glowing lights of the downtown skyline, then looked in the backseat. Sage Parker was huddled close to the door, her head resting against the rain-splattered window. She hadn't spoken since they'd left Devon with Reggie at the farmhouse under police protection.

"Turn around," Eden said, an urgent need taking hold; she had to find out for herself if Hope was at the Old Canal Motel.

The old place was only minutes away. Hope could be there. Eden couldn't just drive away in the other direction. If Hope was close by, Eden had to find her.

"What are you talking about?" Leo asked, his eyes still on the slippery road ahead. "What did Nessa tell you?"

Eden hesitated. Would Leo drive to the motel if he knew there might be an active police investigation in progress? Or would he tell her they should wait at the police station as Nessa had instructed? She couldn't take the chance he'd balk at what she was planning.

"Nessa said we should meet her at the Old Canal Motel," Eden said before she could change her mind. "Now turn around here and head back toward the interstate."

Leo looked over at Eden with narrowed eyes. She thought for a minute he could see right through her lie, but then he began to slow the car, pulling into a side street before turning the car around and heading back toward the overpass and the dilapidated motel beyond.

Eden fidgeted in her seat, her breathing starting to come fast and heavy.

What if Hope is there, and I'm too late to save her?

"Please hurry, Leo," Eden said, biting her lip as she stared ahead, desperate to see the sign for the motel.

"What exactly is going on at the motel?" Leo asked, his tone suspicious as he accelerated.

"Nessa says it's the motel where Star had...had stayed. Although, um, I guess I should call her Stacey now," Eden stammered, stalling for time as she tried to decide how much she should tell Leo.

"Anyway, Nessa said they've found Stacey, and she told them where she'd been staying. Nessa's there now, checking it out."

"And she wants us to be there, too?" Leo said, raising his eyebrows as if surprised, before suddenly frowning. "So, she thinks that's where they may be holding Hope?"

"Maybe," Eden whispered, too anxious to catch her breath.

She clutched at the purse in her lap, desperate for the pills that would take away her dread and fear. But before she could reach inside, she saw the sign ahead.

"There it is!" she practically shrieked, grabbing Leo's arm. "Pull in here. Don't miss the exit."

The street up to the main parking lot was dark and empty, and Eden turned to Leo with wide, frightened eyes.

"Turn off the headlights," she commanded, her voice shaking. "Don't let anyone know we're here. Not yet. Not before we see who's here."

Leo stared over at her. "You're not making sense, Eden. What are you not telling me?"

"Nessa didn't tell us to come here," Eden blurted out, not caring what Leo thought about her lie, only wanting to find Hope.

"But Hope might be here, and I need to know if she is. I can't wait around for a call telling me it's too late when Hope needs me. I wasn't there for her mother...and...I...I can't make the same mistake again."

Eden's chest heaved, and she felt as if her throat was closing up. She felt as if she were suffocating. As if she were dying.

Just stop it, she scolded herself, inhaling deeply and then exhaling. *You can't afford to have a panic attack now. You've got to save Hope.*

Leo brought the car to a stop, turned off the lights, and looked at Eden. She expected to see reproach in his eyes, but she saw only sympathy. He took her trembling hand in his and squeezed it.

"You didn't have to lie to me, Eden. I want to find Hope, too, and I'll do anything I can to help you. But whatever happens, it won't be your fault. You didn't fail Mercy and you won't fail Hope."

Eden felt hot tears on her cheeks as Leo turned the car back on but left the lights off. He drove slowly toward the motel. Eden could see lights and a few cars clustered near the rear building, but a grassy median separated the front and rear parking areas.

"There must be a rear entrance as well," Leo said, just as Eden spotted two cars under a lamppost at the edge of the lot.

"Over there," she said, pointing. "I see people standing under that light."

"Is that Nessa?" Leo asked, as Eden strained to see through her window, which was foggy and blurred by the rain. "Can you see who's with her?"

Sage sat up in the backseat and gasped. Eden turned around to see her staring out the window in dismay.

"That's the guy that Trevor works for," Sage said in a horrified whisper, pointing to the man in the black baseball cap beside Nessa. "That's Sig."

Before Eden could react, Leo shook his head and frowned. "Actually, I think that's Detective Reinhardt. He's been on the force for years."

"Well, I never knew his real name," Sage said, sinking lower into the seat. "Trevor did say he was a cop once, but he was high, and he was always lying about things, so I didn't really believe him."

"Maybe Reinhardt just looks like Sig," Eden said. "I mean, why would Nessa be here talking to him if..."

But her words stuck in her throat as she saw Reinhardt extend his arm toward Nessa. A flash of light flared briefly in the dark as a deafening gunshot reverberated through the night.

They watched in silent horror as Nessa slammed backward onto the wet pavement and lay motionless in the falling rain.

CHAPTER FORTY-TWO

Hollywood leaned his head against the motel room door, a wave of nausea washing over him. He hadn't eaten since the day before but still struggled to stop himself from retching. If he was sick now, the only thing that would come up would be the hot bile churning in his stomach.

He turned to face the room, resentment filling him at the sight of Hope, still bound and gagged on the floor. The girl had brought him nothing but trouble. She had screwed up everything.

He glared at her, but she wasn't looking at him. Her wide, terrified eyes followed Vinny's every move as he paced around the room. He had removed his glasses and was watching Hollywood with naked, predatory eyes. Hollywood felt a shiver run down his spine.

"Look, Vinny, I didn't mean for this shit to happen," Hollywood said, putting his hand behind him and feeling for the door.

He needed to be ready to make a quick exit. Although it wasn't easy to make Vinny angry, when he did lose his temper there was no reasoning with him.

"What exactly did you think would happen when you dragged us into this mess?" Vinny demanded, his voice cold.

Gone was the meek sidekick who would take whatever crap was thrown his way. Hollywood knew instinctively that he had finally pushed Vinny too far.

"I know, bro, it was a bad idea." Hollywood reached for the little gun he'd stuck into the back of his waistband earlier.

It was gone. Had it fallen out, or had he put it somewhere when he was too high to remember?

He stalled for time. He needed to talk Vinny down from the ledge. "But we can fix this, man. It'll be okay."

"Fix this? How will we do that?" Vinny asked, moving closer to Hollywood. He gestured toward Hope, who cringed at his attention. "By killing *her*?"

Hollywood tried to think of a witty comeback, but his brain felt thick and slow. He forced himself to raise his chin in defiance and glared at Vinny.

"Yeah, actually. You can save the day. Be a hero for once, instead of a loser. After all, sometimes we gotta do what we gotta do."

"No." Vinny shook his head, offering a bitter smile. "*You* have to do what *you* have to do. You're the addict, not me. You're the one who needs the drugs. You're the one who owes those thugs from Miami. I can walk away tonight, no problem."

"Come on, man," Hollywood said, almost pleading. "After everything I've done for you? After everything my mother has done for you? You're gonna let me down?"

"Everything you've done?" Vinny spit out, his face contorted with rage. "If I really wanted to pay you back for what you and your mother have done, I would have to kill you both. But maybe that's not such a bad idea."

Hollywood blinked in surprise. Didn't Vinny remember the way they'd taken him in after his mother had died? They'd fostered him and given him food and a place to live. Had treated him like a son and a brother. And now here he was acting like they'd done something terrible.

Before Hollywood could respond, a loud bang rang out from the parking lot.

"What the hell? Was that a gunshot?" Hollywood stepped to the window and peered out.

The night was dark, but he could see a figure illuminated by a light pole at the far end of the lot. It was Sig, and it looked like he was holding a gun. A motionless body lay on the ground next to a black Dodge Charger.

"Holy shit," Hollywood said, dropping the curtain and ducking down as if Sig might start shooting in their direction. "Sig just shot someone. I think it was another cop."

He looked around and saw that Vinny was now standing behind him, reaching for the door.

"No, don't go out there!" Hollywood shouted, dragging Vinny back toward the middle of the room. "First, you've gotta take care of her. She knows who we are. She's seen us. Come on, Vinny. I don't want to go to jail."

Vinny looked over at Hope, then back at Hollywood. "Okay, I'll help you."

"Thanks, man, I knew you wouldn't let me down. I owe you one," Hollywood said, then took a double-take. Vinny was holding the little pistol.

"I think you owe me more than one, *Trevor,*" Vinny said, examining the pistol and cocking the hammer.

"Don't call me that around here, you moron," Hollywood snapped, then flinched as Vinny raised the pistol and held it with both hands in front of him.

"Okay, okay, relax. Call me whatever you want. The girl won't be around long enough for it to matter anyway."

"That's right, Trevor," Vinny said, as he brandished the gun. "You don't have to worry about anything, anymore. No more drug problems, no more money problems, no more girl problems. All your problems are over. I'm going to save you."

Hollywood snorted and shook his head, unable to believe what he was hearing. What could Vinny do to save him? Vinny was a loser. A nothing. He'd been a total deadweight for the past twelve years.

But then again, Vinny was a loser with a gun. And Hollywood needed him to use that gun. If they didn't kill Hope, then Sig would just do it himself. And Hollywood and Vinny would become his next targets.

Hollywood didn't want the girl's blood on his hands, but what could he do? He had no choice. He'd have to pretend to go along with Vinny until he could ditch the little loser once and for all.

"Okay, so you're going to save me," Trevor said, trying to keep his voice steady. "How exactly are you going to do that?"

"Just like I saved the others," Vinny replied, pointing the gun in Hollywood's face. "Just like I saved Jess and Brandi and Tiffany."

"Are you *nuts*?" Hollywood couldn't stop the words that spilled out. "Those girls are all dead. Nobody saved them."

"Actually, I did, since I put them out of their misery. I saved them from ruin. And I'm going to do the same for you."

"You mean, *you* killed them? All of them?" Hollywood said, prompting a muffled scream from Hope. "But...why...how?"

"You made them whores, and I saved them from you and all the other lowlifes that used and abused them."

"What the hell are you talking about, man?" Hollywood ran a shaky hand through his hair, unable to take in what he was hearing. Was this some kind of sick joke? Then he saw the crazed gleam in Vinny's eyes. He was telling the truth.

The pathetic loser actually killed those girls.

Hollywood's mind hurt with the effort to make sense of it. But something didn't fit in with Vinny's twisted logic.

"But Tiffany? Why her? That girl was pure," Hollywood said, remembering now how Vinny had urged him not to tell the police that they'd known Tiffany after she'd gone missing.

"She was no whore."

"Not technically, no," Vinny agreed, "but I knew you'd ruin her just like you did everything and everyone else you touched. So, I sent her someplace you could never hurt her."

Vinny stepped closer. Hollywood could smell the cheap soap he always used and tried not to gag.

"Okay, so you want to kill me. But my mom?" Hollywood demanded, trying to stall, hoping Vinny would make a mistake. "You'd really go after the woman who took you in after your whore of a mother abandoned you?"

"First of all, your mother never gave a damn about me. She just cared about the check she got from the state for fostering me."

Vinny's voice vibrated with anger. "And second of all, my mother was a good woman until some scumbag got her hooked on drugs. He ruined her, just like you've ruined the girls here."

"That's always the excuse. *It wasn't my fault. He made me do it.*"

Hollywood heard sirens approaching in the distance. He'd have to get the gun off Vinny if he was going to make it out alive. If he could just get out of here, he could talk his mother into giving him enough money to leave town and disappear. Maybe he'd even kick his habit and start over, without his nagging mother and loser Vinny to drag him down.

If he could make Vinny mad enough, the weakling would take a swing and give him a chance to grab the gun. Given enough time Vinny was bound to make a mistake. He was a loser, always had been.

"Your mother was a no-good whore. Stop whining about it like a little bitch and just deal with it." Hollywood braced himself for a punch, ready to grab for the pistol.

But for once Vinny seemed not to hear Hollywood's insults. He pointed the gun between Hollywood's dark, disbelieving eyes and pulled the trigger.

CHAPTER FORTY-THREE

The wipers sluiced the rain off the BMW's windshield, briefly revealing Nessa's body sprawled on the ground before the rain again blurred the macabre scene. Eden shook her head in disbelief, her mind not fully convinced that she had in fact just seen someone gunned down in front of her.

This can't be happening again; it has to be a hallucination.

"This is Leo Steele, calling from my car outside the Old Canal Motel. I've just witnessed a shooting and there's a police officer down. The shooter is Detective Kirk Reinhardt, and he's still on the loose."

Eden turned to see Leo holding his phone to his ear, his eyes blazing as he looked into the dark night beyond the window, his big hand gripped so tightly around the phone she could see the veins bulging. He tapped on the phone, disconnecting the call, and then leaned over to open the glove compartment.

Her heart thumped in her chest as he withdrew the gun and laid it on his lap.

"What are you going to do, Leo?" Eden asked, her eyes glued to the weapon, feeling the phantom weight of a gun in her own hand.

"I'm going to help Nessa," Leo said, and the rock-hard conviction in his voice penetrated her shock. Leo was right. Nessa had been shot, but she may still be alive. They might be able to save her if they could get past Reinhardt. They had to try.

"But how can we get close enough without him seeing us? He might panic and start shooting."

Eden surveyed the dark parking lot. How could they get to Reinhardt undetected? Her eyes were drawn to the far building. A light pole showed a handful of cars parked outside. Did that mean people were in there? Did they have Hope?

Just then Leo started the car. The soft purr of the engine was inaudible under the wind of the storm. Eden felt the car begin to glide forward, and she heard Sage protest from the backseat. The fear in the young woman's voice was palpable, but Eden didn't look back.

She had to stay focused on what lay ahead. Leo was inching directly toward Reinhardt, who was still standing over Nessa's body. They wouldn't be able to remain undetected for long.

"When we get closer, I'll turn on the lights and scare Reinhardt away so that we can get to Nessa," he said, the hitch in his breathing the only outward sign that he was aware his plan may not work.

"But what if he isn't scared away?" Eden asked. "What if he charges straight at us? What will we do then?"

Leo patted the gun. "That's what this is for. If he won't get out of the way, then I'll have to use this."

Eden recoiled, turning her eyes away. She had always disliked guns and refused to let her father have one in the house when she was growing up. But that dislike had turned to pure terror the night Mercy and Preston had died, and the sight and sound of a gun, even in movies or on television, now had the power to incite a tidal wave of anxiety inside her.

Eden looked through the windshield at the gun in Reinhardt's hand. His throat tightened and her chest squeezed. Was this how it would end for her, too? Would she be killed by a rage-driven man wielding a gun, just as Mercy had been killed? Preston's hate-filled face loomed in her memory, and she felt the rage ignite inside her just as it had when she'd seen him standing over Mercy's prone body.

"Okay, I'm going to switch on the high beams," Leo said, talking in a low voice, as if Reinhardt may hear them.

But before he could move his hand to the console, they heard police sirens begin to wail in the dark, and then, only moments later, a gunshot sounded from within the motel's rear building.

Reinhardt must have also heard the sirens and then the gunshot. He froze, first looking toward the interstate, where blue and red flashing lights could be seen in the distance, and then turning toward the motel, where the shot had been fired.

As he hesitated, illuminated by the harsh light above him, Nessa raised an arm off the ground and pointed it up at Reinhardt. He didn't look down, and he didn't see her pull the trigger. His head jerked back, and a burst of blood filled the night and sprayed down on Nessa like crimson rain.

* * *

Eden's scream reverberated inside the car. She squeezed her eyes shut and put her head on the dashboard, rocking back and forth.

"This isn't happening," she murmured. "This isn't real."

Eden raised her head and stared out the window in disbelief. Reinhardt had fallen next to Nessa; he lay face down in a puddle of water and blood. There would be no saving him, but Nessa was moving, her head turning to face Reinhardt.

Leo shoved the gun back in the glove compartment. He opened the car door and ran forward, the high beams acting as a spotlight on the bodies of the two fallen detectives. As he bent over Nessa, Eden opened the door to follow him and caught movement out of the corner of her eye.

A man in a dark hoodie had exited one of the motel rooms. The overhead light in the corridor was dim, but she could see that the man was carrying a backpack and seemed to be pulling someone behind him. Her heart stopped as she recognized Hope's slender frame and long, brown hair. The man pushed Hope toward a silver sedan parked under a flickering light post.

Without thinking, Eden splashed around the back of the car and jumped into the driver's seat. She shifted the gear into drive and pressed her foot down hard on the gas pedal as she steered the car toward the grassy median that separated the front and rear parking lots.

She didn't have time to drive around and find the back entrance. She had one last chance to save Hope. As the front tires bumped up and over the concrete curb that bordered the grass, Eden saw a police car race into the lot behind her.

"Good, they'll help Leo and Nessa," Eden said.

She wasn't sure if she was speaking to Sage or to herself. But she wasn't stopping, whatever happened. Either she'd get to Hope on time, or she'd die trying.

"I think that's Vinny," Sage said from the backseat. She sounded dazed. "He...he took Hope."

Maybe she's in shock, too, Eden thought. *I think we all are.*

Ahead of her, the man in the hoodie jerked his head around as the headlights started bumping toward him over the grass. He shoved Hope's head down and thrust her into the backseat before jumping into the driver's seat and slamming the door. The car roared to life and squealed backward just as the BMW jolted down onto the concrete of the rear lot.

Eden followed the taillights of the silver car as it pulled out onto a deserted road lined on both sides by thick, untamed underbrush and battered palm trees. She didn't know where the road might lead, and as she looked again in her rearview mirror, she saw that no one was following her. It was up to her to save Hope now.

Eden kept her foot smashed on the gas, determined not to lose sight of the silver car. Vinny would have to stop at some point, and when he did, she'd be right behind him.

She glanced toward the glove compartment, picturing the dangerous gleam of the gun inside. Her stomach churned at the thought of picking it up and pointing it at Vinny.

Will I have the courage to use it if I do catch up with them? she wondered, bumping over a deep pothole and struggling to keep control of the car on the uneven road. She had worked so hard to save lives during the last four years, desperate for redemption. Would redemption come at the end of gun?

A long, deep horn shattered the night, igniting a spark of terror in Eden's chest. It was the horn from an approaching train. They must be heading toward the train tracks that bisected the city, delineating what was considered the east side and west side of Willow Bay.

If Vinny made it past the train tracks, he'd quickly reach the on-ramp to the interstate, and from there could head up north toward Tampa, or southeast to Miami. Either way, he and Hope would soon disappear into the stormy night, and she may never see her niece again.

Eden strained to see the road, the dark clouds and rain making it difficult to see more than a few feet ahead of her. She had to stay focused on Vinny's taillights. But the BMW's wheels found another deep pothole and Eden bounced up with the impact. She struggled to regain her balance, her foot instinctively lifting up and off the gas pedal as the car jerked forward.

The silver car was pulling away, hurtling down the pitted asphalt with dangerous speed, taking several sharp bends without slowing down. Vinny was driving like he had nothing to lose, and Eden feared she wouldn't be able to catch up to him before he wrecked the car, perhaps killing Hope in the process.

The dark road had no street lights, and it was only the growing rumble ahead that let her know the train was getting closer. As she rounded a bend, she saw the blinking lights of the railroad crossing. The deafening horn sounded again, and the intense headlight of the train raced toward the crossing at high speed, but the silver car plowed ahead.

"Oh my god," Sage whispered from the backseat. "He's going to try to beat the train."

Eden watched in horror as the silver car approached the red and white barriers. Her breath caught in her throat as she fought the instinct to turn away from the impending crash. She had to keep her eyes on the tracks ahead. On the spot where Hope would either die or would pass from her view, perhaps forever.

The silver car burst through the old wooden barriers, cracking them into pieces as it flew over the tracks only seconds before the big train roared through. Eden skidded to a stop and jumped out of the car. Her knees buckled under her as she watched the endless line of freight cars rattle past.

As the last freight car came into view, Eden turned frightened eyes to the far side of the track. Would it make sense to climb back in the car and continue the chase? How would she know which way they'd gone?

It took a minute for Eden to register what she was seeing. The silver car sat at an angle about fifty yards away, the front driver's side tire flat. Flashing red and blue lights lit up a semicircle of police cars and barricades that blocked the street ahead. Eden gasped as she saw a policeman with a shotgun crouched behind the barricade. Another policeman with a megaphone stood behind a cruiser.

"Exit the vehicle with your hands up!" the officer with the megaphone commanded, his voice vibrating through the night. The man with the shotgun took careful aim.

"Wait! My niece is in that car!" Eden screamed, but her voice was obliterated by the rain.

She climbed back into the BMW and put the car into gear, keeping the headlights off and ignoring Sage's pleas to know what was going on. She drove the car across the now empty tracks, following angry black skid marks that led toward the silver car.

The officer with the megaphone turned toward the BMW and waved his arms, gesturing for Eden to turn back.

"Stop now! Turn around!" the officer yelled into the megaphone, and Eden saw the shotgun swing in her direction.

She took a deep breath and continued to roll slowly toward the stranded car, stopping only a few yards away. Leaning over to the glove compartment, she opened the latch and looked at the gun nestled inside. With trembling hands, Eden picked up the gun. The shape and weight of it felt familiar in her grasp as she prepared to open the door. She was going to save Hope.

CHAPTER FORTY-FOUR

Vinny looked in his rearview mirror and watched the last railcar thunder out of view. He wondered what it would be like to be on the train, headed somewhere far away from the dead-end town he'd grown up in.

Would I have been somebody? he wondered, looking at his eyes in the mirror, now bare without his glasses.

If my mother had lived, and if we'd made it out of this town? Would things have been different?

He met Hope's wide, blue eyes in the mirror. They were kind eyes. Not the cruel eyes he'd seen so often in the many girls that had rejected or ignored him his whole life. He hadn't been good-looking like Trevor, and he hadn't been witty or smart.

When girls looked at him they either saw a loser or a nobody. Or, if they were more perceptive, they saw something disturbing, something damaged, that hid just below the surface.

A voice roared through the night, demanding they exit the car, but Vinny chose not to hear. They wouldn't approach the car yet, not with Hope as his hostage. They'd try to talk him into surrendering. He still had a little time.

"What are you going to do?" Hope asked. He could tell from the slight tremor in her voice that she was scared, but she was also calm. Almost resigned.

"I'm going to save you, just like I promised," Vinny said, picking up the little gun that lay on the passenger's seat next to him. "You and I are moving on to a better place."

He glanced back, assuring himself that she was still tied up, although the makeshift gag had fallen off in the dash to the car.

The voice on the megaphone yelled out again, telling him to stop and turn around. They must be able to see him in the car. Must be able to see he had turned to talk to Hope. Would they take a shot at him? He sunk lower in his seat.

"Where are we going? The police are waiting up there for us," Hope said, fixing her gaze on the flashing lights in the distance.

"They'll stop us if we try to leave."

"The police can't stop us...not where we're going." Vinny cocked the gun. "I'm done with this town. I'm finally leaving. Should have left years ago."

"But...what about me? What are you going to do with me?" Hope's voice finally broke, and she swallowed hard.

"I'm going to take you with me. Can't leave you here with the kind of men that run the place." Vinny looked back at her with narrow eyes.

"You do know about this town, right? That some of the cops run the operation at that old motel?"

Hope shook her head, her eyes filling with tears.

"They just want to make a buck off the girls. They sell drugs and girls to men who come into town off the interstate. It's disgusting." Vinny hit the steering wheel with his fist. "Men like that ruin everything."

He thought of the father he never knew. His mother had never admitted who he was, but Vinny suspected his father was just another user. Someone who had taken what he'd wanted and left them behind.

Vinny saw Hope's eyes flick to the rear window, and then glance back at him. Her breathing had quickened, and her pupils seemed to dilate as he watched. She'd seen something.

He strained to see through the rain-spattered glass and glimpsed blonde hair moving toward the rear of the car. Eden Winthrop hadn't given up the chase after all. A surge of anger filled him, making his head throb with the pressure.

That nosy bitch is the reason you're in this mess, the cold voice in his head told him. *If she hadn't gotten involved, you wouldn't be trapped here like an animal waiting to die. She's ruined everything.*

"And it's not just the men in this town who ruin everything," Vinny said, turning his eyes to the side mirror, waiting for Eden to come up beside the car. "The women are just as bad."

Hope sat up straighter, as if on alert. "Which women?"

"My mother, for one. She chose drugs over her own son. Abandoned me so she could get high."

Vinny tightened his fingers around the gun, knowing Hope was trying to distract him, but unable to resist responding.

"And my foster mother? She only cared about Trevor. Pretty much ignored me as long as the checks from the state kept coming."

"I'm sorry for you," Hope said, clearing her throat. "I know how it feels to lose your mother. My little brother and I lost both our parents a few years ago. My dad killed my mom."

Vinny frowned and looked over at Hope. Was she lying to get his sympathy? Did she think he'd let her go now, just because she had some sob story? No, she had a brother and an aunt who loved her. She had a whole police force ready to kill to get her back. What did he have? Nothing, that's what.

Resentment boiled over as he saw Eden creep around the corner of the car and head toward the door. He lifted the gun and held it by his shoulder, waiting for Eden to draw nearer.

"Drop your weapon!" the policeman with the megaphone yelled. "Get on the ground!"

"Please, Vinny," Hope begged from the backseat, tears in her voice. "Put down the gun before you get hurt. It doesn't have to end this way. I'll tell them you were only trying to help me. Only trying to get me away from those bad men."

Vinny paused, considering the idea that he could somehow escape the mess he was in. Maybe he could even come out of this a hero. Win an award instead of a trip to the gas chamber.

He pictured his mother's thin, plain face in the dim light of one of the many generic motel rooms they'd stayed in as she struggled to make ends meet. At bedtime, she would read from the only book available, the Bible that could always be found in a drawer by the bed. He liked the parable about the Good Samaritan; at the end, she always told him he was destined to do good deeds and save people in need.

All thoughts of his mother vanished when Eden's face appeared in the window beside him, the big gun in her hand aimed at the glass. He dismissed any chance of convincing the enraged woman beside him that he'd been trying to protect her niece.

So, I'm not going to be a hero, he thought, *but if I'm going down, I'm taking her with me.*

He put his hand on the doorknob, preparing to smash open the door and knock Eden off balance. Once she was on the ground he'd put a bullet into her nosy brain.

Let the cops shoot me, what does it matter?

Just as he pulled the handle, he felt the belt loop around his neck and tighten as his head was forced back against the headrest. He dropped the gun and grabbed at the belt with both hands; his eyes scanned to the rearview mirror, and he saw Hope's blue eyes pinned on his in fierce triumph, her teeth bared from the exertion of holding the belt in place as he struggled.

His mind reeled in panic. How had she gotten her hands free? Would he be strangled to death by his own belt?

Eden wrenched the car door open. Vinny writhed in the driver's seat, unarmed and unable to get free from the belt wrapped around his throat. He stared into blazing green eyes. They were filled with the same murderous fury that he had seen before in his own reflection. He felt the car start to spin and let his arms fall to his side before the world went dark.

* * *

When Vinny opened his eyes, a burly man in a rain-soaked shirt and tie was leaning in the door, cuffing his hands and reading him his rights.

"He need an ambulance, Detective Jankowski?" a uniformed officer called over, and the big detective shook his head. "No, I'll drive him over to the station and book him. It'll be a pleasure."

Vinny's throat burned, and it was hard to swallow. He wanted to turn his head to see if Hope was still in the backseat, but his neck muscles hurt too much. He groaned as Jankowski pulled him out of the car and hoisted him onto his feet.

As Vinny hobbled toward an awaiting police car, he saw Sage Parker sitting in the back of another police cruiser. She looked straight ahead as the car pulled away.

Jankowski pushed his head down and into the back of the cruiser. Vinny looked out the back window and saw Eden Winthrop standing beside a muddy BMW. She had her arm around Hope, who was wrapped in a navy-blue blanket. They watched as the police car pulled away.

Vinny turned and stared with dead eyes into the night beyond his window. The rain had stopped, and a few bright lights appeared to float in the black sky.

CHAPTER FORTY-FIVE

Reggie pulled onto Gladstone Drive and parked in front of a modest white house. She opened the door of the Mini Cooper to let Duke out of the backseat and smiled when she saw Milo jump out after him. The smaller dog had taken to Duke right away and followed him, tail wagging, wherever he went.

Eden climbed out of the passenger seat and joined Reggie on the sidewalk. She surveyed the house, eyes resting on the flowering magnolia tree in the front yard and the cheerful blue shutters framing the windows.

"This is nice, Reggie. You did good." But even as Eden murmured her approval, her eyes returned to the quiet street, scanning for suspicious cars or people lurking nearby.

Reggie took Eden's hand and squeezed. She knew that even though Trevor Bane and Detective Reinhardt were dead, and Vinny was now in jail, Eden was still jumpy, still paranoid that someone would be following her. She wasn't going to have an easy path to recovery, but she was on her way, and today's visit might help.

Duke and Milo trotted toward the front porch, and Reggie followed. Before she could knock, a balding man in a gray polo shirt and khaki pants opened the door. He smiled at Reggie and beamed down at the two golden retrievers.

"Morning, Quinn," Reggie said, relieved to see the security company had sent over a familiar face. Oliver Quinn had worked for the foundation before. He was well prepared to deal with dangerous stalkers and violent abusers. In this case, he was standing watch over Stacey Moore, along with her mother and little brother.

Although Buddy Jones was no longer a threat to the family, some of the men from the Old Canal Motel operation were still on the loose. They knew Stacey would be able to identify them, and that meant she could still be in danger.

"Good morning, Dr. Horn," Quinn responded, bending down to scratch both of the dogs behind their silky ears. He looked over at Eden, who had stepped into the house after Reggie. "How are you holding up, Ms. Winthrop?"

"I'm good, Quinn," Eden said, smiling as she watched the dogs enjoying the attention. "Everything okay here?"

Quinn nodded. "Things have been quiet so far. But I'm keeping my guard up, and we have cameras on the street and backyard."

Trisha Moore appeared in the doorway, her thin, strained face breaking into a smile when she saw Reggie and Eden. She crossed the room and hugged each of them tightly, then turned to call into the other room.

"Zane, come out here, honey, you've got visitors!" She looked at Reggie with a grateful smile.

A small boy with bright red hair darted into the front room and crashed into his mother's legs. He wrapped his arms around her waist and looked over at Reggie and Eden with scared eyes.

"You remember Dr. Horn, don't you, Zane?" Trisha prompted, as Zane buried his face against her stomach. "And Ms. Winthrop?"

"Hi, Zane. You know, I was just wondering about something." Reggie knelt in front of the boy and smiled. "Do you like dogs?"

Zane nodded and looked over at the dogs still sitting at Quinn's feet. Reggie saw his blue eyes follow Milo as he jostled for position next to Duke.

"The big one is named Duke, and the smaller one is Milo," Reggie said, and both dogs turned interested eyes toward Reggie upon hearing her say their names.

Trisha pulled Zane's arms from around her waist and nodded toward the dogs. "Go on, Zane. Say hello to Duke and Milo."

For a minute Reggie worried that Zane would turn and run out of the room, but then she saw him begin to take tentative steps forward. As he got closer, he held out a small hand.

"Hi there, Duke. Hi there, Milo." His voice was high-pitched and gentle, and both dogs wagged their tails and sniffed at his hand. Soon Zane was kneeling between them, stroking their golden fur and talking in a happy tone.

"Quinn, can you keep an eye on Zane and his new friends if they go play in the backyard?" Reggie asked.

She opened her purse and pulled out a small bag of dog treats and handed them to Zane. "Take these as well."

Once Zane had followed the two wagging tails out of the room, Reggie turned back to Trisha.

"So, how are you doing?" she asked. "And how is Stacey?"

Trisha swallowed hard. "I'm doing okay, I guess. Mainly worried about Stacey. She acts tough, but I can tell she's suffering. She's been having nightmares; we all have."

"Has she been asked to testify against the men arrested so far?" Reggie asked. She knew several men had been taken into custody at the Old Canal Motel the night Hope had been rescued.

"They asked her to identify the men in some pictures," Trisha said, biting her lip. "She was able to pick out the men in custody, so the next step is an actual line-up at the jail, but she's scared."

"I don't blame her," Eden spoke up. "It won't be easy for her to see the men that exploited and threatened her."

"Well, the local police have brought in the FBI. And one of the agents said he can get our family into the witness protection program if Stacey agrees to testify."

Trisha looked over her shoulder as if Stacey might be at the door listening. "The men worked for a group in Miami that's already under investigation. Organized crime the agent called it."

Reggie shuddered at the image Trisha's words raised. Grown men working together to organize the capture and assault of young girls. It was appalling, and she felt a burning hatred rise inside her at the thought of the men profiting from the trafficked girls.

"She has to testify if she can help put those bastards away," Reggie found herself saying, her words uncharacteristically bitter.

Trisha's eyes widened at Reggie's tone, but then she sighed and nodded. "That's what I told her. There are other girls out there now, and they're suffering the same fate she just escaped. She can't just turn her back if she can help them."

Trisha sank into an armchair with a deep sigh. "Besides, they may be after us as well. That dirty cop, Detective Reinhardt, they think he sent the guy that killed Buddy, and that he was connected with the group in Miami. So, who knows who may come knocking next, wanting to shut Stacey up."

Reggie hesitated, then said, "I don't want to upset you, but can you tell me about Buddy? I mean, I know he was shot and killed, but why was he at your house to begin with? I thought you were hiding from him."

Trisha looked down at her hands. "What can I say? I was an idiot. Buddy requested to speak with me as part of his rehabilitation plan. To admit he had hurt me and apologize. Kind of like the twelve-step program for abusers I guess. The jail counselor contacted me through the court, and I agreed to meet him in a supervised setting. After that, I wanted to give him a second chance. I thought he'd changed."

"And had he?" Reggie asked, her voice gentle.

"At first it seemed like it. I think he did try. But no, he didn't change. Not really. By the time Stacey came home, he was back to the old ways. Drinking and hitting out whenever he got mad."

Trisha blinked hard, her eyes wet. She turned to Eden.

"I was too ashamed to come back to Mercy Harbor asking for help again. I mean, you guys helped me once already, and I just screwed everything up again."

"We would never have judged you," Eden said, her eyes sad. "Only you know what really happened, and why you made the decisions you made."

"In the end, I guess Buddy actually helped save us," Trisha said, looking up at Reggie. "You could say that he took a bullet for us. Even if he didn't intend to. He was just in the wrong place at the wrong time. At least for him. But that extra few minutes the shooter took to get through Buddy gave me time to get my gun. That allowed me to hold off the guy until Detective Jankowski could show up."

"Thank goodness the police showed up in time," Reggie said. "You must be very grateful."

"Yes, Detective Jankowski saved my life and saved my children. There's no way I can ever thank him enough," Trisha said, allowing a small smile to appear. "Although I'd love to try. He is a fine-looking man."

Reggie stared at Trisha in surprise and then let out a giggle. "He is a hunk, isn't he?"

"When I first met him, I thought he was very rude," Eden said, before raising her eyebrows and grinning. "But now I know, underneath that tough attitude, he's just a teddy bear."

"I wouldn't go that far," Reggie laughed, "but we do owe him a lot."

Reggie studied Eden's face, enjoying the happy blush that had appeared. It made her look young and vibrant and pretty enough to turn any man's head. Reggie's optimism wilted as she remembered the way Leo Steele had looked at Eden.

It was obvious that he was more than a little interested. And the handsome womanizer might make Eden happy for a little while if given the chance, but Reggie wanted something more for her friend. Eden deserved a good man. A man like her Wayne. A man you could live and die for. Not a man who would be gone when the next pretty face walked by.

"Eden?" Stacey stood in the doorway, tears in her eyes. Her platinum curls had been restyled into a light brown bob.

"You don't know how glad I am to see you," Eden said, holding out her arms. Reggie felt her own eyes well up as she watched Eden comfort the weeping girl.

Then Eden spoke in a soft voice. "I'm sorry I let them find you, Stacey. I tried so hard to protect you."

"No, you *saved* me. And you saved my family. If it wasn't for you, no one would have even known to look for me," Stacey insisted. "Sig, I mean Detective Reinhardt, would have found me eventually, and he would have killed me and my family."

Stacy looked down and bit her lip, then used the back of her hand to wipe away tears. "I just feel so guilty that I almost got Zane killed," she whispered. "I've been so selfish. So stupid."

"There's no use thinking like that." Eden looked into Stacey's eyes and held her gaze. "Blaming yourself won't help anything. Just make sure you use what you've learned to help others. That's the only thing that's gotten me through the tough times."

Reggie's heart swelled with emotion. It had taken her friend a long time to get to the place where she could believe those words. She felt a surge of relief. Eden was going to be all right after all.

CHAPTER FORTY-SIX

Stacey walked to the window and looked out onto the quiet street. Although she'd escaped from the motel room weeks ago, part of her still felt like a prisoner. She knew there were still men out there who would silence her if they got the chance, or perhaps even try to take revenge for what they must see as a betrayal, but the true force that kept her hiding behind locked doors was her own fear.

As she watched, a small gray bird settled onto a branch of the magnolia tree, its head cocked to one side as if listening to a silent tune. Delicate white flowers trembled as the bird fluttered away, and Stacey felt a wave of sadness. Something deep inside of her had changed; she was no longer the innocent, trusting girl she'd once been.

Somehow, she was going to have to learn to trust again. She had lost faith in everyone besides the few people that were with her in the little house. And, worst of all, she had lost faith in herself.

She wondered if she would ever be able to forgive herself for the foolish choices she'd made. For putting her family in danger. Could she ever learn to trust her instincts again?

Stacey turned toward the room and saw Eden watching her. The woman's bright green eyes looked thoughtful, and Stacey wondered what had happened to Eden that caused her to dedicate her life to helping strangers. Maybe she too was trying to earn her own forgiveness.

"Why don't you go into the backyard and meet Zane's new friends," Reggie said, a mischievous look in her eye. "I'm thinking you and your little brother could use a new friend right about now."

Stacey heard laughter as she stepped through the back door. Zane was running beside a small golden retriever, a smile on his face and a stick in his little hand.

"Get the stick, Milo," Zane called out. The joy in his voice was contagious, and Stacey couldn't stop a smile from spreading across her own face as he threw the stick across the thick green lawn and squealed in delight.

Oliver Quinn sat in a lawn chair wiping sweat off his face with a big hand. The summer day was hot, and he looked a bit red in the cheeks. He waved over at Stacey but left her to her own thoughts as she sat down on the top step and wrapped her arms around her knees.

It was good to see Zane happy and to know her mother was safe inside. It was good to know that Buddy would never hit her mother again and that she would never have to go back to the horror of the motel. As the sun soaked into her skin, she felt her shoulders relax and the tension in her neck soften.

The back door opened, and Eden sat down on the step next to her. She didn't say anything for a few minutes, just sat and watched Zane and the dogs.

"Looks like Zane and Milo are getting along," Eden finally said. "My dog, Duke, he's been a real comfort to me in the last few years. He's what you call an ESA, which means he's an emotional support animal. Milo is an ESA, too."

"Yeah? Well, Zane seems really happy. Thanks for bringing the dogs." Stacey bit her lip and glanced over at Eden. "Can I ask you a question? I mean, if it's too personal you don't have to answer."

"Sure," Eden said. "Ask me anything you want."

"What happened to you?" Stacey asked, not daring to meet Eden's eyes. "I mean, why do you try to help people, and why do you need a support dog?'

Eden paused, and Stacey felt a rush of embarrassment. She'd gone too far. But then Eden cleared her throat and said in a soft voice,

"My younger sister, Mercy, was killed almost five years ago. Her husband shot her, and I...I found her. After that, I started having panic attacks and lots of anxiety. Duke helped me cope."

Stacey wanted to say something to comfort Eden, but her throat felt tight, and she just listened.

"I felt guilty that I hadn't saved Mercy," Eden continued, "and I wanted to do something to...to make up for it. I wanted to help save other women because that would make me feel better about myself, I guess."

"That makes sense," Stacey said, wishing she had a plan to make herself feel better.

"I hear you may be going into the witness protection program." Eden looked over at Stacey and held her gaze. "How are you feeling about that? You scared?"

"A little," Stacey admitted. "But also a little relieved. I want my mom and Zane to be safe, so I'm glad someone's going to be watching out for them. And I want to help stop these guys from doing the same thing to other girls. I keep thinking about Jess and Brandi, and the other girls I left back in the motel."

"And what about you?" Eden asked. "What do you want for yourself?"

"I don't know," Stacey murmured, looking down at her feet. "I guess I just want to feel okay again. To not feel ashamed or scared. That's about it right now."

"Hey Stacey, look at me!" Zane raced ahead of Milo to touch the fence. He jumped up and down in glee. "I won! I won!"

"Good job, Squirt!" Stacey yelled back as the door again opened behind her.

"What's all the commotion about?" Reggie asked. "Zane enjoying his new dog a little too much?"

"His dog?" Stacey looked around at Reggie with wide eyes. "You mean you're giving that dog to Zane?"

"Yep, I've already gotten approval from your mom. Milo is now part of your family," Reggie said, a smile lighting up her eyes. "He's a good little guy and he needs a family to love and take care of."

"Why don't you go tell Zane the good news," Eden prompted, her hand warm on Stacey's shoulder.

And as Stacey ran across the grass, the sunshine warm in her hair, she felt her eyes well with tears, and for the first time in a long time, they were the happy kind.

CHAPTER FORTY-SEVEN

Nessa winced as she lowered herself into the lawn chair next to Pete Barker, silently cursing her cracked and bruised ribs. She slid on her sunglasses and tried to distract herself from the ache in her chest by counting backward from one hundred by sevens. That was the test the doctors had used after she'd been shot to determine if the head injury she'd sustained had caused brain trauma. She'd gotten to sixty-five before she'd given up and pretended to doze off. She'd never been good at math anyway.

"I'm the one who's had a heart attack and angioplasty," Barker said with a raised eyebrow. "So how come you're the one with chest pains."

"No, you had a myocardial infarction. That's what you told me before. You said it's not really a heart attack." Nessa ran an irritable hand through her newly close-cropped curls and paused to rub a still-tender patch of stubble. Her head injury had been serious enough to require the medics to shave a patch of skin around the wound.

"And you were wearing a bulletproof vest, so you weren't really shot," Barker replied, earning a glare from Nessa. His tone softened. "I guess that means neither of us have an excuse to sit around here slacking off anymore."

"I'm going back to work as soon as I get the doc's sign-off," Nessa assured him. "I can't stand sitting around and twiddling my thumbs with everything that's going on."

"So, in the meantime, you thought you'd twiddle your thumbs with me?" Barker asked. "I don't mind the free time too much, really. Gives me time to think."

"Actually, I'm here because I had questions about a couple of your old cases."

Nessa took off her sunglasses and turned to Barker. He looked pretty good. The heart stent and all the rest he'd gotten had brought some color back into his skin.

"Oh, yeah?" Barker stretched and yawned. "Which ones you been thinking about?"

"Ingram said I should ask you about Eden Winthrop," Nessa said, watching Barker's face.

He suddenly looked alert.

"What about her?" he asked.

A frown appeared on his face for the first time that day.

"Well, she was Mercy's Lancaster's sister. She found the body," Nessa offered up. "And that was the last case you and Ingram partnered on, right?"

"Okay, so what does that matter?" Baker looked toward the street as if hoping someone or something would come along and save him from the conversation.

"Well, Ingram had a bad reaction to Eden's name. Seemed like he had a problem with her, but he just said to ask you."

"Ingram's old-school. He follows the code, you know? He didn't agree with the way I handled that case, but he didn't lodge a complaint. That's not the way he works. He just requested a different partner."

Barker smiled and sighed. "I thought it was probably a good idea. He was a pain in the ass."

Nessa agreed, but she let the comment pass.

"So, what did you do that pissed him off?"

"It's what I didn't do," Barker said. "I didn't push for a full investigation into what happened. I accepted the murder-suicide theory and closed the case."

"And Ingram didn't buy it?" Nessa was confused. "What did he think happened?"

"He thought Eden Winthrop was involved," Barker said. "He thought she was faking her amnesia, and he wanted to go after her."

"He thought she killed her own sister and brother-in-law?" Nessa asked in surprise. "Did any of the evidence support his suspicions?"

Barker looked uncomfortable. "I shouldn't be saying all this. It's water under the bridge."

"Off the record, Barker," Nessa said, her interest piqued.

"It doesn't matter anyway," Barker said. "We didn't process the crime scene as a homicide scene. None of the evidence would hold up in court now."

Nessa felt her heart sink at the mention of evidence. So, there *had* been evidence linking Eden to the scene?

"Let's just say Ms. Winthrop had blood on her hands when we arrived, even though she couldn't remember being in the apartment. And the gun had blood on the grip. Of course, it could have been the victim's blood, but...well, the scene suggested a different scenario."

"So why didn't you flag it as a possible double homicide?"

"Because Mercy Lancaster had been beaten so badly, she was unrecognizable, and Preston Lancaster had stalked and abused his wife prior to that day. It just made sense that he had killed her."

"But the blood on Eden's hands?" Nessa wondered aloud. "How would it have gotten there?"

"I don't know. I have my ideas but that's all they are. No facts to back them up. But I believe Preston Lancaster beat and shot his wife. And, however he ended up dead, he had it coming."

Nessa stared at Barker with an open mouth.

"I told you I shouldn't be saying this," Barker said. "But when you face down death, you start saying all the things you always wanted to say but were too scared to say."

Nessa could see Barker was getting upset. She hadn't come to cause problems, and it wasn't her business what had happened before they were partners. Some things were better left buried.

"You said there was another case you wanted to ask me about?" Barker said, clearly ready to change the subject.

"I've been thinking about the Natalie Lorenzo investigation. You were the lead detective on that as well."

Barker just nodded, his face grim.

"Well, now that we know Vinny Lorenzo killed those girls, I keep asking myself why his prints were in the room where someone strangled his mother. Do you think he could have killed her? His own mother? And at that age?"

"No, I don't think the kid killed his mom," Barker said, his forehead furrowing into deep wrinkles. He looked at Nessa and sighed. "I've tried to forget the case. Tried to forget the kid."

The raw emotion in Barker's voice surprised Nessa. She knew he was a big softie under the gruff exterior. That wasn't a secret to anyone who had known him more than five minutes. But she'd never heard him talk about the Lorenzo case before or mention any kid that had gotten under his skin.

"You see, that day, the day I told the kid his mother had died? That was the day I realized I didn't want to be a cop anymore." He drew in a long, shaky breath.

Nessa raised her eyebrows but didn't speak.

"I'd suspected I wasn't cut out for the work early on, but I didn't want to admit it. I wanted to be a cop like my dad and my uncles, even though they never pressured me. *I pressured myself.* And then once I was in, well, it was hard to get out. Kids, bills, debts, obligations, expectations. You know how it is. But after that day, after Vinny Lorenzo, I knew eventually I'd have to get out."

"What was it about Vinny that changed things?"

"You know what happened to his mother. She had drug problems. Had been arrested a few times for solicitation. I guess she was trying to earn money for drugs and trying to take care of the kid. I don't know. But when she was found like that, we figured she'd been killed by a john that took things too far."

Nessa wasn't so sure Natalie Lorenzo had been killed by a john. The River Girls Investigation had raised new questions and doubts. But she knew she needed to let Barker have his say. He'd sat on his feelings for twelve years; he needed to get them out. Bottling up his feelings obviously hadn't been good for his heart.

"Anyway, when we finally realized her next of kin was her son, a twelve-year-old kid, I offered to be the one to notify him. I thought I could handle it." Barker paused and cleared his throat.

"When I told him, he just looked at me with dead eyes. Like the life had already been kicked out of him and there was nothing left of him that could grieve. His eyes stayed with me after that. You know, sort of like when you see your first dead body? Well, this felt like I'd seen my first dead soul. I couldn't shake it. It ate at me, and I had to admit I wasn't cut out for the work. Maybe I'm not hard enough."

"Caring about a kid, and hating what the world did to him, doesn't mean you aren't cut out for the job, Barker. It just means you're human. It means you're decent."

Nessa felt tears sting her eyes as she thought of her own doubts about being strong enough to handle the pain and suffering she witnessed on a regular basis.

"I'm sorry, Nessa," Barker said, his voice low. "I guess I'm trying to justify my decision to leave the force. That kid made me see the world differently, and after that, I couldn't un-see it."

"I guess it's no big surprise Vinny Lorenzo turned into a killer," Nessa said, realizing with a sick stomach that nothing she could say would convince Pete Barker to come back to the department.

"It's a screwed-up world, sometimes, Pete."

"Yeah, it is." Pete nodded, looking up toward the bright blue sky. "But we're both still here, and we're lucky to be alive. Let's stop complaining and just enjoy the day."

Nessa leaned back into the lawn chair, ignoring the stab of pain in her chest, and began to count backward from one hundred by sevens. This time she made it all the way to fifty-eight before dozing off.

* * *

Eden Winthrop's house looked different in the daylight, without the drama of flashing lights and yellow crime scene tape. The house looked peaceful. Nessa hoped her visit wouldn't disturb that peace as she walked slowly up the path, Jankowski close behind her.

She wasn't sure why he'd insisted he come with her to check on Eden and Hope, but she hadn't objected. He was her partner now, and she was going to have to get used to him.

As they approached the door, Nessa glanced over at Jankowski's stony profile, wondering what was going on behind his impassive exterior. Just two weeks earlier he'd killed a man on the same night he had arrested a serial killer and his partner had been shot at point-blank range. Did any of that bother him? Was he secretly suffering from PTSD? He certainly didn't appear to be.

Nessa didn't know what was going on inside the brawny detective's head, but on the outside, he looked fit and healthy, like he didn't have a care in the world.

He knocked on the door and looked up into the newly-installed security camera as footsteps approached. The door swung open to reveal Hope. She had her long hair pulled back into a simple ponytail and wore baggy shorts and a Florida Gators hoodie.

She led them inside, calling up the stairs, "Aunt Eden, Nessa's here, and Detective Jankowski."

"It's good to see you safe at home," Nessa said as she followed Hope into the living room.

She remembered looking at the school picture of Hope and wondering if the girl's picture would end up on her investigation room's whiteboard.

Some things work out after all, she thought. *Sometimes they really do come home.*

"Thanks, Nessa." Hope's voice was solemn. "I'm really glad to be home, too. If it wasn't for you guys, and for Aunt Eden, I wouldn't be here now."

"Well, let's not think about that," Nessa urged, putting a reassuring hand on Hope's arm. "All that matters now is that you're here and you're safe."

Devon appeared behind them without warning. "And she's got a new boyfriend that won't stop calling!" he teased, his eyes lighting up as he watched his sister's face.

"Devon, how many times do I have to tell you that Luke and I are just friends?" Hope smiled then, and Nessa was relieved to see the girl was finding her way back to normal.

"Nessa, how are you?" Eden hurried down the stairs and walked straight over to Nessa and pulled her into a gentle embrace. Nessa's ribs throbbed at the slight touch, but she hugged Eden back.

"I'm doing pretty good all things considered," Nessa answered, her hand self-consciously rising to cover the shaved patch on the side of her head.

"Well, I love the new haircut." Eden stepped back to consider Nessa's shorter style. "It really suits you."

Eden turned her attention to Jankowski, and Nessa studied the pretty blonde's profile, remembering her talk with Barker.

Could this kind, elegant woman be a killer?

"Thank you, Detective Jankowski, for everything you've done. I visited Stacey and Trisha Moore this morning and they told me how grateful they are. We all are."

"It's my job to catch the bad guys," Jankowski said, then cleared his throat and shifted his weight around as if he couldn't get comfortable.

Nessa looked over at her new partner, surprised to see a flush of color in his cheeks. Was he flustered by Eden's compliments? Or was he interested in more than just praise? Maybe that was why he'd insisted he come along.

Nessa raised her eyebrows and smiled at Jankowski, already anticipating the fun she would have teasing him about his crush on Eden.

Hope excused herself to make a phone call, and Devon ran upstairs, taking the steps two at a time. Nessa watched them leave with a satisfied smile.

They're just normal kids again, she thought. *Who'd have thought normal could be such a blessing?*

She imagined Cole and Cooper waiting at home for her. Imagined Jerry pacing, anxious about her being out of the house again. Hopefully, her family would soon get back to normal, too, or at least their version of it.

Eden ushered them into the kitchen, where Duke was curled up by the back door. He raised his head at their entrance and stretched before trotting over to greet them. Once they were settled around the kitchen table, Nessa turned to Eden.

"It's great to see y'all safe and well, but I came by because I imagine you have questions, and I think you deserve to know whatever we know." Nessa glanced at Jankowski. He was looking at Eden, his gaze unfathomable.

"Yes, I have lots of questions. It's all been so confusing." Eden clasped her fingers in her lap and exhaled deeply. "I've tried to understand how these men...these terrible men...were able to operate out of that motel without getting caught. Why didn't the police stop them sooner?"

Jankowski shook his head, as if frustrated, and Nessa worried he would get defensive and take Eden's question as an attack on the department. But his words were tinged with regret.

"I'm really sorry about that," he said. "It's unforgivable when a cop betrays his department and his community. But that's what happened here. Detective Reinhardt was dirty, and he shielded the crooks that were running drugs and trafficking girls."

"But why would he do that?" Eden asked, anger finally surfacing.

"I'm not sure exactly how it all got started. We're still investigating, but it looks like he was deeply involved with a criminal organization." Jankowski looked over at Nessa, his expression wary.

"In fact, we were already investigating Reinhardt and the guys in the Miami organization prior to recent events. We suspected Reinhardt might be involved with distributing drugs, based on an informant that turned on him."

Jankowski stood and paced over to look out the back window.

"And we'd heard rumors about underage girls in south Florida being offered up on the internet, but we had just started looking into it. Chief Kramer wanted us to complete our own internal investigation before calling in the state bureau or the feds. He didn't want to destroy the department's reputation until we were sure."

Nessa stared at Jankowski in disbelief. He had known all along that Reinhardt might be dirty, and yet he hadn't warned her? The room spun, and Nessa felt hot blood rush to her head, making her wound throb. She put both elbows on the table and took a deep breath. What other secrets had Jankowski hidden from her? Could she really be his partner after this? Could she ever truly trust him to watch her back?

Jankowski shot Nessa a look of remorse, then turned to Eden.

"We've determined that Detective Reinhardt had picked up Trevor Bane on a minor drug charge and struck a deal with him. Reinhardt would let Trevor off if he agreed to recruit young girls for the Miami organization. We think that's when Trevor started using the street name Hollywood to hide his real identity."

"And he exploited the girls at Clear Horizons," Eden stated, understanding the connection now. "He used his position there to gain their trust, and then got them hooked on drugs and delivered them to these criminals."

"Yeah, that's what it looks like," Jankowski said, rubbing the back of his neck. "Of course, we've got to prove all this in court if we're going to convict the men we have in custody or have any hope of stopping the guys who are running things in Miami."

Nessa felt Duke nudge her hand, and she turned to see him staring up at her, his eyes worried.

He must know an emotional basket case when he sees one, she mused, as she began to stroke his soft fur.

"What about Trevor's mother?" Eden asked. "What about that horrible woman. Was she involved somehow?'

"Denise Bane must have at least suspected what was going on and did nothing to stop it. But we haven't found any evidence that she was involved, and we can't yet prove what she actually knew."

"And Vinny Lorenzo?" Eden asked. "How did he figure into all this? Why did he try to strangle Hope? Why did he abduct her?"

Nessa cleared her throat and motioned to Jankowski that she would take this one. He'd taken her by surprise with his admission that Reinhardt had already been the subject of an internal investigation, but she was still the lead detective on the River Girls case.

"Vinny Lorenzo was placed in Denise Bane's home as a foster child after his mother was declared unfit. She'd been arrested for drug possession and solicitation. When Vinny was twelve his mother died. The case was never solved, but Vinny had already been living with Denise Bane, and he was then permanently assigned to her care. So, he grew up with Trevor."

"It's clear that Vinny was involved with the crime ring, but what about the killings?" Eden's delicate brow furrowed in doubt. "Why would he kill all those girls? Are you sure it was him?"

"He's confessed to killing Tiffany Clarke, Jessica Carmichael, and Brandi Long. And, of course, we caught him red-handed trying to abduct Hope."

Nessa considered her next words, then decided Eden had a right to know it all.

"Vinny told us that he planned to kill Hope. Planned to *save her*, as he called it. He said he strangled all the girls to prevent them from suffering."

Eden raised a trembling hand to her mouth.

"I knew he was probably planning on killing Hope. But to have him admit it? It's incomprehensible. He must be mentally ill. How else could you explain such twisted logic?"

"Yes, he's a sick young man," Nessa agreed. "It will take time to understand why he acted in the way he did. Maybe we'll never be sure. But we have found his fingerprints at the scene of his mother's homicide. So, we think he may have witnessed the murder of his mother. Perhaps that trauma ultimately turned him into a killer."

Nessa watched as Eden tried to absorb the information. Could anyone really understand the motives of a serial killer? She turned as Jankowski's phone rang and he left the room to answer it.

She watched her new partner exit the room, curious if he'd kept other secrets from her. She glanced back to see an inscrutable look on Eden's face. Barker's words spun in her head, prompting an unwelcome thought.

Can we ever fully understand the secret motives in the mind of another? Do we truly know anyone?

CHAPTER FORTY-EIGHT

Jankowski jabbed at his cell phone screen, ending the call. He wished he could end all connections to his soon-to-be ex-wife, Gabby, so easily. She'd called to inform him the divorce papers would be ready to sign by the end of the week. His stomach clenched at the thought of seeing Gabby again. Of formally ending the marriage that had started with so much love, that had been expected to last happily ever after. He let himself sink into self-pity. Were there ever any real happy endings in this world?

The empty feeling in his chest expanded, and for a minute he couldn't catch his breath. Then he saw his reflection in the mirror above the fireplace, and a thought flashed through his mind.

There stands a broken man.

The idea irritated him. He didn't have a right to feel broken. So, his wife hadn't been able to handle being married to a cop. She had gotten lonely and sought comfort elsewhere. It happened all the time. He'd done nothing to prevent it. Now he had to live with it.

Innocent people were out there now, at the mercy of criminals and killers. He didn't have time to pity himself. No, he had a job to do, and feeling sorry for himself wasn't in his job description. Besides, somewhere inside him, he had known Gabby wasn't a forever kind of woman. Maybe that's why he'd resisted having kids. Maybe he'd known, deep down, that she wouldn't stick around when the going got tough. Maybe now he could find a woman that understood the kind of world they lived in and would respect his need to make it better.

A vision of Eden Winthrop's blazing green eyes made him smile. Now *that* was a woman with a heart. Maybe, someday, he'd find someone like her.

Sticking his phone back in his pocket, Jankowski walked back into the kitchen just as Eden was asking Nessa a question.

"Why did no one find out Detective Reinhardt was involved with the crime ring?"

"He was pretty good at hiding it," Jankowski cut in, sitting down at the table. "He used a street name to hide who he was. Called himself Sig. He always bragged about carrying a Sig Sauer P226, so he must have picked the name because of his weapon."

Nessa rolled her eyes and shook her head. "The good news is that eight girls were rescued from the Old Canal Motel that night. Reinhardt was getting ready to ship them out to Miami. Your quick-thinking actions saved those girls from further exploitation and suffering."

Jankowski bit his lip, debating how much he should admit to Eden and Nessa. He knew Nessa would have a hard time trusting him after he'd kept the internal investigation from her. Could he afford to alienate her even more if the whole story came out?

"Actually, Reinhardt had been suspended a few years back for a gambling addiction," he blurted out. Nessa and Eden stared at him, and he cleared his throat, already regretting his words.

"But Reinhardt said he'd gotten treatment and was no longer gambling, so Chief Kramer brought him back in as a detective in Vice. But we now know that Reinhardt never stopped gambling. He owed a bigshot criminal in Miami lots of money. We think that's why he was helping these crooks to traffic drugs and girls. He kept the heat off them. Protected them. He was paying off a debt."

Nessa narrowed her eyes at Jankowski, and he knew she was restraining herself from lashing out at him for keeping her in the dark as to Reinhardt's true character. Nessa might be fuming mad, but she was still a professional, and she wouldn't allow herself to go off in front of a victim.

"But why wouldn't someone at the motel raise the alarm?" Eden asked, and Jankowski felt a bolt of admiration pass through him. She was sharp and persistent. Like him."

"Yeah, that was a big question in our minds as well," Jankowski said. "We've since found out that the manager of the motel, Hiram Ewell, or Big Red as everyone calls him, was aware and in some ways involved. He's been charged with aiding and abetting on a multitude of charges."

"And Sage?" Eden asked, her eyes dropping to focus on her hands. "What happens to Sage now?"

Jankowski met Nessa's eyes and shrugged. Her hard expression softened, and she nodded.

"The D.A. is considering what charges, if any, to file against her," Jankowski said. "He could charge her with making a false statement or impeding an investigation. But considering that she had been threatened and was under duress, he doesn't think the charges would stick."

Eden nodded but kept her eyes on her hands. "Will Sage be asked to testify? Will Hope and I have to testify?"

"Vinny has confessed, and it's likely he'll agree to a plea deal if the DA offers him life without parole instead of the death penalty," Nessa answered. "So, with luck, none of you will need to testify, and you can get back to normal."

Eden pulled Duke to her and hugged him. Her eyes misting over as she spoke. "I'm not sure what normal is any more. But I'm so grateful to have Hope back with the family. I know that it could have ended differently, and that happy endings aren't guaranteed. After losing Mercy, I know that better than anyone."

Jankowski felt a sudden urge to pull Eden to him, to comfort her. What would it feel like to have her arms around him? He knew it was a pathetic question. He stood and turned to Nessa, knowing her appraising eyes were still on him.

"I think we'd better go," Jankowski said, putting out a big hand to Eden.

Her fingers were soft and warm as she took his hand and squeezed it, and he couldn't resist looking into her green eyes one last time.

CHAPTER FORTY-NINE

Pat Monahan stepped into Leo's office and crossed her arms over her ample chest, the silent disapproval on her face impossible to ignore.

"What have I done this time, Pat?" Leo asked, his dark eyes flicking to his phone. "Have I missed an appointment?"

"No, but you missed a call from the public defender's office. They say it's regarding your work with Vincent Lorenzo." She pronounced the name with exaggerated disdain.

Everyone in Willow Bay who watched the news or read a newspaper now knew that Vinny Lorenzo had been arrested and charged with three counts of first-degree murder. Based on the grumblings he'd heard around town, Leo wouldn't be surprised if a mob broke into the jail and lynched the accused serial killer. And if the look on Pat's face was any indication, she would be holding the biggest pitchfork.

"Thanks for the message, Pat."

Leo turned to his computer and began shutting down his files. He knew Pat wanted his assurance that he hadn't agreed to represent Vinny Lorenzo, but he wasn't in the mood to satisfy her curiosity. As fond as he was of the good-hearted woman, he had a mission in mind, and he didn't want to get sidetracked or lose his nerve.

As Pat remained standing in his doorway, Leo stood up and pulled on his suit jacket. "I'm leaving for the day. I have an errand to take care of."

Pat looked at her watch in surprise. "But it's only four. You never leave before eight."

"Well, maybe I'm changing my ways, Pat," Leo said, picking up his briefcase and sliding in his laptop and a few file folders. "Maybe I've finally realized some things are more important than work."

"About time," Pat said, nodding in satisfaction. "And I hope she's the right one this time."

"She?" Leo raised an eyebrow. "What do you mean?"

"I mean I hope the woman you're going to see is the right one for you. It's about time you settle down." She turned and walked back to her desk before Leo could think of a reply.

He walked out to his BMW, welcoming the intense heat of the June sun after the chill of his air-conditioned office. As the car headed away from downtown, he selected a mellow playlist and opened the sunroof. He hoped the music would calm his nerves, but it was no use.

He'd given himself two weeks to try to get past his infatuation with Eden Winthrop, and it hadn't worked. Her green eyes and sad smile had stayed with him. He knew it was pathetic, but he had to see her. Had to know if she was okay.

And he needed to know if she hated him again, now that Hope was safely home, and Stacey Moore had been found alive and well. Now that the trauma was over, would she regret the things she'd told him? Would she blame him again for defending Preston Lancaster? Or would she remember the connection they'd felt as they had searched for a killer together?

He supposed that even the absence of hate would be enough to encourage him. One way or another he had to find out how she was. And he had to know how she felt about him.

As Leo neared Eden's street, the urge to turn around and drive home washed over him. This was crazy. He didn't even really know the woman. What could he possibly say to her after two weeks of silence? But when he stood on her doorstep, and she opened the door to him, a warm smile lighting up her face, he knew it would have been even crazier to stay away.

"I wondered where you'd gone," Eden said, stepping back so he could enter. "I didn't have your number. I wanted to call and thank you."

"I thought you'd need time to take care of Hope. Time to get her and Devon back to some sort of normal schedule. And, well, I didn't have your number either," Leo lied.

He'd gotten her phone number by reviewing the police report she'd filed when Stacey Moore had gone missing. He'd looked at the number so many times in the last two weeks that he now knew it by heart, although he'd never actually dialed it.

"Well, I'm glad you've stopped by." Eden led him into the living room and motioned for him to sit next to her on the sofa.

"I would have had to track you down eventually to thank you for everything you did. I know I was a mess, and you helped me hold it together long enough to find Hope."

"Don't forget what you did for me. You helped catch Jessica's killer," Leo said, drinking in the sight of her next to him. How had he managed to stay away for two weeks?

"Thanks to you I was able to tell Jessica's mother what happened. At least now Beth knows her daughter's killer will be brought to justice."

"I just hope it brings her some measure of peace," Eden murmured, her smile dimming at the thought of Beth Carmichael's grief.

"After coming so close to losing Hope, I can't imagine how she's getting through it."

Leo wanted to take Eden's hand, but he wasn't sure how she'd react. So far, she'd been polite, even friendly, but that didn't mean she was ready to start holding hands. Just seeing her again made him realize how much she'd been through, and how fragile she must still be emotionally.

If he had any hope of winning her trust, he'd have to be patient. Have to take things slowly. That is if she'd give him the chance.

"And Hope is well?" Leo asked. "And Devon?"

"Yes, it's amazing how resilient they are. Reggie's been meeting with them, counseling them I guess you could say. She thinks they're doing really well. Although Hope does have nightmares sometimes."

Eden looked down at her hands and sighed. "We all do really. But that's to be expected after...everything."

Leo's phone rang in his pocket, but he ignored it. "That's probably the public defender's office again. I offer my services to them pro bono like most of the defense attorneys in town. We're all on rotation, and I guess my turn came up when it came time to assign a public defender to Vinny Lorenzo."

Eden's eyes widened in horror. She stood up abruptly and walked to the window before turning to face Leo, her face drawn and pale. Leo hurried across the room and took her hand, forgetting his own advice to take things slowly.

"Don't worry, Eden," he said, instantly regretting his choice of words. "I would never take the case. For one, it would be a conflict of interest, since he's accused of killing my client's daughter."

"And two?" Eden asked, a challenge in her voice. "What is the other reason you would never take the case?"

"And two is because I already hurt you once by defending someone that turned out to be a killer. I regret that, and I would never forgive myself if I hurt you again."

Eden swallowed hard, and Leo saw the glint of tears in her eyes as she turned her head away. Had he ruined his chance to win her trust already?

"I'm sorry, Eden," Leo said, knowing that his actions had played a part in her sister's death, and hating himself for it.

"So am I, Leo," Eden said, squeezing his hand gently, then releasing it. "I know you didn't want Preston to kill Mercy. And I know you just want to help people like your father. I understand how much it hurts not to be able to save someone you love. It eats away at you. So, I do forgive you, if that's what you're asking. But..."

Leo's heart dropped at the look in her eyes. "But you can't forget that I was there helping Preston?"

"I'm sorry, Leo," Eden said again, finally raising her haunted eyes to meet his. "I want to forget about it. Hell, I'd like to forget everything about Preston and what he did, but I'm not sure I ever will."

Leo looked into her eyes and saw that she understood his pain. She felt it, too. Maybe she was the only one that could. And he could understand her pain as well. She wasn't the only one who had a hard time forgetting the past. Perhaps they could help each other if only she'd let him in.

"You know, I've been thinking a lot these last two weeks," Leo said, knowing he couldn't tell her that most of his thoughts had been about her.

"And one of the things I've been thinking about is how Natalie Lorenzo was murdered only a few weeks before my mother was killed. And neither murder has been solved, at least not to my satisfaction."

"What are you saying, Leo?" Eden asked, her brow furrowed. "Do you think the murders could be related? That the same person killed both your mother and Natalie Lorenzo?"

"I don't know," Leo said, knowing he had no evidence to link the cases. "But I imagine the police will be delving into the Natalie Lorenzo case, trying to get answers, so I might reopen my own investigation into my mother's murder. See if I can find a link."

Eden looked thoughtful, then nodded. "I think you should. I think you need to know. I'd want to know."

Later, as Leo stood in the hallway preparing to leave, he felt a soft nudge on his hand and looked down to see Duke sitting beside him.

"Hiya, Duke. You doing okay, big guy?" Leo said, ruffling the dog's fur.

"He's been a lifesaver, as usual," Eden answered, kneeling beside Duke and hugging him to her. "He's always there to support me. And he's been great with the kids. We're lucky to have him."

"And Duke is lucky to have you." Leo wondered if he was actually jealous of a dog. "Looks like he gets a lot of love around here. But you know..."

Eden opened the door and looked over at him, eyebrows raised, waiting for him to finish his sentence. He stepped onto the front stoop and looked back, not wanting to leave.

"Well, if you ever need emotional support from a human, I'd be happy to help out."

Leo handed her his business card and grinned, his heart beating like a caged bird in his chest.

"In fact, if there's ever anything you need, you have my number now. Feel free to use it anytime."

As he pulled out of the driveway, Leo looked in his rearview mirror and saw that Eden, outlined by the warm glow of the setting sun, was standing on the front steps, watching him drive away.

CHAPTER FIFTY

Leo's car had disappeared into the sunset, but Eden remained standing on the front steps, her eyes turned to the horizon, transfixed by the exquisite shades of blue and pink that painted the sky before her.

She wondered where Leo would go. Did he have someone waiting at home for him? He had never mentioned a wife or girlfriend, but then, why would he? So far, they'd only shared stories of their tragic past. She knew in many ways they were both still trapped in that past, unable to find a way to live fully in the present.

Eden pictured Leo's dark eyes, so hard to read, and yet somehow vulnerable. She looked at his business card, still clutched in her hand. How long should she wait until she called him?

Leo had opened his heart to her and she suspected, whether she liked it or not, a bond had formed between them. Life had damaged him, but she now knew what kind of man he really was, under his brooding exterior and smooth good looks. He was a man who was willing to risk everything to see justice done. That kind of passion could be dangerous, and it both scared and thrilled her.

Eden doubted she could ever forget how Leo had helped Mercy's killer, but maybe she could learn to accept it someday. And maybe someday she would even be ready to share her deepest secret with him. She had a strong sense that, even though he'd just driven off into the sunset, their story wasn't over. It was just beginning, and she had no idea how it would end.

If she'd learned anything in life, it was that you can never be sure how anything will end. She thought of Nathan, and the red-eye flight he'd taken to get to her when he'd heard Hope had been abducted. She'd broken down in tears when he'd knocked on her door the morning after Hope had been rescued, his face pale and drawn with worry.

She realized then that she could never give up Nathan, and she'd been foolish to think she could. He was her oldest and dearest friend, and while they were no longer a couple, Nathan had assured her that he would always be a part of her life. In his own gentle way, he'd set her free.

The pink in the sky deepened into violet as Eden watched. Duke whined in his throat beside her, not liking the way she stood so still, staring into the distance. He nudged her hand and she looked down into his worried eyes.

"You want to go for a walk, boy?"

She heard a soft voice behind her.

"Can I come, too?'"

Hope stood in the doorway, her blue eyes shining like sapphires in the dusky light.

"I'd like that," Eden said, reaching for Hope's hand.

They led Duke down the familiar street, waving at neighbors and stopping here and there to let Duke sniff around or mark his territory.

"You remember now, don't you?" Hope asked, keeping her eyes on the horizon. "You remember what happened that day Mom died."

Eden's heart began to thump in her chest, but she didn't feel anxious. The panic and anxiety were behind her now. She'd been forced to face her demons when she picked up Leo's gun, ready to kill a man if it meant saving her niece. And she had known then that it wasn't the first time she'd held a gun.

"I guess some part of me refused to admit what happened. A part of me that wouldn't let me remember," Eden said. "For the longest time, I believed the nightmares were just nightmares. Now I know they were flashbacks."

"I was there, you know," Hope said. She stopped under a streetlight and turned to look at Eden. "I saw what happened. I saw what you did to Dad."

"Whatever I did, I did for you and Devon." Eden squared her shoulders. "And I don't regret it."

"You saved us," Hope said with grim certainty. "You saw that he'd shot Mom. When you ran to her, tried to save her, he pointed the gun at you and told you to leave."

Eden closed her eyes at the memory. Mercy had been bleeding. There was blood everywhere. Eden had tried to put pressure on the chest wound, but she could feel right away that her sister's chest was still. There was no heartbeat.

She had turned away in despair, desperate to find Hope and Devon, not sure if they were even still alive, but Preston had blocked her path.

"Dad said he was going to kill us, too. That way we would all be together."

Eden's head spun at the words.

Get out of here, Eden. I'm not leaving this world without my kids, Preston had said, his eyes crazed. *We'll all be together on the other side.*

"I was so scared." Hope's voice trembled. "But you didn't leave. You charged at him, caught him off guard. He didn't think you'd fight back. But you grabbed the gun and shot him. Just like that."

Eden nodded. Her throat had closed, and for a minute she couldn't speak. She'd made her choice that night, and it had been the right choice. She'd saved her niece and nephew. She'd taken revenge on the animal that had killed her sister. The time for denial and self-recrimination was over.

"I couldn't let him hurt you or your brother," Eden finally said, the words spilling out. "I couldn't let him get away with what he'd done to your mother. So, yes, I killed him."

She looked at Hope with haunted eyes. "I took a life."

Hope squeezed her hand. "But you saved two lives. I think that means you don't have to feel guilty anymore. You can let it go now. You can move on."

Eden looked into the night sky, breathing in the sultry air, searching for a sign that Mercy was still out there, somewhere. She saw only pinpoints of stars. The moon must be hiding behind the clouds.

She knew she should be content. She'd been through hell but had made it through to the other side. Hope and Devon were safe. She had her memory and her sanity back. But she still felt restless.

The lovely colors she'd seen in the sky had now faded into darkness, and she shivered in the warm night air. She now knew that the world was full of monsters that walked on two legs and hunted in the night.

Although she'd been lucky enough to bring Hope safely home, there were other girls out there still in danger, other families still missing loved ones. Her work wasn't done. It likely never would be.

"Come on," she said, pulling Hope by the hand as Duke ran ahead. "Let's go home."

Continue the Mercy Harbor Series Now...

Want to find out what happens next with Eden, Leo, and the rest of the gang in Willow Bay? Then continue reading the Mercy Harbor Thriller Series now with:

Girl Eight: A Mercy Harbor Thriller, Book Two
by Melinda Woodhall.

And don't forget to sign up for the Melinda Woodhall Newsletter to receive bonus scenes and insider details at www.melindawoodhall.com/newsletter

ACKNOWLEDGEMENTS

MY MOTHER RAISED ME IN A HOUSE FULL OF BOOKS and instilled a love of reading and storytelling in all her daughters. Upon her death, I turned to books for solace and found comfort in the magic of a good story. I am so grateful to have had a mother who believed that one day I would be a writer. As always, she was right.

I wake up each morning and give thanks for the unconditional love and support of my wonderful husband and my five beautiful, brilliant children. I would never have finished this book without their constant love and encouragement.

Writing a book is often a solitary process that can be somewhat isolating. Luckily, I am blessed with two fabulous sisters, who are always close by when I need them, and the enthusiastic support of my amazing in-laws.

And finally, I have to acknowledge and thank all the writers that have offered up their hearts, souls, and stories in the books they have written, and which have inspired, entertained, and delighted me throughout a lifetime of reading.

ABOUT THE AUTHOR

Melinda Woodhall is the author of the page-turning *Mercy Harbor Thriller* series. After leaving a career in corporate software sales to focus on writing, Melinda now spends her time writing romantic thrillers and police procedurals. She also writes women's contemporary fiction as M.M. Arvin.

When she's not writing, Melinda can be found reading, gardening, chauffeuring her children around town, and updating her vegetarian lifestyle website.

Melinda is a native Floridian and the proud mother of five children. She lives with her family in Orlando. Visit Melinda's website at www.melindawoodhall.com.

Other Books by Melinda Woodhall

The River Girls
Girl Eight
Catch the Girl
Girls Who Lie
Her Last Summer
Her Final Fall
Her Winter of Darkness
Her Silent Spring
Her Day to Die

Made in the USA
Middletown, DE
06 May 2024

53954069R10203